Praise for *Chasing Cleopatra*

"Tina Sloan creates the perfect cocktail of spy thriller and romance in *Chasing Cleopatra*. Equal parts sexy and intriguing, this mystery of betrayal keeps you breathless and guessing until the very last page. And Sloan's glamorous Cleopatra will keep you awake all night."

— DANIELLE PAIGE, *New York Times* Bestselling Author of the *Dorothy Must Die Series,* and *Mera: Tidebreaker*

"I love Tina Sloan and her writing! I'm a huge fan and enthralled with Tina Sloan's new novel, *Chasing Cleopatra*. Her fab heroine foils plots, romances younger men, eats pancakes, and fight terrorists!! My kind of gal!"

— BETTY BUCKLEY, Tony Award winning "Broadway Legend" and "The Voice of Broadway"

"I stayed up all night to finish *Chasing Cleopatra*. A breathtaking, pulse-pounding tale of romance and intrigue, as glamorous and sophisticated as the author herself."

— CRISTINA ALGER, *New York Times* bestselling author of *Girls Like Us* and *Banker's Wife*

"I read *Chasing Cleopatra* in two days and was so taken with the story line I read it all over again. It truly is a novel of intense love and intriguing suspense and betrayal. I am hoping for a sequel."

— ANNE FORD, Author of *Laughing Allegra* and *The Forgotten Child*

CHASING CLEOPATRA

A Novel of Love, Betrayal, and Suspense

All the best

TINA SLOAN

Tina Sloan

December 21–25, 2011—Honolulu

To Steve, Renny, Helen, Hazel, and Mather

Life would not be as wonderful as it is without you.

*To Serena Turner – This book would not
be here without your help.*

MOHAMMED ABDUL RAHMAN

It has been years. But we are so close now. To the end.

When I first saw Cleo, I was on a mission. But her face got in the way. I tried to ignore her beauty. But it was more than that—she was more than that. I knew when I saw her that I was compromised. I was undone.

Yet the moment of my undoing was the same as her own. I knew immediately that I wanted to do the one thing that I was not supposed to do, to see the one thing that I wasn't supposed to see. I wanted to see what her face looked like when I told her the truth. *About her father. About herself. About me.* And now, after all these years and all these secrets and all these lies, we will come to the end. And I will see the truth finally written upon her beautiful face. And then I will bash that face in. And sever her hold on me for good.

It has been years. But we are so close now. Almost time to say goodbye, dear Cleo.

Chapter One
December 21, 2011

CLEO

It was all because of a man, but then again… it always is.

I was very young when I learned it was necessary to protect myself. As I grew up, I kept up the barriers, though they were certainly not visible to others. I choreographed a life that kept me safe and looked so normal to those on the outside. I lived alone in a spectacular, breathtakingly beautiful house, an oasis. And I trained constantly in the martial arts, primarily Krav Maga. Krav Maga is a military self-defense and fighting system that was developed for the Israeli Defense Forces. Not only is it self-defense, more importantly, Krav Maga is a fighting system that can be used to kill. I had work I loved and was very glamorous. I surrounded myself with wonderful people who enjoyed me but would not get too close. No one knew what I was not letting in.

Then in a day, no, in an hour, everything changed. It changed forever and kept changing at an enormously fast pace. Things turned upside down and I became me. A nightmare?

Or a dream? Both, I think. Let's go back to the beginning. To the hour that changed it all.

The accident is all my fault. I had just finished an especially grueling Krav Maga session with Walter, the Navy SEAL who trains me three days a week. Usually, Walter eases me into the hour with a series of explosive calisthenic exercises to get my heart jumping. But today, I was feeling anxious and so I asked if we could go straight into combat work. Having been a Navy SEAL for nine years, Walter was more than happy to indulge my request and skip the jumping jacks, push-ups, and sit-ups.

"Okay, Cleo. Pretend you're at the ATM down at First Hawaiian when someone approaches you from behind," Walter said as he slid his arm pads on. "It's dark and you don't know whether it's a friend or foe."

I knew what to do. I balled my hands into two tight fists and turned to the left before punching Walter hard in the throat. In real life, Walter would not have the luxury of defensive pads. He would have been stunned by the force of my fist first, choked second, and gone down on the ground third. After practicing turning to the left side first, I turned to the right and did the same.

"Okay, now you're on the street, texting, when someone questionable approaches you head on. Go."

Without hesitation, I hit Walter with fast, effective kicks to the groin until he threw his hands up in the air and conceded that the threat had been neutralized. And on and on we went. I loved our sessions, and on days off, I couldn't wait for the next one. Krav Maga is my drug and oh, I am addicted for sure. When I first started seeing Walter four years ago, I had the feeling that someone was out to get me. My trainer before Walter was also a former Navy SEAL but had decided after two years in Honolulu that it was better to raise his young family on the mainland back in Nebraska, where his parents were.

"Fear is common, Cleo. And it's real," Walter assured me. "Our objective is to get past that fear. The hope is to train your body and mind so relentlessly that you are capable of making tough, split-second decisions to defend yourself."

"And it doesn't hurt getting in a good workout as well," I joked.

My skills sharpened as the hours and years went on but unfortunately, I am not immune to injury. Toward the end of today's session, I was practicing an inside chop and hurt my neck, which often triggers a migraine.

I am rifling inside my purse for a small bottle of Excedrin, which works on my migraines if I take it right away, and at the same time my car is rolling out of my driveway, rolling straight into his car and meeting his temper head-on. My whole body jolts forward as metal crashes into metal. He is yelling at me before he is even out of his Jeep. "What the hell, lady?!"

As I step out of my newly-dented yellow convertible to assess the damage, I catch my lavender sundress on the door handle and rip it. It is almost comical. Not a great day so far... I don't say a word, letting him blow off steam before I try to explain my side of the story. Of course, I don't really have a side of the story and, of course, I am completely at fault.

He kneels by the trunk of his Jeep, surveying the damage I had done. It is bad. There is a sizable dent in the fender, trunk, and on part of the back door. It's a miracle that neither of us are injured. His car looks drivable but rather pitiful. If I were him, I would probably be screaming at me, too.

"Jesus. Were you even looking?" he seethes, half to me and half to himself.

I approach him silently. He hasn't even glanced over at me yet.

"Seriously, what were you thinking?! Well, clearly you weren't... It's a fucking rental, you know. I'm gonna have to go all the way back there and explain this. Do you have any idea how long that's gonna take? And on my vacation?!" He glances at me briefly but not long enough to get a good look.

Still, I keep quiet, riding out the worst of his temper, hoping that like a storm, it will pass if I wait long enough. He marches over to the driver's seat, leans down and presses a button. The trunk doesn't budge and just makes a sad, whirring noise. *Oh, dear.*

"Oh, great. Wonderful. Now I can't even open the trunk!" he continues to fume, pacing back along the car. "Where am I going to put all the tennis racquets and golf clubs? On our laps?!"

He sounds like a spoiled three-year-old child who refuses to go down for naptime. He leans down by the large dent, surveying the damage again.

"I'm so sorry," I apologize finally.

Then, oddly, I start to laugh. Nerves? I seldom get nervous, but for some reason, right now, I am more nervous than I've been in a very long time. My laughter infuriates him enough that he finally looks away from his precious Jeep and up at me. Looking at me seems to temper his temper. He gets up off his knees.

He stares at me. And keeps staring at me. We stand in silence for so long that it becomes disconcerting. But also, rather exciting. I know I should break the moment, but I can't. He is so devastatingly handsome and suddenly, I don't care at all about social graces. His dark, curly hair is combed straight back like some sort of Greek god or an ad for Giorgio Armani cologne. He's younger than I am. Oh yes, he's much younger, that I know for sure. Probably fifteen years. I turn forty-four in four days, on Christmas, and he can't be any older than thirty. Twenty-eight or twenty-nine, more likely. No wonder he's acting like such a spoiled child. He removes his sunglasses, showing me his piercing blue eyes.

He almost smiles and sort of whispers, "Jesus. Who are you?"

My heart starts to beat so hard that it fills my ears. "I'm so sorry," I apologize again. "It was my fault... I am just glad you seem alright."

Grumpy and spoiled, but alright.

"Right," he murmurs, clearing his throat. "Well, do you have your insurance? I should probably take down your info," he struggles to sound businesslike. He keeps staring at me, which takes away from the professional façade.

"Everything is at my house. It's at the top of this driveway," I point behind me.

"Okay, I'll follow you." He waits a moment before delivering the punchline. "From a safe distance..."

He cracks a real smile for the first time. And this smile devastates me. Part of me wants to start sobbing. There is something about his smile, something brand new... and yet something so very familiar. He's shaken me. He walks back to his damaged car and jumps into it. It starts up, thank heaven. I get into my car. And I think about the men in my life and the way I have forbidden them to really touch me. But he seems so familiar to me—like a dream. My barriers seem to be cracking like a volcanic fault. He is stirring something in me that I recognize. *Oh God.*

He follows me back to my house, up the long, curving driveway. As we get out of our cars, Jimbo Isom bikes past and gives us a friendly wave, pointing to the dented cars. I smile and wave back. There is always something a trifle dangerous in Jimbo's demeanor, even when he smiles. This makes him very exciting to women, though not to me. Never to me. Well, that's not entirely true. When I first saw him, I thought he was glorious with his platinum blonde hair and lean, muscular build, but I found out quickly that he has little interest in the women who are so interested in him. His Ironman competition is his mistress and he is a very loyal lover.

Shortly after becoming my friend, Jimbo became my tenant too. My property is quite isolated, so knowing that Jimbo is a mile down the path in the gardener's cottage is a huge comfort to me. Years ago, I had a man stalking me, presumably a fan of my local talk show, *Close Encounters*. Jimbo saw the stalker a couple times but never was able to catch him. But he is omnipresent, all over the island training for his beloved Ironman contest. It's his *raison d'être* and consumes him totally. His only goal in life is to be in the top five of the Ironman. So far, he has come in eleventh, ninth, and ninth. He thinks this will be his year and oh, I hope it will be.

"Who's that?" my accident victim asks.

"Oh, that's just Jimbo," I tell him.

"*Jim-bo?*"

"Yes, he's my tenant," I smile. "He lives down the road in an old gardener's cottage that he redid."

"How quaint..."

"Yes, he did a great job. It's quite gorgeous."

"Just like its owner..."

He's flirting with me.

"It's perched on a cliff and overlooks the ocean," I say, doing my best to remain matter-of-fact and to not flirt back. "He has a far better view than I have."

"Not better than me," he smiles.

Hmmm, oh, so definitely flirting with me. There is an awkward silence as we walk toward my house.

"Have you ever been spelunking?" I ask him, trying to fill the silence.

He looks over at me as if I'm speaking ancient Greek.

"Spe-whatting?"

"Spelunking," I laugh. "There are cliffs here on my property that are actually pretty wonderful for it."

"Oh. Right. Yeah, I've heard of it. A British friend of mine is pretty into it."

"Jimbo could show you around them if you like. Or perhaps you prefer sticking to country club sports?" I ask, perhaps flirting a bit myself. *But I mean, spelunking? Really, Cleo?*

He shrugs, not the least bit interested in the world of spelunking or in Jimbo either. Who can blame him? As we head toward my main entrance, his head keeps turning, taking stock of my property, which isn't the only thing that he's checking out. He tries to be subtle through the cover of his sunglasses, but his Ray-Bans aren't nearly as tinted as he thinks. I can see exactly what he wants to do, starting with the top pearl button on my newly ripped sundress.

"What's your name?" I ask him, realizing I don't know it.

"Jake Regan."

Jake. I used to hate that name. So trendy and without any real substance behind it. But for the moment, I love it. I really, really love it.

"Come on in, Jake. I'll get my papers."

But he lingers, looking at the huge French doors with their pale green shutters. I wish I could take credit for choosing that wonderful shade of green myself, but it was selected by the owners before me. Quite aptly, it's called Sweet Dreams, as is the house. The house, a nineteenth-century villa, has four wide stone steps leading up to the front door. Six years ago, when I was first introduced to the property, I fell madly in love with it even before I stepped inside. And when those French doors opened into a huge inner courtyard with a happily spouting fountain as the centerpiece, I was in thrall. Now the courtyard's fountain is surrounded by cascading, white, flowering trees that my father gave me as a housewarming gift when he came to help me move in. The tiny white lights are this year's Christmas addition, so it is a fairyland by day and night.

And the flowers. My father, Didier Gallier, loves to remind me of my mother's favorite saying, *"the earth laughs in flowers."* He was always sending them to me after she died. Didier also bought me my vintage, pale yellow convertible and himself a beat-up old MGB-GT, which stays in the garage for when he visits. I would've bought my house for the courtyard alone but the Tuscan architecture, which rambled all over, was a fortress of solitude and peace. Nothing jarred; it was pure serenity. I have my mother, who was never serene, to thank for this tranquility. She left me one of Matisse's Odalisques, auctioned at Christie's by my friend Anne Bracegirdle for an amazing sum of money. This single painting allowed me to buy Sweet Dreams and generally afforded my self-sufficiency too.

Finally, Jake follows me inside. The interior is full of fresh air and flowers and sunlight. No animals, no children, but filled with photos of my family and travels. I am seeing it through his eyes and recognizing what a blessed life I have.

When I return with the papers, Jake has already made himself very much at home on the long white sofa in my living room. There are huge bouquets of white roses decorating the room, and it's my favorite part of the house. He takes the papers, takes my arm, and then takes me onto his lap. I stop breathing. The air between us is so heavy, I feel like I'm going to pass out. How dare he... but also, how dare he not.

I wanted this. I wanted a man who would just take me and not be afraid. A man who would push me up against a wall and kiss me, hard. A man who would not stop kissing me until my legs would crumble and I was lying on the floor waiting for him. A man who would melt my unrelenting frigidity.

I wanted this very much. I am shocked by how much... This goes against the entire life I've carefully cultivated. I am terrified, but for good reason, for very good reason. This time, the real collision occurred. I collided with more than I could have imagined. I collided with some part of myself that I'd always kept hidden away. The part of myself that had never been opened. Only one other time have I let myself get this close to a man and now, here, it is happening again. Happening with this man I don't even know and who is so many years younger than me. He's simply glorious. Jake looks at me and I'm stunned. The hugeness of him smashes my hard won protection. I had fought long and hard for peace and serenity, and his masculine presence derails it in less than a second's time. The force field—that's what it feels like, a space, outer space capture of my life—the force field expels such sexual tension that I can't speak, I can't breathe. I become someone else; someone I never knew existed. And I like her. Oh, I like her very much. I have slept with men, of course, but never really let go until now. I had wept at how isolated that made me, but that was how I'd chosen to live my life.

He wins me over completely with his kiss. He dazes me at the rightness of it, the first clue to who he is. The kinetic life force, the kiss introducing him to me with such breathtaking power; I'm paralyzed. His hands are all over me like he owns my body, and that's exactly who he is—my keeper for this moment in time. No fear, no polite chatter. Beginning at the top, he very slowly begins to unbutton the tiny pearl buttons on my dress. Unable to speak, I watch, fascinated.

"Can I have a tour of your place?" he asks, undoing button number five. Still unable to speak, I nod.

He leads me away to stand in hallways. He kisses me so hard and rubs his very aroused body against me so often that I'm silently begging for him to come into me. We make our way through more hallways until we arrive in the wing where my father stays when he comes to visit every season. He stores his clothes in the closets here. I catch Jake glancing in one of them, and then back at me. I know what's he's worried about. *Am I married? Is there a husband who could walk in on us now that he had popped off all the tiny buttons?* A husband who would catch this mysterious young man with a massive erection pulling my dress apart? This seems to excite him so much, he drags me onto the floor and starts kissing me all over. I could have assured him that the clothes were only my father's and that he wasn't even in Hawaii. But I didn't want to.

I tremble so much and he finally can't stand it anymore. He comes into me, though he has the presence of mind to pull out a condom. He must be used to this. He comes so fast, it couldn't have been much more than a minute, and then smiles and starts again as we finally stumble, kissing blindly now and touching furiously, into my bedroom. We grapple with what is left of our clothes. Nothing matters except that in this moment, we had to be together again and this time slowly.

We make love on my queen bed with the sun streaming in and the smell of white roses surrounding us. I smile at him.

"I can't believe this happened," I laugh, finally. My self-consciousness and self-awareness suddenly wash over me like a tidal wave. I can't have a hit and run. I can't be sleeping with a man whose name I only learned a minute ago. I can't be sleeping with a child.

"What do you mean?" Jake asks, turning over toward me.

"You don't even know my name!"

"Cleopatra. I saw it on your papers."

I turn away to cover how wonderful what just happened was for me. I want to do it again and again and again, but—

"I can't, I can't, I can't."

"Oh, I think you can. I think you can very well..." he says, admiring the emerald ring that my father gave me after my mother died.

A rather perfect response.

All flashes of me as a woman who protects herself, who keeps her distance from any man who tries to get too close, fizzle. I'm so taken with him, so overwhelmed by pure lust, I would have risked anything. My mind disappears. My body is stunned by the rightness of him. I am having an out-of-body experience. I feel I am in a movie or a book but not in my own life. No migraine and I never even took my medicine. This must be the medicine I really needed.

"This is going to sound corny, but you know that old saying, 'to hear bells ring?' I feel like I finally heard 'em." He smiles at me. He must have instantly felt self-conscious because he laughs and adds, "but if you mention that to anyone I'll deny it. Not that we have a whole lot of mutual friends..."

What do you say to something like that?

"Come to my hotel for lunch. Who knows, maybe more bells will ring..." He doesn't ask me, he tells.

He assumes. He's right to assume. He breaks off one of the white roses and puts it in my hair. How could I go? Was I becoming some sort of modern day Mrs. Robinson? Mrs. Robinson was looking for lust, but that wasn't all, surely. She needed a way out of her boredom and liquored life. I wasn't bored or liquored and I certainly wasn't searching for this. I have my life in order. Because of something in my past, I had been totally terrified and undone by the idea of sex. And here I am having this awakening, finding it for the first time with a very young man that I don't even know.

A challenge beckons me, a chance to open the one door I have kept closed until now. Perhaps I would understand what I'd missed in my earlier days when I'd felt such pain and insanity and obsession over another man, a man who didn't have piercing blue eyes, but piercing brown ones. Danny.

Chapter Two
December 21, 2011

JULIA

I can barely sit still as I whisper-sing track sixteen of my 'I'm Nearly Engaged!' playlist. My feet want to salsa (I'm in a heavy Shakira phase, don't judge) across the ugly, synthetic carpet but I don't think 4A or 4C would appreciate an impromptu dance number. I'm fully aware that naming a playlist 'I'm Nearly Engaged!' makes me a huge loser but hey, sue me. I'm excited. Despite having sung choir all through Lemania, my boarding school in Lausanne, I decide to spare my fellow Delta passengers. There's a special place in hell for the type of person who inflicts their cell phone conversation or musical taste onto everyone within a twenty-foot radius in a public setting. *No, ma'am, shockingly, I don't need to hear all the exhilarating details of your eight year old's orthodontist appointment. And, sir, I'm perfectly cool not jamming out to "Apple Bottom Jeans" (the boots with the furrr) on my seven a.m. subway ride, thanks very much.*

It sounds lame, but I have an excuse to sing today. I'm en route to meet my boyfriend, Jake, and his whole family in a tropical paradise. They're one of those families who do a big family trip every year at Christmas, and I'm not one to complain. Jake has a wonderful family. So yeah, at thirty-thousand feet, I'm in a pretty decent mood. But being the good, rule-abiding gal that I am, I can't help but feel a twinge of guilt, so I assuage my balding seatmate, who's already shot me the evil-eye, and switch off my iPhone.

Jessica, the business class flight attendant whom I've become quite close to over the last five hours—Jess is a Capricorn, from Dallas, and her natural hair color is red—prances over and puts on a big toothy smile.

"Sure you don't want anything, darlin'?" she asks me in her Texas drawl.

My British accent sounds downright proper in contrast. "A bottle of water would be great, actually. Thank you."

"I was picturing something with a little more kick, but suit yourself..." she smiles. "Gotta be on your best behavior for Jake and the rest of the Regans, huh?" she says, before scurrying up toward the galley.

Okay, I've overshared. But wouldn't something be a bit off if I wasn't on cloud ten before the man of my dreams put a ring on it? I sit back and drift into fantasyland, where I've been spending a lot of time lately. Too much time. I wonder when Jake will do it... Sunset? That'd be cool. What about where? Definitely not opposed to the beach. And I guess it doesn't really matter *how*. Shit, which outfit should I wear? After a very expensive stroll down Madison Avenue yesterday, I don't think I'll be able to eat for the next three to five years. But it's worth it. A wise woman—or, at least a vain one—once said, "when you look good, you feel good." Or maybe it was the guy from The Men's Warehouse?

I switch on the television and select one of my all-time favorite movies to get me in the Christmas spirit, *Love Actually.*

Chapter Three

CLEO

It was all because of a man, but, then again... it always is.

The man, Didier Olivier Gallier, epitomized the famed Camus phrase, "charm is the ability to get the answer 'yes' without ever having to ask the question." The little he used to see of me, those treasured few weeks a year, he taught me how to find the keys to unlock people. When my father saw an elderly matron out at a restaurant alone, he would stop at her table on the way to the men's room and offer her a compliment. When Didier returned to our table, he'd test me.

"*Mon chaton*, what do you think I just told her?"

"I don't know, Daddy. That she looks nice?"

"No, it has to be more specific. Don't you see her pretty pin? Always find one thing and mention that. And if she smiles, Cleopatra, you know you picked the right thing."

He said I would always have the advantage that way. My father would do the same with doormen, children, maitre d's, concierges, and everyone in between. He has all the keys. He is simply one of those charismatic men whom people want to please.

I would do anything for his attention. He believed attention was the greatest gift you could give someone, a belief I have never forgotten. Whenever he bought me a gift or took me on a trip, it was pure delight. He made me feel like a princess, and in those moments, I was euphoric. I prayed that he loved me the most. And, when he was with me, he *did* love me the most. He would wrap me in tissue paper, name a star after me, and leave silly notes on my pillow.

As a girl, I always wanted to engage him about whatever interested him, and he found in me a most perfect audience for his philosophizing. Anything he said or did was entrancing. He has such power over me and is so terribly wise. He can still talk me into anything.

In 1977, Didier took over his family's vineyards in France and Algeria. On his father's side, the French side, he was a Marquis, his aristocratic Gallier lineage dating all the way back to the fifteenth century. Didier's father, Eduoard Alexander Gallier, was thought of as a rebel when he veered off the traditional path of marrying a woman of the same class. Instead his choice to marry Raina Lellouche, an Algerian peasant, stunned his family and friends. But Edouard did as he wanted. And this mixture of his parents, a French aristocrat and an Algerian peasant, made their son Didier a far more enchanting man than most.

I loved visiting the Gallier vineyards. Didier loved showing them to me, and he loved his work, but he was a harsh taskmaster. If he was happy with you, which was most of the time, he was warm and encompassing and generous. But if he was angry, his coal-black eyes would slice right through you. Once, when I was twelve years old, I overheard him speaking on the phone to someone who had not pleased him. I picked up the extension in the library, scared stiff, but so wanting to know with whom he was so deadly furious.

"You've been a bad boy, Leon," Didier said. His voice was icy and terrifying.

"Didier, it'll be done by Friday. I just need the extra time to tie up loose ends," the mysterious caller—Leon—said from the other end of the line.

"See that you do. If you don't..." The quiet threat dangled there for a moment.

I was always surprised by Didier's dark side. I had seen him go from light to dark in an instant, but this was darker, crueler than I'd ever known him to be.

On the lighter days, large, romantic gestures appealed to him. Our favorite shared moment was a tragic one we witnessed while walking together one afternoon on the beach in Algeria. After hearing a commotion, we looked up to see a parachute artist whose chute had failed to open. There was nothing he could do to save himself as he plummeted to his death from twelve thousand feet above the earth.

Instead of panicking enroute to his certain end, the parachute artist chose to perform the series he had orchestrated for his audience as if his chute had opened. He gave his all—executing front flips, backflips, twists, and turns all in the face of his imminent end. He, like the orchestra on the Titanic, played on. Didier was transfixed by the man's choice to die with such grace, to laugh at fate, and to overcome fear in his last moment on Earth. We talked all through dinner about the choices one makes in life and what they mean.

He left the vineyards the next day for a business meeting, of course—he always gave me a day here and there, whenever it was most convenient for him. His visits were often cancelled at the last moment, and his excuses were historically terrible.

Didier never ever *put* me down, but he used to *let* me down so often. I always blamed myself, thinking I wasn't interesting enough, smart enough, or sophisticated enough. I would never do anything negative or critical to turn him away from me. Scared of saying anything that might make his absences a bit longer, my response to his ridiculous excuses was always, "Oh, yes. I understand." As the saying goes, "when he looks at you, you are the center of the universe, but when he turns away, you're cold." And I never want to be cold. Not for a minute.

Whenever he failed me in the past, he'd say something like, "Cleopatra, you understand I have been away for two weeks and have all my mail to go through, so we'll do (insert: dinner, lunch, any outing whatsoever) another time."

On my eighteenth birthday, which was Christmas Day, he'd promised to fly me to Paris to be with him. The day before my birthday—three hours before I was to leave for the airport—he reneged.

"You understand, mon chaton, I need to meet with a friend who came all the way to see me from Istanbul. But be a good girl and I will buy you a gold watch for your birthday." He never did buy me that watch and I would never ask. Maybe he forgot.

Even now, at forty-four years old, I have never bought myself a watch and have never let anyone else buy me one. I keep waiting for my father to call and tell me my watch is on its way. I know he will someday. I am still making him up to fit my needs.

Chapter Four
December 21, 2011

MIRANDA

My son Jake is especially buoyant when he returns to the hotel. He comes to find me poolside, where I'm reading chapter eight of Agatha Christie's *The Locked Room* on a chaise lounge. I offer him my cheek to kiss. He does, then sits next to me. He looks as joyful as when he lost twelve pounds for crew at boarding school and could eat angel hair pasta again.

"So... bad news."

Uh oh. I put my book down and brace for impact. Bad news. Since becoming a mother over twenty-eight years ago—to three boys, mind you—I've had my fair share of, "hey, Mom. Bad news..." I accidentally threw away my retainer on the flight back from Palm Beach. I tore my ACL coming down a black diamond. Mrs. Trevor caught us stealing Budweisers from their fridge. The moment after the confession but before the details, that sense of dread never disappoints.

"I was... in an accident. With the rental," he says, not able to look me in the eye.

I shoot up in my chair. "You weren't hurt, were you? You look fine... Was there damage? Was the other person hurt? Oh, I hope not."

"Mom, chill."

Chill. I hate it when they tell me to "chill," as if being wound up like a coiled spring was some sort of choice I made a long time ago. "You know I hate that expression, Jake... Anyway, whose fault was it?"

He smiles.

I want to strangle him. Of my three boys, Jake has always been the most secretive. It's a trait that can drive a mother mad. "Why are you smiling like that? Did you hit your head?"

"Mom, relax. I'm fine and so's she. Her—oh, her name's Cleo—Cleo's car was yellow. Looked kinda like a bumble bee. Or maybe a Thanksgiving Day parade balloon. Remember those when we were little and you'd take us to see the parade?"

Like a bumble bee? A Thanksgiving Day parade balloon? Has he hit his head? I don't know what to make of him. A concussion, probably.

"Her car looked like a 'bumble bee?' That doesn't sound like you, Jake... Very imaginative, to say the least."

He just shrugs.

"Okay, are you sure everything's okay with the car though?"

"Yup. I mean, there are a few dents but it drives fine. The trunk wasn't opening at first but I fixed it."

"You're sure? I don't know how your father will feel about driving around with a damaged car."

"He's renting another one, remember? Everything's cool, mother dear. Promise!" He nudges me playfully, still beaming like a Fourth of July firework.

Oh, I get it. I know what's going on.

"I think I know why you're in such a good mood..."

"What? Why?" he says, defensively.

"... Because Julia's getting here soon."

His smile fades a touch. Odd.

"You know what, I think I'm gonna go fishing before she gets here. Julia hates to fish."

"That sounds nice. Why don't you ask Matt to join you?"

Jake is already out of his chair.

"Wait, what time does Julia get in again?" I call to him, trying to get into his happy mood.

"Should be here in time for dinner. She texted me that her plane was on time," he tells me, turning back around.

"Wonderful."

"FYI, I think I'll go fishing solo. Unless you wanna come and get burnt. The conditions will be harsh on gingers with pale skin like you and Matt," he jokes.

Jake bends over and kisses my red hair. He is being uncharacteristically sweet. Suspiciously sweet. His car crash certainly seems to be the last thing on his mind. Since he's in such good spirits, I decide to risk it...

"Honey, will we be hearing any bells in your near future?"

He freezes. "What?"

"Wedding bells, Jakey."

"Let's not go there, Mom. See ya."

And he's off. Part of me wants to chase after him and tell him how happy his father and I have been all these years and how I hope he and Julia will be too. But he usually bolts when I get "sappy" about Tripp and our wonderful life together.

Chapter Five
December 21, 2011

TRIPP

I traveled to Miami as my real-life persona, Tripp Regan: lawyer, husband of Miranda, father to Jake, Matt, and Ricky. But in the Sunshine State, I transform into the University of Miami ENG 319: Shakespeare professor, Dr. Marcus Pearson. The real Dr. Pearson doesn't even know my real identity. To him, I'm just some guy named James Howard.

With his gray hair and brown eyes, Dr. Marcus Pearson looks nothing like me. He's got two inches on me in height— *lucky bastard*—and another fifty in weight. *Not so lucky, bastard.* The professor stays at home alone when I travel. My organization pays him handsomely to do whatever he pleases for forty-eight hours while I'm out in the world pretending to be him. This guy can do whatever his little heart desires and he chooses to write books. Books on Shakespeare. Go figure. At the moment, his chubby fingers are hard at work on book number four. Part of me admires Dr. Marcus Pearson. If I was on paid vacation within the comfort of my own home, I'd probably just watch the news and old reruns of *The Rockford Files.*

I ring the bell at his Coral Gables apartment building. When he doesn't answer thirty seconds later, I ring it again. I'm buzzed in and hustle up to the fifth floor. From the stairway, I can hear him schlepping toward the door.

"James!" Pearson whispers as he swings open the door and bear-hugs me. "How the hell are ya?" he asks, hunched in the doorway and chomping on some variation of a mystery meat sandwich.

Sometimes I marvel at the fact that this man has a PhD.

"I'm—"

"Come in, come in," Pearson demands before I can get a second word out.

"Listen Marcus, I hate to run in and out but I don't have a whole lotta time. My flight from New York was delayed two hours, and—"

"You're in a rush to start saving the world again, one homicidal terrorist at a time," he jokes, his mouth full of ham. Or bologna. Or turkey.

"Something like that..."

"Say no more. You know the way, big guy."

I smile at the professor, who, to be clear, is a far "bigger guy" than I'll ever be.

In the bathroom, my eye color changes from blue to brown with the aid of colored contacts. I put a lift in my shoes, glasses on my nose, and prosthetics in my cheeks to make my jowls heavy. I own a well-shaped white beard that I adhere with glue. It goes on crookedly the first time so I have to yank it off and reapply. I add spray, taking the dark out of my hair and leaving it gray. I step into a padded body suit, which adds Pearson's fifty pounds. For the past three years, I've made it a habit of having one of my men check in with the professor about his current weight the week prior to an operation. His weight tends to fluctuate at a fairly alarming rate, which I learned the hard way during year two, when upon arrival, I discovered he was twenty pounds heavier than he was the previous trip. Little heads-up would've been nice, *big guy*. Working with the materials at hand, I stuffed a pillow under my sweater so I wouldn't raise suspicion among his students if I happened to be seen exiting his building. I couldn't take the risk.

Lastly, I top off the whole look with a green and orange University of Miami visor. Stepping into Pearson's clothes and sneakers, I'm fully transformed.

As I head back toward the living room, my gait slows to mirror Dr. Pearson's. I find the professor holed up at his messy desk, working away on his laptop. A wry smile dances across his face when he looks up and sees me standing there.

"I get the distinct feeling we're not using this little trick of yours to its full potential, James..."

I smile back at him, wondering exactly what the hell he's implying. I stay serious, focused. "By now, you know the drill, but just to recap—"

He interrupts me for the twenty-fifth time today. "I know, I know. No phone calls. My out-of-office message is already set up and says I'm out of town at the Manila Conference. Food's been delivered. I won't make a peep and I certainly won't answer the door, even if it's Lady Macbeth herself back from the grave and needing to wash her hands."

Laughing, I shake the professor's hand.

"Good. And as always, the money will be wired into your account on day three."

"Yes, siree. Works for moi," Pearson nods.

"You need anything, *anything*, call this number," I tell Pearson, handing him a card.

"Merci."

"And here's your temp phone." I hand him a black iPhone.

"Ooh, new iPhone. Can I keep?"

I shoot him a look.

"You're no fun..."

"Your country thanks you, Professor. Now go finish that book. Your fans are eagerly anticipating its arrival."

"Yeah, all six of them," he jokes. "Okay, now scram. Better get out of here before you miss my flight to Manila. No professor would ever be late for a conference."

Something feels out of place when I arrive at Miami International. As I board, I get the feeling I'm being followed.

AFTER A TEN-HOUR FLIGHT, we arrive at Manila Ninoy Aquino International Airport at just after 9:00 p.m. As I always do, even though my seat is in the first row, I wait to deplane and watch as the other passengers get off. They're all just happy to be on solid ground after a long, bumpy ride, so most of them don't even glance my way. I study each of their faces, memorize each of their walks.

For the past twelve years, we've been infiltrating Jemaah Islamiyah, the Al Qaeda group in the Philippines. The network's existence was discovered in late 2001 after Singaporean authorities disrupted a cell planning to attack targets associated with the U.S. Navy.

In Manila, I'm to check in with my new contact, J.R. Ocampo. He has a lead on the whereabouts of the charismatic JI-AQ leader, Mohammed Abdul Rahman, who's been off our radar for almost four years after he bombed a busy market in Bali and fled. Ocampo tipped us off that Rahman had entered the U.S. to stage bombings, but where exactly, we don't know. Ocampo, a member of Jemaah Islamiyah, will be attending my guest presentation at the Shakespeare conference and we have reason to believe the source can provide us with Rahman's U.S. residence and what he's plotting. Ocampo, whom I'll meet face to face for the first time at my presentation of *Henry V*, had turned on Rahman after Rahman callously murdered his two younger brothers when they changed their minds about becoming suicide bombers. Rahman doesn't take rejection lightly.

THE NEXT DAY, posing as University of Miami's Professor Marcus Pearson, I lecture on the famous St. Crispin's Day speech from *Henry V*. During the Q&A, I wait for the code phrase from my contact, "but if it be a sin to covet honour, I am the most offending soul alive." But I never hear it. With only fifteen minutes left, I still haven't. The clock ticks five minutes more, leaving only ten remaining. *Five, four, three, two, one.* The sentence is never uttered. The contact isn't here.

After class, I pack up my briefcase and hustle back to the hotel. I try and keep calm even though my gut tells me something is very, *very* wrong. My instinct at Miami International, and now no Ocampo. I pass the sitting area in the hotel lobby and give Chris Castillo, my CIA backup—reading the sports section of *The New York Times*—a nod, signaling him to join me in the elevator. When we get to the door of my hotel room, all the hairs on the back of my neck stand up. That feeling again. Castillo and I both raise our guns before I slide my key card into the lock and push open the door.

This ain't my first time at the dance, but still, it's never easy. In the middle of the room, there's a young man, twenty-two years old tops, seated facing the window. His head is positioned at a strange angle, all the life from his eyes is gone and there's a metal garrote around his neck. And there's the code, the quote from *Henry V*, written in black Sharpie in two rows across his neck: "but if it be a sin to covet honour, I am the most offending soul alive."

"Jesus…" I remove the garrote from J.R. Ocampo's neck. "No eyes or ears anywhere?"

"No, sir," says Chris Castillo, who is staying in the room next to mine.

"And why not? Why didn't we have someone stationed up here?" I bark.

"We didn't think it was necessary, sir."

"Well, *we* were very wrong, weren't we? I want to see all security footage from management. If Ocampo walked through the front door, it's on tape. You didn't see anything suspicious? The entire time you were sitting out there?"

"No, sir," Castillo says sheepishly.

"This is a huge fucking fuck-up. Get his body to the coroner immediately, please. I want an autopsy done, ASAP."

Castillo nods. I shake his hand as I turn and start to go. Castillo hands me a suitcase that matches the one I came in with, but this one is filled with Tripp Regan's clothes. Tripp Regan is the real me. The me who has a family waiting to celebrate Christmas vacation in Hawaii. Seeing this poor kid's dead body doesn't exactly get me in the holiday spirit.

Chapter Six

MOHAMMED ABDUL RAHMAN

Born an American in Cleveland, Ohio, in 1973, I was a very surly child. At age twelve, my parents, Patricia and Jim Olsen, moved to the Philippines for work in the oil business and became close friends of Imelda and Ferdinand Marcos. Imelda and Patricia quickly bonded over a pair of my mother's expensive shoes during a dinner at the Palace. At the next party, Patricia and Imelda arrived in matching shoes and a deep friendship was formed. To go from Cleveland to the Palace was the pinnacle of success for my social-climbing mother who spent every day after that with "Aunt Issie," shopping and lunching or shopping and gossiping or shopping and traveling on the Marcos's plane. Patricia and Jim joyfully went to the Palace many evenings for State dinners and parties, leaving my brother, Paul, and I alone in our house, beginning when I was twelve and Paul nine. Every night, my mother was outfitted in a new designer gown just so she could keep up with the proverbial Joneses, or in this case, Marcoses.

One night after I finished my homework and Paul went to bed, I was bored and wandered into my father's study where I came upon a book about the Marathon Monks of Hiei. I snuggled up in my father's brown leather chair and read it cover to cover until three in the morning, just before Jim and Patricia finally stumbled in. To run more than twenty-six miles every day for a thousand days... (at that time, my biggest accomplishment was winning Most Valuable Player for my school's soccer league). Having such devotion, mental toughness and purity of purpose was a foreign concept. The Marathon Monks of Hiei changed everything, and I felt a great calling to find my own purpose, a real one, not just wanting to win a stupid soccer game or go to an Ivy League college someday.

In 1988, three years after we arrived in Manila, the Marcoses were thrown out of the country, indicted by a grand jury on charges of racketeering, conspiracy, fraud, and obstruction of justice. At fifteen, I was too young to fully understand the gravity of the charges, but I was certain they weren't good. And by association, neither were my parents. The Marcoses fled to Honolulu where Patricia and Jim followed like two loyal sheepdogs, leaving Paul and me in Manila to finish school with vacation breaks in Honolulu. My soccer coach, Rashid, who, at this point, was like a father to me, was put in charge of my brother and me along with the household help and our teachers.

Rashid said I was one of the best soccer players he'd ever seen. After team practice, he'd coach me one on one and often invite me to dinner at his house afterward. Being at an all-boys school, I wasn't around girls my age often, and so I naturally developed a crush on his daughter, Afsheen. Her name means "shines like a star." On our wedding day six years later, I thanked Rashid, whom I realized had brought me to meet her on purpose. He was not only grooming me to be a jihadist, but also his future son.

On weekends, Rashid took me to visit his cousins in the ghetto. They lived in dirt huts with garbage in the street and no bathrooms. In America, I had blinders on. The slums of Manila made East Cleveland look like Beverly Hills. I felt stupid and ashamed of my ignorance. How could these shacks be only a few miles from my home? The cousins blithely played stickball without shoes or a ball, just a measly piece of rotten fruit. Rashid gave them soccer balls every visit, but by the next time, they'd be gone. Stolen by the other kids or maybe sold for a few scraps of food.

"Welcome to the real world," he said in a hushed tone.

"What?" I was so naïve.

"Look around. They're all victims of the Marcoses, who live in palaces with two hundred rooms while their countrymen starve on the streets. They don't care. Do you think that's right?"

I was ashamed of my parents' close connection to such people. I looked to Rashid as a god, and so, when he asked, I agreed to go with him to his mosque, Masjid Al Dahab, in the Muslim section of Manila. I was scared and excited. Paul chose never to go to Rashid's house and never to meet Afsheen. He hated the smell of Muslim food and the look of women covered head to toe frightened him. He was so small-minded, planting himself with his mouth gaped open in front of our television for the American programs. Paul was attracted to all those whorish women on *Miami Vice* and *Dallas*. But the burkas, the thought of a woman that no one but their family could see, fascinated and excited me.

At the mosque, I was greeted by men who seemed glad to talk to me. They encouraged me to come often to meetings where they discussed the government's failure to provide food, security, or basic services. Nothing causes greater resentment than poor governance. Rashid continued to cleverly take me into the poor neighborhoods, where the taste of resentment and anger became more bitter. Afsheen looked at me with such admiration when she heard I was at the mosque almost every day doing ablutions and talking to men who were trying to mitigate the poor's living conditions with food and medical care. I thrived on those looks she gave me.

Slowly, Rashid introduced me to members of the mosque who were also in a group called Al Qaeda. As a boy, I hadn't heard of this group but I instantly felt the most at home when I was with them. I could tell that others in the mosque looked up to the men in Al Qaeda as if they were gods. After speaking with them, I realized I found my purpose. I wanted to be a god too. And just like that, my whole life transformed. My previous existence of soccer games, homework, and Walkmans seemed like a waste. Like the marathon monks, it was the mental fortitude, iron will, and monomania of the Al Qaeda soldiers that set me on my righteous path to Islam. The jihadists fought injustice not just with words but with their lives. Is there anything more courageous? They had an obsession for good and took their obsession in a different direction than the monks did. They stopped at nothing to fulfill their mission and to remove the invaders, the Westerners, even if it meant paying for it with their lives. And so, it began.

My existence as Patrick Olson ended abruptly, and I was sent to a training camp in the southern jungles of Mindanao. There I underwent daily weapons and combat training, as well as teachings from the Koran. I went from cashmere to camouflage, from a very large house with central air conditioning to the stifling desert, from my own private bedroom and bathroom to sharing a cold floor with no showers. I went from chasing after a soccer ball and memorizing the dates of the Spanish American War to learning bomb-building and to shooting AK-47s. I went from being sure of my place in society to being an outcast and having to prove myself to these men daily. With my dark hair and tan, sometimes I passed as having been born in the east. Then, when the soldiers took a closer look, there was no mistaking my blue eyes and midwest American accent. As was expected, I was met with suspicion and dirty looks at first. *Go home, stupid American. Go home.* As the daily Koran teachings and bomb-building continued, my birthplace, blue eyes, and Episcopalian upbringing slowly vanished and my comrades grew to recognize their own mission in me. An American who wasn't dedicated to the cause wouldn't have made it past the first week.

Why did I subject myself to this? I was never happier. At sixteen, I walked away from a life of great wealth to one of poverty. I left my friends, family, and school and proudly substituted it with jihad. Now I have a purpose that is good and pure and I'm truly fulfilled. I laugh when I think of Jim and Patricia with their shoes and parties and martinis. Or Paul, with his idiotic television. I was the only one who actually made something of himself. Today, I am one of AQ-JIs most fervent leaders and one of the most feared. If it means furthering the cause of Islam, I will kill with no regret. And I have one good thing inherited from my infidel parents, a sense of how to fund our attacks. Before I left home, I got all the money in my trust fund and put it in my new name so I was able to fund attacks. The other high AQ leaders saw my benefit and willingly funded me as I succeeded in one attack after another.

MOHAMMED ABDUL RAHMAN

Allah is on my side. I will succeed and there will be another date of infamy for the infidels. On December 25th, there will be bloodshed in retaliation for their pursuit of extreme Islamic factions in Indonesia. Bloodshed in Honolulu. After the Christian holiday, all of the injustices in Indonesia will be seen by the world. The Special Operations Command Pacific will no longer persecute our oppressed people. And we will celebrate. I will finally leave this island and return to my home in the Philippines and to Afsheen. Young recruits will line up for blocks to fight with us. And afterward, Al Qaeda will channel their violence into another worthy cause of removing invaders and injustices.

Chapter Seven
December 21, 2011

CLEO

I change into a pale green sleeveless dress with a very low neck and add some very high-heeled gold sandals. All the things I'd left back East seven years ago came out of my trunk like silk scarves gaily coloring everything around me. It is as though I am a great courtesan in a play. And I am going to act it brilliantly, I decide, as I drive my dented yellow convertible to meet my "lunch date" at the Halekelani Hotel. What is happening to me? Whatever it is, it's heaven.

There is no lunch. Jake takes me to his room where we tear off one another's clothes and are together smashing, crashing, and rumbling. The windows and doors to his balcony are wide open and we can hear the voices of people chattering and lunching, children shouting, couples laughing and plates clattering down below. It is another world, cocooned in his huge, white bed. I catch glimpses of us in his mirror—he's so perfect and uninhibited. How glorious to be so encompassed by this incredible drive, this total immersion in one another. We shower and make love again—and then again. His phone rings but he ignores it. Four hours later, I get up to go, staggered by and rejoicing in the sheer sexuality I have encountered with him, sexuality I'd submerged, had never known. I had to beg him to stop. It was too much but such an amazing too much. Like Marlon Brando in *Last Tango in Paris*, I joined him in the dance across the time warp, joined him in the bacchanals in ancient Greece.

As I am dressing, Jake turns to me sheepishly.

"So, this is kinda awkward... but my girlfriend gets here on the afternoon plane. She should be here in about an hour."

The wind is knocked out of me. I am standing up but scared I will fall down. How could he make love to me for hours and hours and at the same time have a girlfriend and know that girlfriend is about to walk in the door? *Of course, he has a girlfriend. He's gorgeous.* I put on a huge smile to act as though everything is fine. But of course, it is not. I am devastated. How could he do this to me? Or to her?

Glancing at the bed, I force a laugh, "Well, you better call Housekeeping and get them up here right away. Fresh towels are in order, too." I am sounding so wonderfully blase, even to myself. I sound like I do this all the time. The problem is I'm now totally obsessed with him and have to see him again. Girlfriend or not, I need to see him again. I don't care.

"Come to dinner with me on the beach at the Outrigger Canoe Club. Bring your whole family. Your *girlfriend*, too."

He looks at me. "Really?"

"Yes, really. I do owe you for the car damage..."

The girlfriend. I can't very well invite him without the girlfriend and I admit, I actually want to meet her and size up the "competition." What would she be like? During the short drive home from his hotel, I fantasize about her. What a ridiculous waste of time... What "type" does he find attractive when he was not catapulted into an older woman?

I've always disdained the type of women who were predators, who were like my mother. But when I slept with Jake, I had no idea he had a girlfriend. I am not the predator. He wins that title.

Chapter Eight
December 21, 2011

JULIA

About an hour out from landing, my transformation begins. See ya, Lululemon leggings and lumpy white sweater. Aloha, sexy Reformation sundress. I shake out my messy bun and run a brush through it a few times, but I don't want it to look *too* coiffed. I'm definitely not going for that pristine Kate Middleton vibe. I fish out my cosmetics case and apply some cherry ChapStick—I've always thought lipstick is too severe against my pale skin. I wish I could pull it off, but alas. I spritz my neck and wrists with Jo Malone. Jake's favorite.

I check myself out in the mirror one last time. There she is. A new woman. The future Mrs. Jake Regan. Has a nice ring to it, don't you think? Hope he remembered that I love the emerald cut... I've certainly been dropping hints for months. Okay, I'm obsessing. But, ah, I can't wait to jump into his big, muscular arms at the airport. I wonder if he'll have a lei around his neck and one for me too. Who doesn't love an airport reunion scene? *Love, Actually,* anyone? Colin Firth? Hugh Grant? *Yes, Jake Regan. I do.*

Jessica gives me a thumbs up when I finally reemerge from the bathroom a whole fifteen minutes later. I feel like celebrating. Oh, what the hell.

"You know what… I will have that glass of champagne."

"Yeah, girl!" she hollers back at me.

"But just one!"

When we land forty-five minutes later, I no longer feel like celebrating. My phone buzzes—*oohlala, a text from Jake.* I instantly feel a pit in my stomach. "Went fishing. Sent you a driver, Raul." Just like that. No punctuation, no "xo," not even a lame emoji. Quite the wordsmith, that Jakey. I clench my jaw so I don't burst into tears and ruin my newly made-up face. It's not the end of the world. *Suck it up, Julia.*

When I deplane, there's no Colin Firth or even that weird-looking, gangly blonde one. Just Raul with a "Julia Turnor" placard. This trip isn't exactly starting off the way I'd hoped… Jessica catches up to me and puts the cherry on top of my chocolate humiliation cake. I feel like the sad, lonely girl in high school who's just been stood up by the hot lacrosse captain on prom night.

"Well, where is he?! I wanna meet the famous Jake Regan!" she squeals in all her Texas belle glory.

All I can do is point to Raul, holding up the placard—with my last name misspelled, by the way. Jess shakes her frizzy head and pats my shoulder.

"Sorry, honey," Jess mumbles. And then she prances off in her four-inch, knock-off Jimmy Choos.

Chapter Nine
December 21, 2011

CLEO

The "type" I was, was not the same type as my mother or my sisters, Tree and Beebe. They were all so physically alike it made people laugh. And since we all have different fathers, mother, with her eyes looking down so the world could see her thick, dark eyelashes, admitted to very assertive genes. All three of us inherited her dimples and amazing violet eyes. My sisters got her blonde hair and tiny stature, while my father passed his height and dark wavy hair down to me.

My mother, the predatory lioness, brilliantly capitalized on the way she looked and played the delicate flower to perfection. This feeling of being linked to her, who was always most alive when she had a new lover and who invariably used men as her alchemy, excites me. Men had been the bookmarks of her life. "1963? Oh, yes, I was in love with Alan then." Never, "Oh, yes, JFK was shot that year." "1974 was one of the worst years of my life. James and I broke apart that year." No mention of Watergate or Nixon resigning. But maybe she was right. I feel alive and it is living the drama of a soap opera that energizes me.

I call my two sisters often and our cell phone bills can attest to that. I can't wait to speak to them as soon as I am home.

Including her name, everything about my sister Tree is outrageous. As a child, her swim coach told mother she ought to be an Olympian. Mother demurred, "but it would limit her dreadfully..." Her tennis pro and her singing teacher both begged mother to turn her over to be a champion on the court or at the opera and again my mother would fear Tree being "limited."

When we were growing up, at Christmas—which also happens to be my birthday—my favorite game, and Beebe's too, was to decorate Tree with all our favorite ornaments. We wrapped her in lights and one year she even let us put a star atop her head. Our very own Christmas "Tree." She lit up our lives just like a Christmas tree. Tree's short, curly, platinum blonde hair, which rarely saw a brush, always looked like a crooked halo. Beebe and I encouraged Tree to be naughty. No one could ever punish Tree. She was too loveable.

She inherited that lovability from her father who always came on Wednesday nights and would whisk us out of the convent school, where mother had sent us, to the nearest hamburger joint in his old station wagon and regale us with stories. He was married to our mother in her do-gooder phase and was the nicest man I have ever known. She met him and "made" my sister, whom she gave the distinction of naming Tree because she was conceived against a silver birch tree at Woodstock in 1975.

Beebe, our baby sister, was Tree's exact opposite in personality. As Beebe was so lovely, Sandrine, our mother, loved her best, calling her pet names that always reflected some level of royalty, as it actually was in her blood—"her fairy princess" and "my baby Duchess" were Sandrine's favorites.

Beebe's father, a duke and a member of the Church of England, raised bees as a hobby—hence the name Beebe, since she was conceived near the beehives at his estate in England. Bees give honey and Beebe is so very sweet.

In the end, she married one of her father's distant cousins and is now Lady Beebe with two sons at Eton. She acquiesces to her children's and especially her husband's whims easily. If her husband, Lord Philip, wants to go to Rome, she smiles and goes along with him. And if, when they arrive at their villa, he decides he'd rather shoot in Scotland, she just smiles, repacks his bags, has the secretary change the reservations and accompanies him to the shooting lodge in Perthshire. It is in her nature to be so very agreeable. Beebe is delicate and petite; her life is lived quietly, serenely.

I can tell my sisters are glued to their phones as we conference call the way we always do, never wanting to miss out on one another's lives.

I jump in. "I think something is happening to me"

"Something… wonderful or something dreadful?" Beebe asks, warily.

"Something wonderful."

"Go on…" says Tree, her interest piqued.

I hesitate, working out the best way to explain the outrageousness of Jake and what he has done to me in an instant. There's no point in dancing around the lust, the desire, the pure primalness of it all. "It is pure lust and I have to say, it's climactic."

"Oh, Cleo!" Beebe cries.

Tree *ahaa*'s, "sounds like you finally came over to my side…"

"Your side? Dare I ask?"

"And fell in love with a woman!"

I laugh. "Not a woman but a very, *very* young man."

Tree and her partner Crystal love to visit me from Portland, Oregon, where they live and work. They arrive with their two sons and their four black labs, Bronco, Leroy, Edgrrr, and Macho, and a tiny black terrier, Beauregard, who is convinced that he too is a lab. I have two guest wings and they take over both. The house is full of chaos in minutes—clothes, tennis rackets, baseballs, and sneakers are thrown about; swimsuits, skateboards, surf equipment, dropped wherever they feel like dropping them.

Crystal and Tree's sons are Ash and Alex—each carried one child and used the same sperm donor, so the boys are actually biological brothers. The boys are totally wild, leaping off boulders or out of trees like Tarzan. But their mothers don't ever seem the least bit disturbed. The labs, on the other hand, watch the boys with diligent eyes.

When they visit, Crystal and Tree use a private plane that Tree pays for with mother's inheritance. There is no one less pretentious than Tree but flying private is the only way they can bring the dogs. Crystal would rather die one-hundred deaths than be without her dogs for more than twenty-four hours. And Tree would rather die one-hundred deaths than be without Crystal for twenty-four minutes.

"This all sounds so unlike you, Cleo. When it comes to men, you're typically so..." Beebe falters, flustered.

Tree cuts her off. "Chilly?"

"Who, me?" I laugh.

My sisters are right. Ever since I was toddling about at three years old, I was always incredibly independent and self-sufficient. Being reliant made me feel weak. I watched my girlfriends become so attached, so beholden to the boys they were dating. And my mother, oh, she was by far the worst. The bouts of depression every few years like clock-work. I never wanted to be like that. And now, I have never felt so beholden to a man, as I do to Jake. Well, that's not true. There was one other time. Just one.

"Actually, Tree, I was going to say 'aloof,' but 'chilly' works too!" Beebe goes on. "So, tell us who you're feeling this way about, Cleo?"

"Jake, his name is Jake. He's very handsome, and may I say again, very much younger."

"How young?" Beebe asks suspiciously.

"At least thirty…"

"Thirty?!" my sisters scream in unison.

"Okay, maybe twenty-nine…"

"Twenty-nine?!" both sisters say together again. I can tell that Beebe is absolutely horrified and Tree is delighted. Their reactions are a microcosm of their entire beings.

"Yes, I know. He's young, but—but I can't help it!" I laugh, acutely aware of how ridiculous I sound.

A beat of silence.

"I'm having dinner with him, his family, and his girlfriend tonight."

"Girlfriend?!" shouts Beebe.

"Oh, boy…" Tree giggles.

"Mother would love doing something daring like this, wouldn't she? Meeting his entire family and girlfriend after hours and hours of sex."

"Cleo!" Beebe chimes in. "What are you thinking?"

I'm not thinking. That's the point.

Chapter Ten
December 21, 2011

TRIPP

As my 757 sails over the South Pacific Ocean, I start to backtrack, to remind myself why I chose this life and why I need to keep going. And as much as I don't want to admit it, maybe it's finally time to transition out of being the op and into becoming the officer in charge. It was nearly thirty years ago when I was recruited for covert ops by a University of Michigan drama professor I'd met as an unfocused undergrad. I'd taken only two drama courses but that was enough to make quite an impression on wily ol' Mrs. Huneke. She knew how adept I was at characters, costumes, voice patterns, and movement. She also had the good sense to realize just how much I hated the spotlight and would never pursue acting as an actual career. How right she was.

The law has served as my cover for the last twenty-five years. Once I finished college, I was about to start law school but was stopped cold after a traumatic accident took my first wife's young life. My beautiful Cindy and I had played, partied, fallen in love, and married. She was elegant, smart, fun, and so beautiful with that thick, long, blonde hair. Ironically, we met in Mrs. Huneke's drama class doing a scene from *Barefoot In The Park*, which every drama student performs at one point or another. Cindy and I lived a life filled with the romance only your first love gives you.

The summer we married, after our senior year of undergrad, we were on a sailboat off the coast of Maine in a freak storm when an unexpected jib maneuver caused the boom to hit her in the head with such force that she died instantly. I was a mess after Cindy's death; I slept from 4:00 a.m. (after somehow stumbling home) until noon when I began the vicious cycle of drinking all over again. Fortunately, I snapped out of it when I ran into Andy Gustin, an old college buddy, at one of my regular spots. The look on his face when he recognized me was one of sheer horror. I don't know why, but that look forced me to clean up my act. Maybe it was time or maybe I just knew I couldn't go on this way.

Representing my country and working black ops seemed like the most extreme, and therefore most logical, move. I called up Professor Huneke and asked her to put me in touch with the CIA recruiting people she'd spoken to me about years before. It was the perfect fit. For more than two-and-a-half years, the training was so consuming that I eventually came back to life. Once I graduated, I went to law school at the University of Michigan. This is where Miranda reentered my life and where I decided to marry her. Being a married lawyer would be and still is my cover in the real world.

Located in midtown on 49th & Park, Weinstein, Forbes, Regan & Lowe is a midsized firm that specializes in corporate law. Bill Weinstein, the founding partner, is a fossil and graces the rest of us lowly office dwellers with his presence every quarter if we're lucky. He hasn't missed one Christmas party though. Larry Forbes has since taken over the reins and now acts as managing partner. Every other word out of the native Staten Islander's mouth is crude, but damn, does the guy know his way around a courtroom. Compared to the rest of us, Marina Lowe is the new kid on the block but that isn't saying a whole lot. She's been schlepping cases at the firm for sixteen—no, seventeen—years now and has gone through double the number of paralegals. Which leaves yours truly.

If I can avoid it, which most of the time I manage to, I stay out of the courtroom. 'Settle' has become my own personal mantra, and so far, it's served me well. Forbes, the managing partner, knows about my second job and is very cooperative when I need to take some time off. About two years ago, I was knee-deep in a class-action suit—the defendant, an online retail destination, was mine. Said online retail destination had their website hacked, which resulted in many unfortunate side effects—the most egregious being that it leaked the personal banking information of its loyal customers. When the CIA needed me on a plane to the Philippines in the middle of trial to track down a lead on AQ-JI, Forbes came to the rescue and saved my ass. He's a true Budweiser-drinking, gun-toting, God Bless America singing patriot. That said, he didn't hesitate lobbing several four-letter words my way.

My wife Miranda has no idea. Every now and then, she'll happily drop by with a tray of homemade cookies for the whole office or a bowl of chicken soup for me—also, homemade—if I have even the slightest sign of a cold coming on. Over the course of my twenty-five years at 49th & Park, she has always befriended my secretaries but that's only her way of being nice. She and my secretary Shelley are very friendly, and play tennis together every few months. She's had the partners over for dinner often, and just as everyone who meets her does, they all love her. Sweet, innocent, and lacking in curiosity is Miranda.

I needed a wife who didn't ask questions and that is certainly one of the reasons why our marriage is still going strong.

After Cindy's death, I couldn't talk about her and Miranda was the only woman I dated who didn't pry. I knew she wanted to know what I'd been up to since Cindy died, but she had the decency and common sense not to ask. If a man is avoiding an issue, it's because he doesn't want to talk about it. We're uncomplicated creatures. Eat, love, sleep, repeat.

At the deli when Miranda and I bumped into one another again, I hadn't seen her since my undergrad days. The summer we met we were both in Bryce National Park where her father was studying stalagmite formations. Her father was one of my geology professors, so during that summer we chatted often and she would come in and join us. She was to enter college that Fall. I would see her occasionally around campus my senior year and wave. But now, in the deli eating tuna sandwiches on rye toast, we sat at a table together and discussed the National Parks, our childhoods, and topics pre-Cindy, pre-tragedy, pre-black op training.

Women were chasing me and complicating things. Miranda was the healthy choice and one I'm still glad I made since I need her to help me stay away from some part of myself—the drinking, partying side that deep down I always blamed for Cindy's death. I suppose the pursuit of law called to me for the same reason. I stayed away from anyone who could make me love them so much I would drown. Miranda kept me afloat.

No one in my circle of friends and certainly no one in my family knows what I really do. Nor do they suspect. When I see them tonight, I'm sure they'll all ask, or at least Miranda will, about my "legal work in China's capital," which was my cover story for my time on the botched black-op mission in Manila.

As always, I'll divert the conversation back to them with false modesty, making up an excuse about not wanting to bore them. It wouldn't bore them for a second if they knew the truth—that a young man was murdered in my Manila hotel room while I was chasing down a top JI-AQ agent.

But they don't know. And they never will.

Chapter Eleven
December 21, 2011

MIRANDA

We are all to meet for cocktails at six on the hotel veranda. There are festive poinsettias all around—as centerpieces on the round tables, on the overhang that looks out onto the ocean and in white ceramic planters. The sun is just setting as I sit on a plush green cushion atop a wicker chair. The only person missing is my husband, Tripp, who's landing in a few hours. He's coming to join us a day earlier than expected, which is a wonderful surprise.

As always, Ricky is the first to arrive. He looks so handsome in his pink shirt, white trousers, and blue blazer.

"Lookin' sharp, Mamacita," my youngest tells me as he kisses my cheek.

"Aw, honey..." I smile.

It's a mystery how this child, this A-plus child of mine, does not have a girlfriend.

Julia and Jake come strolling out next. Julia looks so fresh, so happy, so chic. I think I spot a new dress on the girl whom I hope will be my daughter-in-law very soon. She must've had a nap after her plane arrived or perhaps it's just her youth.

How I'd love to be her dress size, have her wrinkle-free skin. These days, I could afford a face lift and even liposuction but I've always believed in the au natural look. As does Tripp.

"Hey, Jules! How was the flight? Look at you... wowza," Ricky says, bringing in Julia for a hug.

"Thanks, Ricky. It was—" She smiles as Jake cuts her off.

"Okay, so, I know the plan was to eat here but I've taken the liberty of accepting an invitation for us tonight."

The rest of us look at each other, perplexed. *Huh?*

"You did?" Julia asks.

"Yeah, the woman I got into the accident with offered to take us to The Outrigger Canoe Club for dinner."

"Why?" Matt asks.

Matt is my middle child. By relative standards, he's still a handsome boy but he lacks the striking features of his older and younger brothers. You wouldn't know it just from looking at him but Matt suffers from a mild case of Asperger's syndrome.

"Why? Honestly, I think she was feeling pretty guilty... I kind of laid into her afterward." Jake tells us.

"Why are you changing everything, Jake?" Matt asks with no filter, as always.

"Because she's cool and we're in Hawaii, Matt. God forbid we do something a little different from what Trip Advisor says!" Jake snaps.

Julia squeezes Jake's arm and shoots him a sweet but firm look that says, *calm down.*

Ricky steps in, "Dude, relax. You just caught us off guard is all."

"Oh, Jake, I'd love to go there! I read all about it in *Travel & Leisure*. It's a private club. But I can't go like this..." I glance down at my flowered top and white pants.

"Ugh, no way, Jose. I don't want to get dressed up," Matt complains.

"I'll do whatever," says Ricky.

"Same. But if you ask me, this woman has a lot of making up to do… crashing into this one," she jokes, leaning into Jake possessively.

I understand the second I see Cleopatra why Jake had accepted. She is simply exquisite. A dark-haired, Grace Kelly beautiful. She is that woman from those movies we all watched again and again as a family: *Rear Window, To Catch a Thief, High Society, Dial M for Murder.* She's radiant, beaming at Jake, flirting with my son, flirting with us all. I wonder what it would be like to see her face instead of mine in the mirror each morning. Her face instead of mine with my pug nose and short, red-gold curls. I know I am plain but I also know I have a perfect life.

She takes us on a tour of her club, smiling at us, and charming us. She's incredibly buoyant, exactly as Jake was earlier today. She leads us into a small, cozy dining room named Koa Lanai. We all take our seats, our hostess sandwiched between Jake and Matt.

She must have orchestrated the table setting. White roses upon more white roses and white, flickering, votive candles. She is dressed in white too—in a flowing ankle length dress, which is quite body-hugging. You couldn't pay me to wear something so revealing. But she looks like a Greek goddess in that dress and with that face and body.

"White roses are my favorite flower," Jake informs Cleo.

She smiles and dazzles and glistens. And he smiles and dazzles and glistens back.

I know for a fact that Jake doesn't give a damn about flowers. He calls them all petunias. This Cleo has placed quite the spell over my son. But when? How? During a fender bender and an exchange of insurance information? He's been fishing all afternoon, then picked up Julia. Maybe I'm overthinking this. Perhaps she's just one of those people who likes to extend herself. I'm sure that's it.

"So, Ricky, are you a big golfer? I noticed all those clubs in Jake's car when I crashed into it!" Cleo asks.

"I am! Yeah, I definitely plan on spending a lot of our time here out on the course."

She keeps on and on like a windshield wiper that is stuck. Giddy. People are... different here. My own son is different. I feel a hundred years old even though Cleo and I must be only a few years apart. But my sons all act like she's their contemporary. It's like she was handed a Regan family list of likes and dislikes prior to dinner, knowing precisely what to say and to whom. Though I suppose seeing my sons, it's easy enough to guess what their interests would be. But what stuns me is even Matt vies for her attention. Matt, in his own blunt way, asks her who she is married to.

She answers, "I would have gotten married but he died in a plane crash."

Matt takes her hand. *Really?* I'm almost glad my husband had to miss this dinner, though knowing him, he might see through her.

She looks my way, turning her spotlight on me. And she knows just what to say too.

"What a lovely family you have, Miranda. You must be so proud of your three guys."

I smile. This is my power. Somehow, every wonderful thing in my life has come to me through it. My husband said it was pure goodness and kindness—he would never be afraid if he could see my smile every day.

"Four, actually. My husband, Tripp, gets in tonight. He finished a business trip early so he's on his way," I tell her.

"Oh, how nice. Were you in love the moment you saw him?" she asks. "I bet you were."

"Well, yes," I smile as I realize she just reeled me in. "I was in love. But sadly, he didn't even notice me then."

Cleo smiles and says, "But obviously, he realized his mistake."

Jake picks up a white rose from the centerpiece and smells it. He looks intimately at Cleo. When could he have had time with her? A pit forms suddenly in my stomach. *Ahhhh... I know.*

"How many fish did you catch today, Jake?" I ask my son.

He smiles. "Just one beauty," he says. "But I had to let it go."

"Really, why?" Julia asks.

"It got so wet, it slipped away." He laughs.

I catch Cleo's face—the intimacy mirrored in it. She's been with him all afternoon, I just know it. My stomach is doing somersaults and I think I might be sick.

Chapter Twelve
December 21, 2011

CLEO

"I want to propose a toast to the Regan family. Oh, and Julia too! I'm so delighted to meet you all. As we say here on the island, hipahipa! Cheers!"

Jake flashes a sexy grin as his glass clinks mine.

I turn to Julia, not quite sure how to do this. "I just love the name Julia—like Julia Child. Do you cook?"

"God, no. I'm a nightmare in the kitchen. Jake can attest to that."

"She's not wrong..." Jake smiles.

Julia frowns a bit as if she was half-expecting him to come to her defense. But I can tell she's a smart girl, and she doesn't say a word. She just laughs. Julia strikes me as one of those girls who gets people to laugh and to like her by being modest and self-deprecating.

Ricky, the youngest brother, chimes in, "Don't listen to Jake, Jules. Your man's idea of fine dining is Chipotle..."

Julia and Ricky share a laugh at Jake's expense.

Oh, this is interesting. Jake's brother Ricky is in love with Julia and Jake doesn't have a clue. Ricky is a touch more handsome than Jake, but he lacks the intensity. And sweet Matt. Well, I like Matt. I think he must have a mild form of Asperger's. He's so honest, too honest. A symptom of his condition, I would imagine. His brothers must always protect him.

"Where are you from, Julia?" I feel compelled to get to know her for a number of reasons. One of which is that I rather like her. And the other...

"Well, I was born on the Rock—sorry, I always do that, of Gibraltar."

"Oh, how wonderful."

Ricky adds, "Her dad owns the only newspaper over there."

Julia turns to him, seemingly surprised he knows this. Oh, he is so definitely in love with her. I suspect she might have an inkling but gravely avoids the topic so as not to embarrass Ricky or anger Jake. I imagine Jake was the leader of the pack in school, captain of all his sports teams, Homecoming King, and perhaps a bit of a bully to the less popular kids. Ricky, on the other hand, would be friends with everyone regardless of social standing, GPA, team, or club.

Turning to me, Ricky explains, "I work at *Slate,* an online magazine. I like to know how other countries view the world."

Julia smartly steers the subject back to me, "What about you, Cleo? Where are you from?"

"I was born in Paris. I grew up there and in Algeria and New York. I studied at the Sorbonne."

"No way, small world! I went to the Sorbonne too." she smiles congenially.

"We have a lot in common..." I smile back.

She furrows her brow, slightly confused. But I can tell Julia is no dummy.

"Yes, spelunking! Jake came to my house after our little crash as I didn't have any of my papers with me... Anyway,

I mentioned the caves on my property and he told me his very pretty girlfriend loved to spelunk," I say, smiling. Lying through my teeth.

Okay, well, he didn't say that exactly, but having grown up on The Rock, I figured that "his British friend" had to be her. Suddenly, Miranda chokes on her wine. Jake smiles at me as everyone else turns to Miranda, concerned.

"You okay, mom?" Matt asks, patting her back.

"Yes. Fine," she answers hoarsely, politely wiping her mouth with a napkin.

"Oh, wow. You have caves *on* your property? That's convenient... Gibraltar has great caves. When I was little, my father would take me into them and I wanted to stay all day." She pauses. "I have friends, I swear." Julia laughs at herself.

We all laugh with her. She is quite charming.

"You are welcome to use the ones on my property."

Julia leans into Jake. "I don't think I'll have time. But thank you."

During a true Hawaiian dinner of pineapples, mahi-mahi, and a native Hawaiian rose wine from the Volcano winery called Lokelani, I keep gazing at Jake. I find his stillness magnetic. And I am transfixed with the hairs on his wrist where his shirt ends. What is he thinking, feeling? I pray he'll come to me later. How could we have a day like this and not want to extend it forever? But maybe now, compared to his young girlfriend, he sees me as too old. Well, I am too old but we'll see.

I CONTINUE TO PLY JULIA with my questions. I must admit, I'm quite fascinated by her. Part of this whole new world I find myself in.

"Where do you work, Julia?"

"At the bank with Jake."

"Tell Cleo how you met, Julia. It's such a darling story…" Miranda chirps.

"Mom…" grumbles Jake.

"What?"

"Everyone's heard it a thousand times," snaps Jake.

Julia smirks at Jake and nudges him playfully. "It's fine, Oscar The Grouch. I'll tell it," she offers, trying to please Miranda. "My first day at the office, I was going down the escalator and Jake was going up. We smiled at each other as we passed and before I knew it, this really cute—if not slightly creepy—guy was running down the up escalator to catch me. People were starting to notice and look over at us, which isn't exactly the type of attention you want on your first day. Then, to make matters worse, he started shouting, 'Hey! You with the long brown hair!'" Julia turns to me. "I know, what a charmer… So, finally, he caught up with me and refused to let me off until I agreed to go out with him."

Hmmm, Jake sees what he wants and goes for it. And yes, Julia is lovely but I think she'd have much more fun with Ricky. Then she can leave Jake here with me! In another world, I would adore Julia, but not here and not tonight. Tonight, she is my gladiator opponent. She has youth and history with him. I have passion and although this is new to me, there seems to be a tremendous power in passion.

Miranda, Jake's very cute, short, chunky, red-gold-haired mother, starts making polite conversation, mumbling as she gobbles down the coconut cake.

"Can you tell us more about Hawaii?"

"Well, as the legend goes, Hawaii was made of volcanic eruptions by the goddess, Pele."

Jake moves his seat closer to mine when I mention Pele.

"The soccer player?" he asks innocently.

Oh, boy. Really?

"Noooo, Jake. The goddess Pele, Pelehonuamea, the maker of this island."

"Right. I knew that..." He and Julia both laugh.

I talk about the islands I love as I sip my iced coffee. Up until tonight, my work, my Krav Maga, my friends, and Hawaii were enough. So much has changed.

"People feel it's necessary to assuage Pele, who is extremely vindictive. When She's angered, Pele sends fiery lava to smolder down the sides of the volcano, and She is the one who initiates the trembling and the earthquakes. Pele's a very jealous goddess who has clashed and fought with her own sister over a handsome lover."

I glance at Jake. I can't help myself.

"Pele's sister is the snow-capped mountain goddess, Poliahu," I continue. "Pele gets jealous if her lover is with Poliahu and shakes the earth. Her fires erupt so intensely that Poliahu leaves the island. But Poliahu regroups and brings a massive snowstorm to put out Pele's fire. Some days you can see Pele, the volcano, snowcapped by Poliahu, the snow goddess."

Jake smiles that astounding smile. I imagine he sees me as Pele fighting Julia over him, the handsome stranger. Then I feel his hand on my knee and our legs tangle and I can't breathe.

"Tell us more..." he says.

"Well, let's see... I have a friend, Jimbo, who does this yearly race in Hawaii called the Ironman. He gets down and kisses the black lava road before he begins the race, whispering to Pele that he bears her no ill will and hopes she will let him run and ride over her. He has a poetic streak in him."

Jake allows a small smile. Fortunately, as I was on the brink of kissing him, his mother interrupts, "we should be getting back to our hotel. Your father will be arriving soon. His plane landed forty-five minutes ago."

What a good wife, wanting to be home for her husband.

"Miranda, whenever I leave Hawaii my plane shakes and rumbles with turbulence. My friend Jimbo says it's because Pele hates me or anyone to leave her. He says if Pele has blessed you by allowing you to come to her island, she expects you to stay." Then I murmur to Jake as everyone starts to get up from the table, "maybe you better stay here..."

Jake takes his hand off my leg and whispers, "Jimbo... he looked kinda unhappy when he saw us together."

"No, no," I whisper back. "He was probably just surprised to see a stranger on the property. He likes everything in its place. He keeps an eye on my house."

"And on you?"

I smile and he leans in close.

"Do you hear any bells?" he whispers.

Ah, he is still in thrall to me as I am to him.

"Not now. But perhaps I will later?" I whisper back.

Chapter Thirteen
December 21, 2011

JULIA

After we thank Cleo profusely and leave the Outrigger, Miranda cheerily (the woman is constantly cheery, I don't know how she does it) reminds us that we're meeting Mr. Regan at the piano bar back at The Halekulani. I'm so jetlagged that I'd rather swan dive directly into our king-size bed instead of making polite conversation with the whole family Regan. But, alas, Mr. Regan has just flown in from China, Miranda reminds us again, so this gal really doesn't have a choice.

By the time we get to the bar twenty minutes later, my Stuart Weitzmans are dragging across the tile floor and my head feels like there's a one-hundred-pound weight anchored to it. Mr. Regan stands when he sees us coming. It isn't *that* creepy to think my boyfriend's father, a.k.a. my future father-in-law, is sexy, is it? He and Jake have very similar features so *technically*, he's just an older version of Jake. Basically, I'm just being smart and thinking about my future.

Mr. and Mrs. Regan greet each other with a sweet little kiss. "A day early. What a treat," Miranda coos.

"Yeah, what's the deal? They fire your ass?" Ricky jokes, shaking his father's hand.

"Not yet..." He smiles.

The first thing I always notice about Mr. Regan are his perfect teeth. Color me jealous. He must have had work done. Lately, I've been toying with the notion of Invisalign in order to fix a few slightly unruly bottom teeth, though I'm not sure Jake would take kindly to making out with a girl who has a mouthful of plastic and the occasional lisp.

"And Julia, you look as pretty as ever." Mr. Regan kisses my cheek.

"Thanks, Mr. Regan." *You, handsome devil, you.*

I put on a big smile as we all plop down in the bar's gorgeous and sumptuously cozy furniture.

Miranda turns to the pianist. "I wonder if you'd mind playing some Christmas carols? Our family would love to sing along!"

Here we go...

The pianist nods and starts playing "Jingle Bells." Jake, Ricky, Matt, and I all exchange looks. Forced family fun, here we come! Thankfully, Mr. Regan comes to the rescue.

"Mir, why don't we postpone the tra-la-las? I'm sure the kids are exhausted."

"Oh, alright..." Miranda concedes. Then she turns to me and takes my hand in hers.

"Sweetheart, why don't you tell us all about your first date with Jake? It's one of my favorite stories," she pleads.

I open my mouth to start the story—it's actually pretty cute—when I notice Jake rolling his eyes again.

"Mom... c'mon. First how we met and now our first date. No one cares," Jake protests.

Awkward. We all look around, taken aback by Jake's brusqueness. He's probably right, but still, I can't help feeling a little offended. Sure, I'm biased, but the story does make Jake look like the leading man in our very own rom-com.

"Gee, thanks," I laugh.

"Sorry... but everyone's heard the story, like, a gazillion times," Jake pats my bare thigh, realizing how brash he must have sounded.

"So, anyway, how was dinner? Did I miss a great night at The Outrigger?" Mr. Regan cuts in, elegantly changing the subject.

"Yeah, we missed you, big guy," says Ricky.

"You would've loved it, sweetheart. I had some mahi mahi in your honor," says Miranda.

"The food was delicious," I say, finally pitching into the conversation despite already being in sleep mode.

But Jake says nothing and he's still holding that dumb flower from The Outrigger. So weird. Mr. Regan watches him too. He's even more observant than I am half the time.

"She's gorgeous. And her favorite movie is the same as yours, Dad. *Chariots of Fire,*" states Matt in his cute, completely non sequitur way.

Ricky concurs, "Total babe."

To that, Miranda and I stay mum. Miranda just smiles that pleasant little smile she's so goddamned good at. I wonder if her mouth ever gets sore. Mine starts to shake uncontrollably if I try holding a smile for more than ten seconds. Just ask any of the brides whose wedding parties I've been a part of. Being a bridesmaid is cool and all, and obviously an honor, but I can't stand taking all the photos with the bride, with the bride and the groom, with the bride and all the other bridesmaids, with the bride and her family. I could go on. By the end of the big day, my whole mouth is sore from all the constant grinning. I could never be one of those girls who competes in those Miss America pageants. Well, for several reasons, not just all the smiling, I could never be one of those girls.

Matt gets up to explore a grouping of red poinsettias that decorate the piano bar.

"You know, these poinsettias get a bad reputation. They're not even poisonous but everyone thinks they are. And nobody would really eat them anyway. They're really bitter," Matt points out earnestly.

Mr. Regan nibbles goofily on a leaf then promptly spits it out. He laughs with Matt. Everyone agrees with Matt in matters of botany. The poinsettias, the big, red, velvet chairs, and burning fire. It's all so wonderfully Christmas-y. I glance over at the fireplace, the dancing flames lulling me to sleep.

"Yo, Jules. Why do you think they need fireplaces in Hawaii?" Ricky asks me.

I think this is just his nice, underhanded way of keeping my eyes open. There's no way he actually gives a rat's arse about Hawaiian fireplaces.

"I don't know, because Hawaiian nights can be quite cool?" I answer through a yawn.

"How was your flight, Julia?" asks Mr. Regan who, like me, is still watching Jake holding that weird white rose. "Less bumpy than mine, I hope."

"Oh, it was fine. I indulged in one whole glass of champagne. I'm so wild."

"It's the only way to fly." Mr. Regan laughs.

"I watched a few movies. None of them were especially memorable, except have you ever seen *Love, Actually?* I've probably watched it twenty-five times since it came out but I was feeling adventurous and decided to go for twenty-six. It's so good. Always gets me in the holiday spirit!"

"Of course. I love the burnt-out old guy who's still in the game."

"Bill Nighy," Miranda points out.

"Hey, I'm not a crier, but that scene at the end where all the couples reunite at the airport... Gets me everytime," Ricky chimes in.

Can I get an amen? Preach, Ricky. Kind, sweet, attentive, calculating Ricky. I knew I can count on him to do my dirty work. I smile and he winks back at me. I wonder if he knows Jake ditched me and didn't pick me up at the airport...

"That's my favorite part too. I *love* a good airport reunion," I add with purpose, nodding to Jake.

He impishly rolls his eyes, realizing what I'm driving at.

"Jake," I whisper, "I'm too tired to do the family thing right now. Would it be okay if we went up to bed?" I make the pouty face that I know he loves.

But tonight, he just stares blankly at me. "Yeah, you go ahead. I'll be up soon."

When I got to the hotel earlier today, he hardly even looked at me. Drawing myself a much needed bubble bath, I asked him about fishing as I stripped down to my (intentionally worn) red lacy Hanky Pankys. Not once did Jake take his eyes off ESPN as I pranced back and forth making idiotic excuse after idiotic excuse about things I needed from across the room. Public Service Announcement: do not try this at home. I'm here to tell you how mortifying it is leaning over your suitcase and strategically wiggling your ass in the air without even so much as being glanced at.

Deep breath, Jules. Be the "cool girlfriend." Except, breaking news: I'm already the "cool girlfriend" just by going on yet another Regan family holiday! Not that I'm complaining, but I've never missed one. Not. A. One. And Miranda puts on a *lot* of family get-togethers. Her purpose in life is organizing family vacations, family dinners, family tennis round-robins, family game nights, family discussions. Family, family, family. Everything, everything, *everything*. Poor Miranda. She's never had a career, let alone a real adult job, but I do think she would've been so good as an executive assistant to a high-powered CEO or big-time hedge fund manager. Say what you want about her, the woman is organized. Her grocery lists are practically typed out in an Excel doc. In a screwed up way, I guess she's Tripp's assistant and even the boys' sometimes too. It's safe to say that she hasn't adapted third-wave feminism like many of us. But she's always been incredibly nice to me. Nicer than her son is being at this moment...

Since I met Jake two years ago, I haven't been home on holiday once. And when I do go for a brief visit, God forbid Jake be by my side. It's Gibraltar, yes, and so it's far, sure, but it's amazing and it's my home. I can tell my father already doesn't like Jake. He makes zero effort.

Not to ramble, but a perfect example is Jake could've stayed with me in the city one extra night for my MOMA Young Members ball. But *no-o*, he just had to be on the same flight as his precious family. I imagine Miranda played a part in that. Side note: she still books all her sons' travel. Talk about mama's boys. All I wanted was for him to *want* to come to my party. And, okay, even if he doesn't, would it kill him to at least pretend he's up for doing something because it's important to me? Like coming up to bed with me right now.

But he doesn't, so I crawl into the gorgeous, five-hundred count Egyptian cotton sheets alone. See you on the flip, Honolulu.

Chapter Fourteen
December 22, 2011

CLEO

I am certain Jake will come to me later. But he doesn't come and I stay awake all night waiting, anger building to fury like Pele the fire goddess wondering if he's with Poliahu, the snow goddess. Pacing, and alternately laughing at myself for thinking he'd come and despairing as I picture him in bed with her. I am beside myself. I try to sleep. On the one hand, I am loving this sexual awakening and the merry-go-round I'm on, but on the other, the spinning is so fast that it scares me. I hate how his actions or inactions can affect me this much after just one day.

I like Julia and I hate to hurt her. But I want Jake in a way I myself can't understand. It's changing me. The feelings are so new and yet there's something that makes me feel I've known Jake always. Confusingly different than the orderly relationships I have with my friends and coworkers, my sisters and Jimbo. This is my mother, not me, who loved to hurl passion around—tossing it like a huge vase of flowers at a cowering lover. This almost primal reaction to Jake is pulling me out of control—it's dangerous and I can't afford the explosiveness, the

Pele fire raging, burning me up. I don't want him to consume my life. He will be gone soon. But like the alcoholic, I yearn for one last binge. I want him to come to me tonight. I tell myself I can afford this as my drug of choice will be gone on a 747 back to New York soon. Oh, my mother is up there applauding me. She is thrilled to see her daughter following so fully in her footsteps of fantasy.

Her daughter who fought her whole life to be without a man. It made my mother so sad to see my choices. She sent me to shrinks and hypnotists and set me up on constant dates, but nothing could eradicate my trauma of being raped by a friend of my father's whom I had adored and who nearly suffocated me that night with his hand over my mouth and nose. I still wake up in the night, trying to breathe, and decades have passed. I still scream in the night and sleep with lights on and occasionally put a chair in front of my door should someone enter uninvited. I own a gun that I can get to very fast and my training in self-defense with Krav Maga has achieved the highest level now. It takes a serious force of will to be brutalized in these training sessions but, until finally having an orgasm with Jake, until leaving my frigid self behind, it was the most important thing I did. I know the training keeps danger away but Jake is danger too and I don't want to ever keep him away.

I still can't sleep. To dip into slumber, my mother would count men she had made love to instead of sheep. My mother, ah, my mother. She who quoted Camus to my father the moment they met. Their fairytale; my favorite story. I tell it to myself over and over. When they met they were both single and were attending a reception in Paris at the Hotel de Salm, the National Museum of the Legionne D'Honor. He was dressed in white tie and tails and she in a yellow, draped, silk chiffon Stavropoulos gown with huge Bulgari yellow diamond earrings. They were, undisputedly, perfectly mismatched. He was tall; she was slight. He was dark and strong; she was pale and fragile. He had thick dark hair curling around his neck, and she platinum blonde hair pulled back in a chignon. His eyes were coal black; hers, violet. He was a smart, spoiled, charming French Algerian and she was a rich, spoiled, charming American. So, of course, they fell passionately in love.

When she found out he was French Algerian, she said, "Ah, Camus."

"I know of only one duty, and that is to love," he responded.

Then she, with her killer smile, intoning that favorite Camus line, countered, "Charm is a way of getting the answer 'yes' without ever having asked any clear question."

Nothing more needed to be said. With that, he put his arm around her waist, and took her from the party. He claimed her and she loved it. His friends, who followed him everywhere, yelled out as they departed but he kept going, with not the slightest nod to them.

He lived around the corner from the Salm Mansion on the Rue de Verneuil where they spent the next four months. They married and a few years later I was born. His only child. Her first of three daughters.

My mother never tried to please him or any husband. For my mother, every husband was a rebirth. Each divorce, a death. She certainly had a cycle not unlike the Church with Christmas, Lent, Easter. Hers was a 3–5 year cycle: courtship, wedding, redecorate. The latter was her favorite phase and so telling as to how she was viewing herself, what role she was playing at the time. She was like a blank slate and reflected whatever she saw or read or heard. After reading *Shibumi*, she wrote Haiku verses; after seeing *Dr. Zhivago* she began collecting Faberge eggs.

She was like a well-tended garden, blossoming in the sun. Her sunlight, her vitamin D, just happened to come in the form of men. She allowed them to open her petals. It was as though Mother had a lesson to learn from each of these men and once she learned it, on she went to her next lesson. She was indefatigable and perhaps we adored her and always talked about her because she was never there to scold us. She just was. And at the core, she was untamed. But she feared the untamed outside herself. When she once bought a tiny black kitten for us for Christmas, it arched its tiny back and she flew into such a panic she made us shut it up in the kitchen and had the housekeeper take it back. She preferred animals in the zoos, in controlled environments. The contrast between a total child and a brave woman was elemental in her nature, and our lives pivoted around which one predominated. If her fears took control, as they did after a divorce, we'd have to spend hours calming her down by singing as she played the piano. She loved music; before she left for her death in Switzerland, she kept listening to, "Don't Cry for Me, Argentina." She saw herself as Evita, certainly.

Nature was never her "thing." She had flowers everywhere, but the country scared her—it was too lonely and she'd rush back to the city. Trees bored her, they didn't reflect her. She admitted feeling most mortal, most alone, when she saw farmhouses in Vermont with acres between them at night. Each house with its lights on seemed so vulnerable without crowding neighbors on either side. She could never be alone at night without calling a friend to come stay with her. Just about anyone would do and they could sleep wherever. Many a night when the help was out, she'd bribe one of us to stay with her. Once we were ensconced, she'd forget all about us and go to sleep. But she would have been hearing voices, looking in closets and behind shower curtains, bolting herself in her room with a light on until she'd relent, admit she was a child and go get someone to sleep in the house. If a robber entered then, she'd go right out to meet him, but alone she'd cower, the robbers in her mind far more devilish than any flesh-and-blood man.

I know why my mother, Sandrine, left my father, Didier. He was simply too much competition for her. He was so very handsome. He looked like a movie star and his ever-present sunglasses and cigarette dangling out of his mouth did not diminish his image. His energy was more contained—he didn't strain to take in everyone he met. When I was grown, he tried to explain her to me. He told me she once gave all his ski sweaters away to the bums in Central Park and suggested he go over to see them all lined up on the benches at 59th Street. Her enthusiasm spilled over to infringe on all of us, he explained.

Our infrequent family dinners were ruined when she added the man fixing the bathroom tiles, who barely spoke English and hadn't showered. I hated those dinners. My sisters and I used to try with all her "collections," as she called them—but soon we'd close ranks and she'd exhaust herself being kindly when we abandoned her to her "poor things," her dinner guests who themselves felt so out of place.

She'd take her earrings off and put them on again and again. It was her signal to us to help her out—but we wouldn't. She loved her gestures of blithely asking anyone to join us. But she hated dealing with the "guests" herself, so she called upon her private secretary, Rosie. Rosie began appearing at dinner to handle her collections when we rebelled. Her "guests" included people from all ranks of life who didn't quite fit in. An opera singer who was very obese, a woman who had been left by her husband and could talk of nothing else were all brought into her life and once they were there she didn't know what to do with them and in her typical fashion, she wanted others to rescue her. She didn't want to deal with the reality of their problems. Somehow, she thought just by having them to dinner they would be happy. And when that wasn't so, she collapsed and sent others in to do the work.

Mother was pure passion, a broken thermometer, always turned on high. And right now, with Jake, I am turned on high, so very high, and so addicted to this new sensation of heat.

Chapter Fifteen

DIDIER

As a little girl, my daughter Cleopatra would fuss over my photographs of the men from The Club—a dining club I had the privilege of joining during my tenure at Oxford in the early sixties.

"Who's that one, Daddy?" she'd ask, pointing to one of my celluloid cronies.

"You know who that is, Cleopatra..." I'd tell her, trying to pry the old photograph away from her fingers.

"But I forget..." she'd lie, with stars in her dazzling violet eyes.

Silence is an official rule and I am very discreet. I respect the law of omerta and have never spoken openly about what happens in smoky back rooms or behind closed doors of The Club. Cleopatra is the only person I've discussed The Club with and even then, she only knows the tip of the iceberg.

The Club alumnus reads like a who's who of past, present, and future world leaders. In our brethren, there are kings of tiny countries, princes of large ones, lords, earls, CEOs of trillion-dollar tech companies. My father's royal French lineage and my famous dry sense of humor granted me entrance into the ultraexclusive club. Former members often go onto great-ness and the contacts you make are priceless.

I had other reasons to keep the goings on at The Club close to the vest. It was here, during my third year, when I was recruited to one of the most elite organizations in the world by the then president. One afternoon, while I was studying for a Political Science exam in the upper reading room at Old Bodleian Library, Nathan "Fenny" Fennebresque slipped a note inside the pocket of my sports coat. The most beautiful women at our parties were always drawn to him—and it wasn't because he was president or his family owned a goodly portion of the Earth. He just had that *je ne sais quoi* that everyone always finds so goddamn irresistible.

I reached into my jacket and pulled out the note. I figured he was simply trying to break up the monotony of my political science studying. But then, I read the note. *Walton's. 11pm.*

Walton's was a pub on an eponymous street that I'd heard of but never visited. It was a bit off the beaten path for Oxford students with their noses upturned into the air. Sitting there in the muted four-hundred-year-old library, somehow, I knew. I knew that my meeting that night would change my life for-ever. Since my intuition was so very right about that night, I've learned to trust it in future moments.

The front door at Walton's closed behind me with a creak. I glanced around the pub, looking for Fenny's blonde head. At first, I didn't see him so I glanced down at my watch—10:56. I was early. I started toward the bar and was about to sit.

"Gallier," said a voice to my right.

I turned and saw Fenny there in the shadows, at a table in the very back. He was sipping something dark from a rock's glass. The scene was all so sinister that I almost laughed to myself as I walked over to him. I slid into the seat across from him and noticed a newspaper on the table. Afraid that I might say the wrong thing, I waited for Fenny to speak first. He raised his glass and made a movement with his fingers. Two drinks with the same brown liquid were delivered to our table by the young bartender within seconds. Still, not a word had passed between us. Fenny waited until the barkeep was back behind the bar to take a sip from his drink. He slid the newspaper toward me and tapped his index finger twice on an article with the headline, "Nazi General Dies In His Sleep."

I read the headline aloud.

"That's us."

Us. The club within The Club. Also known as, The Business. So top secret that there is no other name for it. We don't have a company letterhead, business cards, or even headquarters. The dark corners around the world are our main office. We are the people working behind the people *working behind* the people pulling the strings. We are not the puppet masters, we are the executors. The Business works with all of the world's major intelligence agencies—MI6, The CIA, RAW, GRU, all of them—and pulls off the riskiest and most confidential missions. We are the real-life spies that James Bond and *The Man from U.N.C.L.E.* wish they were. You have been led to believe that the undercover agents who toil and tinker away at MI6 or the CIA or any other of the world's secret crime-fighting organizations are as deep as it goes. But you have been had, hoodwinked. To quote Baudelaire, "the finest trick of the devil is to persuade you that he doesn't exist." And that, my friend, is exactly the point.

There is a great need for all of the top intelligence agencies of the world, they've been around for decades and have saved us more times than any of us will ever know from extremists, xenophobes, terrorists, and God knows who else. The Business needs them as they—good people that they are—do most of the legwork. And that's when it's time to call someone from The Business. It is paramount that employees at traditional intelligence agencies build cover identities in order to succeed at missions. Duality reigns supreme over there, but anonymity—hell, *invisibility*—is king here at The Business. We have the network of such power no one can touch us and we use it wisely for the good of the World.

Fenny paused. "So, Gallier. Any grand plans after graduation?"

"Yes, I think I'll work in my family's vineyards. In Algeria."

Fenny looked at me for a long while. He drained the last of his brown liquid, then folded his hands. A small smile washed across his face.

"Do you think that'll be enough?"

"Enough?"

"We've been watching you. Studying you. Something tells us that the vineyards of Algeria might become, well... a trifle dull after a while."

That night changed my life and it would change Cleopatra's too.

The horror of what had happened to our nine-year-old Cleopatra was mitigated by Sandrine holding her and never leaving her side. After asking her if she needed to talk, Cleopatra said no, she never ever was going to talk about it. Sandrine understood. Our nine-year-old daughter had been raped while she was sleeping at my house in Algeria where I was entertaining some of my Oxford clubmates. Three had left after a long boozy dinner and the other three of us went running to her room when the screams sounded. She was lying there with her nightie up around her hips and blood all over. She was screaming and screaming and shaking so hard. She kept saying he, whoever he was, had put his hand over her mouth and she kept biting it. She couldn't see him as it was so dark and he put something over her eyes. She woke to a body on top of hers and a pain rushing through her. She thought she was being smothered to death by his hand.

Three weeks later, her mother, who had come over to stay as soon as she heard, left to go back to her newest lover in the States. I was furious that Sandrine would abandon her daughter in such a time of need, but that was Sandrine. In her defense, she had dropped her whole world to be by her daughter's bedside for twenty-one days straight. While Sandrine was here, she was the best mother a daughter could ask for. But when she wasn't, well, she wasn't. You might say the same about me... Cleopatra needed her mother here and Sandrine understood that. But my Cleopatra was used to having an expiration date on their time together, and on ours too.

One day shortly after Sandrine left, when we felt we had no clues left to follow up on, Cleopatra came down to breakfast. She sat there a long while in silence then looked over at me with big violet eyes that were about to break my heart.

"Daddy..." she said, her tiny voice trembling.

"What is it?" I asked her, sensing something was very wrong.

"I think... I think it was a friend of yours."

My heart sank. My world shattered. My fists clenched. I knew exactly what she meant and instantly, I knew exactly what I had to do.

"When I bit into his finger, Daddy, I felt... I felt the ring you all wear."

She would say nothing more. Obviously, it had to have been one of my "friends" who had "left" after dinner. My job was to find which one, and kill him. And I did. I went to "visit" each of my three friends who had retreated early that night. I saw them separately. I kept hoping she was wrong.

The first one, William Van Ingen, lived in Holland. I noticed in an instant that he didn't have his ring on. And when I asked him about it, he said he'd given it to his son, William Jr. upon his graduation from Harrow years ago. I had someone find his son who, at the time, was at Erasmus University in Rotterdam. He was, indeed, wearing the ring and when asked how long he had had it, confirmed his father's story. William was not the one.

The second, Henry Guernier, lived in Paris as did I, when I wasn't in Algeria. When I dropped by for a drink, we embarked on an hour of small talk about God knows what. I was on autopilot and couldn't focus for more than one minute at a time. Eventually, I saw an opening and queried where he had gone after our drunken dinner.

"Don't you remember I blew out of there? My plane was waiting to take me back here. I had to meet with the PM at eight in the goddamn morning," Henry laughed, draining the rest of his forty-year old scotch.

Now that he mentioned it, that did sound familiar. But still, he could be lying. Everyone in the club is a very, *very* good liar.

"Christ, I was still a bit tipsy when I met him that morning. Don't think I left a spectacular impression." Henry chuckled again as he got up to make himself another drink.

Of course, I had someone check the log, and indeed Henry was on board minutes after leaving the party. My heart dropped and my chest tightened. Part of me, a big part, wanted it to be Henry. Because then, it wouldn't have to be Richard. Every time I tried to set up a meeting with Richard, he was off to Rio or

Tokyo or the States. Finally, a few months later, I walked into one of our clubs in London and saw him sitting there. When Richard Rensasslear saw me, he looked toward the exit. But Richard knew that in doing that, in glancing for a way out, that he'd made his second mistake. He'd acknowledged his guilt with just a glimpse. Richard got up and came over to me.

"Give me a few hours," Richard whispered.

That night, he went upstairs, wrote a farewell to his wife and shot himself in the mouth. I never asked Genevieve what Richard said in the note. When she asked me to speak at his funeral, I made up an excuse and made sure I was out of town on the day he was laid to rest.

Cleopatra smiled for me briefly when I told her he was dead. She slept in a room well lit with a servant next to her who held her hand until she slept. I had moved her room next to mine. Her life force was so diminished. I found someone to teach her self-defense and she worked at it fiendishly. I would remind her that change is constant, but discipline is the only form of permanence, so she must always work at her training. Once she asked which man it had been. I hated to tell her because Richard was her favorite, as he was mine. It was nearly a year before she laughed again.

Chapter Sixteen
December 22, 2011

JULIA

I turn on my side, waiting for Jake to come into our room and climb into bed—knowing that all he has to do is put his muscular arm around me and his chiseled bare chest against my back. I'll turn toward him and we'll have hot reunion sex. We always do.

I lie awake, waiting. And waiting. Thirty minutes later, stillll waitinggg. Finally, after an hour, he tiptoes into the room. But when he gets in bed, he doesn't touch me.

"Hiii," I whisper softly, in my sweet, sexy, half-tired voice.

Crickets. He doesn't say a word but I can hear him mouth-breathing on the other end of our king bed, fast asleep from the moment his head hits the pillow. Well, this is just swell. Feelings of pure hatred course through my entire size-two body. I'm going to make his life miserable for the next foreseeable twenty-four hours. At least! But just as soon as I think this, I change my mind and extend his deadline until morning. We'll wake up, have mind-blowing morning sex, and everything will be just fine and dandy.

When my eyes open at 8:00 a.m. on the dot, Jake isn't here. I repeat: *well, this is just fucking swell.* I wait for him to come out of the bathroom, readjusting myself into a "come hither" position as I pretend to be asleep. Lying on my side, I lower the bed sheet so that my whole naked back is exposed, giving Jake just a hint of my upper buttocks. And I position my arms so my cleavage looks as bodacious as possible (which isn't saying much). After half an hour of pretending, of constantly readjusting and repositioning, I finally call Jake's name and realize he's not even in the damn bathroom in the first place.

Uh...

There must be a note. I look around.

Nope, no note.

Okay, there has to be a text. I check my phone.

No text.

This isn't like Jake. He always tells me where he's going and for how long. He always checks in. He's such a devout checker-inner. It's one of the things I love about him. I guess it's possible he was hungry and went to breakfast, thinking I needed sleep. To be fair, I couldn't shut my yap about how effing exhausted I was last night. Or, another theory... he's gone running. I get up and check Jake's suitcase for his running shoes.

Voila, mystery solved. No shoes. He's gone for an early morning run. Just call me Angela Lansbury, ladies and gentlemen. I start to close Jake's suitcase when I notice a Tiffany-blue box tucked under one of his dress shirts. *Oh my God, oh my God, OH MY GOD.* This is it! My (better be emerald cut) engagement ring! I know I shouldn't, but there's no way in hell that I'm not going to open it. Carefully, I slide off the signature white bow so I can slide it right back on once I've had my peek. My heart rate is jumping. Slowly, I open the box to reveal a slender, gold chain necklace with a beautiful bar of diamonds. My heart sinks into my chest like a five-pound weight. Okay, so it isn't an engagement ring but it's certainly the last stop *before* the engagement ring. It's like a warm-up gift. A pregame. And who doesn't love a good pregame? Crazy people, that's who!

And on the bright side, he remembered. One day, after a very boozy brunch with Jake's Cornell friends, we were passing that famous Tiffany window when this gem of a necklace caught my eye. I told Jake how beautiful I thought it was, hoping but not actually believing in a million years, that he'd buy it for me.

Smiling like a fool, I slide the necklace out and try it on. Like, not to brag or anything, but it looks pret-ty darn great on me. Faint footsteps. *Shit.* I panic that Jake will waltz into the room with me standing here like a real dope wearing the necklace he hasn't even given me yet. Quickly, I take it off and back it goes into its Tiffany blue box wrapped in the white bow. I stuff it back into Jake's suitcase and like a madwoman on a fistful of uppers, zip it shut. I jump back into bed, pull the covers up over me, shut my eyes, and pretend to be asleep yet again.

One minute later, no Jake. False alarm. But one thing's for sure, I'm not so upset with him anymore.

Until next time, Tiff...

Over an hour later, Jake struts back into the room sweaty and red-faced. The door slams, jolting me out of my slumber. I glance over at the digital clock on the bedside table—9:22.

Jake sits on the edge of the bed and starts to unlace his Nikes.

"That was some run..." I say groggily, sitting up and wiping beneath my eyes.

He turns toward me, strips off his sweaty T-shirt and throws it at my face, flirtatiously.

"Jake, ew!" I giggle and toss the Cornell Lacrosse shirt back at him. He catches it, then drops it on the floor for the maids to clean up.

"How'd you sleep?"

"Good! These beds are so comfy... Why don't you come on in and we—"

"You looked so cute lying there, I didn't want to wake you up..."

That isn't like him. Usually, he looks forward to waking me up with sweet kisses on my neck, chest, and mouth. Jake is the king of jolting me out of a slumber, no matter how deep, for a preoffice workout between the sheets. A good boink rarely starts the day off wrong.

"What about you? Seems like you didn't even sleep for long..." I ask, trying to...

"Yeah, the time change has got me all screwed up. Couldn't really sleep so I figured I'd just get up and go for a run."

"Good for you. Where'd you go?"

"Eh, all over really," he tells me, starting toward the bathroom.

"Was it pretty?"

"Gorgeous."

He goes into the bathroom and closes the door behind him.

Well, good morning to you, too.

Chapter Seventeen
December 22, 2011

CLEO

At six in the morning, I walk outside. I am restless. I cannot get Jake out of my head and am hoping that a walk might distract or at least tire me out. I see Jimbo heading out on his morning bike ride with that very determined pumping in his legs. Jimbo, so methodical in everything he does, and yet so graceful, too. He looks up at me and seems surprised. He has one of his food bags wrapped around his neck. He leaves it on his route, filled with Gatorade and energy bars. Usually, he hangs it from a tree, camouflaged.

"You're up early..." Jimbo smiles as he glides up to me.

"You know, I am always so comforted by the sight of you, Jimbo," I tell him as he pumps closer and closer.

He laughs as he pedals in place. "Oh, yeah. Why's that?"

"Maybe I like having a big, strong man on the premises."

"By the looks of it, seems like you had one of those just yesterday..."

I walked into that one. I was hoping Jimbo had forgotten about seeing Jake but nothing gets by him. It's not as if I mind talking about Jake. I just don't particularly want to talk about him with my old friend, Jimbo, who can be so judgmental. He would feel it a badge of honor to remind me of the age difference. He didn't have to come that close to see that Jake is much younger than I. Jimbo leaps at any opportunity to poke fun at me and most of the time, he does it brilliantly. But I don't want him or anyone to make fun of Jake and me.

"How 'bout dinner tonight?" he asks, biking a bit closer.

"Could we perhaps play it by ear?" I smile. I'd at least like to keep the possibility open to see Jake, even with Julia here.

Playing it by ear isn't exactly in Jimbo's repertoire. I knew it was a mistake the moment it came out of my mouth. Everything about Jimbo's life is scheduled, regimented, and routine. His life is a merry-go-round of timers, alarm clocks, and stopwatches. Changing a dinner reservation from seven to seven thirty is Jimbo's idea of flying by the seat of his pants. He turns and pedals a circle around me on his bicycle, ensnaring me in a small patch of land that must only be two feet wide. I glance down at Jimbo's initials on his bike. His only affectation is monogramming his bike. He circles around me once more, keeping me trapped on my own little island. I know what he is doing. Jimbo is a master in the art of passive aggression. He looks over at me and smiles radiantly. A master.

"Fine. Let's have dinner tonight, Jimbo," I give in so easily.

And off he goes. He dips in for a second and then is gone like a hummingbird. And he really is just like a hummingbird— beautiful male plumage, moving fast, not delving for long into anything, taking what he wants and leaving right after.

"You're an oldie but a goodie, Cleo!" he says before riding off into the sunrise.

I finally go back to my bedroom and allow myself to sleep, giving Jake up with the dawn. But with the dawn, he arrives in his running gear, looking exhausted and scared and young. I no longer apologize to myself for what I want because in my deepest soul, I want him. At forty-four, one doesn't play the games that one does at twenty-four. I don't speak, I don't ask the questions women ask when they have a rival. I am here with him.

I know in three days Jake will be leaving me—he, his brothers, parents, and girlfriend all filing out of Hawaii's heaven to return to New York, to home and safety. I know he knows it is going to be over very soon. He knows it is safe to truly let go for once, and probably only this once. In this moment, he is worshipping me as the goddess of his dark side and I am feeling a huge tug to let myself play this game with him, to grasp his soul with the knowledge of life I have, to call on the goddess Pele to hold him hostage here forever and ever.

But instead, I say nothing. I am silent—sinking into the cliched pools of his eyes. I dive so deeply into those eyes two hours pass before I bolt up, realizing I am late for my job on the local talk show I host three times a week, *Close Encounters.*

The show is live on Tuesday, Wednesday, and Saturday from noon to twelve thirty during the heat of the day, and re-runs from five to five thirty before the news. As I jump out of bed and throw on a sundress, he grabs my arm. His touch makes me shiver as he pulls me into him.

"Not so fast," he whispers, kissing me deeply. "What time's your show?"

"Noon," I respond, kissing him back, but then pulling away. He gives up, lets me go, but not without regret.

"I'll watch," he says before he goes out to meet his taxi, which he just called. After a brief one-mile run, he hailed a taxi on the way here so that he could spend as much time with me as possible.

I leave quickly with the smell of him all over me, dazed in the sun, tummy in turmoil, laughing, wondering what he will say to his family about his extended three-hour run. Had Julia noticed him leaving their bed? She will certainly ask where he'd gone. Ironically, Julia knows more about the give and take of love than I do. One thing I do know is that she is probably sitting on the edge of the bed waiting for him, waiting as I had waited all last night.

Chapter Eighteen
December 22, 2011

MIRANDA

When Julia and Jake come down very late for breakfast, I'm quite relieved. I'm not a total control freak, but I admit, I hate chaos. And Cleo could cause it, I think.

When the boys were young, I did my very best to keep chaos at bay. Everyone on the playground always looked to me for toys, diapers, clean spoons. I carried sweaters if it should grow cold, tidy wipes if they got filthy, snacks and juice, pails and books so they were happy and healthy. I never understood mothers who tolerated messes, who never planned ahead for rain or spills.

I was grateful Jake and Julia had spent the morning together. It looks like they're in love again—Julia with her pretty head burrowed in Jake's chest. They pull chairs up to my table under the pale green umbrella. I'm on my third glass of iced tea enjoying the end of my Agatha Christie, waiting for Matt and Tripp to come back from their hike. I know this will take forever since Matt will point out every botanical species to his father who, in turn, will show great interest. Matt needs to explain obsessively how animals won't survive without the plants they need for food and reproduction. And Tripp does seem to listen. He's a good father.

Ever since we'd first met at Bryce, I'd loved Tripp. I have always put him first. In college, he dated lots of women. When I entered my freshman year, I'd hoped he would call and see me. But he would smile at me, wave, and seemed to always be with the same beautiful girl. He was a senior. I studied his interests, his course schedule, his crew practices, and would often "bump" into him. When I made the cheerleading squad, he was the person I most wanted to tell. I would scan the stadium for his face. I knew I'd marry Tripp one day and be a wonderful wife for him. I wasn't obsessed about it, I just knew he was it for me. When he married someone else and she died, I hoped he'd seek me out. After we married, I felt like Joanne Woodward to his Paul Newman. He elevated me in people's opinion by being with him, and I knew and appreciated this. He's the star, and by pure fate and a tuna sandwich, I got to be his wife. I knew people were surprised when he introduced me as Mrs. Regan.

His loyalty to his sons and to me makes all of our friends shake their heads. All they see is this god-like man immersed in his home life. They don't see the work I put in, the way I appreciate him with the small things I do daily. It may sound very old-fashioned to some, but I never forget to have his beer on ice, his car filled with gas, his evenings planned to engage him with tickets to sporting events or concerts, which he loves. I'm always available if he needs me for anything. I work hard on my marriage. I rub his back, soothe his mind. I calm him. I protect my domain fiercely. I appreciate how honorable he is, how people perk up when he enters a room, his quips with any and everyone.

I love sitting here, glancing over at the green chaise lounges dotting the white sand with the aqua Pacific backdrop. I'm so content and think my family is too. Jake, on the other hand, may be a little too content...

"Good morning, Miranda," Julia smiles.

"Hey, Mom. Where is everyone?"

"Ricky was just here and your father's on a hike with Matt."

Julia beams. "You should be very proud of your son, Mrs. Regan. He went on a very long run already today."

"How long?" I ask, already dreading the answer.

"I don't know, about two hours..." Jake says, guiltily. Very guiltily.

Oh, no.

"Why?" I gasp.

"Why? Well, I got lost, Mom."

"Where on earth were you lost, Jake, for two hours?"

My eldest thinks he's so sly. He doesn't have the slightest idea I'm onto him and forgets I'm his all-knowing mother. I have eyes in the back, top, and sides of my head.

"You got lost running, Jake?" I repeat.

Come on, sweetheart, you can do better than that. When he was a teenager and refused to tell me anything about his life, I crept into his room while he was at lacrosse practice and snooped through his drawers, his desk, under his bed, anywhere, searching for indicators. Much to my relief, I never found much other than unused condoms and empty beer bottles. As a girl, I inhaled Nancy Drew books so detective work gives me a bit of a rush.

"Well, I dunno... I just started running and got so into it I guess I just kinda lost track. Sorry..." he says, looking put out.

How dare he look put out. Julia should own that look.
"How many miles is that?" I query, keeping calm.

Truthfully, I don't think he's glanced at poor Julia since she arrived last night.

"Well, I stopped for a while and rested," says Jake, casting his eyes down.

Look your mother in the eye, Jake.

"Can we please talk about something else? Like how many pancakes I'm gonna mow down? What do you want, Julia?"

"Just an iced cappuccino, please. You know I'm not really a breakfast person," she says with a hint of exasperation.

He nods nonchalantly and orders a huge breakfast from the hovering waiter.

"Hi, yeah, can I please get... scrambled eggs, pancakes with a side of toast, the fruit plate, a coffee, and an orange juice. Oh, and a cappuccino for the lady."

"Iced, please."

"Sorry, ICED..."

Watching the two of them, I start making grandiose plans in my head to fix this crack that could open between them. But only if I can do it unnoticed. I've orchestrated my entire life by accomplishing things quietly, without calling attention to them. Some thrive in the spotlight but I blossom six inches to the left—where no one notices me diligently toiling away.

As a child, my parents—so much older than other parents—sent me to ballet class. My body was much more like a fireplug, close to the ground and solid. I didn't have a lanky ballerina's body, so I adapted, unnoticed, by going next door where there was a tumbling class. I walked in one day and loved it. I found what I could do well. As I grew, my tumbling turned to gymnastics and I became a mascot to the older girls, whom I idolized and were the high school cheerleaders. They taught me how to cheer, which meant how to be popular, though I never really was. They taught me about makeup and clothes and boys.

The cheerleaders were my whole life. I was like a puppy "fetching" for them, following them everywhere, doing errands for them, anything to be part of their lives. Nothing makes me happier still than being given a "chore" to do for Tripp and my boys. *Mom, I need a mattress pad, the egg crate kind—can you find it? Mom, I heard The Book of Mormon is hilarious. Can you get me tickets on the aisle? Hey, Mom, could you pick up a new Tribe 7 lacrosse stick for me?*

I loved to pack for my family and still do for Tripp. My lists were endless, filled with chores to do, photograph albums to fill, cars needing checkups, watchbands needing fixing, dress shirts, jeans, shoelaces to be bought. Even now, with the boys in their own apartments, I light up when they ask me to find some esoteric thing for them. It makes me feel very needed and loved. I love to help them. And Tripp. He loves to be taken care of and appreciated.

My "chore" now is to keep Jake on course. I don't want him veering out to sea. I want him close by, married to lovely Julia. She flew all the way out here. How can he not see how adorable she looks in her red bathing suit with the matching red cover-up, those cute bracelets and, oh, how sweet, she's wearing the diamond studs we gave her last Christmas. Just looking at her makes me realize how dowdy I am in my brown one-piece and the hotel's cotton bathrobe I'm wearing to hide my arms. She's invisible to him—and she doesn't know why. He's totally mooning over Cleo. I could kill him.

"Jake, doesn't that Cleo have her TV show today? She mentioned it after dinner last night when the car attendant asked for her autograph. It's called *Close Meetings,* I think?"

"*Close En-coun-ters,* Mom. Yeah, it's on at twelve." He catches himself, "I mean, I think she said twelve... Why, are you gonna watch it?" he asks.

"I might. Your father's hike with Matt could take forever. And her show could be interesting..." I say, smiling at him.

Jake beams. He looks like a puppy that's just gotten a treat. That smile; he got that from me.

"So, what do you think of *that* Cleo, Jake?" asks Julia, turning to Jake.

Good girl.

"What do you mean?"

"Oh, don't be coy..." Julia nudges him playfully. "I saw her gazing at you last night. She seemed very smitten."

If she only knew.

"Well, can you blame her?" he sneers. "Lest I remind you, I took home MVP for Cornell lax in '01 *and* '02, babe."

"How could I possibly forget? The plastic trophies are in your front hall."

Jake and Julia laugh. They have such a fun, witty rapport. At cocktail parties, everyone of all ages loves to be around them. It'd be such a shame for that to go to waste.

"I'm gonna go work on my tan. Have to catch up with the rest of you sun-worshipping Regans..." Julia says as she starts down toward the beach, taking her iced cappuccino with her. She approaches Ricky who's already down there listening to his iPhone. Hopefully he'll give her some attention.

"Enjoy..." Jake says listlessly as his girlfriend leaves.

I stare at him as he gobbles down his scrambled eggs and wonder what exactly is going through that thick head of his. On second thought, I'm not sure I want to know.

A few minutes later, Ricky and Julia run up from the beach. Julia looks so animated.

"Jake, we're going scuba diving. Come!"

Jake grumbles a disinterested response through his eggs.

"C'mon, dude. You love diving!" Ricky points out.

"I'm really tired, okay? Had a long morning." Jake barks.

"Oh, don't be such a Debbie Downer!" Julia keeps on, starting to pull him out of his chair. She's stronger than I thought, but he doesn't budge.

"Julia, I'm sorry. I'm just really beat, you know? Rain check?"

She nods, doing her best to disguise her disappointment. Poor girl.

"I wanna be game for our chopper ride later too. And maybe we can play a few sets afterward if we're up for it. I just need to lie down after I eat or I won't make it."

"No worries. Ricky will keep me company..." says Julia, nonchalantly.

Good girl.

She smiles at me and then at Jake before heading off with Ricky.

Chapter Nineteen
December 22, 2011

CLEO

Today, I have five guests on *Close Encounters*. Today, I need to be especially clever and charming and camera ready. Today, Jake will be turning on the TV, tuning to my station and watching me.

One of my guests is a visitor to the island, a rodeo star, whose agent booked her in advance. Another is a friend of mine who was planning to run the Honolulu Marathon backward, carrying a bottle of Perrier on a tray, for the eighth time. He needed an ego boost and had island color, so I scheduled him with the Broadway actors who had fallen in love with each other while starring in a play and were here on their honeymoon. But I am most looking forward to my favorite guest, the Hawaiian Senator, John Hamada. I have him on once a month. He does a wonderful segment called *Safety Tips!* Oh, how the viewers love him.

I'm dressed in a pale lime green sweater and skirt, having changed my outfit that the poor wardrobe department selected for me many, many times. Usually, I'm easy with the clothes they put out for me, but not today. And poor Peach in makeup; I'm a lot of work since I've had no sleep.

She, who is so instinctual, looks at me suspiciously, "what's with you today? You look... different."

"Oh, I know. I got virtually no sleep last night. I look awful, don't I?" I can't control my blushing.

Peach doesn't let up. "No, actually... Your skin's glowing."

We share a conspiratorial smile and I can tell that Peach knows. There are people who can walk down the street and know in an instant by the way someone is walking or smiling that they had a great time in bed last night; or even this morning! Someone brilliantly instinctive like Peach *just knows*. I am so caught and so thrilled to be caught. Finally.

"Make me beautiful," I plead.

Peach scrunches her nose. "Oh, if I must..."

"I know, I know. You're a makeup artist and not a magician."

This is our favorite exchange and it never fails to make us giggle. Today as we do our routine jokes, I smear my makeup with tears of laughter and have to be fixed. And then fixed again. I am still giddy from Jake coming to me this morning. I didn't know how much fun it could be to share a romance with a friend. Of course, I don't give Peach details, but how much I enjoyed it is written all over my face. Oh, I have missed out on so many of these conversations.

I hear the Senator before I see him.

"Ah, the famous Cleo..." flirts John Hamada as he sits down in Ralphie's chair. He's unusually tall, at least 6'5", with a receding salt-and-pepper hairline and a rather large, bulbous nose. He looks so safe and fatherly, like Steve Martin or Sam Waterston.

"Hi, Senator," I respond, turning my head ever so slightly, careful not to disrupt Peach as she works her magic.

"What's the latest?" he asks me as Ralphie takes out a comb and starts working with what's left of the senator's hair.

"Oh, just business as usual..."

"Well, you look better than ever. Tell a craggy, old senator your secret."

Peach stifles a laugh and I ignore it, trying to draw as little attention to her as possible.

I shoot Peach a smile and leave it at that.

"Hey, question. You big on those acai berries? Or is it a-kay? That one always throws me for a loop... I hear they're all the rage with the kiddos. My teenage daughters gobble 'em down like nobody's business."

Hamada has always been somewhat of a talker, which, depending on the day, makes him either the best guest on the planet or the worst. Sometimes it can be difficult to get a word in edgewise.

"I think it's pronounced ah-sigh-ee. Or at least that's how my health nut friend says it."

"Ah, yes. The famous Ironman..."

Hamada seems to think everyone is famous.

"Has the Ironman finally won your heart?" the senator pries as Ralphie finishes combing his hair.

"Switch," I say, rising out of Peach's chair. I still need to get my hair done, which is a whole other battle, so I move over to Ralphie's chair and sink into the plush leather.

"Looks like I've got my work cut out for me today..." Ralphie pulls at my snarled hair.

"Ralphie, ouch!" I say a bit too loudly.

"So, is that a yes about the Ironman?" Hamada prods.

Peach and I trade looks again. Hamada always asks me this same question, and each time I feel like a high school student. It's so juvenile and very misguided. He and Jimbo know each other as they buy coffee at the same early hour at the same quaint little coffee shop every morning. And, well, the senator is quite a nosy fellow. Ralphie yanks at my hair again.

"Ow, Ralphie, please... Is *what* a 'yes,' Senator?"

"You and Jimbo!"

"Oh, Senator. You know it's not like that and never will be. He's just my friend."

"He's smart, handsome, a great athlete.... All the gals at the coffee shop swoon when they see his bleached blondeness come into Java Joe's, but I don't think the poor bastard even has a clue! I thought maybe that was because you're the lady in his life..."

"Sorry to disappoint you, Senator."

"That makes two of us." He laughs.

"He doesn't work, right?"

I shake my head, starting to grow a bit annoyed by his interrogation tactics. I thought I am the one who is supposed to be asking the questions around here.

"Only the Ironman." I say a bit more strongly than I ought.

"Must be nice... Even unemployed, the ladies still love him! Who supports him then?"

"Senator, really. I–"

"Okay, okay. Methinks the lady doth protesteth too much," Hamada misquotes Hamlet as Peach starts powdering his nose.

"Senator Hamada, are you part Japanese?" I ask, diverting the conversation. This is my talent.

"You betcha."

"Aha, I knew it... Even though you are so much taller than most Japanese."

"Well, aren't you the sleuth, Gallier! There's an opening on the Hill if you're looking for another job," he jokes.

The man is a bit of a flirt. He's in politics after all, so I guess it is not a great surprise.

As Ralphie switches off his curling iron and combs me out, I smile at the senator. "I'll see you out there."

I thank Peach and Ralphie for their intense efforts. I almost look as though I hadn't just spent two fabulous hours with a man half my age in bed! Hamada salutes me as I get up from Ralphie's chair. Making my way over to set, I decide I want to use Jake's name somehow in the interviews. I want to show him I'm thinking of him. I love putting in names of friends who are out there watching me.

When Jake calls the studio after the show ends at twelve thirty, he says, "Hey, this is the 'Rude New Yorker.' Remember me?"

It was such fun calling him that on the show.

"Hmm... yes, it rings a bell," I play, grinning into the receiver.

"I loved watching you."

"Really?"

"You're a good interviewer."

"Thanks; it would be wonderful if you'd come and be a guest on tomorrow's show."

I could hear the smile in his voice. I almost ask how *she* liked watching me, but realize he probably snuck into a room and watched me alone.

"Never been on TV before. Sounds like fun."

"Well, then, it's a date."

"Hey, why don't you join us on a helicopter ride this afternoon. Four p.m., Royal Crown of Oahu."

"I can't, Jake, but I'll see you tomorrow at the studio. I have meetings with my producers and I need to talk over the 'The Rude New Yorker,' segment tomorrow," I joke. I also have my Krav Maga lesson before the meetings but I don't tell Jake about that. I don't tell anyone about that.

The thought of suggesting he just toss Julia into a volcano during the helicopter ride does cross my mind. I can hear the disappointment in his voice as he says goodbye. And oh, yes, I like it.

Chapter Twenty
December 22, 2011

MIRANDA

I go back to our room. Tripp likes it cleaned first thing, so I always call Housekeeping and ask them to do our room early. I make a habit of leaving a very nice tip every day so it's cleaned and straightened and has extra fresh towels and pillows.

When I enter now, it's cool and dark after the bright Honolulu sun. I sit carefully on the perfectly made bed once I turn off the air conditioning and wonder what channel she's on. I call Jake's room.

At first, he feigns ignorance but finally "remembers" and tells me it's channel four. I ask if he'd like to join me in my room—how interesting it would be to watch him watching her.

"No thanks, Mom. I need to nap so gonna stay in here."

Does he think I'm that stupid? There's no way he won't be watching. Of course, I won't let on until checkmate. Until I get him away from her. I imagine there will be something he'll see when he watches her on TV under those lights that will bring him back to reality.

I switch on the television. There she is—I wonder what her weakness must be. She seems to play the innocent card. I guess when you're that beautiful you can be innocent. But how can she have gotten this job if she's so sweet? She must have some manipulation skills. She certainly got Jake, who would've been livid to be in a car crash and waste a single minute of his vacation if he'd been hit by anyone else. Anyone else and he would still be fuming, not watching her on TV in the middle of a gorgeous day.

"I must tell you all... yesterday I was in a car accident with a very rude New Yorker. He was terribly grumpy but so terribly cute too that I forgave the rudeness," Cleo said.

Good heavens, she's flirting with him on air. She's reaching him through electronic waves. I know he must be quite pleased with himself. She looks so damn good too. Gone is my hope he won't be interested once he sees her on TV. The camera certainly doesn't add ten pounds, as the myth goes. Nor does she look old, which I was hoping. I must think of something fast before Julia gets wind of this and breaks up with him.

I'm even a bit taken with Cleo as she interviews some senator about his air travel safety tips. And now I know how she was so adept at talking to us that first night at the Outrigger—it's what she does for a living! I bet she had an assistant research us all before we arrived at her dinner. How clever.

"Senator, in these uncertain times, I am always nervous getting on planes or really in any big, crowded place. Especially if I am in New York or Paris and I see someone who looks a bit sketchy. Is there something I could look out for?"

"It's tricky. We can't very well report every scary, Muslim-leaning Tom, Dick, and Harry."

"No, of course not."

"But we do urge all citizens to take the 'if you see something, say something campaign' seriously."

"Can you elaborate?"

"Of course. Unusual items or situations. For example, if a vehicle is parked in an odd location, a package or luggage is unattended, a window or door is open that is usually closed, or if other out-of-the-ordinary situations occur. Something else to keep an eye out for is when an individual elicits information to a level beyond curiosity about a building's purpose, operations, security procedures and/or personnel, shift changes, etc."

"Because they're figuring out the best way to gain access so that they can presumably blow these buildings up?"

The senator nods. "Then, similarly, incessant observation and surveillance. This could include extended loitering without explanation—particularly in concealed locations—unusual, repeated, and/or prolonged observation of a building, especially with binoculars or video cameras. Taking notes or measurements, counting paces, sketching floor plans, etc."

"Oh, dear. It sounds like the government has its hands full! Probably best to leave this to the professionals."

"Yeah, I fear I shouldn't say anymore as the bad guys could be listening!"

"Oh, not to my show, Senator. I imagine they are hard at work and not tuning into *Close Encounters*. But I appreciate you believing we are that popular! And you can bet, I am going to ask you what the other clues are after the show..." She laughs with him. And of course, he beams back.

And I'm sure she will learn those other clues. I wonder, if I'd been the one in the accident with her, would we have dined together last night? Would we have become friends? Somehow I think we might have. Opposites attract. Women together. Friends. Just like the cheerleading squad had been my close friends. At home, my friends are all couples. Since Tripp and I are inseparable, except when he goes on his long business trips—which are more often than I'd like—we've found couples to go to dinner, movies, and the theater with. I had women friends when the boys were small and we did classroom things or class outings together. But we have drifted apart as our interests changed. There have been women who have tried to become close to me to gain access to Tripp, but I have always taken care of that. He is mine. Checkmate!

But, Cleo and I. She could discuss the Pele myth of the volcano and I could tell her the geology of it. Such different slants. That reminds me, I need to confirm our helicopter ride for the six of us. Tripp wants me to get the dual controls so he can play pilot, which I doubt they'll allow him to do, but I always want to make him happy, so I will be sure to get them for him.

I wonder if Jake will invite Cleo. He's undone over her. Poor Julia.

Chapter Twenty-One
December 22, 2011

TRIPP

Being with Matt this morning is very reassuring. After the incident in Manila, his company is exactly what I need. Matt needs me to pay attention, but really, he's got such a hard time relating to people, I'm not sure he really cares what I say. He never asks anyone questions about their interests, which is actually a lifesaver for my line of work.

He interrupts my musings. "Dad, did you know the canopies of the Hawaiian forests are dominated by very few species compared to the forests on the mainland?"

"I didn't, Matt. But that's very interesting."

"Yeah, and even fewer of these Hawaiian trees provide food for birds. The most specialized Hawaiian birds have gone extinct. I'm worried since it's the plant life that keeps the bird life alive. We really need them, Dad."

Matt springs to life when he starts talking about what matters to him. He's very similar to Miranda's academic parents who didn't care about anything but their specialties.

I first met her parents in Bryce National Park when her father, Wolcott, had been a professor of mine. But when I met

Miranda's mother, Bea, she hardly acknowledged me. She, like Matt, lived more in her field of study—in her case, this was in the time of Cicero, in the first century BC—than in the present. I laughed the first time I saw the walls of Miranda's childhood house. They were covered with the geological formations her father loved and the frescoes from Roman villas that her Mother loved. So Miranda grew up staring at a pretty fresco from a bedroom at the Villa of P. Fannius Synister at Boscoreale. She told me she entered it daily in her imagination—jumping from Roman villa rooftop to rooftop.

Miranda's parents raised her with what we refer to as "benign neglect." They never made appearances at class plays or dance recitals. They were totally unaware of those things. Even Miranda's birth was a surprise. Her parents only wanted solitude to do their work. Matt only wants his plants. The jumble, the messiness of life scares Matt. But he has made his own life and seems happy. I admire that in a way. And every now and then, he'll pick up on something the rest of us miss.

About ten years ago, I took Jake and Matt into a matinee of *The Sixth Sense* at City Cinemas on 60th Street. They were old enough. Jake was about eighteen or nineteen and Matt was probably fourteen. We were supposed to spend the afternoon at Chelsea Piers but the boys wouldn't shut up about the Bruce Willis movie so I relented. To be honest, I had wanted to see the movie for a while myself but I couldn't drag Miranda to see it. The scariest movie she's ever seen is *Titanic*. And that wasn't exactly a twist ending.

"Don't tell Mom," I told the boys as we settled into our seats toward the back of the theater. Digging into our shared bucket of buttery popcorn, Jake and Matt both smiled at me conspiratorially. I probably could've told Miranda the truth,

I doubt she would have given me too much grief, but it was just easier this way.

"He's dead," Matt whispered about halfway through the movie after Haley Joel Osment gave his famous "I see dead people" speech to Bruce Willis.

"Dude!" Jake seethed, so loudly that the irritated couple in front of us turned their heads.

I shushed them both without taking my eyes off the screen. I was riveted but a sense of dread suddenly pumped through my body. *Damn it, Matt.* He'd spoiled movies before, even after his brothers and I have scolded him, but this was the most memorable.

After we left, I asked him how he had possibly figured it out less than an hour into the movie.

"It was obvious, Dad."

Jake and I snuck a look at each other. *Are we idiots?*

"It was?"

"Yeah. Cole, the little boy said it himself. Dead people only see what they want to see. Same as Malcolm, it was so obvious."

Jake and I looked at each other again and both shrugged.

"Didn't you notice how he never touched anything unless he was with the little boy? C'mon, Dad, it was so obvious!" he frowned, pushing the glass door open to the city's noisy Third Avenue.

Matt would go on to spoil *The Others, The Village, Atonement, Memento,* and a whole line-up of other films. Finally, after *Shutter Island,* I learned my lesson and stopped watching movies where there was even a remote possibility of a twist or surprise ending with him.

Chapter Twenty-Two

CLEO

I had been a new Hawaiian resident for two months when I was dining at a typical Hawaiian restaurant with the nontypical name of Fluffy's with my sister, Beebe. As we were leaving, we passed a table where two very chubby, jolly people were smiling up at us. To all the world, they looked like Mr. and Mrs. Claus on an Hawaiian vacation. Big, round cherubs. Such was their mirth and glee I couldn't help smiling back.

Mrs. Claus jumped up, "Please join us!" she thundered, grabbing my hand. She was that kind of woman, the kind who loved people. It was awfully nice to be with someone who was so maternal, having never had a mothering mother of my own.

I was caught off guard by her command, but decided to go with it. I looked to Beebe and sat.

"We've never seen you before—and we know everyone! Tell us, are you new to the island or just visiting?"

"New. Well, relatively speaking. I left the city two months ago and have been here ever since!"

"Which city?" Santa asked me.

"Oh, sorry... I always do that. New York City."

I looked up at my sister, who had made the conscious decision not to sit.

"Would you like to sit, Beebe?"

"Oh, thank you, no. I think I might go back and take a walk in your wonderful gardens," Beebe said sweetly.

That's her—sweet, quiet, lover of gardens. Just last week she sent me her latest gardening articles, for at forty she has become a bit like a serene Martha Stewart. The landscaping of the flowers and bushes in her garden is her masterpiece. And she writes about gardens for a hobby. Shopping is her other hobby. She jokingly will say she is going to see some museums but we all know that they would be the Bulgari Museum, the Chanel Museum, the Ferragamo Museum.

I decided to stay and chat with the "Clauses" as they promised to drive me home so Beebe could take my car. I wanted to meet some people in my new home.

Pudge and Pudding—their real names, no less—answered with perfect "married answers." One would start the story and the other finish.

"So, what keeps you busy on the island?" I asked, crossing my legs and leaning back in my blue wicker chair.

"Business busy or pleasure busy, honey?" Pudding, a.k.a. Mrs. Claus, asked.

"Both! I bet you two know all the best spots..."

"I own a local TV station," Pudge/Santa told me.

"Oh, how exciting! I always thought it would be great fun to work in television. All the lights, camera, action."

"Well, you certainly have the face for it, darlin'," Pudge complimented me.

Pudding turned to her husband, "Hey, has anyone ever told you that you've got a great face for radio?"

We laughed at Pudding's joke, despite all of us probably having heard it one hundred times before. They fascinated me with how seemingly content they both appeared. I was curious if it was just a façade.

"Did you both grow up here? You seem so happy... I hope it's the island living and that it'll eventually rub off on me!" I say.

Pudge began, "Actually I grew up in Newport, Rhode Island, and came to Honolulu for a summer to work on a pineapple plantation."

"He met me, and that was that. I've lived here all my life. Never been much of a mainland gal," Pudding smiled.

"She's right. We met one day at Lucky Belly, this awesome little Asian place that we gotta take you to."

"Best oxtail in the world," Pudding inserted.

"Truth. And then I never left. As the saying goes, this little señorita put a spell on me," Pudge finished, rubbing his wife's cheek sweetly.

I asked another question, "So, was it always Pudding or did there happen to be any, you know... Jell-o or Custard beforehand?"

That got a few chuckles.

Pudding didn't miss a beat. "Maybe a few ding dongs!"

"Or Twinkies!" they both exclaimed simultaneously.

By now, we're all in stitches. People were looking over, watching our little show.

"Nah. I know this might come as a big shocker, but I wasn't much of a 'ladies man' on the mainland," he said, using air quotes. "I'm just so friggin' thankful she actually liked me back."

"He kept me smiling day and night," Pudding shrugged, looking my way.

They both grinned into each other's big doe eyes. In that moment, I was so jealous of them and all their mushy, lovey dovey glory that I had to change the subject before I cried.

"So, what was it you wanted to be when you were young? Did you always know you wanted to work in television?" I asked.

"When I was a kid, hell yeah, I wanted to work in TV. Who didn't? Man, I'd plop my fat ass down in front of my parent's little box and soak it up for as long as they'd let me. But I guess I never really thought about doing the showbiz thing seriously, you know? I mean..."

"It was Rhode Island..." Pudding added.

"Newport's lovely!" I said.

"Right, but it's not exactly a 'booming metropolis,'" Pudge said, using those air quotes again. "Anyway, I took up the family business. We owned a very popular restaurant, which paid the bills. And it sure gave me my love of food! But I knew showbiz was for me, so when the TV station here went on the market, I snatched it up. My family backed me big time."

"Snatched, he did! Would you look at these big hands?" Pudding exclaimed, putting her husband's enormous hands with sausage links for fingers up on full display.

"Tell me something, Cleo, you and your sis don't look at all alike. How's that for a prying question?" Pudge asked.

"Oh, we have different fathers. My father is French Algerian and Beebe's father is an English Lord. And we have another sister, Tree, with yet another father. Tree has the same blonde hair as Beebe. You could say I am the dark horse."

On and on and on we went. The waitress must've come and gone from our table fifty times before we finally got up to go. As we left, I was offered a screen test for a job at the station—a job that if I got, would involve interviewing guests on television for a half-hour each week. Within six months, they gave me a second slot and after eight months, a third. Best of all, I had made two lovely friends. We go to lunch often and every Saturday morning, Pudding and I get our nails and toes polished and go shoe shopping.

Other than Jimbo, they are my closest friends on the whole island. I need them all since my family is so far away. We keep an eye on each other, but respect each other's privacy. It works for us.

Chapter Twenty-Three
December 22, 2011

JULIA

I feel so rejuvenated after scuba diving. Per usual, I had such a blast with Ricky. He's just one of those cool, laid back, down-for-anything kind of guys. Maybe it's a function of that youngest child syndrome—"Hey, guys! Wait for me!" Always having to go along with what his two older (and often, less accommodating) brothers want to do. As an only child, I never had to deal with any of that.

Ricky was trying to point out a dolphin and I don't know what was wrong with me, but I just couldn't spot the thing even though it was maybe six feet away. Knowing the klutz that I am, I think I accidentally rubbed suntan lotion into one of my eyes and so my vision was a little blurry. I laid eyes on Flipper about a half second before my nose shook hands with his dorsal fin. Even six feet below sea level, I'm embarrassed to admit that all I could think about was Jake and what I was going to say to him. It had been decided, I had to confront him. Even with the necklace, I felt too alienated and couldn't stand it any longer. It's better to jump off a cliff than hang off it, waiting for the inevitable. I had to know what was up, even if it was something I didn't want to hear.

The moment of truth (*dun, dun, dun*) arrives as I get out of the lovely Pacific water. I do my best impression of one of the *Baywatch* babes—*hey, I've got the red swimsuit going for me*—as I bounce up the beach toward Jake. I sit down next to him on his beach chair and realize immediately that my *Baywatch* impression did exactly diddly-squat. He's just sitting there, his head buried in his phone and texting rapid fire, 100 percent oblivious to everything around him. I pretend not to notice him tense up when I rub his bare leg. *Chill. The necklace. He got you the necklace. Everything will be fine,* I try to remind myself.

"Ricky and I had so much fun out there. We saw Flipper!" I say breathlessly.

"Who?"

"Oh, come on. You know, the dolphin from—never mind."

"Cool... I ended up going upstairs for a while," he says with as much spirit as a cheerleader on klonopin.

This is hopeless. I texted not one, not two, but five of my girlfriends earlier and the vote came back unanimous. I had to confront Jake. Something was definitely wrong. I can't be the dumb girl who doesn't get it, who willfully turns a blind eye and pretends their life is a goddamn Disney movie when it's really closer to an episode of *The Jersey Shore*. I've never been that girl. I hate that girl. I take another deep breath, then lay out the speech I kept rehearsing in my head while I was underwater with Ricky and the fishies. Ha, that sounds like the name of a hip, new band.

"Okay, be honest..."

He doesn't look up from his phone but he does flirtatiously nudge my shoulder with his hand. "About...?"

I take a breath. "I don't know, I just kinda feel like something's going on with us... Don't get me wrong, I'm having fun, but basically, it just seems like you don't even really want me here. Have I, like, *bothered you* by coming on yet another family trip or something?"

Well, that came out all wrong. My intention was to come off strong and self-respecting but instead, I sound insecure, desperate, and clingy. At least he's finally stopped texting and looks up at me. I think this might be the first time we've made eye contact all day. *Hip, hip, hooray...*

"What? 'Course not, babe, it's great having you here," he says, really effing half-heartedly.

Then he goes straight back to what must be the world's most riveting text conversation.

Okay, at this point, you're probably wondering why I've been dating someone for two years who has more interest in a lounge chair than he does his own girlfriend. I grew up in Gibraltar, went to high school in Switzerland, college in Paris, and spent two years in London at a small financial firm upon graduation. When I moved to New York City two years ago, the only soul I knew even remotely in The Big Apple was my "Aunt" Irene, who was an old friend of my mother's. My first day at a brand new job in a brand new intimidating city, Jake rescued me. In an instant, I had a boyfriend, a fun group of welcoming and popular friends, and a warm, loving family. Jake took me under his wing, doted on me, and loved me. And wow, the boy can make me laugh.

"Jake, seriously. I'm a big girl. What's up? Are you texting to avoid talking to me? Not that I need you to be all over me 24/7 or anything, but you're paying, like, more attention to the sand. You didn't even pick me up from the airport," I point out, sounding a lot whinier and lots more pathetic than I intended. "And we haven't even had sex. *Pas d'intimacie...*"

Somebody shut me up. He loves it when I turn on the Français, but that just sounded idiotic. I need a muzzle or a ball gag, whichever is closer.

"Sorry..." he mumbles, finally putting his phone down. "Full disclosure: I don't want to be a wuss, but I'm pretty sure I have a fever. Here, feel my forehead."

He takes my hand and lifts it up to his forehead. I guess it's a *little* warm but it's also eighty-freaking-five degrees out and he's been sitting in the sun for God knows how long. But still, I go along with it and into full pampering mode, bringing out my inner Miranda, which doesn't always come naturally to me. I blame it on growing up without a mother of my own.

"Oh, no! Can I get you anything? Are you achy? What hurts?"

"Nah, I'll be fine. Honestly, dude, I think I just need to sleep."

Dude? No. I'm not your drinking buddy, bruh.

"Also, this guy I'm texting from work isn't getting back to me so I'm just stressed and taking it out on you. I'm sorry..."

That was his answer to all my pleading and prodding. A guy from work isn't texting him back? Now I'm even more confused about where we stand than I was at the beginning of this pitiful excuse for an adult conversation.

"Who? Glenn?" Glenn is Jake's demanding fossil of a boss.

"No, a client. I don't wanna bore you with the details though." He pauses. "I'm really psyched about the chopper ride later, and tennis and dinner. Just the two of us..."

Then he winks at me. I freakin' love it when Jake winks. Such a turn on. Clean up on Julia's aisle.

JULIA

I head back to the room and check myself out in the mirror. *You have GOT to be kidding me.* I'm mortified that I gave my little speech in this shape. I look like Britney circa 2007, post shaved-head-and-umbrella-freak-out attack. My hair is matted to my head, last night's mascara is running down my cheeks, my nose is a little sunburned, I have a wedgie, and my nail polish is chipped.

At least we have the helicopter in a few hours. I'll have to look better by then. I should have probably gotten to work five minutes ago...

Chapter Twenty-Four
3 Days

MOHAMMED ABDUL RAHMAN

Tripp Regan is about to go down. Literally. And if his whole family is collateral damage, so be it. Here he is on vacation with his family in Honolulu—drinking alcohol, sitting on the beach with the newspaper, and now taking a helicopter ride for tourists.

"Hey, why don't you join us on a helicopter ride this afternoon? Four o'clock, Royal Crown of Oahu," I heard his son say, having tapped all the sons' phones. Jackpot.

Royal Crown of Oahu is one of the island's premier helicopter tours for rich tourists who are trying to make themselves feel more productive after lying in the sand all day. The sightseers are treated to a bird's-eye view of some of Hawaii's most popular landmarks—Diamond Head, The Banzai Pipeline, Hanauma Bay, Pearl Harbor, Koolau Cliffs, Sacred Falls, Makapu'u Lighthouse, and more. The vantage point at Makapu'u Lighthouse is perfect.

There isn't much time. Of all my weapons, I decide that the Glock 19 would be effective enough for taking down a passenger helicopter. A machine gun or, ideally, a rocket launcher, is, of course, the best but there could be other people around so I can't risk getting caught only three days before my big mission. During my training at Mindanao, I was taught that the most efficient method to shoot down a helicopter is by hitting the pilot or the tail. One of the biggest pros in shooting the tail rotor is that it's crucial for stability and usually made of light materials, like fiberglass and hollow aluminum. If I aim correctly, one of the propeller blades could break off, throwing the whole thing into a death spiral—which is precisely what I want. The con of having the tail as a target is that it's small, but unfortunately for Tripp and the whole Regan family, I have excellent aim.

The helicopter will plummet into the ocean where everyone on board will be met with a soggy, suffocating death. If they aren't killed mercifully on impact, infidel Tripp Regan and his family will drown, sucked down to the bottom of the ocean along with the helicopter. And by the time the police and the CIA arrive, I will be long gone, having evaded the authorities once again. Speaking of which, I'm mildly offended by how much Tripp Regan and the CIA have underestimated me all these years. They've been after me for seven years, ever since I orchestrated the bombing of a busy Bali market. Because of me, 232 people perished on that day in 2007, and today, 7 more will perish. All in a day's work.

Chapter Twenty-Five
December 22, 2011

TRIPP

I'm looking at the backs of my family members as they caravan toward the Bell 407 helicopter when my telephone rings. It's my work phone so I have to pick up.

"Sir, the results from the autopsy are in," Agent Chris Castillo tells me as I step to the side of the runway.

"Go on."

"As we assumed, it appears Ocampo died from asphyxiation."

"Okay, that it?"

"Actually, no... The M.E. found something quite unusual in his throat..." Castillo says slowly.

"What?"

I wait for Castillo to go into more detail. I often think that in another life, Chris Castillo would have made a fine public speaker. He often imbues a natural dramatic flair in his speech and you could fit four-lane highways in between his sentences, which, I'm convinced he often does deliberately just for effect. Sometimes it's amusing and sometimes it really pisses me off.

"It's a piece of paper. We don't know what it is yet."

"It's been sent to the lab?"

"Yes, sir. Enroute as we speak."

"It was stuffed inside his throat?" I ask, trying to picture it.

"Yup, and had it not been for the garrote, the poor son of a bitch probably would have swallowed it whole."

"I'd imagine that whatever was on that paper has mostly been dissolved by his saliva and natural juices."

"Yes, sir. I'll give you a call as soon as the results are in."

I can tell Castillo isn't finished.

"Should only be a few hours."

Now he's done and so I hang up.

I watch as my children and wife board the helicopter in such different ways. Jake rushes on board to be next to the pilot. Little does he know, I'll be taking that seat for myself. I want to be near the dual dials. It brings me back to my training. There wouldn't have been enough room for that woman they had dinner with last night. On the way over, Jake announced to the rest of the car that he invited her without consulting with us. It's a good thing she declined or she'd be sitting on one of our laps.

Ricky waits for his mother who, of course, goes directly for the worst seat, leaving the better ones for her brood. She smiles up at Julia and pats the seat next to her.

"Julia, why don't you come sit by me, honey?" Miranda says sweetly.

My wife has always been the best at making others feel included. Unlike some women at the country club or at the boys' schools, she has no interest nor gets any satisfaction out of being exclusive. Julia acquiesces gracefully to Miranda's request, but Jake pulls her toward him and puts her on his lap to look at the dials. He chats with the pilot who seems so bored. Day after day. Tourist after tourist.

"Can we please see the canopy on the other side of the island?" Matt asks the pilot.

"Absolutely."

Matt's making contact with another person, a stranger. I always like to see this.

"Since the plant life is what they need to keep from extinction, is the bird life there in jeopardy too?"

Matt just broached this subject with me earlier today.

"Yeah, I'm a little worried. The Koa Finch birds need to feed on the pods and seeds of koa."

Matt has found a soul mate. Now he won't shut up.

"Did you know the Palila birds depend upon māmane trees and the ʻApapane, ʻIʻiwi, and ʻĀkohekohe birds rely upon ʻōhiʻa trees for nectar."

Good God. Matt must have been studying this for months.

The pilot nods at Matt. "I'll take you to see the forest but better do it tomorrow since there's no plant or much bird life where we're heading now. We might see a Palila bird though."

Before the chopper starts up, surprisingly Ricky is the one who looks skittish. He grabs the armrests of his seat, white knuckling it.

"You okay?" I whisper from the steps, careful not to draw the attention of his brothers, especially Jake, who always revels in Ricky's pain and suffering.

Ricky looks up at me and forces a smile. I can tell I've unintentionally embarrassed him. Damn.

"Oh, me? Yeah, fine! All aboard!" Ricky forces a laugh, then downs the rest of his water bottle.

Knowing him, he'd never say a word and ruin everyone else's fun. Jake has caught wind of our exchange and turns around to face us.

"What's the matter, baby bro? You gonna puke?" Jake pokes at Ricky.

"Quiet, Jake. And please go sit in back. I'm going up front," I command.

Jake rolls his eyes but does as he's told. "Fine. C'mon, Julia." They get up and I get in.

The blades on the Bell 407 rev up and spin as we climb up over Honolulu. I'm so used to hopping into choppers but I can't let my family see this aptitude. I pretend to struggle a little bit as I put on my headset, channeling the inner actor Mrs. Huneke first spotted decades back.

"Like this, right?" I ask the pilot, pointing to my headset.

The pilot nods with a smile. As if there could be a wrong way... Then I turn to my family behind me and act like I'm a complete novice. Playing the part of the goofy, uncool dad never requires much effort in their eyes.

"Hey, guys, isn't this great?!" I shout back at them.

They all nod enthusiastically. I study each of their faces as if I'm searching for a traitor among a group of my peers. An old CIA habit.

Jake chomps at the bit to be up front. He's the bravest of my boys and probably should be in black ops. He'd thrive there. Ricky, on the other hand, his eyes shut, looks like he's still suffering from a nasty upset stomach or vertigo. Matt switches seats with Ricky so Ricky can be in the middle and not have to look out. He certainly is Miranda's son. So thoughtful. Even now, my heart melts a little when I see my kids being good to each other. Makes me feel like Miranda and I have done our jobs. Though most of their character can be accredited to my wife. Sitting behind Ricky now, Miranda is patting him.

My guess is the pilot was in Vietnam and has been flying ever since. So loosey-goosey, and he has such an easy hand as he hovers. Up, up and away. What a rush. We head out toward the jungle for about a mile and a half before heading north toward the shore. Then, it happens suddenly. We get hit with something, and then another something. Both Julia and Miranda scream. There's a loud, cracking sound and the whole helicopter starts spinning like a top. Ricky opens his eyes for the first time in minutes.

"What was that?!" he shouts, in a panic.

The pilot must have hit his head on impact because he's out cold. Luckily, I'm the only passenger who knows this. I don't want to send my family deeper into panic, but simultaneously, I can't reveal my training or they'll all grow suspicious and wonder just when, exactly, I found the time to sneak off and take secret pilot lessons. I immediately go into red alert.

"Sir, what do I do? I can try to help, tell me what to do!" I shout to the unconscious pilot. My family is silent with fear and the chopper starts spinning round and round and heading down. Their terror is so strong it is taking me over for an instant. Then I jump back into rescue mode. I grab hold of the controls as the plane continues to plummet.

"What's wrong with the pilot? Is he alright?" Miranda shouts at me, panicked.

"He's alright, he just hit his head."

"What?! Is he alright?" Ricky, in a panic, shouts.

I could blow a foghorn two inches from the pilot's ear and he still wouldn't wake up. I press one ear of my headset, pretending like he's giving me instructions only I can hear.

"Got it!" I say, continuing the conversation with myself.

"Tripp, what's happening?!" Miranda screams from the rear.

"It's going to be okay, Miranda. The pilot's fine," I lie. "He's telling me what to do. Everything will be just fine."

"You want me to come up there and help, Dad?" Jake asks, already halfway out of his chair.

"No! No, Jake, you stay back there with Julia and your mother," I command. I could almost use Jake's help, and he is so calm that it calms me.

"This button, right?" I pretend to ask him, after I've already pressed it. They can't really hear me in the back over the roar of the engine but I pantomime to soothe them.

"Here, take this," Matt says, handing his brother a barf bag and patting Ricky's back. Matt has proven to be quite even-keeled in a time of crisis. Ricky uses the bag once and then again.

Smoothly, I career over the jungle and double back toward the helipad from where we took off only a few minutes ago.

"See, guys, look!" I say, pointing to the helipad. "We're home free!"

Not entirely true. If this pilot doesn't wake the hell up, I'm going to be in trouble. I look over at him, almost willing him to shake a leg. *Wake up, buddy. Wake up!* My will apparently isn't strong enough. His eyes remain shut and his mouth still open. Thinking fast, I steer the helicopter away from the helipad, buying myself a little more time.

"Where are we going?" Jake asks.

Shit. I was hoping no one was going to notice that. I ignore Jake and keep steering the helicopter further and further away. I look over at the pilot again. *C'mon, buddy. Look alive.*

"Dad? Why are we going this way? The helipad's back there."

Shut up, Jake.

"Yeah, Dad, can we go back?" Ricky groans.

"Tripp, maybe everyone's had enough," Miranda adds to the pile-on.

I ignore them all until Jake gets out of his chair and starts toward the cockpit.

"Jake! Sit down!" I bark.

Jake, shocked by my sudden outburst, does as he's told. My temper has one benefit. Finally, the pilot stirs, reentering the world of the living. His head moves from right to left, to right back to left, regaining his bearings. Now that he's awake, I steer the chopper back to the helipad.

I hear my family breathe a collective sigh of relief. I glance back at their faces. It feels good to save the day. Like some sort of secret Indiana Jones or James Bond. No applause or pat on the back comes with the territory in the CIA. The invisible knight in shining armor, at your service.

"Jesus, what—" the pilot screams, as he takes control of the vehicle.

"What an exciting ride!"

"What the hell happened?"

"I think something hit the tail. It was probably a flock of birds," I say to the pilot in hushed tones.

"But how did you—you know how to fly?"

"One of my many hidden talents," I whisper. "Don't tell my family though. I'm gonna surprise them when we go to Alaska and fly over the glaciers this summer."

The pilot lands the helicopter safely and my family piles out. Like my eldest, I'm pumped up on adrenaline. I crave the rush and try to convince my family to do it again.

"You guys want to charter another one?" I ask them.

They all look at me, blank-faced, amazed their goofy old dad would be up for another round.

"Uh, no thanks, Dad. Have a blast though," says Ricky, still breathing heavily and covered in sweat.

"I think that's enough excitement for one afternoon, Tripp..." Miranda says quite sternly, gesturing at Ricky and Julia.

"I'm game, let's go!" Jake shouts.

"Jake..." Julia pipes in, shooting him a look.

"Yeah, you know what, your mother's probably right." I say.

They have no idea what I did but the pilot does. Still dazed, he stumbles over to thank me.

"Sir, I don't know how to thank you. If you didn't—"

I put my arm around the pilot and turn him away from my family, now straggling over to the cars. "Hey, don't mention it! Literally, don't mention it..."

He shoots me an odd look but goes along with it. The pilot and I walk the helicopter's perimeter to find the point of impact from the bird flock.

"Hope the damage isn't too bad. There can be a lotta paperwork—" He cuts himself off when he notices something about the tail. He shades his eyes, and points. "Jesus."

I follow the pilot's line of vision. The sun shines through two pebble-sized holes in the tail rotor. There was never a flock of birds.

I need to make a call immediately.

Chapter Twenty-Six
December 22, 2011

JULIA

After our near-death experience in the helicopter (I'm still shaking) and tennis with Jake this afternoon, I decide it is time I break out the big guns. I scooped up this particular ensemble from Intermix, my favorite boutique on Madison. I model the sassy outfit for Jake in our hotel room. He glances over at me and smiles his approval but he doesn't wander over and pull it off me as he normally would. Getting dressed in our room is usually so much fun. But tonight, it still feels like Jake is on sabbatical on planet Zulu.

"… You like?" I say with a little twirl.

"Yeah, you always look great, babe," he says, barely glancing away from the baseball game.

It's kind of like he's reading an etiquette book about *How To Be Polite To Your Grandmother.*

As we drive over to the restaurant, our favorite music—Kings of Leon—fills the silence. My eyes drift out the window and I look with wonder at the beautiful island as it whizzes by. It really is a gorgeous place. This is what a holiday should look like—palm trees, convertibles, golf carts, sunsets, the beach. But it doesn't *feel* like one and I'm beginning to dread dinner. If all we do is sit in silence like two morons with nothing to talk about except the weather and the menu, I'm going to—

"This is it." Jake glimpses over at me and forces a smile and bounds out of the car.

I wait for him to open my door as he typically would. I'm such an idiot. Silly ol' me, I should've suspected that his usual chivalrous schtick wouldn't be around tonight. In the side view mirror, I see him texting as he waits for me.

"Yeah, that's cool. I'll just get it myself..." I mutter under my breath as I get out of the car.

(For the record, I don't think I'm above opening and closing my own doors. I just think, as do many women, that as long as men bring home 20 percent more than we do, they can afford to be bothered with such a trivial courtesy). I slam the door as hard as I possibly can—s'up, pilates!—startling Jake. He almost drops his phone on the ground. I wish he had.

"You good?" he asks, sneering.

"Oh, yeah! I'm grrreat!" I lie, plastering on the biggest Miss Congeniality smile I can muster.

I pass him and make my way toward the restaurant, shaking my ass like a Kardashian. *Eat your fucking heart out, Jake.*

The hostess escorts us over to our table and we both take in the view. We're looking out onto the white sand of Kahanamoku Beach where a few stragglers are still lying on towels, enjoying fruity cocktails and the last rays of sun. A gentle breeze drifts off the ocean waves through the palm trees and through my hair. To our left, a short woman with a green lei around her neck starts playing the ukulele to a Hawaiian song that sounds familiar. The white Christmas lights in the palm trees make the the scene look like one of those Corona ads with the happy couple. How ironic...

"I had such a good time this afternoon." I smile, staring toward those baby blues as he types away on his cell phone.

"Yeah, it was nice..."

Earth to Jake. Come in, Jake.

"Well, except for that terrifying helicopter experience..."

He just nods. *Strike one.* Undeterred, I step up to the plate again.

"So, did we even recap about the MOMA party? All our friends were jealous that you were already out here lying on the beach."

"Really? That's nice."

Nice? Stop saying that stupid word. Strike two.

"But no worries, you didn't miss much. I mean, same party, different year."

"Right."

Strike three—he's outta there!

"Jake, c'mon. I'm talking to you.!"

"Sorry, it's just this fucking client..." he says, referring to his phone.

"Can you please just give it a rest while we're at dinner? Let's have a good time together."

I reach across the table, snatch up his cell and drop it into my purse. He looks at me, surprised, maybe even scared, but doesn't say anything. Just raises an eyebrow.

"Ooh. I love it when you tell me what to do..."

"Shut up," I snigger. "I mean, how dope is this view?"

He finally looks around at the ambience. "My assistant found it."

"I know. Caitlin's the best. Sitting outside in the city, I'm always worried some hobo's going to swoop in and steal the food off my plate."

We both chuckle. *Okay, signs of life.*

I playfully tap his forearm, trying to jolt him back to reality. "Admit it, you're a little pissed I finally beat you at tennis..."

"Nah..." he shrugs. "Might that have anything to do with your lessons at The River Club?"

"What?! How'd you know?" A reluctant smile prances across my face.

"Well, Carmen Sandiego... a few weeks ago, when you were in the shower, I noticed "The River Club" was calling. I thought I was being a good, dutiful, little boyfriend by answering on your behalf. It was your friend Hiro calling to confirm your weekly lesson."

Whoops. "Are you mad?"

"Jesus, Julia, who do you think I am? Ike Turner?"

We both laugh again. We stare into each other's eyes. And then, nothing. Boyfriend and girlfriend of two years who are sitting at one of the most romantic restaurants we've ever eaten at and we can't think of a goddamn thing to say to each other.

"Anyway..." says Jake finally, taking his etiquette book out again like he's still chatting with Grandma.

"Yeah, anyway... I still can't get over that helicopter ride."

"Eh."

Eh. Wow, baby, you really reached for the stars with that masterpiece of a sentence. I raise an eyebrow.

"Eh?"

"I told you, I had fun on the chopper... Ricky was really in bad shape though," Jake snipes.

Ah, Jake's Achilles Heel. He and Ricky are always competing. Sometimes when Jake's really irritating me (like now), I like to sneak in a good Ricky jab.

"Hey, has he been working out? He looks fabulous."

"Uh, yeah, if you count walking to the fridge to get another Stella."

"Oh, stop. He rubbed lotion on my back today before we went diving and it felt like I was getting a Swedish massage. Such strong hands..." I twist the knife.

"Whatever. What are you thinking of ordering?"

"Probably just a salad. You?"

"The steak sounds pretty tasty."

And then another silence hangs in the air. Exactly what I was afraid of. Us staring at each other with nothing to say. Time to restrategize. Thinking of our all-time favorite game, I scan the other patrons for a lucky winner. We invented this game on our second date and I always turn to it when I need to lighten the mood. Imagining the other diners having orgasms is usually our failsafe.

Craning my neck, I say, "How 'bout that guy over there? Red shirt."

It takes Jake a moment, but then he smiles shrewdly. He knows what's up. Jake looks over at the man and touches his chin, doing his best thinking man. "Hmm. Homeboy looks like the gracious type. He's just happy to be at the party."

"Woman to your right. Black jeans."

He turns and studies the woman. "Oooh. Definitely a screamer. Bet she howls at the moon."

"Definitely," I laugh.

"Okay, my turn. Blonde in the flowery thing. Nine o'clock."

I turn to my left and study the woman in the pretty floral top. "Great build up. On par with Meg Ryan from *When Harry Met Sally.*"

"I'll have what she's having!" we say at the same time.

For the first time since we sat down, Jake laughs heartily. His laughter is contagious—so much so I almost choke on my water. There's the boyfriend I love and adore.

I smile at the waiter when he comes over to timidly take our order. His plastic name tag says 'Jay' in gold letters. Oh, what the hell. I've been working my ass off this entire dinner so I deserve a reward.

"What can I get you folks?"

"Hi, there. May I please have the Mahi-mahi with a side salad."

What I'd do to swap out the side salad for a big, greasy plate of fries.

"Hi. Yeah, and I'll have the ribeye medium rare with the baked potato—sour cream and melted cheese, please—and maybe also a side of the creamed spinach too." Jake closes the menu and hands it back to our waiter. "Gotta leave a little room for dessert."

How wonderful it must be to stuff whatever you want down your gullet.

"Oh, and a bottle of cabernet please. Unless you want white, Julia?"

"Red's fine."

I've never seen him order so much food except when he's in training for the Head of the Charles Regatta.

When our shy waiter leaves, Jake gestures at him and whispers, "how 'bout him?"

I stay in the spirit of the game.

"Jay might seem shy... but he's a beast in the sack. And he loves to talk dirty at that magic moment."

We both laugh, myself maybe a little bit more than him. I'm just so freakin' ecstatic to have my boyfriend back from his field trip from Never Never Land. The orgasm game always works like a charm.

Dinner and the red wine arrives, and Jake wolfs everything down like a wild animal.

"So, what's on the agenda tomorrow?" I ask through a mouthful o' Mahi.

Jake looks at me sheepishly. I get the distinct feeling I'm not going to like what's about to pour out of his mouth.

"Okay, well, you know that woman, Cleo?"

Yes, I know *that woman*, Cleo. I nod, bracing myself for maximum impact.

"Yeah, so, she randomly asked me to be on her show tomorrow morning. To be honest, I don't really even wanna do it, but I also didn't really know how to say no..." he says, unable to look me in the eye.

"Really? Doesn't she interview, like, actors and writers and acrobats and whatever?"

"I guess..." he shrugs.

"So, what's she going to talk to you about then?"

He shrugs again. "No fucking clue."

Suddenly, I have the urge to hit him but I resist the temptation. Ten bucks he'll be a *terrible* guest. Jake sucks at this sort of thing, always freezing up at the least opportune of moments.

"Well, that's terrific. I've never been to a television studio. What time are we going?"

He takes a big pull from his wine.

"Yeah, so… apparently there's a strict 'no guests' policy." Then he quickly adds, "she says it's a really small studio."

Unless the studio is located inside of a tiny underground bunker, that is by far the worst excuse I've ever heard in my entire life. And then he starts downing even more wine. Guess I'm driving home.

We pile into the Jeep—well, Jake kind of just *falls* into the Jeep. He is really feeling that cabernet.

"Seatbelts," I remind him, starting the engine. He obeys like a good little boy.

In a weird way, I must admit that I like it when Jake's drunk and I'm sober—or, at least *more* sober. He's normally such a control freak, but when he's had a few too many he morphs into this cute little puppy who does whatever I say and he only wants to please me. *Take me home. Take out the trash. Take off your clothes. Take off my clothes.*

We pass a cute, shabby-chic restaurant called Sweet Pea. Lots of wood and palm trees. It being 9:30 at night, there are only two cars parked in the driveway. One of them is a yellow, dented Renault convertible. Jake bolts up in his seat as if he's just been struck by lightning.

"Speak of the devil. Cleo! That's her car!" he says, his speech a bit slurred. His face is pressed against the glass window like he's some kid trying to catch a glimpse of the snow leopard at The San Diego Zoo.

That woman, Cleo. She's everywhere, I tell you. Everywhere! As we drive by, I glance over and notice her sitting in the window with some exotic mystery man. Ah, Jake's not going to like this.

"Wow, her date's gorgeous." I can hardly even see the poor guy from here. He could look like John Candy for all I know.

Jake looks back at them, nodding stupidly. "Yeah, that's what's his name—*Jimbo*. They're just friends." Furious, he settles back into his seat and crosses his arms.

"I don't know, he doesn't look like the type any girl is 'just friends' with..."

Jake looks over at me, puts his fingers up to his lips and shushes me. A smile stretches across his face before he reaches over and puts one hand on my right thigh. His soft, Kiehl's-kissed hands caress my skin and slowly start to move upward toward my black thong.

"You're gonna get it, l'il lady," he smiles again. "You're gonna get it good."

Well, it's about freakin' time.

Chapter Twenty-Seven
December 22, 2011

CLEO

I didn't get to see Jake last night. I wanted to so very much as he was all I could think about during my monthly production meeting with Pudge and Pudding.

The meeting was timely as we went over the production schedule for the New Year. I flashed to how much I would love to be with Jake as 2012 was rung in. There have been rumblings of changing our shoot times from the morning to the afternoon as we would save money that way. But that's all the rumors were—rumblings. While Pudge was saying this, I pictured Jake in his running clothes as he appeared in my bedroom this morning.

"Frankly, we'd save too little to make it worth our while. Plus, the three of us wouldn't be able to go to our lunches afterward!"

Pudge laughs. "Well, that's just another reason not to move forward with the later shoot time…"

Now I am picturing Jake undressed with that gorgeous body and that curling hair. He had a bit of stubble when he arrived and started kissing me. I just love that look.

"Cleo, what say you?" Pudge asks.

I snap out of it. Jake's shirtless body vanishes from my mind.

"Oh, yes. I agree. I much prefer the early start times. Also, don't forget that I'm on vacation after Christmas."

"Don't worry, darlin'. We remember. Production is dark the next three weeks. We can't exactly do the damn thing without you," Pudding says.

I start to think about what I could give Jake for Christmas. My fantasies are making me blush as I hand gifts to Pudge and Pudding.

"I'm sorry to disappoint you, but I'm going to have to skip the annual party this year, so here are your presents. Merry Christmas!"

"Aw, you shouldn't have," says Pudge, shaking the box I have just handed him. He opens it to find a large, cut crystal Tiffany bowl with a huge tin of caviar and the accompanying bellinis and crème fraiche.

"Oh, I think you should have. You always should have…" Pudding laughs as she puts on her new turquoise Oscar de la Renta earrings.

"Make sure you're around after tomorrow's show. I have a guest that I want to introduce you to…" I say as I rise off my chair.

"Dinner plans tonight? We're thinkin' of hittin' up Fluffy's," says Pudge.

"Oh, I'd love to but I'm actually getting salads with the Ironman…"

A running joke between our little trio is that Pudge has a bit of a crush on Jimbo. After our Saturday manicures and our shoe shopping, we always return to my house for my housekeeper Consuelo's pancakes and hot fudge sundaes. Pudding is always on the lookout, hopeful that Jimbo will be biking, running, or swimming around the property. Without his shirt, ideally. I remember one particular Saturday, Pudding and I came back after a successful trip to the nail salon but a less successful one to the shoe stores. I just love coming home and finding a delivery waiting for me. I remember thinking it was my new Krav Maga shin pads, but as I was opening it, I noticed that it was actually for Jimbo. Pudding tore it from my hands and opened it and then wrapped it up again to use it as an excuse to see Jimbo.

"Shall we go deliver it then? I bet my second husband's expecting it!" Pudding batted her eyelashes.

I laughed. I loved this little game. Of course, Pudding is very happily married to Pudge and he is in on the joke too. As is Jimbo, who is a very good sport. We started down the path toward his cottage, his package in tow. As we continued down the white-pebbled path, I looked up and noticed the security cameras Jimbo installed in case my stalker returned. He was so right. After he installed them, I never heard from my stalker again.

"HOW'S YOUR TEENAGER, Cleo?" is Jimbo's opening line as we walk into Sweet Pea. Shockingly, he says it with a straight face, as if he really wants to know.

"He's fabulous... This morning he arrived with stubble," I laugh.

Duncan, the owner, is moving a young, attractive couple away from our favorite table at the window. Duncan loves having us here. Jimbo is by far the restaurant's best customer and since Jimbo is the poster boy of health and I am a local television star on the island, we don't hurt the image of Sweet Pea either. We go there every single time we eat out.

Even though other tables are open, we are guided to sit at our favorite—the one with the crumbs and napkins and glasses still on it from the nice couple who are staring at us, starstruck. They wave and smile. I will pay for their dinner. That's the least I can do as they were rather rudely moved from their table when Duncan saw us. He knows this table is Jimbo's favorite as Jimbo likes to keep an eye on the road from here in case any of his competitors are biking or running past. With everything that's going on, I had forgotten to call today to reserve it for us, which is what I usually do as it makes Jimbo quite happy. I enjoy seeing Jimbo happy and he always takes it as his right. He's disinterested in others, unless, of course, they can run a 2:10 marathon. This singular focus is why he does so well in the Ironman.

"Welcome, you two," says Duncan when he comes over to happily wipe down our table. "Sorry for the mess. Didn't know you were stopping in!"

"Don't be silly." Jimbo claps Duncan on the back. Duncan's chubby cheeks turn the color of a ripe tomato.

As we sit, I look up at Duncan and for the first time notice tiny devices in each of his ears. They're skin-colored and look smaller and more high tech than any hearing aids I've ever seen.

After Duncan goes, I ask Jimbo about them.

"Really? That's weird, I never noticed."

"Duncan's never mentioned anything to you about having poor hearing?"

"Never."

Once again, Jimbo proves me right about his disinterest in others. He changes the subject and regales me with an anecdote about his favorite subject of them all.

"So, the guy who won last year *and* the year before swears by aerodynamics. In the cycling community, there's a saying that aero trumps weight and I totally agree..."

While Jimbo drones on, my eyes float across the restaurant until they land on Walter, eating by himself in the corner. He's told me before that he loves Sweet Pea's quinoa bowls and I believe he and Duncan are on a friendly basis too. Sensing my gaze, Walter looks up and catches me looking at him. I smile, then redirect back to the Ironman.

"You've heard of Jean-Paul Ballard, right? He's this really respected aerodynamicist who founded Swiss Side."

"Um..."

"Anyway, they created these new rim brakes. They're a little pricier than your typical model but naturally, I bought four of them." He pauses, "Hey, do you know that guy?"

"I beg your pardon?"

Krav Maga is my drug but it's also my deep, dark secret. Besides my father, Walter is the only one in on it. Four years ago, Walter and I came to an agreement that if we were ever put in an awkward situation, such as this one potentially, Walter was to be an occasional yoga instructor and I his willing pupil. There is even a rolled-up, purple yoga mat in my front hall to sell this point. I've never done yoga a day in my life...

"That guy over there just nodded at you," Jimbo's tone is suddenly protective. I love it when he gets like this. "He's the Navy SEAL, right?"

I look over at Walter and pretend to be surprised. "Oh, yes. I've taken a few yoga classes with him over the years. How did you know he's a SEAL?"

"We swim at the same spot off Waikiki. Seen him around a few times."

"Oh. You've never told me that."

"There isn't much to tell. I don't really know him. He isn't exactly Mr. Congeniality..."

"Well isn't that the pot calling the kettle black!" I laugh.

Jimbo is smirking at me when Duncan brings our food to the table as he always does. Three kale salads for Jimbo and one Caesar for me.

"Anything else?" Duncan smiles over at Jimbo.

"Think we're all set. Thanks, man." Jimbo smiles back at him. Duncan rarely ever glances in my direction.

Duncan beams at Jimbo one last time and then saunters off. Jimbo has already started on one of his salads.

"Okay, so back to these rim brakes..." he says, taking a big bite.

"Jimbo... I have a wonderful idea, why don't we talk about something else for a change?"

"Well, well, well, Miss Bossy. Okay, like what?" he asks through a mouthful of kale and apples.

"I don't know, anything. How's your family? We never talk about your family."

Finally, he glances up and makes eye contact. "What made you think of that?" he asks as he shoves more green garden into his mouth.

"Every now and then, I deserve some insights into your personal life..."

"They're fine. Same old, same old. At their age, I don't think there's too much excitement in Scottsdale."

"Just you wait. We'll be their age in no time."

"Hey, how 'bout I stop by tomorrow and show you my new rim brakes?" he says. Jimbo thinks he has just given me the best gift imaginable.

I glance out at the small, gravel parking lot. Through the glass wall, I see Walter unlocking the door to his black Honda. Before he hops in the driver's side, he notices me and shoots me a friendly wave.

"Let's go see the start of Chariots, shall we?" *Chariots of Fire* plays once every month down at the art theater and so we go to see it quite regularly. "But first, nature calls..." Jimbo announces as he scoops up the last vegetables from out of his bowl and rises out of the metal, hunter-green chair. Even after three large salads, the man is still a bottomless pit.

"Then you better answer..." I throw down a large tip and mouth to Duncan to put our dinner and the young couple's on my bill. I am the only charge account they have. But Duncan would do anything for Jimbo as he has such a crush on him. *Get in line, Duncan. Along with all the women on the island.* Sometimes I wish Jimbo liked men. What fun it would be to have Duncan or another man around us all the time.

Then, at that moment, Jake texts me. He must be drunk as his words are all weirdly spelled. I get butterflies every time his name flashes up on my screen. I feel the power of this new obsession and I yearn to be with him. He is my Ironman contest. My obsession.

I had experienced this overwhelming feeling of obsession only once before. It was in Africa. But it has been nine years since its power turned on me.

One would hardly think climbing a mountain could change your life so drastically. But the climb up Mount Kilimanjaro in Africa with Outward Bound did just that. It was an ascent to nearly twenty-thousand feet and not only did we climb but we also cooked, built latrines, and assembled our own tents. Mostly though, we slept in caves as big as football fields where noises echoed and bats flew. We were too tired to care unless one was as high-strung as I was when the snores reverberating off the walls and the bats' screams drove me to distraction. So, I moved away from the snoring, near him, near Danny, near silence. Danny, the silence he brought, was like mine. He couldn't sleep either, so we whispered the African nights away.

I told Danny how the image of Peter Fonda in *Easy Rider,* with his hippie looks, long blonde ponytail, and relaxed walk had flashed in my mind when he had walked over to me at the foot of the mountain. And he knew what I was talking about. He was there to scout a location for a movie. Like me, he loved movies. A kindred spirit. We compared our favorites—how we loved *Out of Africa,* and of course, I told him how his devil-may-care attitude also reminded me of Robert Redford flying his plane.

"I fly," Danny told me. "I love being up there."

"Oh, did you ever read *West with the Night?* It's one of my favorite books."

He nodded.

"I adore Beryl Markham daring to fly solo from England to America against the prevailing winds. And I love her remark after she landed in the jungle with Hemingway when she was asked if they'd had an affair. She said, 'No, I just slept with him. There's nothing else to do out there but make love...'"

Danny started to laugh, "I beg to differ. I heard Hemingway called her a 'high-grade bitch' when she wouldn't sleep with him on safari."

Our laughter broke up the sounds of the bats above us. They started screeching and hissing and fluttering about.

"Shhhh. Mon Dieu, *fermez la bouche!*" someone in the darkness hissed.

The reprimand took both of us off guard and killed our mood. Our laughter came to an abrupt halt. Danny and I were both silent for a few moments, taking in our anonymous scolding. Should we go to sleep? Or should we ignore them and whisper even more softly? Since beginning the ascent of

Kilimanjaro, this was the first time I was able to forget about the aching muscles, the wheezing lungs, the trembling fingers. I would have done anything to keep our conversation alive.

I felt his big, calloused hand tap my left thigh and it was as if an electric current pulsed throughout my entire body.

"Who was that?" Danny whispered so quietly that I could barely make it out. When his hot breath hit my neck, I let out a small gasp.

"I..." I started. "It had to be that French woman. Rosalie... something or other, and I know she already doesn't like me. So now, she will really hate me."

"Why do you say that?" he asked.

"I've heard her speaking to her husband. Unfortunately for Madame Rosalie, French is my first language. And I'm sorry but her accent is terrible. A good French accent is non-regional. Hers is Marseille. Uh oh, I think I am sounding like a 'high grade bitch.'"

Danny laughed. He wasn't the type of man I thought I'd ever be interested in. He was sort of hippie and quite rugged. Very much like Sam Shepherd. He wore flannel shirts and Carhartt pants. He did work in the film industry but I can't imagine location scouts lead a very glamorous life. He was in Africa for a location scout but arrived over a week early so that he could fulfill a lifelong dream and climb Kilimanjaro. I'd always pictured myself with someone like my father—well-traveled, well-educated, and wealthy. My father wouldn't think of leaving the house without a bespoke blazer on his back and a pair of polished, black Gucci loafers on his feet.

I could hear a slight rustling to my left. Danny was moving his sleeping bag closer to mine and I was so grateful that the darkness kept our secret.

"Where do you come from, Cleo?" he asked me.

"I beg your pardon?" I knew what he meant but I wanted to hear him say it again. I loved his voice.

"Sorry, I didn't mean it that way. I just—" Danny stumbled.

"Oh, no, I didn't think you did. I was—"

We both fumbled around our words as two people who are trying to say all the right things at all the right moments do.

"I just meant you seem like you're from somewhere... Somewhere, I dunno, *sophisticated*. French is your first language, so probably Paris?"

I loved his Southern drawl as he asked me these questions. And he was being a bit ironic, I think. Laughing at and with me.

"No, tell me about you, Danny," I said, not yet answering his question because a bit of mystery on this mountain with clothes and hair getting filthier each day couldn't hurt.

"Oh, I was born in a charming little hamlet called Lookout Mountain, Tennessee. But now I live in Brooklyn."

"Shh! *Tais-tois!*" a female voice with a French accent seethed. Definitely Rosalie. Very tempting to answer in French. I waited at least sixty seconds before whispering again. Even covered by the cloak of darkness, a part of me was intimidated by her. "Goodnight, Danny," I said at last.

Hopefully he didn't want to stop our conversation either. But it was hard to tell in all of that blackness and bat-ness.

"Goodnight, Cleopatra," he whispered.

The next night, Danny and I met again in another corner of another dark, bat-infested cave. We were now at 14,000 feet and oh, how I was hoping our sleeping arrangement had become an unspoken ritual between us. While everyone was unfurling their sleeping bags, using their flashlights as guides, I looked across the cave at Danny. As if sensing my gaze, he looked over at me too and cracked a small but very sweet smile. My heart rate picked up and I felt lightheaded again, much like I had the night before, as I laid out my sleeping bag on the cold, hard ground.

I needed another night of conversation with Danny. It was an especially tough day on the mountain. It all started out well enough when our fearless and endlessly jovial leader Jabari greeted us as he did every morning—*"Kariba Kula Muta!"* That had put a smile on my face more than usual that morning. I was in high spirits while thoughts of my conversation with Danny danced around in my head like sugarplum fairies on Christmas Eve. The sun was shining and the wind seemed calmer than it had on the earlier days. The calm before the storm. I should have known. Here I was at fourteen-thousand feet, which was already a struggle. As I arrived each day at the new camp, I burst into tears of relief and everyone sort of smiles when I do it. Sort of.

But that day, when I finally arrived—last, as usual—Danny saw how white I was. When I told him I was getting one of my migraines, he went to his Dopp kit and got out the medicine climbers use, diamox, and made me take it.

"Someone told me to have it on hand because of the altitude," he said.

And we had the migraine talk. How it makes you fragile and vulnerable and can leave one in a dark room if they don't catch it right away. I did catch it when he gave me the diamox.

One by one, everyone turned off their flashlights as they began settling in for the night. It was as if a string of Christmas lights had started to malfunction one bulb at a time, indicating that the party was over. My heart was slowly beginning to sink. I had hoped that Danny would make the first move tonight and slide his sleeping bag over to mine. After all, I had made the first move last night. It was his turn. Only fair. I sounded like a six-year-old child. It was the tinge of migraine.

Danny, myself and one other climber—one of the men from Japan—were the only ones with our flashlights still shining. I looked over at him one last time before I shut mine off. Danny was fiddling with the zipper on his black sleeping bag, which appeared to have gotten stuck. I thought about using that as an excuse to go over to him and ask if I could lend a hand but quickly decided against it. *Don't be desperate, Cleo.* I sighed loudly, perhaps secretly hoping that would draw Danny's attention, that he'd pick up on my frustration and come to me. That I was aching for his sleeping bag to be next to mine. I shut off my light, climbed into "bed" and closed my eyes. Moments later, I heard Danny's light click off too. I had purposely put my bag very far away from Rosalie so that we could talk tonight without her angry remonstrances.

Almost immediately on closing my eyes, I found myself in that strange half-lucid, half-dream state. That state came from the migraine, I knew. I was still partially awake, yet at the same time, I was on the mountain again at daylight. Something wasn't quite right. I was alone. No one else was around me, just miles and miles of whiteness that stretched as far as the eye could see. Then something quite perplexing happened—the mountain seamlessly morphed into an ivory, fluffy cloud. Still, no one was here but me.

"Are you alright, Cleo?" a voice whispered.

My eyes exploded open. I said nothing as I couldn't tell if I was still dreaming. I must have been breathing very loudly or God forbid, talking in my sleep.

"Cleo?" the voice whispered again. "Are you okay?"

Danny. He had come to sleep next to me, after all.

"Yes," I answered him, breathless. "Yes, Danny, I think I am."

"Tell me where you come from," he asked. I knew he was worried about me and just wanted to see if I was on track. So, I started talking.

I told him about New York, about France, and about Algeria. About my mother, and my father, and about my sisters. Soon the conversation turned even more personal—he talked about the South, and we laid out our desires, our fears, and even our secrets. There's something about the darkness that draws out everyone's deepest and darkest secrets. Gone is the fear of the other person's eyes looking at you in judgment. I went on such long rambles that night that, at times, I almost forgot Danny was by my side. He let me go on and on and on and on, inferring that it might be therapeutic for me. I explained that this trip—not just the strenuous nature of the climbing itself, but the spreading of some of my mother's ashes at the top—was one of the more difficult things I'd ever had to do. Every once in a while, when I landed on a particularly intimate or painful or humorous detail of my life, I could feel his cold hand on my thigh through the gortex sleeping bag. It was a comforting, supportive hand. It was not a crass or presumptuous or even a sexual hand. I loved that hand.

And then, on that dark African night, I told Danny what no one but my parents knew.

"Ever been married?" Danny asked innocently.

He must have known from my bare wedding finger that I was not married. And I assumed he must be aware of how I felt about him. Before this conversation, my feelings were strong and after this conversation, they only grew and expanded like a big birthday balloon.

"No." I whispered. "You?"

I could hear rustling next to me, coming from Danny's sleeping bag.

"Really, never? An exquisite woman like you. Why not?" Danny asked, avoiding my question and steering the conversation back to me, where it had stayed the entire night. Now I knew what that rustling was—Danny had turned in his sleeping bag; he was now facing me, instead of looking at the ceiling at the bats. I took his lead and turned toward him. Our faces must have only been six inches apart. It felt so insanely intimate.

"Oh, I don't know..." I demurred. Yes, there was a particular reason for that. But I didn't think I was ready to tell him. I didn't want him to look at me differently. We lay there facing each other in the dark for a few long minutes. I wondered how the light would change us. We would never have had the courage to be positioned like this, so very close. Maybe we wouldn't even be talking so personally, had the light shone upon us.

"Is your real name Cleopatra?" Danny finally asked.

"Yes." I said.

"So, I guess... you haven't found your Marc Antony yet?"

"Unless it's you," I blurted out. I couldn't believe I said that. The darkness draws out our secrets like good wine.

"No, but seriously... why not? Something's not adding up." I think Danny meant it as a compliment, but to me, it sounded like an accusation. *Why have you never married? What's wrong with you? Oh, there must be something wrong with you... You're too good to be by yourself!* I knew Danny didn't mean it like that and so I decided to take it as a compliment. Maybe he was offering to be my other half... Oh, what a team we'd make.

"Oh, it's a long story..." I said. I knew I'd started down a road there's no coming back from.

"Hey, I got time."

"Well..." I started, still trying to figure out if I was really going to go through with it.

"C'mon, out with it!"

I didn't even know how to begin so I said it very quickly. "I was raped when I was very young by a friend of my father. He almost killed me," I blurted out.

A long silence.

"What?" Danny said finally, incredulous.

Another long silence.

"It was a long time ago. I've gotten past it. But..."

"I'm so sorry, Cleo. When I asked—I didn't mean to... Shit, I'm really sorry," Danny apologized.

"I know you didn't." I could feel the hot tears rolling down my cold cheeks.

I thought about that night so often but was never really forced to confront it. Not like this.

"Did they ever catch the guy?"

"Yes. My father did. And he and my mother insisted I learn self defense. I studied Krav Maga and I always will. I am really, really good. I could kill anyone."

And that's where we left it. I trusted him with this but the next day, in the strong sunlight, I was so embarrassed, I couldn't look at him. But he walked over and held me close. He knew my secret, and in the daylight, he was still gentle. He had seen into my nightmare.

He would stay with me now every day—never leaving my side as we slogged our way through the ever more monotonous landscape until our final night in a tiny cabin. Unable to sleep, we held hands while waiting to go into the sandy, gravely, icy, knee-deep scree from 16,000 to 19,700 feet under the dark skies of midnight and the freezing blasts of wind. We made it to the top and others didn't. All I knew was together we had performed a baby miracle. He helped me fulfill my mother's last wish as I scattered her ashes there on top of the African world as dawn light blinked awake. I know my mother did this on purpose. *Scattering my ashes atop one of the highest mountains in the world will be so romantic,* she must have thought. And she was right. Danny held me, and held me, and held me, and wouldn't let me go. Our bond was forged.

This is the memory Jake dredges up, and yet I had never even slept with Danny because soon afterward, he died in a plane crash.

Our intimacy, so long ago, was far deeper than the lust I had in the here and now with Jake. But Jake's text makes me smile. It is hard to decipher but I think it said, *looking forward to hearing those bells ring at the studio.*

Chapter Twenty-Eight
December 23, 2011

TRIPP

I had gotten back to The Halekulani more than two hours after my family. Miranda was waiting for me when I walked in the air-conditioned doors of our hotel room. I explained to her that in the event of an accident, it was Royal Crown protocol for one member of the guest group to stay behind and fill out a stack of paperwork.

I didn't tell her that six agents were at the helipad within ten minutes. They confirmed what I had suspected—someone had shot at us. Someone had tried to kill my family and me. While the pilot—whose name I finally learned was Paul—and I waited for them to arrive, I had to explain who I really was.

"Well, that explains a lot..."

The ballistics expert on the scene confided in me that from the size and shape the bullet holes were fired from a Glock. He took several photos of the tail before another agent sawed off the tail to be taken to a local Honolulu lab to confirm the ballistic expert's suspicions.

Another agent questioned Paul, but he couldn't yield any useful witness testimony since he was rendered unconscious for the majority of the ride. The last thing he remembered was seeing Waimanalo Beach beneath us, which I corroborated. Of course, I had no clue what beach it was but I'm certain we were close to the shore when we were hit.

While the CIA is generally a cautious, suspicious bunch, the lead agent suggested that my family was likely just ancillary. Whoever was shooting at us was likely just trying to kill me. But who? That's the $60 million question. As a high-level agent, I'm used to threats on my life. I've pissed off a lot of dangerous people from even more cities and countries. Which psychopathic, homicidal, megalomaniac decided to come after me today is anyone's guess. But this time is even more personal than others. This bastard decided to involve my family.

When the agents were wrapping up their investigation, I pulled the lead agent aside and advised that the CIA buy Royal Crown a new helicopter for their fleet. We were the reason why there were two bullet holes in one of its revenue sources, a revenue source that's now perfectly useless as one of the primary pieces is in the back of a white van on the way to Diagnostic Laboratory Services across town. The "accident" had nothing to do with poor Paul and so it was only right that we make it up to him. I also gave Paul some cash as he was out of work for a while.

"And to be safe, get three agents to tail my family. Discreet ones. I don't want them thinking anything's wrong."

Chapter Twenty-Nine
December 23, 2011

CLEO

I am beside myself. Jake will be at the studio soon, soon, soon. I can't wait. Any minute now. I am so stirred up by him. He's all I can think about and think about all the time.

When he arrives in khakis and a Polo shirt, I bring him over to Peach to show him off and Ralphie goes in for the kill. Ralphie likes to take on straight guys and flirt with them so they get uptight. But Jake, as it turns out, is a good sport. He probably gets hit on a lot at the gym anyway. Then he meets Pudge and Pudding who are hilariously polite.

"A-lo-ha..." Pudding smiles, so obviously checking out Jake's physique.

I introduce them. "Jake, I'd love for you to meet my very good producers and even better friends, Pudge and his wife, Pudding."

I am beaming at them all as they shake each other's hands.

"Welcome to our little studio, bro," says Pudge.

"Thanks for having me."

"Jake, was it?" Pudding asks him. But I know she is making a little joke. She knows *all* about Jake. She's heard the name "Jake" more frequently in the past twenty-four hours than she will in her lifetime.

"Jake, yeah," he nods. "'Pudge' and 'Pudding,' very cool names!"

"Well, we'll let you get ready for your big television debut. Give a holler if you need anything. Water, some grub—" Pudge says.

"A shirtless massage!" jokes Pudding.

We all laugh. It's such fun having Jake here. I also have Alexa McPherson, a snowmaker from Nevada, on the show today. She works for the company that manufactures the fabricated snow for all of the Olympic games. There's also a last-minute change—Ashlyn King, the ballet dancer, had to back out, and so a film director who is shooting a movie in Oahu has thankfully agreed to take her place.

"Here are Spencer's credits. Have you heard of him?" Pudge asks, handing me a printout of Spencer Stone's bio and filmography.

"No, I don't think so. Should I?"

"Maybe not yet. He had one small movie that came out last year. Not a lotta people saw it but it got pretty decent reviews."

"So Jake," I say as I begin the show, "what about you? Do you ski?" I ask, the bright lights shining into my face.

"Mmmhmm," is his one-word response.

Uh oh.

"What fun! Where?"

"All over..."

I'm in trouble.

"I can tell you're an athlete. Is skiing your favorite sport?"

"Nah."

My audience laughs. Giving him the benefit of the doubt, I blame nerves. I switch gears and turn to Alexa, a far more engaging guest.

"Why don't you tell us a funny story about the snowmaking industry, Alexa?"

Alexa is happy to rescue the show's pulse. She goes on to delight the audience and me with a wonderfully entertaining story about the last Olympics in Sochi. Even Jake laughs.

Feeling guilty for having ignored him for the first half of the show, I turn to my third guest. Spencer has a tan, handsome face with a strong jawline. There's gel in his slicked-back hair and sunglasses over his head. He certainly looks the part of a modern Hollywood director. Howard Hawkes in a leather jacket.

"So, Spencer... you're in town shooting a film with Amanda Seyfried, is that right? I just loved her in *Mamma Mia*. What a voice!"

Typically, before every show, I go around to each of the dressing rooms and introduce myself to all of my guests. But since Jake's here, I talked myself into skipping that nicety today.

"That's right. It's a spy thriller called *The Last Touch*." I'm surprised to hear a British accent. "And, actually, one of the reasons I said 'yes' to the project was how much I love Hawaii. It's a dream to shoot here."

"Where do you stay? I hope production has put you up at some fabulous hotel."

"Actually, I bought a house in Waikiki a few years ago. I much prefer the surfing here than in Los Angeles."

And on and on we go about film and life on Hawaii. With his sexy looks and proximity to movie stars, the audience enjoys Spencer even more than they did Alexa. Jake, on the other hand, is so bad, just totally rigid and frozen. But after the show, he follows me back to my dressing room and his rigidity became something else entirely. People keep knocking on my door. This lust, this passion has to be satiated.

My back pushed up against the closed door, Jake up against me, he whispers, "During the whole show, all I wanted was to make love to you."

Oh, so that's why he couldn't speak...

After the live show and the dressing room show, which lasted an hour, I send Jake on his way. On the one hand, I crave normalcy, sanity. But the abnormality, insanity, and restlessness won out yet again. Jake is like a rooster, crowing to the world "I am male! Wake up! Look at me! Look, look, look at me in my prime!"

I remember Saint-Exupéry writing of the barnyard birds who tried to fly and join the wild geese as they flew overhead. The barnyard birds would feel the call of the wild. They would stop pecking at their chicken feed and flap their wings—some primordial instinct beckoning them into another orbit. But after a few futile tries, they would put their heads down and return to pecking their feed, forgetting about their wild side, their instincts blunted. I was thrilled to be in the sky for once, flying with the wild birds.

"Come to lunch. This time we might really eat... And wear a suit," my rooster casually suggests as he drives off. "We could go for a swim."

I'm waving at Jake's taillights when I notice Spencer Stone across the parking lot standing by a black car. He notices me too and we start walking toward each other.

"Thanks again for being part of our little show. And I can't wait for *The Last Touch!*" I say as we meet halfway.

"Of course, it was my pleasure. I was hoping we'd meet beforehand but your producer told me you didn't have time."

"Oh, yes. I'm so sorry about that, Spencer. You must think I'm so rude!"

"No worries. I know you're a very busy woman." He smiles and takes a step closer. "I just wanted to introduce myself since we have an interesting connection..."

"Oh?"

"Yes, well, I didn't want to bring it up on the air but once upon a time, I hear our parents were great friends."

"You're kidding! Who are your parents?"

"Genevieve and Richard Rensasslear," he pauses. "Spencer Stone has a much better ring to it, don't you think?"

My cheeks and chest are suddenly one hundred degrees.

"Well, my father *was* Richard. I don't know how well you knew him, but he actually died a long time ago." He pauses again. "Did you know that?"

My heart is beating so quickly and so loudly, I worry that Spencer can hear it.

"Oh. Yes, I think I recall my father mentioning that..."

Spencer waits for my condolences but I don't give them to him. As a film director, he must know how to read people and I can tell he understands that something is wrong.

"I'm sorry to bother you. I just thought it was a funny blast from the past. Anyway, I'll be here with my kids through Christmas. I hope to see you around the island."

As I drive over to the hotel, I keep thinking about that conversation. *Does Spencer know what his father did? Does he know why he killed himself?* I shudder, worrying that Spencer knows I am the reason why his father is dead, why he grew up all these years without him. Didier told me that Richard had written a note, but I can't imagine that he told the truth. I force myself to focus my mind on more pleasant things, like swimming in the ocean with Jake. I imagine us making love in the surf—the pounding waves, the warm sand.

I put on my favorite purple bathing suit to match my eyes.

When I arrive, Jake is sitting on the starkly lit beach with his brothers and Julia. She is in a navy bikini that compliments her figure. Jake is rubbing lotion on her back. *Breathe, Cleo.*

I smile. "Hello."

Jake drops the sunscreen and grabs my hand instead.

"You haven't met my father yet, Cleo. C'mon."

Chapter Thirty
December 23, 2011

JULIA

"For real?"

"Um, hey, want me to get the rest of your back?" Ricky offers, obviously trying to talk me off a tall ledge.

The rest of your back.

"Yo, tell me you just saw that," I say incredulously, turning to Ricky as we watch my boyfriend frolic off down the beach with the old battle axe.

"Yep..." he responds sheepishly.

"I mean..."

"Don't worry about it. We all know Jake can be kind of a dick."

"True. But, like..." I trailed off.

Ricky picks up right where Jake left off, scooping up the suntan lotion from out of the warm sand.

"Here, turn around. I got you, girl."

Under normal circumstances, I like having suntan lotion rubbed into my back and shoulders. It's so relaxing, and feels so nice, and—

"Ohmygod, he just pulled her hair! Did you guys see that?! Is he on a fucking playground?"

Matt looks out at the two of them. "She has a very nice body and the most beautiful face, like a movie star. And very pretty hair. And she is very nice and I think Jake really likes her," Matt admits earnestly.

"Matt," I say through gritted teeth.

"C'mon, Jake'll hit on anything with two legs," Ricky chimes in.

"Oh, good. In that case, I guess I don't have to worry about octopi and water buffalo."

Ricky and Matt laugh.

"Guys, I'm serious!" I say, giggling inexplicably through my anger.

"Stop, you're fine!" Ricky reassures me as he rubs more lotion into my back. I have to admit, Ricky's pretty good at this massage business....

"Did you see her ears? She has the prettiest ears. They're tiny and she has on these purple earrings with little pearls."

Only Matt would notice her ears. Normally, I appreciate his honest take on the world. But not today.

Ricky soothes me, "Dude, no one would flirt with anyone when they have you."

Aw.

"You're sweet. But wildly delusional."

"Maybe he really just likes her ears?"

Ricky elbows his brother.

"Ow! Why'd you do that?!" Matt cries out, overreacting big time.

Oh my God, I've been so naïve. Now it all makes sense. Has Jake really been sneaking off to be with *that woman,* Cleo?

One, he didn't pick me up at the airport. Two, now that I think about it, I saw the way he looked at her at dinner. Three, it doesn't take a rocket scientist to see he's been ignoring me the entire trip. Even in my red lacy thong. Now I know what his "fever" was all about. He is hot for her! Mrs. Robinson.

Deep breath. We had amazing sex last night. Jake wouldn't stoop that low. He might be terrible at making an effort with my father or at letting me pick what movie we're going to watch (*Die Hard* again? For real?) but he wouldn't do something this insensitive.

Also, he got me the necklace, which is the last stop on the Live-In-Girlfriend Express before I transfer over to the He-Put-A-Ring-On-It Line. But now, the question is, do I want a husband who will upset me like this? Do I want to marry someone who, after two years, makes me question what we have together and what I am to him? I was always told—by my father, my girlfriends, by characters on TV—that once you've found the right one, it should be easy. That everything just falls into place like pieces in a jigsaw puzzle. Had they made it past their sixteenth birthdays, even Romeo and Juliet would've occasionally squabbled over stupid things like who was driving home from the Cox's Christmas Eve party this year. I've always known the *type* of man I've wanted to marry but, until my twenty-fourth birthday, that man's face was completely blurry. Since then, his face has become Jake's. It was Jake's face across the aisle smiling at me in my white dress, Jake's face staring into my bloodshot eyes at my father's funeral in my black dress, and Jake's face flowing tears of joy while I lay sweaty and red-faced in a hospital gown after delivering our first child, named Constance, after my mother.

I guess it's still Jake's face. Jake's face that I want to punch square in the jaw.

Chapter Thirty-One
December 23, 2011

CLEO

Once we're out of sight from his family, Jake takes my hand and we start splashing along the sand as the warm ocean ripples over our feet. Our feet go deep into the sand. The ocean looks glorious and the wind is balmy. A perfect day in Paradise.

Shyly, Jake says, "Cleo, can we stop for a sec? I wanna give you something..."

He awkwardly pulls a delicate, diamond-and-gold necklace out of that little buttoned pocket in his swim trunks and puts it around my neck. How lovely, he must have picked that out for me at one of the shops at the hotel.

"Jake, this is so beautiful. Thank you. I am so touched."

He is looking down, so embarrassed. How sweet of him, the Alpha male, to become so shy when he does something romantic. The first man I have enjoyed making love with and he rewards me with this gift. I should be giving him presents...

As we stroll on to meet his dad, I entertain him by talking about my life here since he seems so utterly unable to speak.

Not that he's ever been a major conversationalist, but he is being so unlike his usual brash, assertive self. I think it's adorable.

"God, what a beautiful day..."

"I know. You're lucky you never have to leave."

"You know, I chose to move to Hawaii because of something that happened during a vacation here. My sisters and I were returning from a hotel on a tiny island in the Hawaiian chain called Lanai. It is filled with sunshine, flowers, heavy rugs on cold stone tile floors, thickly cushioned blue chaises, luxurious baths, and wonderful foods and wines. I sound like a travel agent, don't I?" I laugh.

He laughs with me. "Great. I'll tell my mom."

"Anyway, we were waiting for our boat to take us back to Maui to catch our planes home. And as we stood at the dock in the fading afternoon, this young man who was so reminiscent of freedom—tanned, barefoot, with sun-streaked hair, in an old khaki pair of shorts—jumped aboard his tiny boat and turned up his radio, filling the sky with sounds of Beethoven. You remind me of him actually, Jake."

"He must be devastatingly handsome." Jake twinkles.

"Of course... And when some friends asked when he'd be returning, he shrugged and yelled over the haunting music, 'Don't know. I'm off to Molokai. I'll probably be there for breakfast.' And my world collapsed. The yearning, the youth, the freedom, the strains of music, and the fading day conspired to relegate my, until then, perfect vacation to the abyss of the ridiculous.

"I felt the overwhelming need to get on my own small boat, into uncharted waters, sails unfurled, tasting Molokai, tasting worlds of total abandon, tasting freedom, tasting the stars in complete blackness alone, no one but the sea and Molokai at breakfast. Molokai—those three syllables conjured up every bittersweet thought, every possibility. I held deeply in me that vision of that gorgeous boy, that haunting melody, that run-down old boat, those bare feet, that insouciance in the face of the wide ocean, that careless shrug, that total mystical moment in summation of the uncluttered, unfettered perfectly free life. He made me realize I was frittering my life away and I had to change it, so I moved out here. It just felt right. I am very aware my life out here is hardly me living on a tiny boat in the ocean and fishing for dinner, but it is me free in some real form. I am closer to who I really am out here."

I don't tell Jake that I fixed up a cave which I named Molokai and only I go there to meditate and write. It is my magic place, my tiny boat.

"Well, I'm glad you decided to move. Our paths never would've crossed..."

Dear God, it's a good thing he hardly spoke on the show...

"There's my dad way up the beach. He'll love you, Cleo."

Then I see him, an older Jake, half a mile ahead of us and running with such precision. And I shiver uncontrollably.

Chapter Thirty-Two
December 23, 2011

TRIPP

I can't breathe or think straight when I see her walking toward me. It is almost as if I've been sitting in the sun for forty-eight hours and am suffering from mild heat stroke and hallucinations. There's no way it is her, I think initially. But as she comes closer and closer toward me with my eldest son in tow, there is no denying it. I am looking at the woman I had wanted to be with forever. We bonded with conversation only, under an African sky, a very long time ago. She had told me her darkest secret, a secret no one else but her parents knew. She admitted she had been unable to be close to a man, unable to have rewarding sex—that in truth, she was frigid—a huge admission that embarrassed her so much the next morning she couldn't even look at me and kept avoiding me until I finally reminded her I would never betray her. But I did.

She was climbing Kilimanjaro to fulfill her mother's last wish: to have her ashes spread at the peak. I was in Africa for a black-op mission under the name Danny Mortimer. When the mission was pushed back a full week, I decided to climb

Kilimanjaro. It was something I had always wanted to do. My cover was a location scout for a film shoot in Kenya and Tanzania. I'd gotten the idea from the Argo mission.

I was forty at the time. We were having a late breakfast outside in the warm sun before we were able to check into our separate rooms at The Amboseli Lodge. We'd come with the other climbers to see the lions mate after our ascent.

"Cleopatra is an unusual name. Is there a story?" I had asked her as I poured us both glasses of water from a pitcher left for us on the table by our waiter.

"Oh, yes. My very charming, but very eccentric mother, conceived me at Cleopatra's tomb."

"You're kidding."

Cleopatra had shaken her head. "That's what she always told me... But when I went to Alexandria to see it, I was told Cleopatra was buried with Marc Antony, but no one is sure where their tomb actually is. I think I must have been conceived near *a* tomb and she wanted it to be romantic so she claimed that it was Cleopatra's. Very like my mother."

A black cat with purple eyes just like hers slithered between tables next to us. I pointed down at it, "Great timing. This must be your namesake's cat."

"Excuse me?"

"Check it out, she has your purple eyes and black hair. Just like the first Cleopatra, I think? She had such power and wasn't afraid to use it."

The cat started rubbing her leg. Cleo smiled and stroked the feline's black hair. The cat instantly took to Cleo and started to purr softly. That was the first time in my life I found myself envying a cat.

"I think he rather likes me..." she said, stroking the cat yet locking eyes with me.

"He does," I leaned closer.

We stayed like that for a second or two. By the way we were looking at each other, I'm positive that we could both hear one another's hearts practically pounding out of our chests. It's still one of the most electrifying moments of my entire life.

"Age cannot wither her, nor custom stale her infinite variety," I blurted, desperate to stop the silence that was becoming more unbearable by the second.

She laughed. It wasn't the reaction I was going for but it sure helped lighten the mood.

"You don't like Shakespeare?"

"No, I do. 'They do not love that do not show their love,'" Cleo quoted with a smile that melted my heart. "I know every line of my namesake's play."

For the record, I don't normally talk like this. She's the only woman who would inspire me to quote fucking Shakespeare. That acting class of Mrs. Huenke's came in very handy at that moment.

"I told you so much about me, on the mountain, Danny, so now it's your turn to tell me something."

I would've liked to tell her the truth; that I was a deep undercover agent, here on a mission, using the persona of Danny Mortimer. That I actually lived in New York City with my wife and three sons and not alone in Brooklyn, like I said. But I couldn't or she would have stood up and walked away. While this flashed through my mind, she must've mistaken it for worry. And I was very worried. I was falling in love with a woman who wasn't my wife.

"Just tell me anything, Danny Boy—which, by the way, has just become my favorite song."

I acquiesced and showed her the six small holes in my two front teeth from when I had the measles while my teeth were growing in. Unless I pointed them out, you would never notice them.

Later that day, she dropped me off at the tiny airstrip to get on a single engine plane for my "location scout."

"I'd love to go with you, Danny. I want to see how you work," Cleo told me, grabbing my wrist.

"Me too. But you'd only distract me," I laughed. "And unfortunately, there are only two seats on the plane…"

If only she knew I was on a mission to kill a top Al Qaeda operative and that I'd never been on a single location scout in my life. I had come prepared, however—all the camera equipment and all the guns were on board.

"Well, I could always sit on your lap…" she flirted.

I looked at her. As much as I loved that image, this obviously had to be a solo mission. She could tell the answer was still 'no' from the look on my face.

"Oh, alright… But I'll miss you and the tiny holes in your teeth, Danny Boy."

And then she touched my tiny holed teeth. I'll never forget the way she looked, standing on the rough plane tarmac, in her beige safari outfit. I knew it would happen when I returned in a few hours after killing Fazul Mohammed. She had never enjoyed sex with anyone since the violent assault on her at age nine. I must be so careful not to hurt her. *Jesus, what am I talking about?* I remember thinking to myself. In my real life, I was a married man. I couldn't be the one who had sex with her and then walked away. I knew she wanted me to be the one and I wanted it, too. Hell, I almost made love to her at breakfast. That would have been a real treat for all the other diners at Amboseli… I wanted to swat all the plates and glasses off the table in one fell swoop like they do in the movies she thinks I work on. I wanted to grab her, set her on the messy table and rip off all of her clothes, then mine. I wanted to be inside of her, feel the depths of her, connect with her like no one ever had. To hell with all the others at the restaurant. But I couldn't do any of these things. What I needed to do was focus on my mission.

Fazul Mohammed was one of the masterminds behind the '98 Kenya embassy bombing in Nairobi along with his cronies, Al Qaeda's number one and two, Osama Bin Laden and Zawari. The Agency had discovered the hiding place of Fazul, and the perfect kill plan was in place. But, of course, nothing is perfect.

When Cleopatra and I parted, I tousled her hair and boarded the bush plane. As we taxied down the runway, my asset, the man we thought we bribed and bullied to help us, was acting strangely.

"How are you feeling, Karim?" I asked him.

"Oh, fine," he told me, his dark eyes focused on the tarmac in front of him.

"Need anything?"

Karim shook his head. A few moments later, he tugged on the Cessna 120's joystick, slowly lifting the small plane into the air. We sat in silence for the next few moments.

"You're still clear on the plan?"

Karim was supposed to take me to Fazul's hiding spot in the Somalian highlands. We would touch down on the plains half a mile away and I would walk the rest. Fazul never would have seen me coming.

Without looking at me again, Karim just nodded. All the telltale signs of betrayal were there. Anticipating, manipulating, and controlling those signs are precisely what I was trained for.

"I'm gonna grab some water from my backpack. Want any?" I asked Karim.

"No, thanks."

As if everything was up to code, I casually got up off my seat and headed toward the back of the plane. I grabbed a canteen of water from my pack and took a big swig. A divider separated the cockpit from the rest of plane but still, I always need to sell it. Even in crisis, it was crucial that I always maintain a composed façade. If you panic, they panic. I glanced around the plane and noticed our parachutes a few feet away. Satisfying my suspicions, I grabbed and examined them. The first one was as it should be, normal, but the second was not. When I held it up to the light, I saw several tiny holes. This was to be my parachute if we had an emergency landing. But that wasn't the plan of course. I would be captured and tortured and give up information to Fazul.

It was too late to stop Karim. We were already in the air, cruising at an altitude of five thousand feet. The asset we thought we'd turned was setting me up. Fazul must have had grand plans in store for me. I knew Fazul was about an hour and a half out. I should have noticed Karim's manner before we took off but I had been too engrossed with Cleopatra. Just like the first Cleopatra who deterred both Marc Antony and Caesar Augustus from their battles, she had deterred me from mine and it was going to be very difficult to get out of the plane alive.

When I sat back down next to Karim, I noticed he was sweating, the reality of what he had agreed to do to me presumably setting in.

"Man, the beauty of this place..." I said as we soared over Rahole National Preserve in Kenya. "So different than America."

Karim nodded.

"I hafta admit, I'm excited to get back there. Back to my family. Do you have a family, Karim?"

Karim nodded again.

"I gotta wife, Miranda, and three young boys. Jake, Matt, and Ricky. Couldn't tell you why, but they love their dear old dad..." I smiled and looked over at Karim. His dark eyes were still laser-focused on the blue sky ahead of us. "What about you? Your family?"

"Please. I'm sorry, I need to concentrate," he said finally.

"Oh, of course. Of course. I don't mean to ramble, just trying to pass the time... I get so bored on planes. Here, lemme show you a family photo and then I promise I'll leave you alone!"

When I rose, I turned to go toward the back of the airplane. But then I pivoted quickly and turned again, doubling back to the cockpit and approached Karim from behind. I skimmed the knife's edge in my right hand close around Karim's throat and lodged his trachea in the crook of my elbow. Using my left arm like a fulcrum, I put my left palm flat on the back of his head and pushed forward. I waited for Karim to pass out, and then asphyxiated him—if I released him the blood would flow back and he'd come to.

I hopped in the pilot's seat and scanned my surroundings, looking for a safe place to "crash" while I contacted my backup. I needed it to look like we were burnt to a crisp. After parachuting out and crashing the plane, the CIA came and removed me. They extracted me from the plane using a harness, self-inflating balloon, and an attached lift line to The Fulton surface-to-air recovery system. Fulton is based on a similar system that was used during World War II by American and British forces to retrieve soldiers and downed assault gliders.

Cleopatra was worried sick when I wasn't back for dinner as I said I'd be. She kept calling my hotel room every fifteen minutes, praying that eventually my carefree voice would pick up. After four-and-a-half hours, she finally convinced someone from the hotel to drive her over to the tiny Amboseli Airstrip. Except for one employee working behind the desk and someone waiting for a flight, the airport was a ghost town. That someone was CIA. She waited there for three more hours, pacing around the small room to quell her nerves, unable to sit still. With each passing minute, her anxiety escalated and exacerbated. The cruelest form of torture.

Eventually, the lone employee got a phone call. Cleopatra ran over to his desk and craned her neck, trying to hear the other end of the call.

"What is it?! Is it about Danny? Is he alright?!"

The employee ignored Cleopatra. He just nodded a few times and thanked the caller before he hung up, careful not to let his tone or body language prematurely confirm the news of my "death."

He couldn't look at her.

"What? Just tell me," Cleopatra begged.

"I'm so sorry, missus, but..."

Tears stained Cleopatra's cheeks before the employee could get the rest of his sentence out. Twenty minutes later, he helped her crumpled body off the floor. We had done an excellent job staging the crash, so to everyone but the CIA, it was treated as absolute.

So to her, to beautiful Cleopatra, I was dead. The CIA cleaned out my "apartment" in Brooklyn. The cover I had, Danny Mortimer, location scout, was forever gone. The CIA later alerted me that she had come to my apartment. She spoke with my landlady and asked how she could get in touch with "my brother," whom the landlady, also CIA, told her had cleaned out my stuff.

The last time I saw her, the time I tousled her hair, was just before my identity as Danny Mortimer was compromised. And now, here she is on this Hawaiian beach and I see in an instant that she's having an affair with my son. Well, that explains Jake's recent lack of interest toward his girlfriend... I'd thought of Cleopatra so often at the start and felt so guilty that she presumed I was dead, that she'd had to grieve someone who never even existed. So, like any other normal, red-blooded man, I closed off all my feelings. Early on in black-op school, we were taught to segment our lives. The golden rule was to avoid getting close to anyone at all costs. There's always a chance, if duty called for it, that we'd eventually have to kill their closest relative or in some cases, even them. It's easier to stay closed off. But with Cleopatra, I'd broken that doctrine and now it's come back to haunt me.

Under my Danny Mortimer cover, when I'd first laid eyes on her at Kilimanjaro, our leader on the climb, Jabari, came into the center of a circle we'd formed. He welcomed us and then informed everyone that in the proper Outward Bound tradition, we were to carry our own 70-pound packs. That was A-okay with the rest of the group, but not her. Horrified, she looked up at the daunting mountain and blurted out, "But I have never done more than climb the Stairmaster! I'd never have come on this trip except for my mother, Sandrine's last wish!" Later, Cleo told me all about her mother and the adventures she'd been on in spreading Sandrine's ashes.

On that day, at the start of our climb, she stood there in a pink parka while the rest of us were all in earth tones—khaki, tan, brown, etc. From the faces of the men in the group, I knew they were already hypothesizing that she might, *maybe,* make it to ten-thousand feet, if that. And from the faces of the women in the group, they wanted her gone even sooner. She was that beautiful. I hate to admit it, but I had to agree with the other men—I would've put good money on the fact that she wouldn't make it past the ten-thousand feet camp. She was wearing head-to-toe pink for Christ's sake—*pink!*

Her strength surprised us all. She touched something in me, something I hadn't felt since my younger days with my first wife, Cindy. I walked straight across the circle and offered to help her. I didn't want to lose her at ten thousand feet. I wanted her to stay right next to me for the entire climb. And I wanted her to fulfill her mother's wish to scatter her ashes.

Is her being here, on the beach with my son, just one of those weird coincidences? Or does it signify something greater? Like I did on the plane with Karim the last day I saw her, I immediately go to black-op mode. I believe in coincidences, though many operatives don't. But this feels like more than a simple coincidence. All these years, I thought I was the one who had a secret identity, who had pulled the wool over her eyes—whether or not it was by choice. But what if I had it wrong this entire time? What if she had fooled me too? I almost died in a helicopter that she knew I was on yesterday, the same way I almost died on that bush plane in Africa. That's some coincidence.

I sprint into the water to cool off and to give myself a second before having to greet her. There's no way she could recognize me. I was dead. She'd seen the crashed plane and my "body" that had been burned beyond recognition. I'd had a different name and a totally different look then—long blonde hair tied in a ponytail, with a lasso and a carelessly laid back attitude reflected by my slow Southern drawl. It was Danny Mortimer that she knew and loved so long ago in Africa. Not

Tripp Regan. Back then, I'd worn tinted-brown contact lenses and carried myself so casually. I was a cowboy, even though it wasn't real. Now I'm an uptight lawyer and family man with short, cropped, dark hair and my God-given blue eyes.

The walk is what always gives the covert operator away and I had Danny's gait down perfectly, a lope almost like an African animal. She even commented on the way I walked. So relaxed and slow. In a flash, there are so many things about her that I remember. As I walk toward them—damn that perfume. She's wearing the same perfume that she wore in Africa. I'll never forget the name. Endgame.

She'd told me how her father had had it made specially for her at a shop in Paris where they spend hours finding what works on your skin and with your personality. She wore it every day on the mountain and I couldn't get enough of it. Suddenly, I feel fury at my own son. I never got the chance to sleep with her, and obviously, he already has. I wonder when she got over the repercussions of that awful rape as a little girl. I strain to look calm. My dark hair, my blue eyes, my type-A walk, my clipped voice, and my bearing are my own now. She wouldn't recognize me as Danny even if she didn't believe he had actually died years ago. I'm good at my job, but right now I'm being tested like I never have before. In a way, it's sort of thrilling to be tested by her. Now I'm just the lawyer father of the young buck she's having an affair with. I wonder if she sensed something of me in him when they met. Maybe that's why she is having an affair with him. Same DNA. My ego is begging to believe that.

On this beach in Honolulu, I walk over to her again. I'm so tempted to tousle her hair and ask, "Who's your Marc Antony, Cleopatra?" Unless you count a measly handshake, I can't even touch her.

"Dad, I want you to meet Cleo Gallier. She's the woman I met in the car crash. Cleo, this is my dad, Tripp Regan."

"Lovely to meet you, Tripp. Jake told me you just came back from China on business."

"I did," I nod.

What a heartbreaker.

"I love the Great Wall. Do you get a chance to sightsee while you are on work trips?"

My voice, I need to keep it from the Danny drawl and make it very clean and crisp, "Yes, Cleo, I can usually manage some time off. The Great Wall's pretty daunting though. You've climbed it?"

"Somehow, I can't imagine you being daunted by those stairs!"

Jake eyes her warily, seemingly not a fan of Cleo complimenting another man in his presence. But I smile.

"Let's join the rest of the gang. I'm sure Julia will be missing you, Jake."

I shouldn't have said that. I've reverted to sandbox tactics. Cleo laughs but Jake shoots me a furious look, not appreciating my fatherly advice.

"So, Cleo, have you lived here all your life?"

She smiles so happily and takes Jake's arm to help her over some pebbles.

"No, I was born in Paris, actually. I was raised there and in Algeria and New York. I found my way here about seven years ago and fell madly in love with this place. So, I followed my instincts and stayed."

Well, I fell madly in love with you on Kilimanjaro. I nod politely, scared to speak.

"I think following our instincts makes us happy, don't you?" she continues.

My instinct is to stay silent or I will give myself away. What questions are safe between two people who talked for eight full nights in Africa? What questions will keep us on safe ground and not on slippery footing and ledges? And who betrayed whom? Am I the traitor or is it her?

And Jake. How I envy him right now. Before lunch, I will go to my room and call the agency to see if I should be worried about meeting Cleo Gallier.

"Excuse me, I need to change out of my running clothes," I tell my family as they sit down for lunch.

I need to find out Cleo Gallier's true identity. There are just too many coincidences. Running into her on the beach after nine long years is momentous enough. She was there as I got on the plane in Africa that was to deliver me to the enemy and she is here now. Yesterday, she was invited on our helicopter ride that was nearly doomed. Is she responsible for the tiny bullet holes in the tail? And she's involved with my son, which also gives her access to me.

I WAIT TO CALL AGENT Steve Singer until I'm in the confines of my hotel room. Miranda has mercifully kept the air conditioner on high.

"Singer, hi. I need you to look up someone for me. First name: Cleopatra, last name: Gallier. Currently resides in Honolulu."

"Copy that. Just a moment, sir."

A few terrifying minutes pass. To keep my mind occupied, I strip off my sweaty clothes and change into a clean T-shirt and pair of khakis. *Please keep her out of this. Please, God, keep her out of this.* There's a chance I'm making something out of nothing but I can't cut corners or risk making any assumptions, not when it comes to my family.

"Singer? Anything?"

"Sorry for the delay, sir. Just wanted to make sure. No, Cleopatra Gallier doesn't show up having any red flags. Travels to Europe and Algeria 'bout once a year. Looks like she lived in Algeria in 2004, though." Agent Singer tells me finally. "But, it looks like her father—"

"Is part-Algerian."

"That's correct, sir."

"It seems she's lived a pretty charmed life, especially since she relocated to Honolulu. Occupation: television personality, never been married, no affiliation with any church or other religious groups, though it looks like she went to Catholic school as a child."

"Okay. Thanks, Singer. Any news on that autopsy?"

"Not yet, but you're our first call as soon as the results are in."

"And any word on the bullets that hit the helicopter yesterday?"

"It was a Glock, sir, but we have not found where it was shot from or the gun, itself. We will, though, that's for sure."

Now that I know it's unlikely Cleo isn't anyone other than who she says she is, I can relax a little.

Chapter Thirty-Three
December 23, 2011

MIRANDA

When I see Cleo cascading along the beach with Tripp and Jake, I start to laugh. They all look so perfect together—like the cover of a romance novel or a *Town and Country* magazine or a film poster for *High Society*.

I jump up to meet them.

"Oh. Hello, Miranda. There you are," my husband says to me in a very wooden, almost formal tone.

Oh. Hello Miranda, there you are? Tripp's greeting is so off. He looks like he's in shock. Did Jake tell his father that he's having an affair with Cleo? I doubt it. It's unlike him. He's so secretive and I certainly didn't mention my suspicions.

"What a gorgeous trio you three are!" I exclaim.

"C'mon, let's get something to eat. I'm starving, aren't you?" says Tripp.

As we make our way back up to the hotel, toward the patio restaurant, Tripp looks like he's just had a jolt but covers it by being amazingly, ridiculously glib. Our family takes their seats at the big round table, and he's acting like a caricature of a father in a fifties' sitcom—ordering us all to lunch, clapping and trying to rally us.

"Waiter, can we get some wine? Guys, red or white? What do you want, Cleo, Julia, Miranda? Iced tea, ginger ale, or wine?"

But Julia doesn't answer, she is frozen staring at Cleo.

"Ricky, what about you? Miranda? Whoops, sorry, Matt," Tripp says as he stomps on Matt's foot.

He's acting like he owns the hotel, issuing commands and instructions. My husband, the lawyer, has morphed into a drill sergeant. He helps Cleo into her seat as if she's Baccarat crystal, but she barely acknowledges him. Tripp is overcompensating for something. He's usually so relaxed. What's happened?

"You know what, excuse me, I need to change out of my running clothes," he announces as he leaves us.

"Excuse me, too. I have to... uh, check on something," Julia tells us before running off. Actually running off.

Tripp returns ten minutes later wearing a pressed LaCoste shirt tucked into his shorts with a belt. I must say, he looks a little more buttoned up than he usually does on our vacations. As he sits down, he almost misses his chair entirely. He catches himself gracefully, so that no one notices this but me. But he seems far more relaxed now. He is smiling broadly.

"Sorry I took so long. I had to make a call."

"Everything alright?" I ask.

"Yes, never better. Fortunately, what I was concerned about turned out to be a non-issue."

I nod, leaving it alone.

He turns to Cleo. "I'm really sorry I missed the Outrigger. Jake told me all about your car crash." Tripp clears his throat and takes a sip of water. "Cleo, is that short for something?"

"Yes, it's Cleopatra. My mother named my sisters and me after the places where we were conceived."

"I was conceived in Egypt near Cleopatra's pyramid. Tree, my sister, was conceived in Woodstock against a Silver Birch Tree."

"Woodstock? Your mom sounds wild," Ricky cuts in.

"Oh, yes. And she never told us where my baby sister was conceived, so she was named Beebe for baby, and because her father raises bees as a hobby. Once she slipped and said Beebe was conceived on her father's estate where the bees are. Knowing my mother, perhaps she was conceived in Westminster Abbey, but even my mother wouldn't admit to that."

Tripp laughs. "I think I would've liked your mother."

Cleo smiles, "Yes, you would have. All men did. Always. Her name was Sandrine."

Chapter Thirty-Four

DIDIER

Cleopatra's mother, Sandrine, was my wife for a few, short, wonderful years. She followed our marriage with other marriages as she thrived on men and romance and felt most alive when presented with their newness and the thrill of seducing them. I understood her and I watched her, laughingly, maneuver through a glamorous life.

On one typically gloomy Parisian day, Sandrine called to inform me that she wanted to speak with me in person. I could tell by the tone in her voice, lacking its playful lilt, it was serious. We were to rendezvous at our favorite little bistro, Comptoir de St. Pere, where, decades ago, we breakfasted daily and had supper occasionally when we had been married and lived together in Paris.

On the phone, she told me Paris was no bother, "it was on the way"—but not saying where it was on the way to. Since she mentioned no final destination, it never occurred to me to press her for details. I knew she'd enlighten me when I saw her face to face. Almost as an afterthought, she added she wanted to see Paris one last time and wanted to see it that last time with me. Sandrine always did have a flair for the dramatic, so I didn't take her comment too seriously.

When she arrived the next Tuesday—our last Tuesday together—she looked her usual lovely self. I knew she was very aware of the aging process and the unforgiving toll it takes on every woman of a certain age. She'd always had her small aches and pains but I could see by the way she walked they were front and center now. And her face had wrinkles softly carving it.

"Didier..." she smiled, leaning into me.

"*Bonsoir, mon amour,*" I said, taking her in my arms.

We kissed each other twice on the cheek then smiled as we sat down at our table. She looked up at me and started laughing inexplicably.

"What is it?" I asked her.

"Oh, nothing. It's nothing..." she said, calming herself down.

"... Sandrine?"

Then she burst into laughter again. It always did have quite the contagious effect on me.

"Oh, come on! Out with it!" I demanded, thrilled at the prospect of what she was going to tell me.

Through laughter she began, "Well, I've been thinking lately... about so many things. Our time together."

"Yes, Sandrine..."

"When we met and even when we were married, you remember how much we loved playacting? It was such a huge thrill for us both." She gaily nudged me with her foot.

"Of course, I remember. We just got too good at it..." I smiled, taking her hand.

I'll never erase those images from my head. She was so perfect in her white or pastel swimsuit, sitting at a hotel pool. Sometimes I'd sit in the shade, just watching her. There she'd be—reading, eating, sleeping, it didn't matter. I'd march up to her and open by asking her a completely arbitrary question. Knowing the drill, she'd reply without missing a beat and I'd introduce myself as someone from some far-off place like Moscow or an obscure city in Thailand. I'd make up what I did—netsuke dealer or horse whisperer or dahlia gardener... The game was to trap her and find her ignorant about what I was talking about. Then I'd win. I am an expert at bluffing but unlike most women in my life, Sandrine was more than my match.

Once, I admired a gold necklace she wore, which I had just given her that morning. It had our initials entangled. I was pretending to be a gold dealer from Italy.

Her snappy retort, "This old thing? Oh, it's fake."

And then she heaved it into the pool. I couldn't look upset or Sandrine would win. Admittedly, we were a pretty deadly combination. A child of about seven, maybe eight, dove into the pool and retrieved the necklace for her.

"Excuse me, ma'am? Is this yours?" he asked, his tan little body dripping water onto her chaise.

"Please give it to your mother, darling. I'm sure she'll like it better than I," Sandrine laughed, staring at me. Challenging me. She won that round.

But my favorite was the time I went over to her dressed as a pool boy carrying a tray of food. I "accidentally" spilled it on Sandrine and she retaliated by picking up a handful of the spilled salad, throwing it at me and stalking off. I ran after her, grabbed her, and passionately kissed her while the pool guests looked on, shocked. What a scene the two of us could make. It was as though we were meeting for the first time each time we started up a new game. So, naturally, we ended up in the most torrid encounters.

We laughed and smiled radiantly at one another as we looked back. I saw her then as I always saw her. Young and beautiful.

"You look wonderful, Sandrine," I told her.

"Ah, Didier. What happened with us?" she asked quietly.

"All good things end, Sandrine."

Again, we smiled at our memories as our typically Parisian, typically irritable waiter made his way over to our table with a bottle of our favorite wine from my Algerian vineyard.

"That's actually why I'm here, my love..." Sandrine started. "I've had a good life. But all good things end."

I felt my heart break.

"You see, I won't allow myself to become like Tati, Didier. I won't," she told me, sipping the white wine. "I have made arrangements in Switzerland and nothing you say or do will change my mind—but you know that. To you and to Tree and Beebe's fathers I will tell the truth, however. I have an inoperable brain tumor and while I am fine now, I don't have long. I have given our Cleopatra a job to scatter my ashes and I hope she will see what fun life can be as she wanders through the places where I had such wonderful memories."

She touched my cheek and smiled at me. And I knew there was nothing I could do to talk her out of her decision. Nor did she want me to. I did remind her of Camus's famous opening sentence in *The Myth of Sisyphus,* "There is but one truly serious philosophical problem, and that is suicide."

And she smiled and said "Ah, Didier, I am not choosing suicide. I love life, but I am choosing to end painlessly and not have my family suffer with me."

She referred to her mother whose death at ninety-eight was a relief to all who loved her. Tati genuinely disintegrated before her family's eyes, tottering to death on her martinis. Sandrine once said, "Mother is like a sachet that has been in the drawer too long and lost its fragrance." This was a stark contrast to the Tati I'd first met in 1965. Then, she'd been like a whirling helicopter, but eventually her propellers were permanently damaged by age. I cherished Tati, but Sandrine would sooner become a polar bear than become like her mother.

Toward the end of her life, Tati's favorite trick was to pretend to die when she felt she wasn't getting enough attention. She'd suddenly scream, "Help me, help me!" then collapse conveniently on a nearby bed or a sofa. Always a forgiving surface. Knowing she was simply craving the spotlight, her family tended to ignore her while she just laid there, eyes shut and arms out like Sarah Bernhardt. And knowing her weakness, the girls would mention a martini, and without fail, Tati would perk right up.

No, Sandrine never wanted to be like her mother. I can hardly blame her. In fact, it was hard for me to blame Sandrine for much at all. I never blamed her when she left me either; she felt I was too much competition for her. She always said I looked like a movie star but everytime it came out, it sounded more like an insult than a compliment. We had such high energy, we inflamed one another and blew each other up. But whereas my energy was contained, Sandrine's was frenetic and volatile. This was evidenced in her postmortem chore to our daughter Cleopatra, which she told me about that night, our last night.

After "dying" at the clinic, she left Cleopatra a duty in her will to sprinkle a few of her ashes in all the places men she loved had proposed or given her something she treasured. She aptly titled this little excursion, "The Pilgrimage of Ashes". Sadly, but not surprisingly, none of the places the ashes were to be scattered had anything to do with her three daughters.

She loved them as extensions of herself, but not fervently nor passionately as she did the men who paraded through her existence.

The most imaginative locale she sent Cleopatra to was the San Diego Zoo, where she threw her mother's ashes to the lions—something Sandrine was always so fond of doing to her daughters. She certainly threw them to the lions when she sent the threesome during one of their spring vacations from school to a very dangerous drug rehab center in New York. I was appalled when I learned, after the fact, that Sandrine sent Cleopatra, Tree, and Beebe to work as volunteers at Haze Avenue in Chelsea. I know her intentions were pure—to remind her girls that the cushioned world they live in is foreign to most, a fairy tale. But there, Cleopatra and her sisters could easily learn how to: smoke dope, shoot up heroin, make LSD, and obtain cocaine. The addicts were more than happy to share their war stories with a trio of bright-eyed, Upper East Side teenagers. As I said, Sandrine always did have a flair for the dramatic.

Included in her ash-scattering timetable were several New York City restaurants—One If By Land, Two If By Sea and also the River Café under the Brooklyn Bridge, where we had lapped up several bottles of pink champagne during our last year together. It made me smile that she instructed Cleopatra to pour a bottle of that wonderful pink bubbly into the East River with some of her ashes. And I got a wonderful flash-back when Sandrine added our favorite suite at our favorite hotel—the one with the fireplace—to the list. It was in that room I had given her the emerald in the Faberge egg, which Cleopatra now wears every day.

When Cleo listed all the places of her "Pilgrimage of Ashes," I encountered so many memories that I'd forgotten years ago. Tahiti, where we only went for three days—all that way, but God, it was worth it. She wouldn't let me sleep while we were there. "Didier when we are dead, we can sleep," Sandrine had said. But I really wondered who she was thinking of when she sent Cleo to scatter her ashes at Kilimanjaro's peak? Or who took her on the Peter Pan ride in Disney World? Even in death, Sandrine always kept me guessing.

The bill was put on my charge, our coats were buttoned, and we exited our bistro into the cold Paris night. We wandered the streets of Paris until dawn, just reliving our wonderful times in the City of Love. We said goodbye at dawn, and of course, I knew for certain it was the last time I'd ever see my Sandrine.

"I think you already know this, Didier," she said, her gloved fingers touching my cheek again, "but I'd like to be certain." She paused for what seemed like forever. And then, "It was you. It was always you. You, my dear, were the greatest love of my life."

"And you mine, my darling."

We held on tightly until she started to pull away and then gracefully and predictably turned and smiled at me one last time, and was gone.

But after Sandrine left this earth, the letters that came to her daughters from so many men tell a different story. It seems they all thought they were the only one. Ah, Sandrine! Even in death, you keep surprising me and breaking my heart. Sandrine Smythe Gallier Austin Lady Alastair.

Chapter Thirty-Five
December 23, 2011

JULIA

I'm going to be sick. He gave her my necklace. My necklace. My fucking necklace!

My legs wobble, my heart pounds, and my stomach is in six hundred knots as I hightail it away from the Regan's table as if it's on fire. I hurry into the dark, air-conditioned lobby and beeline over to the bar where a semi-hot blonde guy holds down the fort. I'm not much of a drinker but that's about to change in... *3-2-1, lift off.*

"Hi, I'd like a Mai Tai, please." I smile sweetly at the semi-hot bartender. "Oh, and make it a double."

Semi-hot looks over and smiles back.

Yup, this chick can party. Now hop to, Bud.

"Comin' right up."

Then I giggle inexplicably. I do this sometimes. Giggle when I'm angry. Or nervous. Or on the verge of a total nervous breakdown.

"Charge it to your room, ma'm?" he asks, handing me a cocktail the size of Arnold Schwarzenegger's head. I'm pretty sure I could swim the breaststroke inside this thing.

Call me "ma'am" one more time, buster, and it's your head. "Yes, please. Room 788."

My fingers are shaking as I step into the elevator and press the button for the top floor. The doors shut and we start to whir upward. I take a big sip and immediately gag from all the rum. Semi-hot wasn't messing around... I reach inside my purse and go to fish out my phone but find Jake's instead. *Jackpot.* I forgot he'd given it to me on the beach for safe keeping. *Sucka.* There's a code, but I know it. 8-8-8-8. *How uncrackable, honey.* Idiot.

The elevator doors slide open and I walk down the hall, completely absorbed in Jake's phone. I check his recent call log. 808 something. *Eighteen* outgoing calls to a random 808 number. That nameless client he was trying to get ahold of? Methinks not. But just to confirm, I dial...

"Hello, you've reached Cleo Gall—"

Unbelievable. I hang up and assuage my rage with another big gulp. *Glug, glug, glug.* Fumbling with the room key, I finally open the door. Yikes, my buzz has already kicked in. You know, I think I'll take up day drinking. Everyone's obsessed with brunch anyway. Having a cocktail, or a glass of wine (or ten) during the day is so much more civilized than staying out until 2:00 a.m. and waking up with a pounding headache. There, it's decided. Day drinking is my new thing.

Stepping inside the cool room, I go directly to Jake's suitcase. The Tiffany box is still there but not the necklace. It's official. God, I hate her. But I hate him even more. I want to yank it right off her wrinkly old turkey neck and strangle them both with it. Two birds, one stone. His jumbo box of condoms is still in the suitcase too. There must be at least twenty missing. Gross. I down the rest of my Mai Tai and put the empty glass in the box of condoms. *Take that, shithead.* He slept with me last night too. Twice. And once this morning. Gross, gross, *gross*. Oh, I could kill him with my bare hands.

I happen to glance in the trash can and notice the white ribbon from the Tiffany box is inside. Maybe I should wrap it around my neck and fashion my own necklace? That would get quite the reaction from Jake at the lunch table. I've gotta get out of this room, *tout suite*. There's no way I can sleep next to Jake, that two-timer, now. I storm across the room and start stuffing all my belongings into the dark lavender T.Anthony luggage that Miranda generously gave me last year for my twenty-fifth birthday. From the closet, I grab all my expensive dresses and tops that I'm kicking myself for buying now and hang them over my arms and shoulders, then hurl open the door and enter the hallway.

Okay, now what… I haven't exactly thought this genius plan of mine through. I peek down the hall—once to my left and once to my right like a cautious New York pedestrian—and finally get an idea. Ricky. I'll stay with Ricky. That'll really push Jake's dumb, stupid, lying buttons. For the first time in my life, I can actually sympathize with Lorena Bobbitt for chopping off her husband's selfish little friend. My bag in tow, hangers draped over my arms and shoulders, I roll toward Ricky's room looking like the crazy bag lady that camps out on the corner of my block. There's a petite, elderly maid with a cart across the hall who glances up at me and makes a face.

Keep moving. Nothing to see here, people.

I reach for Ricky's door. It's locked. Of course, it's locked. It's a hotel for Christ's sake, Julia. Across the hall, the maid swipes her card and is about to enter another room.

"Excuse me?" I say to her, my voice high-pitched and shaky.

She turns and looks at me with a raised unibrow. Very Frida Kahlo. I'm digging it.

"I'm so sorry, but I seemed to have forgotten my room key. Would you mind... letting me in, please?"

Homegirl isn't buying it.

"Is this your room, Miss?" she asks, in a thick accent, already knowing the answer.

"Of course it is!"

She looks back at the room I shared with Cheater McLiar. "Are you sure, Miss?"

Change of plans. I start to sob. Literally, sob. Like, not one delicate, glistening tear down my cheek, a whole avalanche. The floodgates have opened. I let it all out in front of this poor, nice maid who probably just wants to do her job well and go home to her nice family on time. I look up at her, and notice her name tag says 'Marta.'

"My—my boyfriend, Marta," I sob. "He's cheating on me right in front of my face! He, he gave her this necklace that he was supposed to give to me... I even picked it out! Stupidly, I thought he was going to propose!" I sniffle, "Gosh, look at me... I'm so sorry, what a mess!"

Marta is looking at me like I'm the little girl who barfed all over everyone in *The Exorcist*.

"I swear, I'm normally a little more put together, Marta!" I manage a laugh. "Anyway, there's no way in sweet hell I can stay in the same room with him now!" I scream, really feeling the full effects of the Mai Tai. "Oh God, I'm gonna be sick..." I've officially deboarded the Live-In-Girlfriend Express and taken a detour onto the Crazy-Psycho-Ex-Girlfriend line. I lean against the wall and, having no strength left, slide down to the ground, all my clothes sprawling around me like I'm having a yard sale. Dignity? Out the window. Pride? Yeah, I don't think so.

"Can you please just let me into this room?" I plead. "It's my boyfriend's, or rather, my *ex*-boyfriend's, brother's room. I just need to put my luggage in here for now, you can even go in and out with me if that makes you feel better. I'm begging you, Marta. I—"

"You ask me, he worth... shit." Marta says, in her thick Latino accent.

Marta looks at me and unlocks the door to Ricky's room. If anyone deserves to be sainted, it's this woman. Saint Marta of The Halekelani Hotel. I smile through my tears as she helps me up.

"Thank you, Marta! You're truly a lifesaver!" I can't help myself and hug Marta so tight, she eventually pats my back as if to say, *okay, time to go.*

I enter Ricky's room and make a beeline for the minibar. *They tried to make me go to rehab but I said no, no, no...*

Chapter Thirty-Six
December 23, 2011

MIRANDA

Our food finally arrives. The boys are all furiously digging into their usual order—club sandwiches with a side of fries. Cleo has a fruit plate, which looks delicious, and Tripp and I are both eating chef's salads. He's now drinking a dark and stormy and I am drinking iced tea... though I could use a strong martini right about now. Speaking of which, Julia finally returns with a large fruity looking cocktail and sits—more like collapses—down next to Ricky. She moves her chair even closer to him.

Jake doesn't acknowledge her return but turns and says to Cleo, "You should join us for dinner tonight."

"Thank you for the invitation, Jake, but I'm sorry, I need to stay in tonight as I'm running part of the Honolulu marathon in the morning."

"Do they start all the old people at the back?" Julia blurts out, slurring.

We all glance around the table, shocked by Julia's remark. I look at the glass in front of her and notice it's now only half full. She's normally so well put together. *Oh, no.* She must have just figured it out. I buckle up my proverbial seat belt. This is going to be one bumpy lunch...

Cleo pretends she hasn't heard Julia's snarky remark, "I've run the marathon every year since I moved out here—"

"Who was the man Jake and I saw you dining with last night?" Julia interjects.

The perfectly composed Cleo looks surprised.

"Man? Oh, that was Jimbo."

"Jimbo?" Tripp asks with a tint of criticism at the man's name.

Julia calls over to the waitress. "I'll have another Mai Tai, please. And tell the bartender to make it a double. He'll know what I mean..." she says sloppily.

Yes, sweetheart. Everyone will know what that means.

I slide a water toward her, hoping she'll take the hint. Take, she does not.

"Last night, Jake and I were having the most romantic dinner in town..." she slurs. "The, uh, I forget the name. D'you know it, Cleo?"

"Sure, I know it very well," Cleo says, going along with Julia gamely.

"Of course you do..."

Whatever that means.

We're all looking at her, wide-eyed. Especially Jake, who most certainly is worried about what's going to spill out of his girlfriend's mouth. Julia looks over at him, catches his dopey deer-in-headlights expression, and smiles.

"What, Jake? Oh, don't worry, I'm not going to tell everyone our little secret..."

Jake braces for impact.

"... That I kicked your asssss in tennis!" she slurs again. It's getting worse.

"You sure did," Jake smiles awkwardly. He looks relieved.

"He was such a good sport about it... I thought he was going to be so mad. But actually, when we got home, we had sex. Twice!" she blurts out. "Oh God, can't believe I said that..."

Neither can I.

"Anyway, Clee-yo, we saw you having dinner with your handsome friend. I don't think you had on that necklace, though. It's Tiffany, right, *Jake?*"

Julia turns and glares at Jake. He's about to say something but clearly thinks better of it. An awkward silence envelops the whole table. The tension is bashing us all over the head.

Tripp gives me a look of *do something.* Matt just keeps gobbling up his sandwich as if we were discussing the weather or traffic.

"Oh, Ricky. I hope you like the surprise I put in your room..."

"Great! Let's go see it!" Ricky pops out of his chair, grabs Julia's arm and practically drags her toward the hotel lobby. Bless Ricky. But before we're in the clear, Julia defiantly turns back around and makes a beeline right to Cleo's chair. *Uh, oh.*

"Oh, and we did it once this morning, too..." Julia tells Cleo, glaring at her. She thinks she's whispering but we've all heard it perfectly. And then, finally, she's gone.

Cleo must be stunned by the idea of Jake sleeping with Julia. But what does she expect? They are a couple. Still, I can't believe Julia said that...

"Have you ever had a garden, Matt?" Cleo asks, smiling at each of us one at a time as she takes the conversation in another direction. Matt feels her interest and lights up.

He's talking to her in his way, head down and not looking at her but still being quite the chatterbox.

"Well... I have an apartment in the Village. It has an open, empty courtyard, and one day, I hung baskets of red geraniums all over the place. Everyone in the building liked them, so I added ivy on the fence, baskets of begonias, a trellis in the middle covered with ivy and tiny roses. Then everyone jumped in and gave me money to get a table with an umbrella, benches, and chairs so they could all enjoy my handiwork. I added exotic plants—rare Aristocratic Lady Palms, Ming Aralias, and more unusual succulents like Albuca and Ledebouria. I even brought in Cycads, the kinds of plants the dinosaurs fed on. The building behind the ivy fence then hired me to do their space."

Oh, thank God. Matt has saved us all with his babblings about his favorite subject.

Ending his monologue, "I think my mom is like a sun-flower. She follows my dad everywhere like he's the sun. And Cleo, you're like a Venus fly trap. Everyone comes to you no matter how dangerous you are; they can't see it because you are so beautiful they don't want to."

Cleo starts laughing happily. Matt looks thrilled with her laughter. I wonder what he meant by "dangerous." Given Matt's condition, there are many times that he doesn't pick up on social graces and nuances like the rest of us do. The accusation certainly doesn't seem to bother Cleo—she seems flattered, or else she's a brilliant actress.

"I'm glad I could make you laugh, Cleo. I know you must have been so sad when the man you loved died in that plane crash."

Tripp lets out some sort of gasp. He seems almost pleased by this. Why in God's name would Tripp be happy that Cleo's love died in a plane crash? What a weird reaction, I must say.

"Matt, that isn't very polite," chides Tripp.

"What? Cleo told us the other night at The Outrigger Canoe Club, Dad." Matt turns to me, "Don't you remember? It was right after the waiter served us our—"

"Yes, Matt. I remember." I pat his knee underneath the table, hoping he'll understand.

"S'cuse me, Mrs. Gallier," says an elderly man who has approached our table.

"It's Ms." Cleo smiles.

"Oh, I'm so sorry, Ms. Gallier. You're just so beautiful, my husband Ernie and I just figured there was a Mr. Gallier!" a woman with the elderly man says, as if she were talking to the pope.

"Thought the smart lookin' fella there was your hubby!" Ernie pipes in, pointing to *my* husband.

Tripp and Cleo turn to each other and both laugh awkwardly. I choose to keep quiet and not make an issue of it. It's an honest mistake. But looking at Jake, he's horrified.

Cleo signs an autograph for the couple who are shaking with excitement and off they go.

"Does that happen often?" Tripp asks, once they're out of earshot.

"No, no. Although I do have one fan story that you might get a kick out of... A few years back a man named Garrett Brock Trapnell wrote me a fan letter. The return address was Marian State Penitentiary. Obviously, prisoners have a lot of time to watch TV, so a letter from a prisoner was not so odd. But what was odd about the prisoner's letter was the intelligence, the tone. He said I reminded him of his former wife and that I should read the story of his life in the book, *The Fox is Crazy Too*. Needless to say, I hustled to get the book. Indeed, he had NINE wives, all unaware—before he was arrested for hijacking United Flight 1—of the existence of the other women. I began to look forward to his letters. He was in for life so I wasn't worried in the least. My friend Jimbo kept insisting it was dangerous to write him. But of course, I didn't agree. But one night, listening to the radio as I was going to sleep, I heard of an escape attempt at Marian State Penitentiary. That woke me up. My pen pal was the inmate they were talking about. Apparently, one of his wives wanted him out. She had gotten a small plane and landed inside the prison yard. Trap, as he was nicknamed, had planned his whole escape. I was terrified. I thought how he might track me down and expect me to help him. After all, I'd be a great cover, a good hideout on Honolulu. Jimbo was very ruffled at the thought of my pen pal on the loose. The next morning, I heard he had been recaptured and was now in solitary confinement. I imagine they took away his writing privileges as I never heard from him again."

"Wow, what a story…" says Tripp. "You have fans around the world."

"No, no." She laughs and promptly gets up to leave. "Thank you for an… interesting lunch, Miranda." Her hand covers the necklace as she looks over at Jake and smiles. "It's time for me to go."

I finally exhale. Goodness, I didn't realize I hadn't been breathing. I study her face. Her jawline is so defined, her lashes so thick, long and dark, and her eyes such a lovely shade of violet. They clash with the enormous square cut emerald she is wearing.

"Cleo, where did you get that gorgeous ring?" I can't help but ask.

"Oh, thank you. It was my mother's—a gift from my father."

"I love it. It's so simple and beautiful."

She puts on lavender-tinted sunglasses to leave. "Thank you again," Cleo says before trailing off, as if she were floating on air.

"Here, I'll walk you to your car," my husband offers. "I might be interested in running part of that marathon with you."

She's like a goddess and I can see why Jake is entranced. But I don't see why Tripp needs to walk her to her car, let alone run the marathon with her. It surprises me. He's being so polite, but then she so obviously affects men that way. Jake is roaring to follow, but I keep him for a bit.

"Jake, what are your plans for the rest of the day?"

He sees Cleo is beyond him today. Then he leaps away, saying, "One sec, I have to talk to Cleo about something."

He sure does.

Chapter Thirty-Seven

DIDIER

In "death," Danny Mortimer left a wake of despair. Cleopatra was inconsolable for well over a year. I tried to cheer her up with old games of mine that never failed to make her laugh as a little girl. Sipping my foamy Pina Colada on our Algerian balcony, I'd point to the sky and say, "I'm pouring the clouds down my throat, Cleopatra!"

But the smile I adore, my favorite smile, the smile that makes *me* smile, never appeared. Nothing could release my daughter from the grip of her darkness and I tried everything—conversation, travel, shopping, good wine, good food, exercise, films. Even therapy. It wasn't until the day when I unwittingly revealed my "other work" that her ears perked up. My "other work" brought the sparkle back to her violet eyes and gave her a reason to live. And right out of the gate, Cleopatra loved the idea of it.

My "other work" was The Business. Having a home and vineyards in Algeria very near Al Qaeda headquarters was a great asset to our group.

Cleopatra found out about my work by mistake. We had just walked through the big lacquered doors of Dolma—proprietors

of the best couscous anyone has ever tasted—when I saw someone whom I recognized and suspected might be an important
Al Qaeda asset. She was tall, wearing a designer blue dress. It
was her slight hook nose that instantly identified her to me.
The gentleman across from her was an older man, the same
difference between Cleopatra's age and mine…

After our waiter took our drink order, I noticed the woman
with the hook nose excuse herself and walk toward the ladies
room. I knew it might be important for me to see what was
happening in that ladies room.

I turned to my daughter who was staring at the menu
blankly. "Cleo, do something for me, will you?"

"What is it, Daddy?" she asked, without glancing up from
the menu.

"Go into the ladies room and tell me what you see. Don't
say a word. Just observe. Do you understand?" I whispered.

Finally, she looked up at me with those violet eyes. Her
brow crinkled, confused.

"What?"

"Go on, hurry," I said with a wisp of urgency in my voice.

She looked at me once more, got up from her chair and
marched obediently toward the ladies room. I sat there, waiting, as the waiter approached. He set down Cleo's pinot grigio
and my cabernet. I thanked him and he was gone. As I raised
the glass and took my first sip, the woman with the hook nose
returned to the older gentleman at her table. They shared a
slight smile but exchanged no words. I waited, sipping my
cabernet until Cleo came back. Her brows were still crinkled,
still bewildered about my cryptic marching orders.

"Well, there was a woman—" she started in as she sat
back down.

"Not now, Cleopatra."

"What do you mean? What's wrong?"

"Later. Do you know what you'd like for dinner? I've been meaning to try the kofta."

I could feel my daughter's eyes burning into the top of my head as I perused the menu, but I ignored her. Not now. Less than an hour later, the couple left. We were the only people left in the restaurant. The waiter gave us our bill and went into the kitchen. We sat in silence for a while until finally I turned to Cleo.

"So, what did you see in the bathroom, Cleopatra?"

"Why do you want to know?" she asked suspiciously.

"Tell me and I'll tell you," I smiled.

She took a breath. "Well, nothing really. There was that woman in the Escada blue dress from a few tables away but nothing else was really all that interesting," she replied with a tinge of exasperation.

"Was this woman doing anything?" I asked as I looked over the bill.

"What do you mean? She was just in there. Putting on some lipstick," Cleopatra explained, more exasperated this time.

"She left the lipstick in there, didn't she? She didn't take it with her, am I right?"

Cleopatra's brow crinkled yet again and she turned her head, trying to remember. I sat there, letting my daughter work it out.

"Now that you mention it... yes, she did leave it in there. I washed my hands and as I threw the towel away, I think I noticed it glint in the wastebasket. I didn't realize that until just now..."

I nodded.

"Why? How did you know that?" Cleo asked with interest, for a change.

I waited a while before I answered my daughter's question, checking to be sure we were alone still.

"Please go back in and see if it is still in the wastebasket."

A minute later, she returned and sat back down in her chair. The expression on her face was stunned. "It's gone," she whispered.

I thanked her and we went out to the car. As I started the engine, I finally broke the silence.

"You've never heard me talk about my 'other work,' have you?"

Cleo shook her head.

"Good. That's because I'm not supposed to. Not to anyone. Not even to you."

"What 'other work?'" she asked.

"Well, I—actually, there's a whole group of us—we work together with various government agencies across the world. We try to keep the world safe from certain... threats, I guess you could say."

I glanced over at my daughter, expecting a look of total and utter shock to be stretched across her lovely face. But instead, there was a smile, a huge smile.

"What kind of threats?" she asked, excitement starting to build in her voice.

"Terrorist threats, mostly," I admitted.

I know I shouldn't have told her that much but I saw life returning to her. And that smile. I welcomed its return with open arms. She was engaging with life again.

"You're James Bond, aren't you?" Cleo joked.

"No," I laughed. "But maybe something like that."

Cleo's smile stretched even further across her face.

"Are your friends from the club involved? I knew you men were always up to something with all your secret, smoke-filled meetings that no one could interrupt."

"Some of them," I confessed. "But I won't tell you which ones."

"Did you take me to that restaurant on purpose, Daddy?"

I looked over at her and smiled. "No, it was serendipitous."

She turned to me and smiled back. "But who took the lipstick and what was in it?"

My daughter had come alive again. I told her the woman she had seen was rumored to be Yana Khouri, part of an Al Qaeda terror group, but no one could prove it. The fact that she had left a lipstick and it disappeared certainly hinted that she was involved in this group and that someone who worked in the restaurant was too. I found out later that she passed on the whereabouts of an AQ double agent on a tiny piece of paper hidden within the lipstick. Now we would watch her carefully.

And it was this influential intelligence ring I was part of that led me to find out that the man she loved and trusted, Danny Mortimer, had not died in a plane crash but was alive, and he too was a black op. I saw no need to tell her that Danny, under his real name, Tripp Regan, was not only alive and well but also married with three children. This would be the ultimate betrayal. So I never told my Cleopatra.

Chapter Thirty-Eight
2 Days

MOHAMMED ABDUL RAHMAN

It's all ready. Pearl Harbor, the holy ground where so many American sailors gloriously lost their lives. Before my parents Jim and Patricia relocated us, the teachers and the textbooks at The Hathaway Brown School in Shaker Heights taught us that American sailors were the victims and the Japanese the unjustified. Americans have frequently been "victim" of attacks, but now, in my wiser age, I recognize that they are never unwarranted. The USS Arizona Memorial marks the grave of over 1,100 sailors who died that day. To the infidel it is hallowed ground. I will be desecrating their graves and all the world will wake up to how foolish and weak the infidel is. It is a sensational target. It will cause major disruptions to PAC Command. Their ridiculous open policy allows anyone to walk in with a camera with a bomb inside if they are willing to die for their beliefs. I am not, as I have more plans to carry out. Therefore, what I have done over the past four years is get to know the guards well, and as an American, they naturally trusted me. They took me at my word when I told them I was a SEAL in Afghanistan in the early 2000s. When plied with questions, I told them we don't talk about what we do. Of course, I knew all about the War in Afghanistan but from the other side, the righteous side. To pull off the ultimate mission, I had to play the long game and my violent mind had to be kept hidden.

During the first phase of my grand plan, I'd started claiming a seat at the end of the bar at Club Pearl, a watering hole right off the base that the security guards would frequent after their shifts ended. I only ordered seltzer water and would rarely engage with the guards, who were busy getting drunk off cheap rum and whiskey. But that wasn't the point. They'd recognize my face as a familiar one when I came by at lunchtime on my break from "work." The naïve bastards warmed to me even easier than anticipated. It only took a few days for the bored guards to strike up small talk with their daily visitor. Everything was going according to plan.

Phase two was having the guards admire me. And with my "naval background," they did. Stupid Americans look up to anyone who's a "winner." After I got them to respect me, I got them to trust me. From then on, every Tuesday and Friday, I'd bring the guards lunch in the same navy Under Armour backpack, and so eventually, after four years, that backpack wasn't even glanced at. We'd eat lunch together, and every once in a while, I'd pepper in questions about Pearl Harbor's security, operations, and layout. These questions were parsed out meticulously, only once a month, and always to a different guard to limit any suspicion. After we'd eaten, I wandered around "to digest." This was also phase three, figuring out where to place the bombs for the biggest explosion. I decided on the USS Arizona Memorial. It was an obvious choice. Like bombing Arlington Cemetery or The Empire State Building or The Twin Towers, it has both emotional and national significance.

Once two full years had passed and I'd gained each of the guards' friendship, respect, and trust, I started to carry a game of Monopoly in my backpack along with the lunches I brought them. I was inspired by a trick that the Brits created during World War II. The German army allowed the International Red Cross to send Allied POWs who were interred in their prison camps games of Monopoly. Like the guards at Pearl Harbor, Hitler's army thought the game was too innocent to raise any suspicions. They both should have known better... My motives differed from the Brits', but they're no less honorable. Whereas the Brits hid secret messages and maps inside the game board intended to guide their comrades to escape and ultimate safety, I hid tiny parts of a bomb inside the game pieces. Each time I visited, I hid a new, teeny fragment of a bomb and snuck it into Pearl Harbor.

Even I can't do everything alone. I was taught bomb building in the mountains of Mindanao, but it had never been my specialty. It was menial and slavish work, whereas I'm the brains behind the operation—the Steve Jobs, the Nikola Tesla, the Osama Bin Laden. Sergeant Koi Kang was merely a foot soldier albeit a necessary one. Four years ago, my cell and I were looking for an accomplice. Besides me, everyone else in my JI-AQ cell of five unsurprisingly claims Middle Eastern lineage. After 9/11, the U.S. Government became a little uptight about hiring anyone who praised Allah. Racial profiling at its finest. The radicalization of American soldiers is more common than Americans will ever admit, but still, Koi Kang was quite the find. He grew up in Pukalani, a small town outside of Maui, had a normal childhood by American standards and enlisted in the army as a means to pay for his college education. During a tour in Iraq in early 2005, Kang saw the same light I had and grew disillusioned with "home." A six-year-old little boy died in Kang's arms after Kang mistook him for an Iraqi soldier during a nighttime raid. The experience moved Kang to an extreme hatred of war, a war that America caused and thus, an extreme hatred of America. But he too knew the value in playing the long game, so when he returned "home" to American soil, he continued his service in the armed forces and got a job as an air traffic controller at Joint Base Pearl Harbor-Hickam.

On May 8th, 2007, at approximately 8:00 p.m., Koi Kang fulfilled his growing curiosity and came to our Mosque. We talked for months about our vision not just for Hawaii, but for all mankind.

I left each monopoly piece at the designated drop point. Because of intense security at Pearl Harbor, even for employees, Kang could never have taken them in himself. The drop point was where I threw out our lunches in the bright bags. Hide in plain sight. One by one, Kang took each piece back to his locker and slowly began to build the bombs. In the back of his locker, there was a poster of Penelope Cruz from the movie *Blow*. The bombs were hidden behind in a false bottom he fashioned one night after everyone left.

Tomorrow night, on December 24th, Kang will distribute the bombs to their designated areas. And then at noon on December 25th, when I'm long gone on a plane back to Manila, Pearl Harbor and The Arizona will cease to exist. I only wish I could be here to see the explosion and to watch as they try to figure how we were able to penetrate the area. There's a flight booked tomorrow night under an alias with Canadian citizenship. I will fly from Honolulu to British Columbia first, then onto Toronto, and then back west to Hong Kong. Finally, I will fly from Hong Kong to my beloved Manila, and into my darling Afsheen's arms.

Chapter Thirty-Nine
December 23, 2011

TRIPP

As promised, less than three hours later, Castillo calls me again at just past six on Christmas Eve Eve.

"Go, Castillo," I say, anxious for the results.

"We're emailing you a copy of the recovered paper now. Most of it is illegible but there's a small area that we may be able to pull something off of."

"Get all hands-on deck. We need as many people on this as possible. You hear me, Castillo? This is critical."

"Yes, sir."

I hang up and head down to the lobby.

"There a printer I can use?" I ask the lanky concierge standing behind the big oak check-in desk.

"Of course, sir. We have several available for all hotel guests in the work station just off the lobby," he points to his left.

"Thanks. It shouldn't be too crowded at this hour, correct?" I glance down at my watch.

"I wouldn't think so, sir."

I thank the congenial concierge and hurry across the lobby and down a carpeted, heavily air-conditioned hallway. *Please be empty, please be empty*, I say to myself like a mantra as I approach the glass-walled room. Printing something of this magnitude and extreme confidentiality goes against protocol but hey, desperate times... Doing it any other way would take way too long and involve far too many moving parts.

It isn't empty. There are three sunburned, gum-chewing teenagers slumped over three big, black Dell desktops. In total, there are eight computers set up in two rows on two long, wooden tables. Hoping to scare them off by my proximity, I sit in the fourth computer next to the teenagers—two girls and one boy. I glance over at each of their screens. As I guessed, they're all checking their Facebook accounts. The swatch of steel blue across the top of their screens is distinct. *Fucking kids*. They look to be around seventeen or eighteen. Their parents have bankrolled an expensive vacation to Honolulu and God forbid, instead of exploring the beaches or Pearl Harbor or Diamond Head, they decide to do the one activity they could also do at home.

"Hey, you guys are over twenty-one, right?"

They look up from their computers and swap intrigued glances.

"Yeah... Why?" says one of the girls, clearly the leader of the pack.

"Some guy just came back from the casino. I think he won a small fortune because he's buying everyone at the bar drinks!"

The teenage trio trade glances again. They all jump out of their chairs like box springs and rush out of the room faster than you can say naïve. A smirk works its way across my face as I log into my second Hotmail account, which I only use for emergencies such as this one. Castillo had to break protocol and send to my personal email account. It was too risky to send to my CIA address. I open Castillo's email and select the attachment.

It's a mess. Whatever's on this little piece of paper is almost impossible to make out. I still feel guilty about his death. The poor kid died on my watch. The paper itself is light blue, similar to an architect's blueprints, and it's laid flat on a sleek, white surface. Whoever took the photo—likely a lowly lab assistant—diligently ironed out the still visible deep folds after it had been crumpled and balled inside Ocampo's throat. His bodily fluids have faded and eroded 90 percent of the black ink, but there's a small area that could potentially be identified or translated. I print one copy normally, then zoom into the somewhat legible section, take a screenshot and print that version too. Of course, I delete the email from Chris.

I've stood up and begun logging out of the computer when the three brainless teenagers of the apocalypse return to the workstation. There are scowls etched on each of their faces and I know what they're all thinking. *Liar, liar, pants on fire.*

"How was it?" I ask innocently.

"Very funny..." leader of the pack snorts.

"What do you mean?"

"Duh. There were no free drinks," leader of the pack snorts again, as if she were the only one to have speaking rights.

"Oh, that's too bad... I guess he'd had enough and went to bed."

The trio of teenagers roll their eyes as I stuff printed copies into my back pocket and hurry back up to my room.

"Anyone have any ideas?" I ask Castillo as I close the heavy hotel door behind me.

"None plausible."

About an hour ago, I had ushered Miranda out of the room before the call I was expecting from Castillo came in. I made up some bullshit about the elusive "China deal."

I pull the prints out of my pocket and lay them flat on a small desk in the corner of the room. It's nearly impossible to decipher.

"Damn it!" I growl into my phone.

"Sir?"

"Nothing, Castillo..." I'm annoyed, mostly at myself. We wouldn't be in this mess in the first place had Ocampo not been killed. "So, which parts are supposed to be legible?"

"The middle area. See?"

No. "Kind of... Okay, stand by. I'll call you back."

My gut tells me we'll never deduce what is on that paper. It's badly discolored and the ink has bled and distorted. From what I can make out, the zoomed-in version resembles a drawing of a flower.

I need air. I slide on my loafers and head back downstairs. The lobby is buzzing with activity. There are couples holding hands, all dressed up, the excitement of a romantic Hawaiian night before them. There are families big and small, some laughing, some bickering, feeling the festive spirit. The teenage trio is also there, sitting in a line on a plush black couch—this time, staring at their cell phone screens instead of computers. *Where are their families? Don't they have parents?*

The pool area is a ghost town. The water, devoid of any screaming children or winded swimmers doing the breaststroke, is completely flat and undisturbed. All of the umbrellas have been tied tight with a burlap fastening and no one sits in any of the chaise lounges, which Miranda tells me are impossible to snag during the daylight hours. The only sounds are the crickets and faint murmur of hotel guests inside the lobby. Ah, peace and quiet.

I take out the two pieces of paper, stare down at them again, and pray for an epiphany.

"Mr. Regan?" a voice booms above me.

I look up, startled. A young, uniformed bellhop stands there. He looks like a local—dark hair, dark skin, and smiling. "Yes?"

"Telephone call for you. The caller says it's urgent."

"Did they say who it is?" I glance down at my cell phone. I have no bars so no service.

"They said they're from your work. That's all the information they gave, I'm afraid."

Well, they wouldn't exactly identify themselves as calling from the Central Intelligence Agency. But who would be calling me on the Halekulani landline? Obviously, someone who couldn't get through on my cell phone number; but who?

"If you'd like, you can take it from the beach bar right over there." The bellhop points. The regularly hopping outdoor bar is dark and vacant at this hour.

"Okay, thanks." I stand.

"Right this way."

Instead of leading the way or walking by my side, the bellhop follows from a few paces behind. The hum of the hotel crowd becomes fainter and fainter. My suspicion grows with every step, and so I glance back at him. My eye catches his and the bellhop brightens instantly, turning on another friendly smile.

"Nice night..."

"Oh, yes, Mr. Regan. Very nice."

But before my eye caught his, there was a flash of something. He was glaring at me, scowling even. Has all of today's chaos just gotten the better of me? For comfort, I finger my glock, hidden as always under my waistband. We arrive at the bar.

"Phone's right there, Mr. Regan." He points toward the far end of the bar. "Press one when you pick up. Would you like me to stay?"

"No, that's alright. Thank you."

I hustle over to the bar, hoping that the voice of this mystery caller will quell my suspicion about the bellhop. As instructed, I press one.

"Hello?"

There's no voice at the other end of the line, just a dial tone. I press the number one again. "Hello?!" I say again, with more urgency.

I look back toward the hotel, to where the bellhop was presumably going. But now, he's gone. He couldn't possibly have gotten to the hotel that quickly, could he? I looked away for two seconds, maybe three. In a split second, I hang up, unholster my gun, and get down in a crouch.

I shuffle quickly toward the right side of the bar, my .45 trained ahead of me. I wait a moment, take a breath, and then turn to the right. Clear. I repeat the same drill with the back and left sides of the bar and then the front again for good measure. Clear, clear, and all clear. All my career, I've relied on my gut. In black op school, I was trained to cultivate and to trust it and soon I grew to rely on it. But now, maybe I'm burnt out or have seen too much or maybe I'm just getting old.

False alarm. I stuff my .45 back into my waistband and follow the lights and hum of the Halekulani Hotel. My footsteps are loud against the concrete path. I hope Miranda and the boys are having a nice time at La Mer. It's a five-star restaurant, so it can't be that miserable without little old me.

I bet Miranda ordered pâté to bring back to me in our room since I had to "work on the China deal" tonight.

I feel it but I don't hear it. A bullet whizzes past my nose, missing the tip by mere centimeters. The bellhop must have put a silencer on his weapon; the only sound is the hotel crowd still happily buzzing. The bullet came from my left. I whip out my gun again, crouch down behind a small ficus bush, and search for the bellhop, my neck craning in all directions like a spastic sprinkler head. With the sun going down considerably since I first came out to the pool, I have to strain and squint to scan my surroundings.

Another bullet whizzes by. This time, it grazes past my right ear, going left. The bellhop has changed locations, and luckily for me, he is a shitty shot. Maybe he skipped target practice day at terrorist camp. I squint again, scouring my surroundings for the bastard bellhop of Halekulani.

Footsteps. I hear them behind me, faint ones, but footsteps. My .45 is spraying bullets before I've even located my target. A dark figure is sprinting toward me and suddenly, the whole weight of his body is on mine and we smash hard onto the concrete. On impact, my gun bounces out of my hand and I hear his do the same. I look up to the bellhop's face, inches away from my own, menace and fearlessness in his dark eyes. He's straddling me, pinning me to the concrete, but he doesn't have my strength. The bellhop swings hard and gets off a blistering left hook to my jaw, putting me in a momentary daze. Like a frog, he bounces off me and chases after his missing gun, which is only a few feet above my head in one of the small patches of grass.

I'd lost my grip on the Glock when he charged into me, but my back-up, the small Beretta Pico that I keep hidden in a holster on my left ankle, has remained in place. As the bellhop gets up to retrieve his gun, I find my opportunity. I reach down, turn, and nail him in the heart before he is able to fire at me. His limp body topples onto the patch of grass but a few splatters of blood are flecked onto the beige pavement. Hardly noticeable unless you are actually looking for it, but still, it has to be dealt with.

"This is special agent, Tripp Regan. Badge number 441789," I say breathlessly to the CIA switchboard operator. "I've just killed an attacker who made an attempt on my life. Most likely AQ. Please send local Honolulu agents to the Halekulani Hotel out on the back patio to assist with clean up and disposal of the body."

Less than ten minutes later, three agents arrive. This isn't the first time I found myself within an inch of my life, but it is the second time my family has been involved. First in their own deaths in the helicopter and now a hundred yards from the attempt on mine.

Two of the agents are dressed as ambulance workers. They lift the bellhop's body from his ankles and underarms onto a stretcher and tuck his corpse in a black body bag as if he were just a regular Joe who died of normal causes. They wheel him away on the concrete toward an ambulance they drove here in.

Once I'm done explaining what happened to the other agents, I hurry inside to the lobby, past the concierge, past the teenage trio, and into La Mer restaurant. Soothing jazz plays on the loudspeakers and it seems as if the patrons are in a constant state of laughter. I've entered a completely different realm than the one I've just come from. My eyes comb the large, jovial dining room for Miranda, Jake, Matt, and Ricky. Bingo. I spot the undercover agents dispatched to protect my family before I notice my family at a large table only a few feet away. Sam and Sam—one female, one male—were playing the part of a married couple with flying colors.

I'm limping a bit from my scuffle with the bellhop. "Got room for one more?"

All four heads Regan whip up from their jumbo shrimp, foie gras, and crab cake appetizers.

"Dad!" exclaims my youngest.

"Hey, why are you walking so funny?" Matt asks me.

"Oh, nothing. Clumsy me just stubbed my toe on the door jamb," I tell them as I flag down a waiter for an extra chair.

Miranda coos, "Oh, Tripp…"

"Where's Julia?" I ask Jake.

"Julia isn't feeling so hot… Happens to the best of us."

"Ah," I say as I sit down with my family. I look at Jake who is so quiet and disengaged. I imagine he wishes he was dining with Cleo instead.

Maybe I should have gone back up to our room and debriefed with Castillo before dinner. Caught my breath, at least. But I don't. Right now, the only place I want to be is with my family.

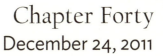

Chapter Forty
December 24, 2011

CLEO

On December 24th, at six in the morning, I stand in downtown Honolulu watching fireworks with Jake's father. They always set them off in the early morning before the marathon begins.

After lunch yesterday, Tripp had walked me out to my car and mentioned that he wanted to run part of the marathon. I thought he was just being polite. But when I pass his hotel, which is on my way to the starting line, there he is on the curb, standing in the pitch dark, waiting as he said he would be.

"Mind if I drive?" he asks.

"Why, don't you trust my driving?" I smile.

"Well, I seem to recall a certain fender bender you may have gotten into, oh, about 72 hours ago with a close relative of mine," he smiles back.

I hop over the gears to the passenger side. Since I know the back roads to the starting line, Tripp follows my directions.

"Take a left here, after the stop sign."

As the car comes to a stop, I notice Tripp pound on the shift three times. Boom, boom, boom.

"You know, I had a friend who had that same tic," I say quietly.

"Tic?" he asks.

"You tap the shift three times at every stop sign. Boom, boom, boom."

"Oh. Yeah, guess I do…"

My mind has wandered back to Africa. To Danny. I first picked up on Danny's tic when we drove to Amboseli. Always boom, boom, boom at every stop. Odd that Tripp has the exact same silly habit.

The early morning hour conjures up the feeling you get when you settle into a car at night before a long trip—telling secrets, blizzard outside, all safe and secure and warm inside.

We join the other runners listening to the National Anthem in the dark, waiting for the howitzer to go off and the front-runners to start. It's a pitch dark, chilly morning with only Christmas tree lights decorating the way along Waikiki Beach as we head out toward Diamond Head. The Hawaiians clap for us but it's so dark I can't make out any of their faces. I am oddly aware of Tripp running next to me. Close. Very close. I wonder if the fabulous sex I have finally had opens me up to all men. If Jake has turned on a magic switch. The thought makes me laugh out loud as we run along with one Santa, eight reindeer, four hula dancers, and one nun. I love the insanity of this island.

In the dark, all my senses are heightened. I can't help but pay special attention to the sound of Tripp's breathing. I notice that sometimes our inhales and exhales are timed perfectly. The two of us keep jogging at a good pace and I suspect we both want to impress the other with our athleticism and stamina. Not a word has passed between us since the race began.

Finally, I speak to him, "So... perhaps you have a question for me."

"Question?" he asks me, in that deep staccato voice of his.

I hold my breath, contemplating whether or not I should say it. And then I do. "About my relationship with Jake."

Why am I doing this, I wonder. Maybe it's the adrenaline of the run, maybe it's just the darkness. Maybe it's both. Though I can't measure his reaction, I think at the very least I've succeeded in shocking him. I can feel his blue eyes on me. It's amazing the things one says in the comfort of the dark, sacred morning. Like the things I said to Danny so long ago when we were in the comfort of the dark, sacred night in Africa.

Tripp doesn't respond. But then I can hear him smile which seems impossible, yet I can. I can hear it in the darkness. The blackness brings out the honesty in both of us, but Tripp's reluctance to answer is very interesting.

We continue to jog along, among a sea of runners in the dark. We are like an enormous school of fish at the bottom of the ocean without our sight, moving with the curves of the terrain instead of the tides of the sea. He laughs. A laugh in the dark either sounds awfully menacing or mysteriously seductive. When he laughs again, I join him.

"What are we laughing at?" I ask, my curiosity getting the best of me.

"Oh, nothing... It's nothing." He clears his throat and his laughter begins to subside.

"Liar." Flirting with him maybe just a bit.

Tripp laughs again.

"I think I know why you're laughing..." I say, perhaps flirting just a little bit more.

"Trust me, it isn't what you're thinking," Tripp tells me.

But I don't believe him. It's exactly what I'm thinking. He's laughing at me and Jake. He's laughing at the notion that his star athlete, investment banker son would engage in an affair with an older, *a much older*, woman. And then he starts laughing all over again. Now I am starting to get a little annoyed.

"If you must know, Tripp," I start in, with a bit more fire in my tongue than I had intended. "It's not as if I have these types of affairs all the time. In fact, I've never really let myself have... what I have with Jake."

His laughter stops. "That's hard to believe. Ever?"

I pause, then... "Well, I don't know."

"You must have. A woman like you..."

"Maybe only once before. A long time ago."

Another long stretch of silence.

"Wanna talk about it?" he asks me, finally.

"No. Do *you* want to talk about it, Tripp?" I ask him back, confused why he'd want to hear about a ghost from a woman he hardly knows.

"It's a marathon, Cleo. We've got a lotta time to kill... Plus, I like your stories. You have quite the way with words, you know."

"You like my stories?"

"Yeah. That one at lunch yesterday about your prison pen pal."

"Well, the only reason I even thought of him—his name was Danny—was when you pounded on the shift..."

"Ah, I see. So, that 'friend' you mentioned was actually... more than a friend?"

My cheeks flush with heat and I know they have turned the color of Audrey Hepburn's most famous Givenchy red dress from *Funny Face*. Once again, I'm grateful for the cover of darkness.

I hesitate, "Yes. He... I fell in love with him... So, when you... the memories started flowing. But it was in Africa a very, very long time ago."

"How exotic." He laughs.

In this moment, once again, I am glad the dark is covering my face. All I can hear are the whoosh of his legs and smack of his sneakers on the pavement as they pick up the pace. It's hard for me to stay with him. But I do. I really do feel free in this darkness and I feel a closeness with the other runners. I hope there are no repercussions to this sober drunkenness.

Tripp seems almost exhilarated as I tell him about my African love affair filled with death and unfulfilled desire. I know he's looking right at me. It's a heavy, thoughtful silence.

I smile and change the subject. "Would you like to stop? There's a fabulous breakfast place nearby and it's close to where we parked the car. I sort of planned on it."

The sun is starting to rise and I can finally make out his body next to mine. I love the dawn of the day.

"Would you like to stop, Cleo?"

"If you do..."

We're both being too polite.

"Yeah. I could eat," he says.

The sun continues to rise and I can see a smile creep across his face as he looks at me. I smile back, which signals us both to slow down, stop, and turn to each other. I can feel the regret seeping into my soul already. My confidences said in darkness suddenly embarrass me now that I can see his face and his expressions.

Beneath his smile though, there is a sadness.

Chapter Forty-One
December 24, 2011

TRIPP

I am disarmed by Cleo's directness. Attracted to it. It takes a certain kind of woman to breach the subject of her relationship with the young—too young—lover's father. My son, for Christ's sake. *Goddamn you, Jake.* How I envy his past few days with her.

We sit down at the little breakfast spot.

"Does this suit you?" Cleo asks as we sit, conspicuously more polite than she was ten minutes ago.

"Yup. It's great."

Our eyes stay locked on each other for a beat longer than they should, and it's Cleo who looks away first, down at her menu. She is so brave in the dark and so shy in the sunlight. Just like she was on Kilimanjaro.

"So, tell me more about this friend of yours," I say, eager for her conversation.

"Friend?"

"Danny."

"Get you folks something to eat?" our very blonde, very tan, very tall waitress interrupts. She looks like that volleyball player with all the gold medals. I forget her name.

After we both order pancakes and coffee, the waitress saunters off. Cleo and I look away from each other.

"I'm sorry, I didn't mean to pry. We can talk about something else if you'd like," I tell her.

"It's alright. It has just been a while since I've spoken about him... And I don't want to bore you."

"You won't." *Trust me.*

Finally, she says, "well, it was a long time ago. In 2003. And it was very brief. Only ten days. Funny how a short time with one person can be far more meaningful than a lifetime spent with someone else."

I nod.

"Have you been to Tanzania, Tripp?"

I shake my head.

"Oh, you need to go. There really is no other place like it."

"It's on my list."

"The primitive African lifestyle left Danny and me both raw, I think. That rawness heightened his ability to grasp my soul. And I grasped his. We were totally encompassed by one another," she says, shaking her head. "He cracked me open and it was the most exciting and wonderful time of my life, like a drug. His charm was electric and his mind shimmered. I remember how I'd sweep the path in front of him, littering it with ideas, so he would feel compelled to bend down and lift one up and engage me in thought. These were my tricks of the trade, my prostitution of soul. You see, I learned mental gymnastics from trying to charm my father, Didier."

"Are you very close to your father?"

I'm intrigued by her father, Didier.

"Oh yes, but then, every girl loves her father. Do you ever wish you had a daughter, Tripp?"

I temper my response, "I used to think up names for a girl."

"Really? That's so sweet."

"Yeah, for some reason, I always loved 'Zelli.' And I'd have loved a girl who looked just like you."

She laughs. "You're charming, Tripp Regan..."

"Yeah, my son gets it from me."

She laughs again.

"Believe it or not, Jake wasn't perfect from the womb. He needed to learn a few things from dear old dad."

"No! Jake certainly isn't perfect. He got completely involved with me before he mentioned there was a girlfriend on her way from New York to be with him here. Of course, had he told me about her, I wouldn't have gotten involved... so I am glad he didn't tell me." She laughs. "But no one is perfect—not even Danny."

"Oh, really? What could possibly be wrong with this Saint Danny fellow?"

"Oh, he had these tiny holes in his front teeth from when he had the measles."

"Weird!" I laugh.

I see her glance at my front teeth. As a true undercover agent, I'd had them capped the day I came back from Africa.

Is all this talk about Danny phony? Does she know that I'm Danny? No, she couldn't but suspicion is pulling me. She'd detest me if she ever found out the truth, that her years of suffering were for someone who didn't even exist. My real life is so different from Danny. I really do have the perfect wife who does all the right things. I love Miranda. She's loyal and uncomplicated and makes me very happy and content. I need that with my work. Cleo stands for passion and lust and insanity. She stands for the side of me that Miranda doesn't even know exists.

At this very inopportune moment, my work phone vibrates. The phone I have to answer.

"Sorry, please excuse me for just a minute. It's work," I tell Cleo before I walk off to take the call.

"Regan," I answer.

"Sir, it's about Mohammed Abdul Rahman," agent Castillo tells me from the other end of the telephone.

Mohammed Abdul Rahman is the high-ranking leader of Jemaah Islamiyah—Al Qaeda (JI-AQ)—who was purported to have gotten into the United States four years ago. I've been after Rahman for nine years in the Philippines and he, or one of his JI-AQ cell, was responsible for terminating my contact in Manila earlier in the week.

"Go ahead," I instruct, holding my breath.

"We found something. Messages between Rahman and another operative in his cell. One Aamir Ahmet," Castillo tells me. He pauses.

"Okay, go on."

"We have reason to believe… that Rahman's in Honolulu, sir. The island's terror threat has just been escalated to red."

My heart sinks and I swallow hard, fearing for my family's safety. That certainly explains the two attempts on my life.

"You're positive?"

"Pretty sure, sir."

"Well now we know who was responsible for the helicopter attack and the attack at the hotel. Go on."

Since 9/11, U.S. intelligence intercepted a series of Al Qaeda plots, including the 2006 transatlantic airline plot, a bombing of U.S. soldiers on German soil in 2007 and the 2009 plot hatched by Najibullah Zazi to bomb New York City. Even before that shithead traitor Snowden leaked NSA capabilities, those intelligence successes were widely reported by the media and that caused a bad ripple effect—terrorists making a big move toward encrypted communication, and thus, making my job nearly impossible. I had not been able to find Mohammed for years and here he is in Honolulu.

"You've heard of Anwar's Secrets, right?" Castillo asks.

"The encryption program, sure."

There are several forms of encryption on our phones and computers that were put in place to protect the public from hackers. Unfortunately, the majority of these measures have not only aided terrorists but galvanized them too. When executed correctly, most encryption cannot be overcome unless the user makes a mistake. Which brings us to our pal, Mohammad Abdul Rahman. Anwar's Secrets is a megalomaniac jihadist's dream come true. In a nutshell, it's a custom encryption tool for terrorists. It's fully compatible with PGP (Pretty Good Privacy, an encryption software giant), which can be used to encrypt other messages. Its developers don't even have to lift a finger or go to the trouble of writing code themselves. They just inherit code written by other actual geniuses.

"Long story short, Aamir's file names didn't have the correct outputs, which got our backs up," Castillo explains. "Maybe he got lazy. Maybe he started to believe he was invincible. All we know is his fuck up is our win."

"Jesus..."

"Yup. That's where we found mention of Rahman's whereabouts being in Honolulu."

"Wonder if this is where he's been hiding out the entire time." I'm thinking out loud now.

"Unless AQ is deliberately trying to lead us down the wrong path—which we don't think is the case—this intel should be treated as 100 percent accurate."

Speaking in absolutes is not taken lightly within the agency.

"Read me the email," I demand.

"Everything set. Date confirmed. Honolulu NS. Meet, same place. Nadia and her friends will be waiting."

"We think 'Nadia and her friends' are bombs?"

"Affirmative, sir. We've seen this before—AQ using female names for weapons of mass destruction."

"They're rounding up the troops. Getting all hands on deck, most likely for Christmas Day. They'd just love to detonate on the day Christ was born," I observe, my mind kicking into high gear. "Arrogant little shits…"

"Yes, sir."

"I'm gonna need a plane out for my family first thing."

"Yes, sir, we're already working on that. The incoming storm is making matters a little tricky, but…"

"Just get it done, Castillo. No excuses. And I want constant updates and a meet with the tactical teams, so please set that up."

"Yes, sir."

I never cared about who would pull the trigger that took Rahman out. Now that I know he was behind my attack last night and most importantly, the helicopter shooting that would have killed my family, that just changed.

"And leak it to all major news outlets right away."

"Sir, are you sure? It may cause unnecessary panic among the locals."

"I'm sure. I want that miscreant to know we're onto him. That's when they trip up. The locals will take the precautions they need and the warning covers our asses."

"Copy that, sir."

"Okay. Updates every half hour, Castillo." I'm about to hang up when I remember. "Wait, one last thing," I whisper. "You're sure Cleo Gallier has no record?"

"Yes, sir. We exercised all resources yesterday and there isn't anything in her travel, criminal record, work history, friends, or family ties that would lead us to that conclusion."

"Okay. Thanks, Chris."

I walk back to Cleo and my pancakes. She sits at our table for two with her delicate hands crossed over the faded yellow wood table. She isn't staring at her telephone screen or pretending to busy herself with reading the menu or even picking at her pancakes, which have been delivered in my absence. Cleo just sits there, looking perfectly content to be alive, to be in Honolulu, and to be at this shabby, little rundown café. As I make my way over to her, she looks up at me with those eyes and smiles.

"Everything alright?" she asks me as I sit down across from her.

I nod curtly. "How are the pancakes?"

"I was waiting for you."

Oh, how I wish that were true. "You didn't have to do that. Dig in. Please."

We both do. The small, outdated Magnavox television screen behind Cleo is playing local news footage of the marathon on mute. As I take my second bite of fluffy pancakes, the programming switches. Bright red block letters that spell out BREAKING NEWS flash across the screen and then Erin Burnett's face appears, all business as usual behind a news desk. A guy sitting at the bar points at the television and looks at our tall, tanned waitress who seems to be the only one working the joint.

"Mind turning that up?"

Our waitress glances at the screen, grabs the remote, and switches on the volume.

"Breaking news out of Honolulu…" Erin starts.

Cleo turns around to face the small television.

I study her closely now. If Cleo isn't who she says she is, maybe she has a tell. The agency has assured me several times that Cleo is a dead end, but I can't help feeling an inkling of suspicion. It's how I've made my living all these years.

"We've just received reports that the island has been elevated from blue to red on the terror threat level chart. Sources from the intelligence community tell us they have good reason to believe a high-ranking member of Al Qaeda has been hiding out on the otherwise tranquil Hawaiian island for reasons that, at this time, remain undisclosed. But stay tuned, we will keep you updated."

There are only a few other patrons in the small café but Erin Burnett has captured everyone's rapt attention. Cleo looks over at me, grave concern in her violet eyes. Is that concern genuine or is she just a talented actor like me? Has she fooled us all?

"As always, we'll continue to keep you updated as soon as we know more," Erin promises. She removes her glasses and shuffles papers.

The footage switches back to the marathon, which now takes on an eerie, doomed quality. The whole marathon could be blown to pieces any minute now and none of the runners have the first clue. An odd silence hangs in the air as everyone in the café tries to swallow what they've just seen—apocalyptic, worse-comes-to-worst scenarios blazing through each of their helpless minds.

"My goodness…" Cleo whispers.

"I know," I nod. "Christ, I wonder what that was about."

"Should we...?" She gestures to the exit. "Get you back to your family?"

Interesting reaction.

"Yeah, this'll probably freak some of them out." I shovel a big bite of pancake into my mouth. "Mind if I finish these really quick?"

"Of course not." She shoves her plate away, having seemingly lost her appetite.

I ram another pancake into my big mouth, taking my time. "Has this ever happened?"

"A terrorist threat? Not since I have lived on the island."

"That's what? Seven years, you said?"

She nods. "Why?"

"Just curious. I thought I heard something about a threat four years ago."

"Related to a terrorist? Here on the island?"

I nod. This is a test. "A guy in my office, Larry, was here on vacation about four years ago, in 2007, and he left early because there were reports of a big-time terrorist being on this island."

"In 2007? I don't remember hearing anything about that."

"Yeah, I think it was 2007..." I pretend to think back. "Yeah, it definitely was. Ricky had just graduated from Middlebury."

"That's so weird. I don't remember that at all... Maybe I was visiting my father or my sisters, but either way, I am amazed I didn't ever hear about it."

"If memory serves, it was some faction of Al Qaeda. It had a funny name." I pretend to comb through the recesses of my brain again. "Jemaah Islamiyah, maybe? Larry called it JI for short, I think. Does that ring any bells?"

"None." There's no reaction from Cleo other than what looks like utter surprise. Surprise that I know all of this? Genuine surprise? She pauses and glances over to the television. Shots of fatigued, sweaty runners continue to fill the small Magnavox screen. "Well, did they ever catch him?"

"I don't think so... Wanna know the scariest part?" I say, my mouth full of pancakes.

Warily, Cleo nods.

I lean in closer. "Apparently, whoever it was, was born an American."

WITH A FULL STOMACH, I follow Cleo back to her little yellow car, parked close to the café. She keeps her eyes downcast, focused on the pavement ahead of her. Her mood has completely shifted since we started running in the dark. She is quiet, distracted, and barely makes eye contact with me.

"Are you alright?" I ask her.

"Just, the red alert..." She looks over at me and trails off. Her hands, resting on her thighs, look like they're trembling.

"Hey, it's out of our control." I try comforting her. Well, not out of mine. And, actually, maybe not out of hers either. Jesus, what a mind fuck.

"It sounds very serious though, Tripp. Don't you think?"

I glance out the window. The wind has picked up considerably since the sun came up almost three hours ago.

Chapter Forty-Two
December 24, 2011

MIRANDA

"Hey, honey."

Tripp just walked in. It's 9:30 in the morning. He'd gone to run part of the Honolulu Marathon with Cleo. He certainly smells like that perfume she wears. He's been gone for nearly four hours. We could have flown halfway back to the States in that time! But I won't question him. No, I won't.

"Tripp, did you see the news? About the red alert?"

"Yeah, I heard about it on the radio on the drive back. Don't let your mind go to any of those dark places, Miranda..."

"But, Tripp, this sounds serious."

"I know." He brings me in for a hug. "But I called Larry—you know how he gets obsessed with this stuff—and he'd already spoken to his guys. Apparently, the CIA or whoever already foiled their plan. I'm sure that'll be on the news soon."

"Phew, what a relief! I was so worried."

Part of me wishes we had to leave Honolulu and get as far away from Cleo as possible. Deep inside, I know she means something important to him. But why, and how important?

Very, or he wouldn't have this look on his face and wouldn't have spent four hours with her this morning. Thank God no one else knows this. It'd be so embarrassing to have anyone see me this vulnerable. My children, especially.

Somehow Cleo seems to be availing herself of my life and getting the outpourings of my husband's and sons' thoughts and dreams. She is my polar opposite—I see it in a flash—I think that may be the reason I feel so scared. I've always reasoned that some women were better cooks, better athletes, better in bed, better looking. Cleo is better at touching something in my men, some place in them that I don't even see. That is what terrifies me.

At 5:00 a.m., Tripp asked me to come with him "if I wanted."

Everyone knows "if you want" is code for, "but if it were up to me, I'd really rather you didn't."

I quickly replied, "No, thanks. But give my best to Cleo."

Normally, he'd throw out a quip here, perhaps a touch cruel, and I waited for it. Nothing. Nothing from my lawyer husband, who can always give the best toasts at parties, teases people no one else dares, touches and relaxes them. He always has his humor, but then he was speechless. His, cool, seductive voice was quiet.

"They have a great fireworks display to kick off the marathon," he added.

"Fireworks?"

Pele the volcano goddess, I thought to myself. Maybe I should've gotten up with him and tagged along. After he left, I wandered around, wondering how long he'd be gone. I started figuring it out in my head. If the marathon starts at six, he'll probably bail at seven and come back to the hotel. But now, four hours later, I don't ask him to explain. I don't want the truth from him because I'm worried it will hurt more than any lie could. I feel checkmated and don't know how or why or when or where. I give him a big smile and a kiss. That damnable perfume.

When he became a runner, so did I. He even encouraged me to join him in a marathon, if you can imagine that. The idea for that brutal 26.2 miles began on a cold Sunday three-mile morning run in Central Park. We were running with our friends, Kay and Rick, as we did every Sunday, huffing and puffing. We, or rather they, were chatting as we jogged and somehow we found we'd run five whole miles. This led Tripp to question whether we could run a marathon! Compared to twenty-six, a five-mile run had never sounded so measly. But this is how Tripp's mind works. Since he could convince anyone to do almost anything, we went to Brooklyn that spring and ran a half marathon of 13.1 long, *long* miles.

Tripp wanted to do Paris next.

"If you have only one marathon in you, wouldn't it be fitting to do it in Paris?" he asked me one night after I brought him his Budweiser.

"I love the idea of running amid beautiful architecture, along the Seine, with Frenchmen cheering us on," I told Kay enthusiastically. But I think my enthusiasm must have been more for my own benefit than for Kay's.

Tripp even came up with a very detailed game plan. He even typed it out on his computer and printed it for me.

"Look, Miranda. On the day, you and Kay can just gab for the first thirteen miles about whatever it is you want to gab about. I mean, Kay works at the U.N., so she can discuss Middle East Policy or any international news that is pressing at the time."

That seemed more appropriate than what he wanted me to talk about at fifteen miles. He suggested, "Miranda, you can cover the economic policy." But, thankfully, only for two miles. Economic policy? He has to be kidding.

"At seventeen, you can discuss movies and TV shows. You're so good at that stuff, I'm sure those miles will whiz by. Then, at nineteen, books. Again, you'll forget you're even running! Twenty, that night's dinner menu. Yum. Twenty-one, tell each other jokes. And for the last five miles, just tell each other how wonderful you are. That won't be hard, will it?"

Tripp didn't mean to sound controlling. Instead, he genuinely thought this little tactic would encourage us and so he even went so far to suggest that we study our topics ahead of time so it'd keep our minds occupied. He didn't take into account how winded and exhausted we'd be. Much too winded and exhausted to "gab" about anything, let alone movies, or books, or economic policy.

At twenty-one miles, Kay felt wonderful. I hated her. I'd hit a wall, a big, tall one made out of brick. She talked happily while I could barely breathe. At one point, I thought the Eiffel Tower, where the finish line was, had been stolen since it never came into sight. I was so enraged by the thought that I didn't even notice when finally, in the pouring rain, we crossed the finish line. Our husbands, who had finished hours earlier, were there smiling at us and cheering us on, just like those flirtatious Frenchmen did the whole way. Tripp was so proud of me and that made it all worthwhile. As I sat on the curb in the deluge of rain, so totally miserable as I tried, unsuccessfully, to stretch my cramped, tight legs, I vowed I'd never run again. *Ever.* I hated it.

Tripp came over and whispered to me, "I'm so happy we did this together, Miranda. Wasn't it great? I'm going to sign us up for the London Marathon next. Don't you think it'd be fun to run all the capitals of Europe?" he said, smiling 26.2 miles wide.

I couldn't believe it. I wanted to sob. But I knew I would join him in this new quest. We are a couple and I get so much from him, that I will give this to him. He was so proud of me.

He was hardly even sweating then, just as he's hardly sweating now in our Honolulu hotel room so many years later.

"Glad you're back. I booked a tennis court and tee times for this afternoon. Doesn't that sound like fun?" I ask as if there's no problem.

Tripp looks distracted as he wanders over to the window and types something on his phone. "I don't know, this weather might cause a change in plans..." He switches on the TV and we spend an hour watching the news and the weather, none of which looks great. There is a storm over the Pacific but it is not expected to hit us, though we might get clouds and a bit of rain.

I GO DOWN TO AN EARLY LUNCH. The wind has, in fact, not died down and blue skies are hidden by dark, gray clouds. Tripp wanted to change and make a phone call and so he meets me down at the table.

"Let's move to that table and sit under an umbrella. I think it might rain any minute," Tripp says, looking up at the gray skies.

I nod agreeably, get up from the uncovered table and follow him over to one that is. Tripp hasn't lost that distracted, worried look he came into our room with. I wonder if the red alert has scared him more than he's letting on. Like me, even if he was stressed, he'd try his best not to let anyone know it.

He only has an iced tea while I order a bacon cheeseburger, french fries, and a double chocolate milkshake. I eat when

I'm upset. And right now, I could have about sixteen double chocolate milk shakes.

"Where is everyone?" Tripp asks me right after I've taken a gigantic bite of my bacon cheeseburger drenched in ketchup.

I chew quickly and swallow hard. "Matt's on the beach. Ricky and Julia are around here somewhere." I pause. "And Jake just left a minute ago for the Banzai Pipeline."

"With whom?" he asks, right after I've taken yet another big bite.

I'm so ravenous I could eat three of these things, no problem. As I chew quickly again, I shoot him an intentional look. *Who do you think?*

"Cleo...?" he asks, already knowing the answer.

I swallow hard and nod. I eye Tripp, trying to gauge his reaction regarding Jake and Cleo's Banzai Pipeline adventure. He looks stricken. Interesting. Exactly why, I'm not sure I want to know. I choose not to deal with that so... I don't.

"Goddamn it, I wanted everyone to stay close. Don't we need him for doubles?"

Tripp is on edge. I wonder if his China deal is stressing him out or if something happened at the marathon this morning with Cleo.

"I told him we needed him but he wouldn't listen."

I am doing everything in my power to keep my son away from that woman but he just wouldn't listen. *Mom, I can play golf and tennis whenever I want, but I can't always see the Banzai Pipeline.*

This morning, I peeked into his and Julia's room and saw no trace of her things. So now I know she officially moved out—as she should have. But I won't ask any questions. It's the same with Tripp and the marathon this morning. Sometimes ignorance really can be bliss. I'll ask the front desk to put her new room on our bill. That's the least I can do. Well, maybe I should give Jake the bill. *An early Christmas present from your loving mother.*

"Tripp, did Cleo mention anything about Jake this morning?"

He flinches. "What? No. Why?"

I stare at him blankly, my eyelids blinking double time. Surely, I'm not the only one besides Julia who knows what's going on here. Jake and Cleo were practically electric yesterday. The term "gaga" comes to mind. And I can't tell if Tripp is playing dumb or if he's just totally clueless. Men can be clueless.

"You know what I mean…"

He turns away from me and drains the rest of his iced tea.

"Tripp, our oldest son is fooling around with this woman, a complete stranger, while he's on our family vacation with his girlfriend of two years."

"That's enough, Miranda. I don't want to get involved. I have enough to think about right now," Tripp snaps.

He never snaps at me. His picture could appear in the dictionary next to the words, "relaxed," "easy going," and laid back." My husband has always been the very definition of calm, cool, and collected.

"Well, I don't *want* to get involved either, Tripp. But I feel terrible for Julia and don't know what we can do. Shouldn't we talk to him?"

My husband looks at me like I've just asked if he'd like to take a barefoot stroll over hot coals.

"Miranda, it isn't any of our damn business. They're not children. They're old enough to work it out themselves."

I'm about to disagree, rare for me, but his phone starts to buzz. The caller's timing is impeccable. Saved by the bell. This isn't the first time Tripp's phone has rung at the most inopportune of moments. Sometimes I wonder if he hides a remote in his pocket, pressing it whenever he wants to get out of a squirrelly conversation. My husband checks the caller ID and looks up at me evenly.

"Sorry, honey, I have to take this," he says, rising out of his chair.

He steps into the empty patio to our right, leaving me to finish my milkshake and order another. Ricky wanders over in his perpetual good mood. He seems particularly happy and at ease today. That makes one of us.

"S'up, Mom. What's the haps?" Ricky asks.

Of my three sons, my relationship with Ricky has always been the easiest. As a child, he'd spend what seemed to be days at a time running around outside with some of the other neighborhood kids. When Ricky would finally return home dirty and exhausted, he'd be thrilled with whatever meal I put on the table. He'd eat it all, thank me, then take it upon himself to wash his own plate. I certainly can't say the same for his two older brothers.

As a teenager, Ricky was like an open book compared to Matt and Jake. He was a breath of fresh air. Jake was so fiercely private; he never wanted to tell me a single detail about school or his day, his love life, or his general thoughts on anything, really. It was like pulling teeth, but I never gave up my questioning, hoping that one day, he'd open up to me and confide in his old mother about something. Anything. Matt was the same way but he had his reasons. His Aspergers is fairly low on the spectrum, but it keeps him from forming close relationships with anyone.

I think Ricky sensed how closed off his older brothers were, and therefore indulged me in a closer, more easygoing relationship. Not that I'd ever dream of asking him about his sex life, but I'm sure if I did, he'd have no problem sharing—up to a certain point. I'm a mother of three very different boys and I love them all equally and for very different reasons. But I've always been the closest with my baby. My Ricky. This has been a secret that I've kept from Jake and Matt, though I'm not sure they'd even care. Jake cares about Jake and Matt is comfortable with his plants.

"... What's the haps?" I repeat, not having the foggiest idea what that even means. Ricky's always on the cutting edge of however the kids are talking, but often it sounds like he's speaking Arabic. I think he does it just to mess with his very out-of-touch mother.

"Yeah, you know... like, what's happenin'?"

"Right. How could I not have put that together?" I smile up at him demurely.

"Anyway, I think Jules and I are gonna go hit some balls but wanted to see what Dad and your plans were before we took off. Guys cool with that?"

"Yes! Yes, that's great! You two have fun," I exclaim, grateful that Ricky has picked up right where Jake left off. I can tell he's a little taken aback by my enthusiasm.

"... Alright, cool. Everything good, Mom?"

No, everything is certainly not good.

"You might want to bring an umbrella," I say, ignoring his question. "It looks like it might rain."

"Okay. But, seriously, mom. You okay?"

How do I put this delicately...

"Will you... Do you think... I mean..." I start in.

"Spit it out, Mom."

"Oh, Ricky, will you just find out how Julia's doing?"

"Ah, yes. You must be referring to my braindead brother, a.k.a. your dumbass son. FYI, she moved into my room last night and I moved into Matt's."

Mystery solved. It's refreshing after everyone else in this family seems to be tiptoeing around the issue.

"Thank God," I say behind clenched teeth.

"I'll keep you posted," my Ricky responds. He kisses my cheek and is off.

Chapter Forty-Three
December 24, 2011

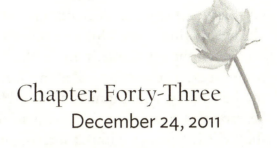

TRIPP

"Sir, I'm sorry to bother you again with bad news."

"Go ahead."

"We just received word that Dr. Pearson was killed," Chris Castillo tells me.

"What?! How could this happen? We had bodyguards on him day and night."

"I know, sir. It appears JI was determined to send us a message. This morning, Pearson was on his way to pick up some food for a get together he was having. Some PBS special or something his buddies were all coming over to watch. Apparently, he was pretty excited to show off the new big screen he just bought—presumably with the money we paid him. Sarkey, the guard stationed around Pearson's residence, said Pearson insisted on showing it to him when it arrived.

"Sarkey was in the middle of a call with his partner when he heard an explosion. There was an incendiary device in the wheel well of Pearson's car that ignited when he turned the key. He didn't suffer. Sarkey's a wreck—he's guessing that JI planted the bomb when he went up to see the new TV. He got pretty attached to Pearson. Hard not to love a guy who's always inviting you up for a sandwich and a beer."

I suck the air through my teeth, thinking. This has been some week. The contact killed in Manila, Cleo on the beach, the helicopter, Mohammed here in Honolulu, and now Dr. Pearson's assassination. My life is at the highest red alert. If they killed Pearson without interrogating him, they must've thought he was an intelligence agent, not realizing that he was only loaning me his identity. I feel completely responsible; we assured Pearson of his safety. In as vague terms as possible, the company advised him to be careful and that they had people watching over him, "just in case."

"They must think we're close to finding Mohammed Abdul Rahman," says Castillo.

"We're not close until he is dead," I grumble.

"Sir, we believe JI thought Ocampo might have given 'Dr. Pearson' something, and whatever intel the contact was supposed to pass on was valuable enough to assassinate him."

I rub my hand over my face. "Animals."

"Where are we on that plane?"

"Working on it, sir. The only complication—"

"I don't give a shit about complications. You hear me, Castillo? This is my family we're talking about. You get a plane out for my family by tonight at the latest. Got me?" I fume.

"Yes, sir. It's just the weather we're concerned about. Planes are grounded from flying across the Pacific. There's supposed to be a typhoon."

"Jesus, Castillo! No excuses! Just get it done!"

I hang up and think about the funny, brilliant professor. He was one of the only people who truly knew who I was. Okay, sure, he only knew me as James Howard, but he knew me. He knew the me that continuously puts my life in danger to keep our country safe. Miranda, the boys—of course, none of them know. They can't. But I wish, if only for a second, that they could understand my work and appreciate my sacrifices in the way Pearson did.

Sacrifices. Pearson made the biggest sacrifice and no one will ever know. No one will realize why he died so unceremoniously. No one will ever get to see the new TV he was so excited about. If only I'd given him one of those big bear hugs back instead of always shrugging him off half-heartedly. If only I'd sat down with him for one of those ham-and-cheese sandwiches. If only he'd been able to publish that book.

A thought dawns on me, and I pick my phone back up. I contemplate apologizing to Castillo for screaming at him earlier too, but decide against it. These young guys need to be put in their place every once in a while, or they'll never learn.

"Chris, I need you to do something else for me. Dr. Pearson was working on a book during his time off. Could you recover it and have it shipped to my office? It'd be nice if we could get it published as a tribute to him."

Chapter Forty-Four
December 24, 2011

JULIA

"Are you okay?"

"Yeah, fine. Why?"

Ricky looks at me, his blue eyes even more turquoise than his older brother's, as he removes both of our clubs from the back of the trunk. *You know what I mean,* is what those eyes are telling me. "Look, we don't have to talk about yesterday and my idiot brother if you don't want to. I'm just putting it out there. If you want to talk, I'm here."

"Thanks. I'm okay for now but I appreciate the offer."

At least one of the Regan brothers was born with the sensitivity chip. Ricky winks at me before he picks up his golf bag with one hand and mine with the other and straps them both in the back of the golf cart. His tanned, toned biceps are practically bulging out of his white Lacoste shirt. *How have I never noticed his perfect arms before?*

"You're not checkin' me out, are you, Jules?"

Maybe...

Ricky turns back and smiles at me, instantly snapping me out of my fantasyland.

"Don't flatter yourself," I laugh.

Last night, while the Regans were eating foie gras and duck breast, I was holed up in my room with room service frantically looking for flights to take me far away from here. After my performance at yesterday's rollicking lunch, I figured it was probably best for all parties involved that I also skip family dinner time. I couldn't see Jake. He and I are so obviously toast, but I'd like to at least *try* and salvage whatever dignity I might have left with the rest of the Regan family. Getting on my merry little way seems like the only solution.

Apparently, that bitch Pele has other plans. According to Kayak, Expedia, Priceline, and every single airline website, all flights out of Honolulu are officially grounded today and tomorrow too. It's not even raining! A few clouds and some wind but that's it. There's a typhoon warning on weather. com over the Pacific. *A typhoon?* Big whoop. A little typhoon never hurt anyone, except maybe The Wicked Witch of The East. Or was that a twister? It doesn't matter. The point is, I'm stuck here. At least Ricky is better company than Jake these days...

"Wanna take the wheel?" he asks, gesturing toward our hunter green golf cart.

"Oh. No, that's okay. We don't need two car accidents on this trip, now, do we?" I joke as I climb into the passenger side.

"Aw, c'mon. Danica Patrick's got nothing on you." Ricky nudges me.

"When have you ever seen me drive?" I ask, suddenly hyper-aware of every single syllable that comes out of my dehydrated mouth.

"For real?"

"... Yeah?"

"You seriously don't remember driving back from the Noguchi that time?"

Oh, boy. Memory refreshed.

"You were a maniac!"

Ah, the wonders of selective memory. Jake and I had just started seeing each other when I got tickets to an exhibit at The Noguchi Museum in Queens one Sunday. Jake was, of course, supposed to come with me but backed out at the last minute because his beloved New York Giants were playing the Dallas Cowboys. Or maybe it was the Indians? Who cares, not important, moving on. Anyway, Ricky stepped in and offered to take Jake's spot so that I didn't have to go to the exhibit by myself. We ended up spending far too much time there, both of us completely absorbed in the Japanese sculptures. That night, as luck would have it, I was supposed to meet Mr. and Mrs. Regan for the very first time at La Grenouille. If I remember correctly, Mr. Regan was probably due in court first thing in the morning, so our reservation was for six thirty. Early bird special, indeed.

At 5:55 sharp, an announcement came over the loudspeaker saying that they were closing in exactly five minutes. I turned to Ricky, mortified at the prospect of being late for my introduction to my new boyfriend's parents. Even if I enchanted them all dinner long with my British charm, they'd never forget that I wasn't there when the clock struck half past six. I could be Queen Elizabeth herself and Mr. and Mrs. Regan would still always remember me fondly as the girl in desperate need of a watch.

Ricky grabbed my arm and we sprinted out to my car. I hopped into the driver side and he into the passenger. Zipping along the East River to the 59th Street Bridge, I accidentally turned *on*to the *off* ramp. I nearly killed us. Cars honked and drivers screamed and my whole life flashed before my eyes. When I realized my stupid mistake, somehow I'd managed to pull all the way over to the right side of the lane, to the shoulder. To safety. But I couldn't move. The cars were still honking and the people inside were flipping us off as they passed like I'd intentionally tried to massacre everyone on the bridge. Ricky fished me out of the driver's seat and escorted me over to the passenger door, rubbing my back. He drove the rest of the way there, cracking jokes the entire time, trying to get my mind off the fact that I'd almost killed us both. I let Ricky take care of me that day. That was the first time that Ricky came to my rescue. Here he is again in Honolulu, taking care of me while Jake is doing what he does best... taking care of himself.

"God, that seems like a million years ago," I tell Ricky as he pulls up to the fourth tee.

"Yeah, your hair was a lot shorter back then."

Look, I admit that it took me a few days to put two and two together regarding Jake and that woman who shall not be named. But, believe it or not, I have learned my fair share about the male species during my twenty-six years on Earth. They don't remember squat about certain details like the length of your hair, or really, details in general unless it directly relates to sex or they like you. Like you, like, more than a friend. And even then, their storage capacity often falls under very basic, very primal categories like hot and not hot, cool or not cool, sexy or not sexy. Unlike us females who remember everything at our own peril, men tend to focus more on the broader strokes. I can rattle off each of the battles in both World Wars (in chronological order, mind you), fill in an entire blank periodic table of elements, quote *Mean Girls, The First*

Wives Club, and *Hocus Pocus* in their entirety and you can bet that if I ever knew a song lyric, I'll know it for life.

"You remember my hair?"

Even I'd completely forgotten that, at the time, I'd been following the latest fashion trend, a horrid Victoria Beckham bob that only Victoria Beckham herself could pull off. I had just cut it, and to say the least, Jake wasn't a big fan. Maybe I just blocked it out entirely; it was pretty tragic looking.

Ricky's face turns fifty shades of red as he catches himself, realizing that he's accidentally revealed something very telling. And he knows I've caught it too.

Awk-ward.

"I mean, I think? Right? Who knows, I could be making that up." He laughs nervously, pulling out the driver from his navy golf bag.

Nearby, thunder growls.

"Did you hear that? Is that thunder?"

I smile at his attempt to change the subject.

"Or just the sound of my ego exploding into a million pieces...?"

I laugh. This is the first time I've ever seen Ricky flustered and it's adorable. I smile at him, knowingly. A conspiratorial smile slowly wipes across his face too. He turns away from me.

"Shut up, Jules..."

I burst into laughter again. Ricky's back is turned to me as he sets up his ball and takes a practice swing. But his shoulders are bouncing up and down ever so slightly and I can tell that he's laughing too.

SOMETHING'S SERIOUSLY UP with this island...

Chapter Forty-Five
December 24, 2011

CLEO

There are eight messages on my cell phone from Jake when I get home from the marathon. I decide to call him after my Krav Maga session with Walter, who is waiting for me at our gym.

"How was the marathon?" Walter asks me as he straps on his punch mitts.

"Interesting..."

"You up for this today?"

I nod. I am always up for Krav Maga. I feel so powerful when I am practicing my punches and my kicks and my chops. I will never feel weak or defenseless ever again.

"Whenever you're ready, Cleo," says Walter as he raises both of his hands in a defensive position.

Once I finish bandaging both of my hands in nylon wraps, I step forward with my right leg, raise my back heel so that it's slightly off the ground and bend both of my knees. My elbows rest tightly against my ribs. I raise my arms so that my hands are eight inches away from my face—my hands protect my face and my arms protect my body. My eyes laser in on Walter, ready for battle. As I always see it, Walter's face becomes that of the now deceased Richard Rensasslear.

I advance forward, bursting off the balls of my left foot. Cross body punch. Elbow strike. Eye strike. Axe kick. I step back, get into passive stance and bounce on the balls of my feet. My focus is fastidious and my skills are precise and unassuming.

"Someone's fired up today..." Walter teases me.

I smile and nod.

"I mean, even more so than normal..." He takes a step forward. "Okay, again."

Walter raises his hands and I get into fighting stance once again. Cross body punch, elbow strike, eye strike, axe kick, inside chop. We repeat this sequence eight more times, and each time, I add a new move—hook punch, headbutt, outside chop, uppercut, back kick, front kick, heel kick, leg sweep, and on and on. Walter uses a body shield to protect himself when we practice the kicks so that I don't injure him, which, even though he was a Navy SEAL for nine years, I can. There are endless moves and techniques in Krav Maga and I have mastered them all. After almost thirty years of training, I should.

"Water break?"

"Let's keep going." I shake my head. Fired up, indeed. I am not sure if it is Jake or the marathon or the red alert or what. All I know is that I don't want to stop.

"Roger that." Walter puts down the body shield. "Okay, my turn. Defensive maneuvers. Put on your gear."

"No, I don't need it."

"Cleo, we've been over this," Walter snaps.

"Yes, so you should know how I feel about it. If I need to defend myself in real life, I won't have time to put on my shin guards or helmet!"

Walter takes a breath, acquiescing. "Fine. But you're drea-min' if you think I'm goin' easy on you." He smiles.

"Oh, Walter. You know I don't need you to." I smile back.

We both get into fighting position. He comes at me with the full force of a SEAL—palm heel strike, uppercut. Side kick. But I fend them all off with my defensive moves. Sometimes I think it must bother Walter a bit. He's a six-foot tall, thirty-five-year-old former Navy SEAL hard-body who can probably bench four hundred pounds, yet he has great trouble taking down a forty-four-year-old woman who weighs one hundred and twenty pounds soaking wet. Well, Walter, practice makes perfect.

Our session goes on for a full hour. Sixty minutes of slap-ping, spinning, sweeping, striking, punching, and kicking. Ah, how I love it. It gives me such energy. An energy that I have learned to thrive on and use to my advantage.

"Good work today, Gallier," Walter huffs and puffs as he sprays a stream of water into his mouth.

"Remember, I won't see you the next few weeks, Walter, as I am going to visit my father. Have a great Christmas and I added something to your check for a Christmas present." I smile, undoing the wraps from around my hands. I leave the gym and head back toward the house.

My phone has even more messages from Jake. I pick it up and call him.

"Cleo?!" he says from the other end.

"Hi, Jake," I greet him, breezily.

"Hey! There you are. How are you? Did you see my dad at the marathon?"

He is so polite, too polite.

He is jealous. Jealous! But how funny to be jealous of his father. A father and a son. So alike. Both handsome with those piercing blue eyes and dark curling hair, with similar builds and smiles. The father so lived-in, the son so new and fresh, like a frisky cub. Tripp is like an old leather chair in a good men's club, mingled with cigar smoke and a newspaper; Jake a new barstool, fun to get on and off, but never comfy. One can't relax or fall asleep on the stool. You had to be alert, lest you tumble.

Am I my mother after all? But I don't really want answers or introspection. I want emotion, excitement, passion. If I stopped to think, I would not see him again and I am not going to stop. Like the hausfrau who makes you remove your shoes before stepping on her clean floor, I am going to remove my conscience before seeing him, and the Banzai Pipeline fits my disease. So I ask him to meet me there.

It was overcast when I got there but the surfers were all out. I removed my flip-flops and strolled up to the lifeguard station, blanket in tow. Jake was at the shoreline, transfixed.

"The waves. They're much bigger than I thought they'd be."

Tsunamis are my greatest fear, so I've only ventured over here one other time. The waves roll and curve and crash, unfeeling, uncaring. They will take anything down.

"This is my Christmas present to you, Jake." I hand him a pair of binoculars. "So that you can see the waves close up. I want you to feel the power of Hawaii, to experience the displeasure and the sanctity of the island. I hope this place stays with you when you return home. It is life force at its strongest, and you can use it when you need your blood to surge through your veins, when you need to rev up your soul. It's so much bigger than all of us; it gives such clarity to human love and yet it inspires such fear that it gives a reason to have human love affairs; a place to go to avoid staring in the face of the intolerable."

He doesn't have a clue what to make of my words; he looks panicked so he takes the binoculars and watches the surfers on the waves. He passes them back and forth to me.

"I could watch 'em all day. The waves. They're so... I dunno, interesting."

I turn and look at him. "What really intrigues you, Jake?"

He smiles. "You."

I give him the blanket I brought and head to a sand dune.

He picks me up and kisses me and I no longer care about his thought processes. I'm only wrapped up in him, his looks, his broad shoulders, his curling poet's hair, the way his hands explore me, the smell of him. It is not the technique or the stamina; it's just him. The hours, positions, ability to come back to excitement, to be turned on so much that one begs to stop. I had never thought I'd want to stop, but it is too much. He's boundless. How could any other man be as amazing? I can't think about anything but him... the rest of the world is a blur. I don't know who I am right now.

He is quiet for a moment.

"Do you love me, Cleo?" he blurts innocently.

"Oh, Jake. You'll be gone tomorrow night."

He nods, digesting what a dent in a car has brought him. He touches the necklace he had given me and smiles that I am wearing it.

As we get up to leave, I have to do a double take. Do my eyes deceive me or is that Spencer Stone in a wetsuit, wading out into the water with a yellow surfboard?

"What?" Jake asks, following my eye line.

"Nothing, let's go." I grab Jake's arm and lead him back to my car.

Jake deliberately left his cell phone charging at my house. He claimed the battery was nearly dead but I suspect that he did not want any distractions while we were together at The Pipeline. How sweet. When we get back, it is 4:30. His phone screen illuminates as I detach it from the charger and I see the phone has several missed calls and texts messages—all from "Dad."

"Looks like you may want to call your father..." I tell Jake, handing him his phone.

He just rolls his big, blue eyes and wraps his muscular arms around my waist. "Eh, the old man can sweat it out. I think he might have a thing for you..."

"Jake, seriously," I laugh. "I don't want your father to worry."

Jake rolls his eyes again but does as I tell him. He dials and waits as it rings.

"Hey, Dad," Jake says listlessly.

I can make out Tripp's voice on the other end, "Where have you been, Jake? It's been hours. Your mother was worried."

"I told her we were going to the Banzai Pipeline."

"I know, we just didn't think it'd be this long. I need you to get back here. Now."

"Why?" Jake whines and his face scrunches up.

"Just do it, okay?"

Jake rolls his eyes for a third time, hangs up the phone, then grabs me from behind.

"No. I can't. I have my bike ride with Jimbo. And it sounds like you have to get back to the Halekelani."

"Can't you skip it? I leave tomorrow, Cleo. You and 'Jimbo,'" he uses air quotes for Jimbo's name, "are basically roommates anyway."

"I'm sorry, but we do it every week."

"So? I play squash at The Racquet Club three times a week, but if I were with you, you can bet your ass I'd ditch it. How can a lame bike ride be so important?"

"It's a ritual, okay?"

"No. Not okay..." Jake says, letting go of me. "What is it with you two? Are you in love with him or something? I just don't get why you can't reschedule?"

Jake has reverted to that same spoiled child routine that he did when I slammed my car into his. I don't enjoy this act of his.

"Jake, you have to go. I need to get ready."

Jake touches my necklace then starts in again by kissing me—knowing my response and testing mightily one last time to see if he can keep me from the bike ride.

"I'm serious, Jake. I need you to leave now," I say as I push him toward the door.

He starts to leave, furious and jealous.

"Where do you guys go on your little rides anyway?"

On your little rides. He's being so condescending.

"Up the Pali highway toward the Koolah Cliffs. That's where I turn and come back. Why?"

"Sweet..." Jake says, his voice dripping with sarcasm.

I finally free myself from him. He is so ridiculously, insanely jealous of Jimbo.

I run back to shower and change. I have to jump in the shower, to rinse off Jake and the sand. From the shower, I can hear him leave. After he slams the car door, I hear Jake's dented Jeep pull out of the driveway with a roar. It's rather childish but fun to have someone so insane about me.

Chapter Forty-Six
December 24, 2011

TRIPP

Blood is on my hands again. Poor Professor Pearson—so passionate, so curious, so totally innocent.

"Matt!" I call down to my son on the beach. He doesn't hear me. "Matt! Buddy, over here!"

He's knee-deep in seawater and slumped over, examining something in the sand. He finally looks up from shore and locates me further up on the dunes.

"How 'bout we take a walk?"

Matt doesn't acknowledge what I've said with his speech. He just splashes out of the water and starts marching directly toward me.

"Same place as yesterday?" I ask him.

"Sure, but it's getting windy."

And we start walking. I don't care where we walk. I just need physical activity and I'm not in the mood for chitchat. There are only four guards afforded to six members of my family so taking Matt kills two birds with one stone. Matt is the perfect choice. Before I left, I checked in with each of the agents who are watching my family. Sam and Sam followed Ricky and Julia to the golf course, Rico is on Miranda, Marcus will be on Jake when he returns and now I'm on Matt. Castillo better hurry the fuck up with that plane. Weather, typhoons, my family needs off this island. I take the photo out of my pocket and study it again, hoping to direct my anxiety toward something productive.

"What's that, Dad?" Matt asks, swiping the paper right out of my hands.

"Matt, no."

I try to grab it back, but he's too quick.

"Hmm..." Matt contorts his torso to the right, away from me, while he studies the paper. His eyes dart around the eight-and-a-half-by-eleven sheet like a hawk in search of prey.

"Matt, please. Give that back—"

"What happened to this? Did you spill something on it?"

"...What do you mean?"

"This map. It's all smudged."

"Map?"

"Yeah, of Honolulu. Did you buy this at the gift shop, Dad? You should take it back, I can hardly read the thing. I can't believe they sold this to you, Dad. You're such a sucker!"

I indulge Matt. "How can you tell it's Honolulu?"

"C'mon, Dad. It's, like, so obvious! See, that's Mamala Bay." He points to the center of the map. "It looks kind of like a flower, don't you think?"

I lean over and take a closer look. Jesus Christ, he might be onto something.

"See, and there's little Ford Island and Pearl Harbor, and Middle Loch and... I think that's Pacific Command. See, Dad?"

Holy shit.

"Hey, buddy, I'm a little tired. Mind if we head back?" I ask, taking back the paper.

Once again, Matt anticipated the twist ending coming before any of us. Al Qaeda didn't force Ocampo to swallow the map in some bizarre form of torture, Ocampo did it to prevent JI from discovering its contents. He was trying to save it for us to give us the targets. Pearl Harbor and Pac Command. In all likelihood, those must be their targets.

Chapter Forty-Seven
December 24, 2011

CLEO

I'd stayed far too long at the Banzai Pipeline. But it was just too wonderful to leave. I don't have my bike clothes on when I see Jimbo's lean shadow lingering outside my bedroom window. In my haste to pull on my white sports bra, it goes on the wrong way and gets twisted, sticking to the moisture I neglected to towel off. I pull on my one-piece bike suit but the zipper gets stuck halfway over my chest. Today, I am grateful for the padding in my suit. After my strenuous time with Jake, I need a seat that is comfy and easy on my muscles and joints.

I can see Jimbo impatiently straddling his bike, glancing down at the Nike sports watch I gave him seemingly every ten seconds. He gets off his bike and pushes through the door just as I'm sliding on my bike shoes.

"Cleo? You here?"

"Be right out!" I call out to his nebulous, amorphous voice. "I just have to get my water bottle in the kitchen," I say, sounding as cheery as Cinderella when she is polishing her evil stepmother's hideous jewelry. The last thing I want to do is make Jimbo angry. We're already behind schedule because of me.

"Sounds good," I hear him say.

I hurry out of my bedroom and start to cross the hallway toward the kitchen when I notice Jimbo hovering in the hallway door. I jump, not expecting to see him standing there.

"Ah!" I scream involuntarily.

"I passed your young pool boy on my way in…" He smirks.

My back turns to him as I rush into the kitchen and fill my water bottle at the sink.

"Up for a bike ride or you all tuckered out from your previous exercise?"

Har-dee-har-har. I exit the kitchen and join him at the door, flashing him an amused smile. Noticing my cleavage, he instinctively pulls up my zipper like a protective father and off we go. We both hop on our bikes and start pedaling away happily. Krav Maga workouts may be my drug but bike rides with Jimbo—the exercise, the Honolulu scenery, and the conversations—are very special to me. Krav Maga is my deep, dark secret; these bike rides are my joy.

"Think we can make it to the marina by three fifteen? I'd really like to aim for that, Cleo. The wind seems to be picking up."

"If we hustle!" I say, pedaling harder. When Jimbo says he would 'like' to do something, it's really more of an order. He might as well say, 'this is what we're gonna do.'

"So… how's young Romeo, anyway?" he asks. I can tell he is trying to get under my skin with that playful yet calculated poke. This is hardly new or surprising behavior for my friend Jimbo. In fact, I knew he was going to react this way and I have good reason to fear being late for him. Despite all his charm and inclinations to protect me, Jimbo can also be a sadist. Sometimes I have wondered if, secretly, he wishes for my tardiness as it supplies him with an excuse. An excuse to retaliate and make me pay for the delay in the currency of thinly veiled insults. He is trying to make me feel uncomfortable. But this time, he hasn't. Oh, no, he hasn't at all.

"Wonderful." I smile a mile wide. "I have to say, there's something glorious about a younger man... He's like a whirling dervish! Full of life."

"Sure he is. Before the weight of the world crushes his mind, body, and soul. It's only a matter of time..."

The road begins to incline and our journey becomes an uphill one. My feet, calves, and thighs burn as I push harder on the pedals, trying to keep up with my famous Ironman. Jimbo always makes it look so amazingly easy. Unlike me, he hardly ever breaks a sweat and his breathing is measured and steady. Normally, at this juncture in our ride, I would still be delighting in the scenery and the rush of adrenaline and even Jimbo's company, but today, my body is sore and lethargic from the past four days with Jake.

"Have you ever been with a much younger woman, Jimbo?"

"...What do you think?"

"Really? Tell me about her!" Only rarely do I get a taste of some fascinating morsel about the mysterious life of Jimbo Isom. Pleasant conversation always passes the time so much more enjoyably too.

"Ah... you know me. Locked vault," he responds, taking with him all the wind out of my sails.

He starts pedaling even harder as we approach a big, winding curve. I do the same, leaning into the turn, trying to keep up with the Ironman as we pedal up, up, and up toward the cliffs and through the deliciously lush He'eia State Park. Whenever my father visits, he insists that we take a walk through He'eia.

He just loves it. I reach for my water bottle and take my first gulp of the ride. I'm even more dehydrated than usual.

"So, how was the marathon? Did you finish in first place, as all the experts predicted?"

"Very funny, Jimbo."

"How many miles?"

"Oh, only about eight. I had wonderful company though. Jake's father, actually..." I smile shamelessly.

It takes Jimbo a moment but then he forces a laugh. "You're kidding."

He looks back at me for my reaction but I don't give him the satisfaction of one.

"That's quite a cozy image. Does he know about you and his young pup?"

"Of course. We talked all about it. I think Jake's father might actually be a bit jealous of his son!"

Jimbo turns back to me with his blonde crinkled brows. I've seen this expression before. It is one of pure disapproval, disgust even. He hates when I pay myself any sort of compliment or pat on the back. He finds it unseemly for a woman to be the purveyor of her own "attagirl!" *It's unbecoming, Cleo,* Jimbo always says. I must say he never pats himself on the back. Well, maybe it's unbecoming, but it's also accurate.

"Doesn't Jake have a girlfriend?"

Oh, yes, he's making me pay for being late.

"How do you know that?" I ask, surprised. In all our conversations about Jake over the past few days, I conveniently left out this detail. He can be infuriatingly judgmental about the strangest things.

"Just a good guess, wasn't it?" he turns back to me again. *My goodness, Jimbo, it was only five minutes.*

"Oh, Jimbo. I don't want to talk about that. That has nothing to do with me. Hey, did you hear about the red alert this morning?" I desperately try changing the subject.

"Yeah. Duncan mentioned something when I went over to Sweet Pea." He turns back to the open road.

"Isn't that scary?"

"I guess..." He shrugs.

"Jake's father and I were having breakfast after the marathon when CNN came on and broke the terrible news. You should have been there, Jimbo. The whole café went absolutely silent. I've never seen anything quite like it."

Jimbo doesn't say a word.

"Jake's father says an Al Qaeda leader may have been hiding out here for as long as four years. I had no idea, did you?"

"Well, *Jake's father* sounds like quite the Mensa candidate. I bet he knows who really shot JFK and where Jimmy Hoffa's buried." He laughs, ignoring my question.

"Oh, Jimbo. Don't be like that. Tripp's actually a very smart man."

Jimbo's reaction stuns me. His entire body tenses in an instant. His fists clench, his shoulders tighten, and his back straightens. He mumbles something under his breath but I can't quite make it out.

"You know, now that I think about it—four years, that's exactly how long you've been here! Are you the leader they're looking for?" I laugh.

"Ha. Ha..." he says, looking down to concentrate on his gears.

Jimbo starts to pedal even faster. I try to keep up with him but, he's apparently lost all interest in conversation or biking shoulder to shoulder as we usually do. Instead, I'm treated to a rear view of Jimbo and his midnight black bike. I look out at the glorious foliage, a much better view, trying to take my mind off the grueling and unusually joyless nature of today's ride with the Ironman. Eventually, my eyes drift down to Jimbo's back wheel. I need a focus point and so I choose his white monogrammed initials, JI bright against the back fender. I don't think anything would ever possess me to have CG monogrammed on my bike. Someone once told me, my father, probably, that lots of actors use alliteration for their first and last names—Marilyn Monroe, Greta Garbo, Sylvester Stallone and Tommy Tune all do roll off the tongue quite nicely with the repetition and reiteration.

Now I am really feeling exhausted and wish Jimbo would slow down so we could at least pass the time chattering away as we usually do. But today, he's different and he seems intent on staying a few yards ahead of me. My eyes narrow, fixated on his stupid monogrammed bicycle, reflecting on how much today's crummy attitude is aggravating and gnawing at me.

Tripp. His words at breakfast come flooding back to me like a thirty-foot wave at the Pipeline. *JI*. Jemaah Islamiyah. The same initials as the terror group that has provoked the horrifying red alert. *How ridiculous,* I tell myself as a rush of adrenaline pulses through my body and I start to pedal harder and faster and harder and faster. Paranoid thoughts come to me and start tumbling in my mind. I flash back to Senator Hamada's questions. *He doesn't work, right? Who supports him?* Then Tripp's words start echoing inside me again: *he left early because of reports that a big-time terrorist had arrived on the island.* Is it merely a coincidence that this just happens to match Jimbo Isom's timeline? I am sure I'm being ridiculous. Jimbo spends his days swimming and biking and running, not planning to blow up our little paradise. *No one knows the island like Jimbo,* I always brag to everyone.

I get a chill as I flashback to that day. To that day almost three years ago when a package addressed to Jimbo was delivered to my house by mistake. I had been overjoyed as I was expecting a new pair of Krav Maga pads in the mail from Amazon. Without even checking the box, I started to open it only to discover a delivery that was not meant for me.

"Oh."

"What?" Pudding asked.

"This is for Jimbo."

"Well, hell! I wanna see!" Pudding snagged the box right out of my hands, set it on the grass, ripped off the tape and rummaged inside. She pulled out a large piece of thick paper rolled neatly into a scroll with a ribbon tied around it as if it were a diploma.

"Pudding, please don't," I begged. But it was too late. She had already untied the ribbon and was starting to unfurl the paper.

"Fancy..." she said, studying the sheet. The paper was so large she could only unfold it as far as her pudgy arms stretched. "Look, it's a map of the island. That's so sweet. Jimbo must be settling in nicely. Maybe this is a thank you gift for you!"

"Maybe..."

"Shall we go deliver it then? I bet my second husband's expecting it!" Pudding batted her eyelashes.

When I looked over Pudding's shoulder, what struck me was the great attention to detail. I had never seen anything quite like it. Leaning even closer, I realized that it was a satellite view of Honolulu, and more specifically, Mamala Bay. I was so pleased that my new friend took such pride in where we lived and I felt even more grateful for being able to bestow

Jimbo with the gift of Honolulu. Doing the neighborly thing, Pudding and I walked the box down to his place after some careful repackaging on my part. That was the first time I noticed how the hidden security cameras followed us all the way down to his house. After the incident with my stalker, Jimbo insisted that I get security cameras for my protection and he even oversaw the installation. Right now, those cameras are taking on a whole new reason. Maybe he needed them. Maybe he even made up the stalker to move in near me.

I can't help turning everything into paranoid thoughts as the doubts gather like wind in a tornado. He glances back in my direction but not at me.

"You all right?" he calls back to me.

"Jimbo, I'm feeling a bit dizzy," I huff and puff.

"Dizzy?" He smirks, still not making eye contact. "You should try riding a hundred and twelve miles, then running another twenty-six in 104 degree heat, Cleo. Then you'll see what real dizzy feels like."

"I don't think I ever want to know what that dizzy feels like... You know that degree of physical activity is far too difficult for little ol' me."

"Have you ever done *anything* difficult?" He laughs. There's condescension, maybe even a touch of menace in his voice.

"You mean, because I've never competed in the Ironman?"

"Just in general."

You wanna know the worst part? Whoever it was, was born an American.

"Cleo? Hello? Come in, Cleo..."

I am jolted back to reality, back to our sloping bike ride. "Sorry. No, I am not an Ironman, Jimbo. But, who knows, maybe I will train for it next year!" I answer indirectly. "I will win one of those fabulous huge medals! Remember you gave me yours last year? I love it. I treasure it," I am babbling now. I do this when I am afraid.

My knees suddenly go weak and I involuntarily veer into the road. I am so distracted by all the irrational ideas whirling and swirling and twirling that I do not even hear the little Volkswagen Beetle's engine coming from behind at sixty miles an hour. Its tires screech as it swerves desperately out of the way and nearly collides head-on with an oncoming eighteen-wheeler truck that's screaming down the road. The truck driver lays on the horn and stays on the horn for almost five seconds.

"Ah!" I howl, having just seen my life flash before my eyes.

Balmy summers in Algeria with my father, yellow, orange, and brown autumns in New York City with my mother, champagne-soaked nights in Paris with friends and silly dates, happy Christmases with Beebe and Tree and all their barking dogs, the convent, the bright lights of the show, Molokai, colliding into Jake, and starry African nights with Danny all spool out before me like a roll of endless film, each photo a different memory. And then the one that rings out—pancakes with Tripp this morning. *A big-time terrorist arrived four years ago.* It's just like they tell you, just like it is in the movies.

"Jesus! Cleo, are you alright?!"

It takes me a moment to find my bearings. I pull over on my bike, trying to catch my breath and still my beating heart. After fishtailing from one side and then to the other, the Beetle has thankfully recovered. I turn in the opposite direction, behind me, and am relieved to find that the truck has also righted its course.

"Cleo?!" Jimbo pulls up next to me. He looks worried.

Wanna know the scariest part? He was born American.

I nod and start pedaling again, pumping my legs, harder and faster and harder and faster. Evading death has hopped me up on so much adrenaline that I feel like Popeye after devouring ten cans of spinach.

"You can rest if you want?" Jimbo calls after me.

I shake my head, still out of breath, and in a flash, he's pedaling beside me again. The feat of cheating death earns me Jimbo's extra water bottle. I stare down at the monogram on his bike once again as he hands it to me. I shake my head in a futile attempt to rid myself of all the poisonous, thunderous thoughts and Tripp's words.

"Are you sure you don't need to stop, Cleo? You don't look so hot..."

Well, what do you expect? I was almost smashed to pieces by a goddamn Volkswagen Beetle.

"No, I'm fine," I tell him as I sip from his Swell water bottle. His initials are branded on the steel too.

"Oh, JI just like the name of that terrorist group... Hey, maybe I am just asking this because... well, that." I gesture to the Beetle, now just a small blue speck on the horizon.

"Uh oh..." Jimbo grumbles.

"Do you think I need to do something bigger with my life, like helping the hungry children in Africa, or fighting for world peace or women's rights or I don't know... against terrorism?" I ask, dangling the bait.

More than anything, I am hoping that my suspicions are totally wrong. And that all of these silly clues are merely just happy coincidences and that Jimbo really is just my cranky best friend whose sole life mission is to win the Ironman race.

"I think that's the adrenaline talking..."

"No, Jimbo, I am serious! Don't you care about the greater good?"

He finally looks at me and something in him snaps like a tree branch. "Oh, I care about the greater good, Cleo."

He pauses for a torturous moment. "The problem is not everyone agrees what that greater good is..."

I have never heard him talk like this. We keep pedaling, silently. I remember my father teaching me how to use inductive reasoning when I faced a problem. But now, I have just solved one. Finally, we are about to reach the cliffs where I normally peel off and Jimbo continues on. My senses are so heightened. Up ahead, Jimbo pulls his bike over toward the road, which means I am to pull mine up on the side of the rocky embankment. Always in the past, it was the other way around. Below that embankment is a steep, deadly drop and so Jimbo would always protect me and position himself on the embankment side.

If I turn around to head home, he will catch me in a second's time and in his mind, that will only confirm my realization as to whom he really is. Instead, I pedal up the last part of the hill very slowly. I am smiling. My best friend is a traitor. Just like my father's best friend who raped me and betrayed him.

All my life I have trained for this moment. I feel as if I could lift the eighteen-wheeler truck if I had to. But I act the opposite, pretending as if I were exhausted. I keep smiling as I drop my bike and walk toward him.

Chapter Forty-Eight
1 Day

MOHAMMED ABDUL RAHMAN

She knows. After four long years, Cleo Gallier finally knows who I really am. I'm not some aimless nonbeliever named Jimbo Isom who only lives to run marathons, ride bikes, and eat kale salads. Cleo Gallier was certainly well-traveled, smart in her own kind of way with the occasional one-liner, and beautiful, even to me. Her presence elevated mine with the locals. She could hold her own during conversations about history, religion, literature, travel, and film. Part of me does genuinely enjoy her company and might even miss her. But I could see it all over her face as we rode. She isn't always as subtle as she thinks, that one. She'd obviously put one and one together and realized that Jimbo Isom, JI, was also Jemaah Islamiyah. The tragedy is, her destiny would have looked far different had she not spent the morning with Tripp Regan, who I tried to kill twice this week. Tripp Regan who has been after me for years. Tripp Regan the CIA star. *Jake's father.* Jesus, if I heard the phrase "Jake's father" come out of her mouth one more time, I'd have killed her even sooner. Without knowing it, Tripp Regan had signed her death certificate. I'm sure he thought he was being so fucking clever too, telling Cleo all about me and secretly pumping her for information that she didn't even know she had. Instead, he armed Cleo with information, too much information, making it impossible for her to keep on maintaining plausible deniability. Tripp put a big, bright red target on her back. There is justice in the world after all.

How easily she welcomed me into her home. I had to invent a crazed, horned-up stalker to speed things up, but still, we hadn't known each other for six months before I was building my own private, secluded lookout on her vast property. The fictitious stalker, bless his heart, not only granted me residence but surveillance too.

"They never caught him, Cleo. I'm worried. He could come back, you know. We should install security cameras by the house just in case."

"You're right, Jimbo. Can you handle it? Should I just write you a check?"

American women can be so stupid. There was no nefarious creature, no obsessed fan who would rape her and wear her skin as a suit, as I had told her—jokingly, but she took it seriously. *The threat was coming from inside the house, silly Cleo, and it was you who gave him the keys and a blank check. But don't flatter yourself, you're hardly interesting enough to warrant bugged phones and hidden security cameras for when your father visited. Perhaps the people who buy your house after you're gone will discover the hidden cameras inside the house, too.* It was her father, Didier who really fascinated me, and in finding Cleo, I had won the lottery. As the saying goes, I played her like a fiddle. I reaped as my rewards convenient housing and access to one of the world's premier spies. And he will be after me with a vengeance when he finds his daughter is dead. He will know it was me as I will be gone on a plane tonight, before the bombs detonate tomorrow at noon. It will take him ten minutes to figure it out.

She'll be coming 'round the mountain when she comes. Here she is, huffing and puffing in that tight, tacky, little pink bike outfit. One thing I won't miss about Cleo Gallier is all the goddamn pink. That's another thing I won't have to worry about when I'm back in Manila—the Filipinos aren't big on pastels. I always looked like such a fool riding around with this ridiculous woman in pink. But she gave me the celebrity status I needed at the start. The guards at Pearl Harbor loved that I was her friend and as a local celebrity myself, I was in. I was the local who had come in ninth in the 2010 Ironman Contest—the only local to be in the top ten, and I came in eleventh the two years before that. I needed to calm my anger as I watched the infidels doing nothing but lie on the beach in bikinis and drink while they played video games. I calmed my violence by running and swimming and biking, and the Islanders loved that I wasn't flying in to compete but that I lived here. I was always high fived and given free meals, free coffee. Several times I suggested to Cleo she buy a more serious color—black or navy blue—but she just laughed at me. Good riddance... She'll be walking around hell with all the rest of the infidels covered from head to toe in pink. Fashionable even in the afterlife.

Cleo is smiling at me, trying to diffuse the obvious tension between us. Lightening and softening everything, she always was so good at that. *Was.* I look casual even in the face of being her executioner, ever the good soldier. The past fifteen miles have not been kind to her already weakened body. Cleo giving next year's Ironman a try, what a laugh! Maybe I've underestimated her humor... Even from over here, twelve feet away, I can see her hands and feet quaking. She definitely knows. Her brush with death with the Beetle and the truck was only a premonition of things to come. The perfect warm-up for the main event.

"Wow, I can't remember the last time I felt so exhausted." She sighs, as she drops her bike.

"Well, you did have quite a scare..."

We look at each other briefly, but then look away just as quickly. I stand in the shadows as Cleo comes to me, waiting like a black widow for her to get caught in my sticky web. She's still grinning like a fool as she walks closer and closer, ten and then nine feet away. She was always smiling, that one. Perhaps I will miss her smile... Nearer and nearer she comes. I stand up straight and close in on her. We stand there for a moment, just staring at each other like two sad people who know they're never going to see each other again.

"You know I hate to do this..."

"Hate to do what, Jimbo?" she asks so innocently, as if trying to discourage her murder with docility.

"You really want me to say it?" I grab her arm.

Cleo's eyes lock into mine, the sweet smile disappears from her face and suddenly, I feel intense pain in my groin and then my stomach.

Chapter Forty-Nine
December 24, 2011

TRIPP

"Where are you going?"

As I hustle back to the hotel, I see Miranda walking gingerly from the pool to the parking lot. I notice Rico keeping an eye on her from a safe distance. She turns around, smiles when she sees me coming, and slows to a stop.

"Oh, just to the parking lot. Surprise, surprise, once again I left my sunglasses in the Jeep." She laughs. "Where's Matt?" Miranda looks behind me.

"I left him on the beach. He's fine." Marcus will stay on him.

"Are you? You look a little—" Miranda takes a step toward me and goes to touch my cheek.

"I'm fine. It's just—"

"Let me guess. The infamous China deal?"

"Yup. Hey, let me get your glasses. I could use another walk anyway," I offer like a good, doting husband. Or really, like an undercover CIA agent who needs to report a major break in his case immediately.

"Also, have you heard from Jake? He still isn't back yet," she calls out after me.

My heart sinks. I shake my head, hurry toward the open-air parking lot, whip out my cell phone and dial. Every second counts. A million thoughts are bouncing around in my head as I scan the crowded parking lot for our dented Jeep Cherokee. Not least of all, where the fuck is Jake? If Cleo so much as touches a hair on his—.

"Castillo, listen to me. I know where Mohammed planted the bombs."

"Go ahead, sir."

"The paper inside Ocampo's throat is a map of Mamala Bay. And in Mamala Bay, there's Pearl Harbor. And the Arizona. Those are likely to be the targets, don't you think?"

"Could be. Either way, I'm dispatching SWAT to both locations. Can never be too safe with JI."

"I can meet 'em there," I suggest, finally laying eyes on the dented Jeep.

"No, sir, I'm gonna ask that you hang tight for now. Let SWAT do its thing."

Ding-ding-ding. The rear Cherokee door beeps in my ear while I turn over tennis racquets, golf clubs, and magazines in search of Miranda's Burberry tortoise shells. Now I know why Jake didn't want to get rid of the rental—this dent is the beginning of his affair with Cleo. No sunglasses. My eyes drift over to the cup holder, which has a few coffee stains around the rim. Bingo. My left hand is reaching for them when I notice it. The back of my oldest son's head in the driver's seat.

"Jesus Christ! Jake?!"

He doesn't move a muscle. Doesn't say a word. I slam the rear door, go around the back, open the passenger side—*ding-ding-ding*—and hop in the car next to Jake.

"What are you doing?" It's stifling in here and so I crack a window. Jake is soaked in sweat. If the artery in the side of his neck wasn't pulsating, I'd think my son was dead.

We sit there in silence for at least a minute. Jake doesn't even acknowledge me. I know my sons. Ricky doesn't take much cajoling. If something's going on with him, I'll ask what it is and it'll pour out of his mouth like Niagara Falls. No ego there. Ricky's the easy one. And with Matt, I wouldn't even have to ask. He wouldn't even be sitting in the damn Jeep to begin with. He'd come and give me a full diatribe on whatever was on his mind. But not Jake. Like his old man, Jake takes massaging, coaxing, and convincing.

"Wanna talk about it?" I finally ask him at a half-whisper.

For thirty seconds, Jake doesn't react. He just sits there staring at the huge palm tree in front of us as if it's got North Korea's nuclear launch codes etched onto it.

"Fuuuuuck," he musters eventually. It isn't so much a word as it is a grunt—guttural and carnal.

Cleo. It has to be Cleo. I let Jake take his time, giving him the space he needs to eventually feel safe enough to confide in me. If I panic or smother him with questions the way his mother does, Jake will retreat like a rattlesnake into a dark, dank coal mine. It's then that I glance down and notice that both of his hands are shaking. They're gripping his knees and have turned the color of snow like he was on the world's fastest rollercoaster. But I stick to the plan. Calm, cool, collected.

"That bad?" I ask with an air of deliberate detachment.

"Yeah, Dad. *That bad.*"

Deliberate detachment works wonders on him.

"I..." Jake starts. "I—I just witnessed a fucking murder."

This, I was not expecting. *Cleo just broke things off. Julia just broke things off. I just broke things off with one of them. With both of them.* Not this.

"A murder? What? Are you sure?" I ask. I'm still calm, cool, collected even though my concern for my son's mental state has reached new highs.

He nods several times. "You heard me," he says with firmness in his voice.

"Okay. You wanna tell me what happened?"

For the first time since our little car rendezvous began, Jake's eyes meet with mine. He's staring at me and it's as if he's eight years old all over again. He's looking at me with those big blue eyes, pleading for some sort of fatherly advice as if we're back at little league and he doesn't know whether to pitch a fastball, curveball, or breaking ball. My son has gone with option two—the curveball.

He breaks eye contact and starts to stutter.

"Okay... So, I guess I was feelin' kinda jealous about Cleo not canceling her lame bike ride with that Jimbo dude she can't seem to shut the hell up about. She mentioned they were going to bike over to some place called the Koolah Cliffs. So, fuck it... I drove over there, camped out, and waited for them to bike past."

Jake glances over at me again as if to say, *I know. Not my greatest moment.* I give him a quick nod, encouraging him to continue.

"So, I get outta the car and hide in this like, wooded area, waiting for them. About forty minutes later, they show up. She gave me these binoculars at the Banzai Pipeline, so I used them to see pretty clearly. Anyway, I see Jimbo first. He's a few yards ahead of her but he stops at the side of the road and waits there for her. When Cleo catches up to him, she drops her bike and makes a beeline right for him. He meets her halfway and then takes her arm. They got so close that for a second there, I thought she was gonna fucking kiss this asshole. I was about to run over there and cold cock him. But it turned out there was no need because have no fear... she didn't kiss him, Dad. She did the fucking opposite."

The opposite?

Jake doesn't look over at me again. He takes a few short, deep breaths before he continues. "Cleo... she—she fucking pushed him over the cliff!"

I had a terrible feeling Jake was going to say something like that.

"Yeah, you heard me, Dad. She. Pushed. Him. Over. The cliff! She did some sort of fucking karate move I've never even seen before and then pushed him over the cliff like he was made outta paper!"

Krav Maga, the Israeli defense system. That's what she used to push Jimbo over the cliff. According to Cleo, she is a master at Krav Maga. On Kilimanjaro, she told me many things about her life and I never forgot a single detail. Especially something like this, which seemed so incongruous with her chichi upbringing, fancy boarding schools, and glamorous vacations. I always got a chuckle picturing her suited up in pink shin guards and strike gloves duking it out with some poor instructor. Obviously, she is a master at it.

"Then, after, she went to his bike, looked around for cars, and then she threw that over too. Like she was getting rid of evidence or some shit, you know what I mean? And then, *then*, she just turned around and pedaled away on her stupid bike as if nothing fucking happened. As if shoving a human being over a cliff is some normal thing! Like, hey, it's Tuesday, you know what that means! Someone's getting shoved off a cliff!"

Jake is starting to spiral out of control. But I let him finish spinning his yarn.

"I shit you not, Dad, I literally looked over my shoulder—not once, not twice, but like, a hundred times to see if I'd just gotten *Punk'd*. I waited to see if Jimbo was gonna somehow reappear alive and well like it was just some weird, fucked-up game of theirs. But he never did."

Jimbo. Didn't Cleo say Jimbo's last name was Isom? Jimbo Isom. JI. *Holy shit*. Cleo said that he's American and has been on the island for four years. *Jimbo is Mohammad Abdul Rahman*. Cleo, about sixty-nine inches and one hundred and twenty pounds, killed one of Al Qaeda's deadliest members with her bare hands. She has to be involved, she just has to be. What if he betrayed her and she made him pay for it with his life? Or maybe she was the one who betrayed him and she killed him before he could kill her?

"So, after hiding on the ground for a solid fifteen minutes," Jake goes on, "after I thought the coast was clear, I finally forced myself to crawl on my hands and knees back over to the car because I was afraid that if she saw me I'd be delicate, innocent Cleo's next victim. My hands were shaking so fuck-ing much it took me a while to even start the car." Jake's voice is shaky and unsteady. Nothing like the confident, cocksure son I know and raised.

I know my son is right about what he witnessed, but I can't let him know that. He has to believe that his mind is playing tricks on him, that there's some sort of logical explanation or else his life is in serious danger. Al Qaeda will hunt my son down if they find out that he's just borne witness to one of their leader's executions. But still… I stay calm, cool, collected, which I'm not.

"Jake, was there a road that he could've gone down to? Or, maybe there was a ledge beneath the cliff? Or even, what if—and I'm not making excuses here—what if this really is just a weird thing they do when they get to that place? I mean, I don't know Cleo very well but I can't exactly picture her as a stone-cold killer, can you?"

Jake starts shaking again, "No, Dad. You don't get it. She pushed him off that cliff like it was nothing. And I could see his face from the woods—homeboy did not see it coming. He looked stunned."

I get goosebumps as I remember Cleo on Kilimanjaro the night she told me about being raped as a child. *Krav Maga, the Israeli self-defense. I study and work at it every day, Danny. No one can hurt me again. There is no one I can't defend myself against. And no one knows I study it. No one knows what I am capable of.*

At the time, I remember sort of laughing it off and going along with it to be polite.

Jake looks at me again with those big, blue pleading eyes. I have to convince him that he didn't see what thinks he did.

"There has to be some sort of explanation—"

"Jesus, Dad, you're not listening!"

"I am, Jake. I promise. Okay. Maybe just text her and see what she says. Get a read on her state of mind," I suggest.

Jake looks at me suspiciously. I give him another encouraging nod. He picks up his phone and tries to work his fingers across the Apple keypad, but they're shaking too hard.

"Jesus fucking Christ..." Jake mutters as he hands the phone to me, unable to write the message himself.

"Hey... what... are... you... up... to..." I read aloud as my fingers fly across the keypad. I look over to Jake for his approval. "Seems pretty innocuous, right?"

Jake nods. I send the message. Within seconds, his phone pings.

Jeez, way to play hard to get, Cleo...

Jake jumps and glances down at the phone. A stunned look works its way across his face as he reads her response to himself. "Oh, this is rich. You'll love this..." Jake says, his eyes super-glued to his iPhone. "She is quote, *'baking cookies.'* Baking cookies, Dad. How fucking quaint?! Fucking Betty Crocker over here!"

Jake's phone pings again.

"What's it say?"

"Jesus... She's wondering if we want to come over for Christmas Eve *eggnog* before dinner."

Jake flashes his phone at me, as if I needed proof, and I read the text for myself.

Interesting. She obviously has no clue that Jake saw what she did, but even so, inviting a family you don't know too well over for Christmas Eve after you've just murdered your best friend is questionable behavior. Could she be planning to use us as alibis? Even now, I'm sure she could ask Jake to dive head first off the Empire State Building and he'd comply. Could Castillo have been wrong? Could Cleo be a deep undercover agent? A deep undercover agent hellbent on exacting revenge on the man who broke her heart eight years ago? With Mohammed Abdul Rahman likely dead, there's much less urgency to get my family off this island. Once Jake heads back to the hotel, I'll call the agency and tell them to cancel the chartered plane. An invitation to Cleo's house gives me all sorts of access.

"Say 'yes.'"

"Dad, for real?"

I nod. Jake types his response.

"Okay..." I say calmly. "We'll stop by on our way to dinner tonight. I don't mean to belittle what you think you saw, but maybe your mind was playing tricks on you. It happens. I'll make some calls and see if Jimbo's been reported missing. I'll have the police check out his house and I'll let you know what they find, sound good? Maybe it's just some new fangled training method, or something. He jumps off a cliff and gets on a mountain bike... I don't know. From what Cleo says, this guy sounds like a total freak about this Ironman shit."

Jake looks over at me and snorts a laugh.

"Yeah, that's a nice thought, Dad. But I know what I saw. She pushed Jimbo over that cliff. And now, she's baking cookies! La-dee-fucking-da!"

"How about you go in and shower and I'll go ahead and call the cops. And I'll tell you what, if he isn't there, I'll call your room right away. No, I'll call you either way; and if he is not there, we won't go to Cleo's."

As soon as Jake is out of the car, I call headquarters and tell them I have reason to believe Mohammad Abdul Rahman has been terminated. I won't know for sure though, until a few hours later.

Cleo must be an undercover agent, too, and she just killed one of the world's deadliest terrorists with nothing more than her hands.

Chapter Fifty
December 24, 2011

CLEO

I put on the red satin Valentino my mother gave me on my twenty-first birthday on Christmas Eve. She gave Beebe and Tree each one in green for their blonde hair.

"It's important to have traditions, especially at Christmas, so I'm starting you three out with beautiful dresses. And since Cleo's birthday is Christmas too, she also gets a pin of rubies, diamonds, and emeralds in the shape of a wreath."

On my thirtieth birthday, my father gave me beautiful emerald earrings that I wish I could wear all the time. As I do every Christmas Eve, I put the whole ensemble on. With memories of my mother, sister, and my father, it's always my favorite outfit of the year.

This year's tree is especially enormous and takes up quite a bit of space in the living room. The trees I get each year seem to have distinct personalities. Some are like alcoholics—they drink nonstop; some are like this one—pushy, taking over the entire room, seeming to grow while I sleep. My favorite tree was my first Christmas in Hawaii. She was a very thin one and oh so shy. When I decorated her, she blossomed and twinkled and smelled so wonderful, rewarding me for making her lovely.

I shiver, thinking back to only a week ago when Jimbo was here, alive and thriving, striding around my living room looking at all of my decorations. Jimbo was never one for holidays, but seeing as Christmas is December 25th, he at least didn't hate the day itself as it was his birthday, our birthday, and he loved to open his presents from me. But now I have to wonder if it really was his birthday, as nothing else he said to me was true. Maybe it was just another way for him to ingratiate himself to me.

Damn you, Jimbo. I already miss you, dearly. I know it was either you or me—you had to die or it would have been my bruised body at the bottom of that cliff. Were there small clues along the way to who you really were? That you had a secret life as an Al Qaeda leader will always be impossible for me to grasp. All those times we spent together, were you detesting and resenting me? My womanly figure on display in sundresses and bathing suits and tight bike outfits must have disgusted you. Did you just use me as a cover while all you really wanted was to wrap your big, strong hands around my neck each time I regaled you with stories about boarding school and being on a yacht in St. Barths? The memories keep flooding back to me. You should be here right now making fun of my love of Christmas decorations, stubbornly limiting yourself to only one measly sugar cookie. I walk to my jewelry box and pull out the Ironman medal you won last year and presented me with. You were so loyal, I thought. But now I know it was all just a front.

"You're an oldie but a goodie, Cleo!" Oh, I will miss your good-byes. I am on a seesaw of missing my friend and hating you for being a traitor and for being willing to kill me. I start to shake all over again just thinking of that moment and the stunned look on your face as you went over. I know you were working for Jemaah Islamiyah but I have no idea what you were going to do here. I will call my father. His intelligence agency tops any other and he will know. I can't stand up, the shock of the last few hours setting in. As I was dressing tonight, I thought I had no regrets, but now I feel so nauseous as I pick up my cell phone.

"Ah, mon petit chou chou. Happy almost birthday!"

I hate when he calls me his little cabbage. Cabbages are round and cute and I am neither.

"Thank you, Daddy." My voice is edgy.

"Do you have plans for the night? I hope you're wearing your lovely red dress and my earrings?"

"I am..."

I am nervous to tell my father about Jimbo and what I have done to him. I never want to let him down and I worry that he'll be disappointed in me for not figuring out Jimbo's true identity earlier on. He taught me so much better than this. He'll be horrified by the thought of his sweet, precious daughter as a killer.

"Wonderful. Tell me what you have planned."

"Oh, I'm just having a family I met recently over for egg-nog. The Regans, who are spending their Christmas vacation here all the way from New York."

My father says nothing. Didier is only silent when he's working something out in his head. This is my moment. I have to tell him about Jimbo.

"Daddy, I—"

"Mon petit chou chou..." he interrupts. "Tell me more about these Regans?"

"Oh, they're just a nice family I met. But Daddy, the reason I called is I need to tell you something about Jimbo."

"Please, just entertain your father on Christmas Eve."

I knew Didier was going to do this. Whenever I have had something urgent to tell him, he gravitates toward small talk. Sometimes it's best to let him have some of that.

"Alright, but then you have to listen about Jimbo, okay?" He agrees.

So, I tell him, "The parents, Tripp and Miranda, are in their fifties, I'd guess. Both very nice. He's a lawyer and she's one of those loving, professional mothers. But it is their son Jake, whom I especially like. He and I got into a car acci—" I catch myself.

"Yes, go on, Cleopatra,"

"No, really, this is not why I called. I have something to tell you about Jimbo. It's important." I pause for his reaction.

"Very well then. Tell me about Jimbo."

Here I go. I start pacing around the room.

"I killed him," I say for the very first time aloud. I pause for my father's reaction.

"What? Why, Cleo?"

"He was about to kill me! It was after our bike ride at the cliffs. Presumably, you know about Jemaah Islamiyah? They're—"

"Slow down, Cleopatra. Tell me what happened."

I take a breath. "Jimbo—my friend and neighbor, Jimbo Isom—was an Al Qaeda leader. And so I killed him."

"You're absolutely positive?"

"That he was Al Qaeda? Yes, Daddy! Tripp Regan said—well, it's a long story, but I know Jimbo was. If I hadn't pushed him off the Koolah Cliffs, he'd have pushed me!"

"Did you use your Krav Maga?"

"Yes, of course." I continue to pace around my living room, circling my couch for the fourth time.

"Let me see if I've got this right. He was going to kill you, presumably because he realized you had figured out his identity, but you managed to kill him first?"

"Yes." I pause for his reaction again.

"Your Krav Maga served you well then. All those years of practice. And of course Jimbo had no idea of your defense weapon."

"So, you're not angry?" I stop pacing for a moment and pause by the bar.

"Cleopatra, you're alive. Of course I'm not angry. If Jimbo was JI, then he deserved to die. No one saw you, did they?"

"No, I was very careful." I start pacing again, catching my reflection in the gilded mirror.

"Very good. I'll make contact with my side and see what I can muster up. I mean, Cleopatra, Jemaah Islamiyah… my God. I don't know how I missed this; I feel partially responsible."

"No, it's alright. He was my best friend for the last four years. How would you know? You never even met him. Interesting he was always busy when you were here, isn't it? That should have told me something."

"It doesn't matter now, but I should have realized as well. I should have looked into your 'neighbor.' You remember what happened to Richard Rensasslear, of course?"

"Yes, Daddy."

"Leave it to me. I will do everything in my power to make this right. Are you alright, Cleopatra? I don't like hearing you like this. Please remember you did what you had to. It was either you or him. You understand that?"

I nod even though my father can't see me. "Yes. I did what I had to."

"And now, I'm afraid I've got some bad news for you, Cleopatra." He pauses. "It's about Tripp Regan, actually."

I start to sit on my white couch, the same couch where Jake pulled me onto his lap before we made love for the very first time, but Tripp's name jolts me up. My heart rate instantly picks up; *pump, pump, pump.* And I start to pace around the room all over again.

"He..." My father pauses again. "He is an undercover CIA operative... And... well, he had a black op in Africa."

No.

"Under the name of Danny Mortimer. It was compromised and Danny Mortimer had to feign a plane crash. Danny Mortimer is Tripp Regan."

I don't say a word. I can't breathe.

"Cleopatra?"

"You cannot be serious. Why would you even say something like that?!" I scream. I want to scream so much louder. But some part of me, deep down, knows my father is telling the truth. Now it makes sense, now I understand why both Tripp and Jake seem so familiar to me on a deeper level. Jake is the son of a man I once loved. And Tripp, that bastard, is the man I once loved.

"Because I'm afraid that it's true."

"How long have you known this?"

"Well..." He pauses. "For a while, but you must trust me that there was no reason to tell you before. But now, I wish I had..."

And now I am furious with my father. I'm suddenly dizzy. My vision becomes spotty and my heart rate accelerates.

He had his teeth capped. That was the only thing that comes to my mind.

"I know this is a terribly insensitive way to tell you, Cleopatra."

"I have to go."

"Cleopatra, please. Stay with me on the phone. Let's talk about this."

"No, I have to get the house ready, but I am *fine*. Just absolutely *fine!*" I smile. I'm borderline hysteric.

I have to get off the phone immediately.

"Yes, Cleopatra, I know you will be fine. But, listen to me, I'm worried about your safety."

I stare at my Christmas tree. My life was so much simpler before this tree was here. I hadn't met Jake, Jimbo was alive, and Danny Mortimer was dead.

"Daddy, I'll be fine. But really, I have to go."

"Wait a minute, Cleopatra. I want you to remember that you killed Jimbo in self-defense. You said it yourself, he was a terrorist. But now you need to be very careful that his AQ cell doesn't know you did it and come after you. I can get on a plane right now, or better yet, you get on a plane to me."

"No, it's fine. I'll be fine. I will stay with our plan and come see you the day after Christmas. I haven't been to Dubai in years. Let's meet there as we planned. Please?"

"Yes, yes, of course. But Cleo, really, I'm worried about you there all alone in that big house. Can you go stay with Pudge and Pudding tonight?"

"I am not alone. I told you, the Regans are coming over shortly. And no one knows I killed Jimbo. No one saw us. No one came by. When they find him at the bottom of the cliff, it will look as if he skidded off the road and over the cliff. Okay, Daddy, I'll see you in Dubai," I tell my father and get off the phone.

I'm shaking. In one single day, I have killed my best friend and found out that the man I loved so long ago and whose death I've mourned ever since has been alive all this time with a family and a job in New York City. I walk over to my bar in the corner of the room and pour myself a huge vodka and tonic. How could Tripp keep asking me about Danny? The nerve. How dare he deceive me all these years. Jimbo isn't the only person who deserves to die today. Danny Mortimer is a black op and the father of the boy who has liberated me sexually. I start laughing and crying hysterically, merging them together just like Danny and Tripp.

The fact that Danny Mortimer is alive and about to walk into my house trumps everything, even Jimbo's death. Tripp knows who I am. What a shock he must have had when he saw his old love from the mountain, on a beach frolicking with his eldest son. I hope it drives him absolutely crazy that I am having a fabulous affair with Jake. I wonder if he was scared I would somehow recognize him or maybe he was just so sure of himself that he didn't give it a second's thought. Damn him for wanting to hear all about Danny on our run. He must not only be in Honolulu for a vacation, but also for Jimbo too. Jimbo, oh, Jimbo. He was so stunned when I turned on him. My training had finally found a worthy opponent in him. And now, my next opponent is Tripp Regan.

Danny is Tripp. And Danny is fucking alive. And Tripp is married and has three sons, and yet as Danny, he acted as though he was in love with me. How could he pretend he loved me and be married? Well, like father, like son. He is just like Jake, who made love to me while he never even mentioned his girlfriend... What a brilliant op if I never recognized him. How well he played Danny Mortimer, with his blonde ponytail and his Southern drawl and that loping gait. And he capped the little holes in his teeth. How well he played me. But he doesn't know Jimbo is dead. And I do. I will set up Jimbo's photo for him to see and worry about. And Tripp doesn't know I know who he is, that is my advantage. Oh, I loathe you Danny and Tripp. I loathe you.

But I love my country and I will do anything to protect it.

Chapter Fifty-One
December 24, 2011

JULIA

*A*rchitectural *Digest?*

For the longest time, I thought Jake was under the impression that *Architectural Digest* was an art history class that I took at The Sorbonne. *Her house looks like something straight out of Architectural Digest!* As we all climbed into the car on the way here, I heard Miranda excitedly whisper that to Tripp. I remember that was the proclamation Jake made to us all when we were in the car enroute to Cleo's Outrigger Canoe Club my first night here. That should have been my first clue. Comparatively, it would be like if I had suddenly rattled off Eli Manning's passing statistics. I vividly remember this one time when he was over at our friends Jen and Greg's apartment. They have this gorgeous butler's pantry that I'd give my left ear for. I was supposed to meet Jake there after work but ended up getting held up at the office doing expense reports for my saint of a boss. I dreamed of having a pantry just like theirs one day, so I wanted to snap a few reference photos for when Jake and I eventually rented our very own apartment (with both of our names actually on the lease, this time).

JULIA

For most of our relationship, I'd always been schlepping my stuff back and forth from my apartment to his. We always stayed at his. He didn't like "away games." By now, we all know that future apartment exists on a mystical island along with Tinkerbell and a peplum top that doesn't make me look fat. So, it occurred to me while I was stuck at the office to text Jake and ask if he could take the pictures for me.

His response: "Sure, babe. Just one problem... What the hell's a butler's pantry?" Such a typical guy. *I am alpha male, hear me roar.*

Jake has barely glanced in my direction nor uttered my name since the now infamous necklace episode of December 23rd, 2011. At this point, it's comical how he makes such a concerted effort to ensure he's sitting at the exact opposite end of the table, or how he scampers off to take the far back seat of the car with Matt. The cat is out of the bag and the jig is officially up. And tonight something seems *especially* up with him. All through the car ride, Miranda keeps asking Jake inane questions to join in on the conversation but he hardly says one word. Not one word.

At the wheel, Mr. Regan has already turned left through a pair of gates and heads up what appears to be a never ending driveway. Suddenly, I feel my nose tingle and the warm liquid pool in the corners of my eyes. I immediately turn and face the window, away from all the Regans.

My mother, Constance, died from lung cancer when I was only four, so the only memories I have of her are from the wonders of technology. The only reason I know how she looks and what her voice sounds like is because of a VHS camcorder that was strapped to my father's shoulder during the last few years of her short life. From the celluloid versions, she reminds me of Natalie Wood, had Natalie been taller and without much of a fashion sense. Her name is anything but accurate. Constance. Constant is the very last thing she was. According to my poor, grieving father, one minute she was fine and the next, she wasn't. What I'd give to talk to her in times like these. *You'll never guess what Jake did, Mom... Mommy, I need your help. If you were me, Mom, what would you do?* I like to think that she'd always know exactly what to say and exactly what to do. She'd always know precisely what drink was called for during any given crisis. When I was a kid, I imagine she would have known that warm chocolate milk would have been just the thing to help me sleep. When I was a confused, insecure teenager, the bubbles and cherry hints in Diet Dr. Pepper always had a strange way of lifting my spirits and so I know she'd always have our refrigerator stocked. And when I broke up with my first boyfriend in London after those weird, transitional years out of college, my mother would have a big glass of rosé (with ice) waiting without me even having to ask. Oh, Constance. How I wish you could've lived up to your name. But, I digress...

Unless you count Mai Tai's with Marta, I haven't shed a real tear over Jake yet. I quickly wipe them away and take a deep breath. The property finally comes into focus.

"I'm surprised she has such intense security," Mr. Regan muses, eyeing the row of "hidden" security cameras that line her driveway.

I wonder if her obsession with security cameras has something to do with stealing other girls' boyfriends. I'd be scared if I was a homewrecker too. Maybe I can unionize with the other women she's screwed over and put together some sort of street gang. "The Outsiders" in heels. Let's kill her, girls. Let's burn her at the stake like the angry townspeople of Salem did to the witches. The only difference is Cleo (by the way, this can no longer be ignored... but *Cleo?* Stupidest name ever) is actually not guilty of "witchcraft," but of having no regard for her fellow woman. What happened to the spirit of the sisterhood? Didn't Grandma grow up in the first feminist era with Susan B. Anthony and Elizabeth Cady Stanton? Another fun option could be tar and feather... The searing hot tar burning her entire perfect body—*okay, chill, Julia. You're veering into "Single White Female" territory.* I must admit that's a pretty heartwarming image though—Cleo covered head to toe in black tar and fluffy feathers.

I accidentally let out a little giggle. Ricky turns to me expectantly.

"Sorry. Just... Never mind."

I looked into flights again earlier today but this weather continues to ground nearly all airplanes over the Pacific. I thought typhoons were just mystical meteorological phenomenons that really only existed in disaster movies to take out the likes of the Empire State Building and the Eiffel Tower. But apparently not. I looked at tickets from all airlines on Kayak, Expedia, and Priceline to literally *anywhere but here*, but nothing was flying out. Nothing. For about five minutes, I briefly considered calling in the coast guard. Then I realized I was being insane. I needed to be a big girl and suck it up. Before we came here, Miranda called my room and said she completely understood if I wanted to skip drinks at Cleo's and just meet us at the restaurant for dinner. And if I wasn't even up for dinner, that was more than fine and she would see me tomorrow on Christmas. I appreciated the gesture, though knowing Miranda, she was probably just trying to avoid any further drama. I certainly considered ditching. But then, something else came over me. *Nobody puts Baby in the corner.* The Regans invited me on this trip, Goddamn it. Jake had been my boyfriend for two years. I haven't done anything wrong (if you don't count lunch yesterday). It may be her turf but I have every right to be here, to hold my head up high and not be intimidated by some geriatric local talk show host.

When we arrive at Cleo's house, I reluctantly go to unbuckle my seatbelt and Ricky, next to me, does the same. Our fingers happen to graze. *Whoa.* Electricity. I wonder if he felt it too... I pull away fast but I loved that jolt. I needed that jolt. We lock eyes and there's the slightest smile on his face too as he gets out of the car. I snap out of it and look at the house. *Damn.* Even I have to admit, the old bag's house is pretty spectacular. Mr. Regan presses a buzzer; the green-shuttered French doors unlock, and he holds them open for Miranda and me. We enter a big courtyard and my eyes are immediately violated by bright white flowering trees glittering with white lights. Big whoop, it's basically a bleached blonde version of Rockefeller Center at Christmas. Bitch, if you want to live in the city so badly, why don't you just move there? Actually, scratch that. Stay far away from us, devil woman.

"This reminds me of a house in Marrakesh," Mr. Regan observes.

"We've never been there," says Miranda, looking offended.

He takes a deep breath, as if suppressing some level of annoyance, and forces a fake smile. "Miranda. *Travel Channel.*"

Oh, goodie. I think everyone's finally getting as touchy as I've been since midyesterday. *Come on in, guys. Join the club. It's warm inside. And we have cookies.* We enter the house and there she is. The devil wears Valentino. She's also wearing earrings that cost more than my education. *FML.* Suddenly, my Brock Collection frock doesn't feel as fabulous. The barrenness and over-the-top perfection of the house is stunning. Unlike her reputation, everything here is pristine and pearly white. Even the roses, from Jake no doubt. Someone once told me, probably Matt, that a name for one of the white roses is 'iceberg.' Seems fitting for Lady Devil—you only see a nice, tiny part of an iceberg on the surface, but underneath, they're deadly. I must say her tree is lovely and all those presents... I should steal a few and punish her. She's already stolen something very dear from me. Call it even.

Cleo smiles. "What can I get everyone to drink? Champagne? Eggnog?"

Arsenic?

Ricky sidles up to me and hands me a drink. "Sadly, Cleo's out of Mai Tais..."

"Shut up." I nudge him flirtatiously.

After golf, Ricky and I decided to meet for a drink half an hour before we were to leave for Lady Devil's. We laughed and laughed and laughed.

"I think the phrase you're looking for, Miss Turner, is actually, 'why, thank you!'"

I smile and take a big sip of the eggnog, pretending to ignore him. Then, finally, I smile. "Thank you..."

"... Ricky, you handsome devil, you."

We both laugh.

"That's what you were gonna say anyway, right?"

"Sure, something like that..."

"I'll be back," he whispers into my ear. He's so close I can smell his Old Spice. Original scent, same as Jake's. It's my favorite smell in the whole, wide world. Sometimes, when Jake wasn't around, I'd take a whiff of his deodorant just to feel close to him. Okay, yeah, I need help...

Left alone, I turn to one wall that's doubling as her own private Sotheby's with all the paintings displayed perfectly with little spotlights over them. These paintings can't be real.

They're most likely fakes, just like Cleo. And if they are real, they belong in a museum. Also just like Cleo. A mummified Cleopatra in the Egyptian wing. Okay, sorry. I swear, I'm a good person...

I catch Jake looking at the mistletoe. He hasn't spoken to anyone and looks scared to death.

Matt warns him, "mistletoe is a parasitic plant and the berries are poisonous. Better be careful, big brother."

That seems to paralyze Jake even more than he is already. *High five to Matty.*

I step closer to Miranda and Cleopatra who are mooning over old photos.

"Where was this taken, Cleo?" Miranda asks, picking up one.

"Corsica." Cleo smiles.

We get it, bitch. You're worldly.

"Oh, look at your dimples! How cute!" Miranda points to one of Cleo as a baby. "You must've gotten them from your mother. All your sisters seem to have them too... Oh, and how precious. These aren't yours are they, Cleo?"

Miranda picks up a photo of two young boys. If I had to guess, they're probably eight and ten.

"Oh, no. Those are actually my sister, Tree's."

Hold the phone. Her sister's name is Tree? You can't make this shit up, people.

"Well, aren't they just adorable..."

"Yes, they are." Cleo smiles.

"They remind me of you and Matt when you were their age, Jake," Miranda adds, nudging her first born.

"Which wasn't that long ago!" I spit out.

All three of them turn to me, thrown by my sudden outburst. I force an awkward laugh. Miranda shoots me a smile and I think she's secretly proud that I'm starting to stand up for myself. The three of them turn back to the photo gallery.

"I'm assuming you don't have any children of your own, Cleo?" Miranda asks.

"Sadly not." Her eyes are downcast. She's lost in thought. Well, wait a gosh darn second here. Is that... Is that a speck of vulnerability I see? Could it be that the great and powerful Cleopatra Virunia Petunia Princess Buttercup Gallier has emotions and regrets like an actual human? JK about her middle names. They sound fitting though.

"May I ask why not?"

"Well, I guess...I guess I just never met my Marc Antony," Cleo answers and smiles/glares across the room at Mr. Regan. Weird.

I'm impressed with her honesty. She could've fudged the truth and made up some B.S. about never wanting kids as most childless women of a certain age do. Part of me feels sorry for her. Not that I want to start popping out kids tomorrow, but if I wanted to, at least it's an option.

Miranda doesn't let it go. "That's too bad. Having children is the greatest joy anyone could ever experience."

Jeez, Miranda. Way to twist the knife. Aha, maybe this is why she wanted to come... To find some way to repay Cleo for ruining our vacation.

"Yes, I'm sure it's very fulfilling. I would have really loved them." Cleo smiles.

I turn and head toward the door. I need to get outside, away from this insanity. As I get closer to the doorway, I feel a hand—Ricky's hand—on my arm, and another jolt of electricity courses through my body as he leads me back to the entryway. He stops in front of the arch.

"Merry Christmas, Jules," he says in a hushed voice.

JULIA

I look up at the mistletoe, that wonderful parasitic plant. He kisses me and I kiss him. And, *wow.* The thought that Cleo did this on purpose crosses my mind. Did she deliberately help me get away from Jake to be with Ricky? Something is seriously up with this island. We kiss again.

Merry Christmas to moi.

Chapter Fifty-Two
December 24, 2011

MIRANDA

I am glad we are going to Cleo's house before dinner. I know it sounds crazy, but I need to understand how she is capable of taking over Jake's life. Before this vacation, he was so in love with Julia. For heaven's sake, I thought he was almost ready to propose. And that was just four days ago. And on top of that mess, what was going on with Tripp and Cleo baffled me, and it even scared me. I want to know where this Cleo eats, sleeps, and does whatever the heck else she does.

Driving over, Tripp and Jake are in weird moods, foggy. The only time Tripp sprung to life during cocktail hour at the hotel was during a discussion about Pele, the goddess of the volcano.

Matt parroted Cleo's mythology report from the night at the Outrigger to his father, who finally perked up. When my mother was alive, she'd had a fascination with all the Roman gods and goddesses and would sometimes dominate our dinner discussions with tales about Jupiter, Venus, and the panoply of Mount Olympus gods. Tripp didn't exactly hide his boredom and would always find excuses to politely bow out during my mother's meanderings.

"Seconds, anyone?" "Can I refresh any drinks?" "I'll get a head start on these dishes."

But tonight, he's mesmerized.

The song "Danny Boy" is softly playing when we walk into Cleo's exquisite open-air house.

"Hello, Regans. Welcome." She sparkles.

"Thanks for having us. I like your taste in music," says Tripp.

"Oh, it's my favorite song."

He looks stunned. But why? Why would he care? My questions continue to multiply.

Cleo starts singing along as she leads us further inside. She's all dressed up in a red dress and emerald earrings like she's about to accept an Academy Award. Compared to her glamour, I look as if I've been at work all day in my garden. I feel like Alice in Wonderland, having just fallen through the rabbit hole into another dimension where all the rules are amorphous and keep changing on me. I brace myself, ready for Tweedledee and Tweedledum to pop out from behind the white-and-blue curtains.

Sizing up my competition, I peek around at all the luxury surrounding me. But it is Hawaii, after all. I bet it costs about the same as a one-bedroom apartment in the West Village. Listen to me… I've never had to compete for Tripp before, but I fear she may be checkmating me.

There's a Neoclassical marble-top table filled with silver framed photos. I head over to them for a closer look. The table is jammed with smiling faces and a huge mirror—also, Neoclassical—hangs above it with a frieze of Cleopatra on her throne in ancient Egypt. She's flanked by two huge black cats. Either Cleo has a wicked sense of humor or she's truly obsessed with herself.

"Who's this?" Tripp asks, pointing to a very handsome younger man in a photo.

Still humming "Danny Boy," Cleo blinks. "Oh, that's Jimbo. My friend and tenant that I told you about. The Ironman. You just missed him, actually."

Jake stares at her, his mouth having just dropped two flights of stairs. Tripp just stares at Jimbo's picture. What's going on with them? I glance over at the curtains, again bracing myself for the Tweedles to make their grand entrance.

Tripp seems unable to take his proverbial eyes off her. Jake, on the other hand, looks like he's in a trance.

"Does he do well in these competitions?" Tripp asks.

"Let's see... He's come in eleventh, ninth, ninth in the past three years. All he wants is to place in the top five. No one knows the island better than Jimbo Isom..." She seems to glare at Tripp, who hangs on her every word.

I feel completely invisible.

"Well, he's very handsome. How'd you and Jimbo meet?" I chime in, as if to remind my husband that I still have a pulse.

"We met about four years ago when he first came to live on the Island. He was working for a florist at the time and delivered a huge bouquet of flowers from my father. It was my birthday the next day and he told me it was his birthday then too. So, we celebrated together."

"Oh, yes, tomorrow," Tripp says, almost as a throwaway line.

Oh, yes, tomorrow? I must be hearing things. Did he see her birth date on the accident report? Had I missed some story at lunch about birthdays? Maybe she told him during their marathon run. It's Christmas, after all, so one would remember. Yes, I'm sure that's it. They had four hours to learn each other's birthdays.

"And, this... this is your father?" he asks, picking up another photo of a charismatic looking man in a blazer and turtleneck. I wonder if she only allows gorgeous people to be put in her heavy silver frames, banishing all the ugly creatures to the bathroom or guest rooms. Her father, who appears to be in his early seventies, looks like a French movie star with his exotic looks and cigarette hanging out of his mouth.

"It is. How did you guess?" Cleo asks, but with a bit of a nasty look directed at Tripp.

"Good looking man. Like father, like daughter."

I feel a little sick to my stomach.

"'Scuse me a second." Tripp takes his phone from out of his pocket and exits toward the back door.

"Cleo, I'd love a tour of your beautiful home."

With Tripp outside, this is a good time for me to look around. There must be a clue somewhere if she'd somehow known Tripp prior to this visit. And I'll know when I see it. I need to understand why he looked so shocked on the beach the day he first saw her, and how tonight, he knew her birthday. I doubt my husband has even the foggiest idea I suspect anything.

"Of course, Miranda. My house is your house. Help yourself." Cleo smiles graciously at me.

She's given me free rein to look anywhere I please. Cleo's quite busy twinkling at everyone, just like her perfectly decorated Christmas tree.

I smile, then wander off, doing my best Nancy Drew impression. I study every single face in every single photo. I look through her glamorous bedroom. What lovely furniture she has and such glamorous clothing. A pale green nightie that I wouldn't have dared to wear even in my twenties hangs on a bathroom hook. It's so flimsy and her high-heeled sandals at its feet are so dainty. I usually wear a graying, flannel nightie and socks to bed. Tripp doesn't seem to mind. I swing open the doors to her medicine cabinet and furiously pick up each bottle, identifying each label; she has all the same Kiehl products we have at home. I do full inventory on her makeup, her books, but don't find anything suspicious.

Growing up as a little girl, the Nancy Drew books were it for me. *The Bungalow Mystery, The Secret in the Old Attic, The Clue in the Crossword Cipher.* Each one better than the next. I could read an entire book in one sitting. But unlike my old friend Nancy, I never get to solve any real mysteries. *The Mystery of the Missing Wool Sock. The Clue to Removing An Ink Stain. The Secret to Hosting The Perfect Dinner Party.* These are the mysteries of my life. Trying to find a clue in Cleo's seemingly endless house, my adrenaline is pumping and I'm thriving on it.

I go to the wings that must be reserved for guests and find an entire man's wardrobe in one closet. Wonder who that man is… maybe her father. Or maybe this is just Cleo's collection of men and the item of clothing each left behind—a sweater here and a dress shirt there, culminating in an entire closet. I can't imagine leaving a pair of pants or a shoe. But it is Cleo after all.

Maybe I'm imagining this whole thing. Why didn't her beau, Jimbo, stay and have eggnog with us? I know it wasn't he who filled her living room and bedroom with all these white roses—they seem to be her own, personal symbol. I search for the card. Ah, there it is. It's signed "The Rude New Yorker." I see that my son has finally expanded his knowledge of flowers beyond petunias. I snatch the card. She'll notice, of course, and I want her to. I think my friend Nancy would've done the same...

I finish the grand tour, coming up empty-handed. If I take any more time rummaging through drawers or combing through closets, Matt or Ricky will come looking for me and I'll have to make up an excuse. Is my mind playing tricks on me? Have I completely imagined this secret relationship between Cleo and my husband? No. No, I learned a long time ago to trust my instincts. If something's wrong, I've always been able to sniff it out like a bloodhound before it bubbles to the surface. I know something is wrong, but for now, I don't have any proof.

I find everyone except Tripp gathered in her kitchen. The perfect Christmas scene is set: Cleo, in her red satin dress, putting out Christmas cookies and eggnog, as holly jolly carols play in the background. It briefly feels like an out-of-body experience, like what my family would look like had I never entered the picture.

Cleo smiles. "Miranda, there you are. How was your tour?"

"Lovely, thank you!"

"Your children were wondering if you ran away!"

"Well... here I am!"

"Yes, there you are!" She laughs, offering me a tray of Christmas cookies.

"Reindeers," Jake says sheepishly as he takes a bite out of one.

Interestingly, Jake seems to have kept a safer distance from Cleo than he has previously. It's not like he needs to pretend anymore for Julia's sake. She and Ricky wandered off soon after we arrived. Ah, I bet I know what it is. He knows that we're leaving tomorrow and so he's begun to detach himself. Jake and Cleo can't actually be kidding themselves and believe they're going to carry on a relationship while she's in Hawaii and he's five thousand miles away in New York? Yes, he's already begun to disentangle himself from her.

"Did you make them yourself, Cleo?" I ask.

"Heavens, no. I never bake; but I bet you're a terrific cook, Miranda!"

Jake spins around and looks at her as if she has sprung hind legs while she demures about her baking, or lack thereof, habits. And then he bolts outside. To where, I wonder.

I get it. Cleo's implying that her life is far more interesting than mine. She's *way* too busy with things like spelunking and volcano goddesses and starring on her own television show to be bothered with such trivial things like domesticity. Oh, and having an insane affair with my eldest son while bewitching the rest of my family must keep her awfully busy too. How could she possibly have time to bake a goddamn cookie?

"Thank you," I say, politely taking one of what must be ridiculously expensive store-bought cookies.

"Can I ask you a question, Miranda?" Cleo asks, taking a sensual bite from a cookie.

Her eyes stay on me and I can tell she's got something up her red satin sleeve.

"Of course."

I wait patiently for it.

"Have you ever wanted to change your life?"

There it is. I assume this is her version of getting back at me after I made those comments about children earlier. Forgive me for not wanting to live all alone on an Hawaiian island with all the bad shirts and bonsai trees.

"Heavens, no. I love my life with my family and friends around me all the time. I wouldn't have it any other way! How brave you are, Cleo, to move so far away from your roots and family all the way out to Honolulu. But then, you don't have any children. Such an... interesting choice." I wait a beat before delivering my final blow. "Are you in hiding from someone?"

She laughs and I wonder again about her life and her secrets and how Tripp knows her birthday.

Chapter Fifty-Three
December 24, 2011

TRIPP

Somehow, Cleo is involved. She must have known who I was all along. I wonder if she started an affair with Jake just to get access to me. She's out-op'd me. As I climb into the Jeep, I stare down at the photo of "Jimbo Isom" that I just took on my cell. I told my family I needed to get "a breath of fresh air." No one except Miranda seemed to notice, but Cleo smiled as though she knew just what I was going out to do. *To play Danny Boy and to mention Marc Antony.*

I ask for my pal Matt Stone who is a genius at photo recognition. "Matt, I just sent you a photo. Please confirm it's Mohammed Abdul Rahman ASAP. I'm 90 percent sure that it is."

"Running facial recognition now, sir. Please hold. Will just be a few seconds…"

Will just be a few seconds. The longest few seconds of your damn life, but sure, just a few seconds. As I wait for my pal, Matt Stone, to give me the answer I need, I look out at Cleopatra's property. One thing's for sure, Honolulu definitely suits her—beautiful, vibrant, and full of mystery. I do what I've so rarely allowed myself to do over the last seven years—think about what my life would have been like had I left Miranda and the boys after Kilimanjaro. Would we have completely abandoned our lives on the mainland or stayed close to home so that I could visit the boys? Or would we have said to hell with consequence and just—

"Yes, sir. I've confirmed. It's Mohammed Abdul Rahman."

"Copy that. That corroborates my suspicions earlier. Rahman's dead."

"Proof?"

"Soon. I need a team to meet me at the Koolah Cliffs in..." I glance down at my watch. "In an hour."

"Copy."

"Okay, and did you get the other photos I just sent? Of the security cameras on his property? Take a look now, please."

"Wait... Where are you, sir?"

"I'm here. Abdul Rahman's using the name Jimbo Isom as a cover—note the clever initials. Pretty fucking ballsy."

"Sir, with all due respect, I'm not sure you being there's the best—"

"Never mind that. I just sent you another photo. I need his identity confirmed as well."

"Okay, this might take a while, sir. I'll get back to you."

"No, Matt. I need it now!" I snap. "This is top priority. I'll hold."

"Okay, copy. One moment."

I take a deep breath, trying to calm my nerves. I hear Matt breathing as he works his magic. He's one of the new young tech experts we've been bringing into the company. They all sort of look alike—scrawny, mousy, like those nerdy types in the Geek Squad ads on TV. But Matt's bright red hair sets him apart from the herd. A few minutes later, he comes back on the line.

"Sir, that appears to be Didier Gallier. Cleo Gallier's father. I pulled his background info. You want it all or just the bare facts for now?"

"All. Now," I demand.

"Okay... 1939, born in Paris to Edouard Gallier and Rania Hakeem. In 1960, he graduated with honors from Oxford University. 1965, married Sandrine Smyth. 1967, one daughter born. His only child, Cleopatra Gallier. 1972, divorced from Sandrine Smyth.

"Gallier's father, Edouard, wealthy French aristocrat, royal heritage, had a winery in Algeria, and while out there, married an Algerian woman, Rania Hakeem. They had three children, including Didier. Didier's mother, Rania Gallier was murdered on 17 October 1961 in the Paris Massacre of Algerians. But wait, this is interesting, sir... There's a very high clearance on him. I'm blocked from going any deeper."

"What sort of clearance?"

"High. Just came on this second as I was reading to you."

"Jesus. Okay, can you see when he was in Hawaii last?"

Matt whistles to himself as he hammers away on his keyboard, scouring his database.

"According to his passports... this October. Before that, August 2010. And before that, Christmas 2009. Seems he visits every year or so."

"And when did she last visit him in Algeria?"

"Pulling up her passport, sir. Last visit was..." Matt pauses for a few dramatic moments. "Four years. But she did stay in Algeria for over a year from 2004–2005. But, Jesus..."

"What?"

"I'm blocked out of her full profile too. Just went into effect a few minutes ago."

Who the hell is she? Over the years, I'd often fantasized about Cleo and who she'd become since our last lunch at the Amboseli lodge. Many scenarios crossed my mind, but secret agent or international terrorist never made the list.

"Okay, now what about these cameras? Those pictures that I sent you?"

"Definitely top of the line. Real high-tech shit, sir."

"Okay, this is what we're going to do. Send a car to the Halekelani Hotel in thirty minutes. But be sure to have two Chinese agents—Chinese, that is crucial—come to pick me up," I command.

"Copy that."

"Thanks, Matt. And please keep trying to get more details on Didier Gallier's clearance. We need to know how high up it goes. And more importantly, why," I tell Matt Stone as I hang up.

What the fuck clearance could her father have that's above mine? Who are these people?

Jake's knuckles rap on the window.

"Dad, Cleo just told Mom she doesn't bake!" he screams as he crawls into the passenger seat.

"Jake, Jesus, we've been over this. I talked to the cops," I lie. Then I lie some more, "I told you, when they got there, he was apparently in his house doing sit-ups. Trust me, the cops all know him well around here."

"I know, but Dad—"

"No. No 'but Dad,' Jake! Jimbo is alive, end of story. I know it's difficult but you gotta trust me on this, okay?"

He doesn't say anything.

"And, Jake, this is critical—you can't say anything to any-one about what you think you saw, no matter what. Promise me, okay? I'll explain eventually, but just know how impor-tant it is that you don't say a peep until we leave Hawaii. You understand?"

"Okay, but see, Dad, that doesn't make any sense. If what you're saying is true, then why do I need to keep my mouth shut? It doesn't—"

"Goddamn it, Jake! What'd I say?! No 'but Dad!' Just trust me on this, will ya?!"

That snaps Jake into silence. He looks forward at the glove compartment and nods.

"Tell no one. Remember how brave you were in the heli-copter? You need to be brave now and, under no circumstances, speak of what you saw." I pat his knee.

I take Jake gently by the arm and lead him back inside to the others. Miranda and Cleo seem to be having a nice conversation; they're both smiling. Miranda won't be for long though...

"I'm so sorry, but we have to leave. Larry just called..." I tell the room, but I'm looking at Miranda.

"The China deal," she says knowingly.

I nod. "I'm happy to drop you off at the restaurant or back at the hotel and you can eat there. Whatever everyone prefers."

"What happened?" asks Miranda, ignoring the dinner issue.

"It's a long story but unfortunately, it looks like we have to work through the night and probably into tomorrow too."

"Really? On Christmas?" Miranda asks, the smile from her face gone.

"Yeah, it's gotta be done by the 26th no matter what."

"Oh, that's too bad..." Cleo smiles at me.

She seems pleased by our quick leave-taking. I turn to her.

"Thanks, Cleo, for letting us stop by. And Merry Christmas," I say, leaning in to peck her on the cheek. Then I whisper, "Kariba Kula Muta."

She pulls away from me and looks at me with fury in her eyes. Her hand on my shoulder gives me a small shove so that no one else can see.

"Don't forget Happy Birthday too," Miranda adds.

Jake approaches Cleo apprehensively, as if he was walking straight into the lion's den. "'Bye, Cleo. It was really nice to meet you."

"Oh, I loved meeting you, Jake." She takes him in her arms and hugs him tight. But he just stiffens, barely hugging her back. He has completely shut down.

"I want to thank you all for coming and keeping a *lonely, childless old lady* company on Christmas Eve." Cleo smiles. She seems to be saying this for Miranda's benefit especially.

"Where are Julia and Ricky?" I ask Miranda.

"I think they went outside."

Cleo leads us out into her courtyard where Matt is busy studying the flowering trees by moonlight. He kneels in his khakis, not noticing or really giving a damn that they're covered with dirt.

"For these flowering trees, Cleo, a good way to acidify the soil is with leftover coffee or tea grounds. Or even pickle juice."

"What a great tip!" she says, kissing Matt on the cheek. He lets her kiss him. Surprising since he hates being touched, even by his own family.

As we pull out of her long driveway, Cleo stands alone, serene in her courtyard as "Silent Night" plays from unseen speakers.

"I'm sorry, guys, to have to leave so abruptly."

"That's okay, Tripp. We understand," Miranda says perkily, from the backseat. I can tell she wanted to get the hell outta Dodge.

No one says anything.

Chapter Fifty-Four
December 24, 2011

CLEO

I change into a pair of jeans after the Regans leave. Forty-five minutes later, I watch as all the black cars go down to Jimbo's cabin. I know, of course, that they won't find him there.

A few hours later, my phone rings. I stare down at it, not recognizing the number but I know that it must be him. I pick up but I don't say anything.

"Cleo? It's Tripp."

Still, I don't say a word. For once, I would like him to do all of the heavy lifting. If Danny Mortimer owes me, Tripp Regan really does.

After a long pause, Tripp finally speaks. "Where is he?"

"Who?" I ask, betraying nothing.

"C'mon."

"*Who?*"

"He's dead, isn't he?"

"Who, Tripp?"

"Your friend Jimbo Isom."

"And why would you think that?"

"Because my son can be very jealous. He saw you."

Oh God.

"He thought you and 'Jimbo' might be lovers so he spied on your bike ride. He saw you throw him over the cliffs."

How is that even possible? Where could he have been hiding? I looked and looked and didn't see anyone else around.

"Then, when he texted you, you said you were baking cookies. But the cookies tonight were bought in a store."

Oh, Jake. No wonder he looked so undone and was so off from his usual carefree self. Poor Jake. It must have terrified him, watching me push Jimbo off that cliff. Well, it would terrify anyone. It even terrified me.

"I convinced Jake it wasn't real. That it must be some stupid stunt you pulled every day and that Jimbo's alive." He pauses. "But I remember about the Krav Maga…"

"Yes. Jimbo is dead," I confess after a long pause. "What was his plan?"

"Same as he did in the Philippines. He hid bombs around Pearl Harbor. They were all going to detonate at the same time tomorrow. We're not sure how he gained access to all of the stations, but—"

"The Ironman," I blurt out. "Pearl Harbor is on his daily route. He knows all of the guards by first name."

"He had tickets out tonight to Manila under a different name. But Cleo, we have to be really careful about how we move forward."

"What do you mean?"

"No one else can know what you did. We need a cover story or else Al Qaeda's coming after you."

"Yes, okay."

Tripp is quiet for a few moments.

"How long have you known?"

"Known?"

Tripp could mean two things, both involving not-so-classic cases of mistaken identity. Is he referring to the one where he and the love of my life are the same person? Or the other, where my best friend was actually an undercover operative for one of the world's deadliest terror organizations and had planned to slaughter God knows how many innocent people on Christmas Day?

"Who I am," he says finally.

"I found out just tonight." I try not to cry.

"Ah. I knew it."

"What?"

"When we were at your house earlier, it seemed like you'd just found out."

"I was trying to scare you. To show you I could play your little game too. Which, I can, by the way. Having "Danny Boy" on when you walked in should have been all you needed, but then, I couldn't resist mentioning Marc Antony."

Tripp is silent.

"And you know, of course, that I had no idea until tonight or I wouldn't have babbled on and on about Danny during the marathon. Actually, I would have had nothing to do with you."

"I know."

"I really hate you, you know."

Tripp remains silent then finally he says, "If it makes you feel better, I loved hearing every detail."

My turn for silence.

"I'm so sorry, Cleopatra. I'm so, so sorry."

"That's not good enough, Tripp."

Not good enough at all. I understand being an undercover agent and having to pretend you were dead. But why, as a married man, did you seduce me and act as if you loved me when you had a wife and three children at home? I wasted years. Years in depression for someone who never even existed. Oh, how I hate you.

"I know it isn't. I really know it isn't. Cleo, I have to ask for your help. Can you help us recover Jimbo's body? My men haven't been able to find him yet. You know how important this is. We need to find him to be sure he's dead."

Chapter Fifty-Five
December 25, 2011

JULIA

I wake up in Ricky's bed alone. I'm stark naked and the last thing I remember is our make-out session—which, from what I remember, was pretty hot. We were underneath the mistletoe and then again, at the hotel bar. I vaguely remember a lot of foot action... touching and twisting around each other's legs and toes under the table. And I'm pretty sure, Semi-Hot, my ol' faithful bartender friend from the other day, was there too, taking in the scene... But then what? One thing I know, I'm never drinking again for as long as I live. R.I.P. alcohol. We had a good run.

There's a knock at the door. *Please don't be Ricky.* I'm really not ready to deal with that radioactive danger zone quite yet. I beg for room service to magically appear with a warm plate of eggs and cheese danishes to last me for days. Warily, I look out the peephole. Annnd... it's Ricky. Of course, it's Ricky. The way this holiday's shaped up, I'm surprised my physics teacher, Monsieur Revelle, who lived to fail me, hasn't popped out of the closet to quiz me on the formula of motion. *Chill, Julia. Be cool.*

"Uh, who is it?!" I call out, not sounding the least bit chill or cool.

"Ric-ky," he answers in a sing-song tone from the other side of the door.

"Oh! Hey! Just a minute please," I call again, scrambling to find clothes, any clothes.

The closest "garment" I find is a towel. I wrap it around myself, swing open the door and plaster on a grin to find Ricky standing there with two coffees.

"Coffee, anyone?"

"Oh. Thank you. That's so sweet," I say, taking one of the cups off his hands.

There's an awkward silence. There's always an awkward silence.

"Well, hey, Merry Christmas!" he says.

I casually take a sip of the coffee, searing the roof of my mouth.

"Hot! Ow, hot!" I yelp.

"That you are..."

I grab my lip in pain.

"Sorry, stupid joke. Are you okay?" he asks, taking a step closer to me.

"Oh, yes. Yup-eroo, I'm fine. Totally good."

Yup-eroo? Jesus. Ricky looks at me like I have ten heads.

"Yeah, I'm fine. Merry Christmas to you too," I "cheers" my coffee to his.

Another awkward silence.

"So, um, what..."

"... The hell happened last night? Nothing really. I tucked you in, then crashed in Matt's room again."

I can't tell if I'm relieved or disappointed. Maybe a little bit of both.

"By the way, you were fully clothed when I left..." He smiles, gesturing to my heap of clothes at the foot of the bed.

"Oh. Okay, phew."

We lock eyes. I'm seeing Ricky in a whole different light. That *kiss*. Has he always been this handsome, sweet, funny, attentive guy and I was just too brain dead and in love with Jake to even notice? Have I been with the wrong brother all this time? Maybe my life is a girly rom-com, after all.

"Look..." I begin.

"I know, I know. I'm just Jake's little brother. You still love him and want to work it out, blah, blah blah. I get it, Jules. No sweat."

"Actually... What I was going to say, before I was so rudely interrupted..." I smile up at him. "Is that I was wondering if you wanted to have a proper breakfast. Like, together."

He tries to control his rapidly spreading grin. "I'd love to. Except... my mom's asked that we all gather for a Christmas brunch."

"One big happy family..." We both laugh. "Well, that's fine. Let's make Miranda happy."

"You might wanna consider throwing on some clothes first. Not that I'd mind, or really anyone down there..." he flirts.

This feels right. And easy. Like I can finally be myself and not have to stress about every single word I say, move I make, food I eat, outfit I wear. And he's perfect too. Well, apart from being in desperate need of a haircut.

"I'll meet you downstairs in ten. I just need to get changed and I'd like to call my dad and wish him a Happy Christmas. It's already... Shit"—I glance down at my watch—"night time over there."

"Oh, hey. Tell him I loved his article about Gibraltar International."

My eyes bulge to the size of donuts.

"It was in the newspaper the other day?"

He has misinterpreted my surprise for confusion. "Oh, right..."

I've become so accustomed to having a boyfriend who makes minimal effort, who has showed very little interest in getting to know my family, which is hilarious because Jake is the ultimate mama's boy. It's partly my fault. I let Jake get away with his carelessness and disinterest because I was so charmed by his humor, looks, athleticism, and bedside manner. Jake is genuinely a fun guy to be around. But I see now that we aren't meant to be together.

"See you downstairs in ten."

And he's off. My knight in shining khakis. Poll for the audience: do you think it's possible to be in love with one person, fall out of love with said person, and then fall back in love with someone new (ahem, his brother) all inside of four days? Yes, no? Like I said, this island is crazy...

After I speak to my father, I put on a sundress, a little makeup, and comb my hair. I leave the room with a grin bigger than all of the Hawaiian Islands combined and head toward the elevator bank. For now, I held off on telling my father about the Jake break-up, but I have a feeling he'll be quite thrilled. The elevator doors whiz open, revealing, well, speak of the devil—my evil ex-boyfriend on his cell phone, among a crowd. He glances over at me as he exits the elevator and then not so subtly puts on his Ray-Bans.

"Dad, it's me. Are you paying attention to the news?" I hear him say into his phone.

The news? What a joke. That doesn't sound like the ignorant Jake I know. He's seen me out of the corner of his eye, I'm sure. Oh, he's so busted. I step aside as a large family shuffles out. Jake ducks and tries to go unnoticed in the middle of them. I may have turned a blind eye the past few days but the jig's up, buddy boy.

"Jake?"

He keeps moving.

"Jake!" I say louder. "Yoohoo, I can see you. Those aren't invisibility sunglasses, you know."

Finally, he turns to face me. We are now completely alone in the hallway.

"Oh, hey, Julia. Sorry, didn't see you there," he mumbles as if he were speaking to a fire hydrant.

That's the first time he's said my name in two whole days, mind you. Jake visibly braces for impact.

"Yeah, I'm so easy to miss..." I pause for effect. "Merry Christmas. I hope you got everything you wanted."

"Jesus, Julia..." He looks up at me briefly but then his eyes redirect to safer ground down on the carpet. "So, Matt told me you've been shacking up in Ricky's room?"

"Yup," I answer, defiantly. Popping my "p" to knock my point home.

How dare he admonish me? Now it's my turn for one syllable responses. See how he likes a tasty little dollop of his own medicine.

"Oh. Cool..." Is all he gives me.

"Problem?"

He looks at me, still hiding behind the green tint of his Ray-Bans. He had to know this moment was going to come sooner or later.

"Serious question: did you not think I knew you were shagging that woman or did you just not give a shit that I knew?"

Relief lifts off my chest. Finally, it's out in the open.

"Jules—"

"Don't call me that."

"Oh, right. I guess only Ricky is bestowed that honor?" He tries to smile at me, hoping that will somehow diffuse the tension. *Try again.*

"Yup," I say again. Again, popping my "p."

"Sorry, *Ju-li-a*. I don't know what you want me to say... It just happened."

It's just happened. I loathe when anyone uses that cop-out as an excuse for anything. *Whoops, sorry! It just happened!* Nothing *just happens*. Things happen, dummy, because you want them to and decide to put those things into motion.

"I don't want you to *say* anything, Jake. There's nothing you could possibly say."

So, he doesn't. He just stands there. I should walk away, there's nothing left to say. Our relationship is a horse that's been dead since the Civil War. There's no use in kicking it now. But I can't go just yet. I feel as if my shoes are glued to the carpet, or like the carpet is quicksand and I'm sinking further and further, keeping me from leaving the hallway. Keeping me from being the mature one and letting sleeping dogs lie. That's a lot of analogies.

"Only weak people can't end things themselves, Jake. They just wait for someone else to do it. Which makes you a huge coward." I smile at him, shaking my head. I couldn't resist.

Finally, his glasses come off. Yikes, he looks awful. Like he hasn't slept in months. "Fine!" he says, like a child told he can't have a second dessert.

Fine? I burst into laughter. It's as if I've been wearing foggy, ugly, rose-colored glasses for the past two years and they've only just been cleaned. Finally, I see Jake as the spoiled, self-ish, aimless jerk that he really is. *He's all yours, Cleo.* His face turns the color of a perfectly ripe tomato, ready for the picking.

"You could've just told me, you know. I'm a big girl, Jake. And I admit, I didn't always treat you like gold... I treated you like platinum! I adored you, and now I just feel like such an idiot because you've thrown it all away for some woman you've only known a few days."

Jakes takes another breath. "Julia, you're comparing yourself to someone when you don't know any of the details. It's not that simple."

"Okay, so then why don't you simplify it for me, Jake?" I am unblinking.

He just looks back at me. No words come out of his mouth, because he can't. He can simplify it, alright, but not without hurting my feelings. *I don't want you anymore, I want her.* Told you he is a coward.

He takes a step back. "I swear, Julia, I didn't mean to hurt you."

Famous last words.

"Hey, I'm on my way to meet Ricky and everyone for Christmas breakfast. Are you not joining?" I ask him, suddenly being sweet and charming again, batting my L'Oreal lathered lashes.

"Eh, I'm not really feeling the holly jolly spirit," he says, having a staring contest with the hallway carpet. "I'm going back to lie down for a bit."

I had a sneaking suspicion he was going to decline that invite. Still looking down at the carpet, I can tell he wants to say something else but he isn't sure how.

"Look, Julia..." He pauses. "I don't—I mean—it just—like I said—it just—kinda—"

Jesus, Porky Pig. S-s-s-spit it out!

"... Happened?" I mercifully finish his sentence for him.

"I'm sorry," he musters finally. "You didn't deserve that, though you seem to be bouncing back pretty well..." A pause. "Anyway, I'm gonna, uh, yeah..." he mumbles before he starts to walk away.

"Merry Christmas, Jake."

Before leaving, Jake gives a very small smile.

I press the button for the lobby, already fantasizing about the greasy bacon, egg, and cheese sandwich I'm about to devour. It's a relief to be the real me for a change. No more egg whites and all that health nut stuff I ate for Jake. Brave new me, real me. Me, who will see my father and not need to make excuses for Jake. Me, who will have a boyfriend at the MOMA parties. *Me.*

Chapter Fifty-Six
December 25, 2011

TRIPP

It's already been a long night and I'm still at Jimbo Isom a.k.a. Mohammed Abdul Rahman a.k.a. Patrick Olson's cabin. He has a trapdoor leading down to the caves below where there are maps, computers, bomb materials, photos of the guards, and the layout of Pacific Command and Pearl Harbor. There are several different passports and ready cash in different currencies, which are all removed from the premises by the agency. They've rounded up his AQ JI cell, and the bombs he planted at Pearl Harbor are being diffused at this moment.

I go get Cleopatra. Once she gets in the car, she can't even look at me. Instead, she just looks straight ahead through the windshield.

"Put on your seatbelt," I stupidly suggest.

She laughs sarcastically as she jams it on. I'm about to put the car in drive when I stop.

"Cleo, I'm worried about you."

"Oh?" she asks with a note of amusement. Her eyes are still fixated on the front windshield.

"I'm serious... I'm worried they're gonna find out you killed him."

"Who?"

"Al Qaeda, the U.S. Government, fucking everyone, Cleo!"

She snaps at me so fast. "No, they won't. And if YOU had actually done your job, maybe I wouldn't have had to be the one to kill him!" Gone is the charming, smiling woman who greeted my family in her red gown and jewels with "Danny Boy" playing. Instead, is this other raging Cleo. The rage is as red as the dress she'd worn earlier tonight. I find it equally appealing.

"Cleo..."

Silence from her.

It is difficult for me to get out: "Are you... I can't help but think that you must be some sort of agent. I mean, to have taken down a top Al Qaeda leader..."

She lowers her eyes in anger and takes a deep breath. "Yes, Tripp, you've finally figured me out. I am Mata Hari and Krystyna Skarbek and Virginia Hall all rolled into one! So, don't you dare fuck with me or I will take you out next, and you better believe that's what I want to do. Go left at the bottom of the driveway."

This time, I listen to her. My men are following us in black Suburbans with their high beams on. I told them that Cleo was a friend and that my wife and I happened to be at her house when she came back from her bike ride. She was terribly upset and about to call the police when she showed me a photo of her friend who had the accident. I recognized him right away and asked her to keep quiet for the time being. The guys nodded. *I think they believed me.* Mohammed Abdul Rahman was dead and that was all that mattered.

She directs me out to the Koolah Cliffs. Except for her intermittent direction-giving, we drive there in total silence.

"Pull over here."

I do as I'm told. I park the car, we climb out and I follow her to the edge of the cliff, along with the other agents who are tailing us.

"It was right about here, I think. Jimbo was going so fast, he must have just lost control as he turned the corner and skidded off the road." She points to the base that's way the hell down there. It must be at least a two, three hundred foot drop.

Don Durita and Chester Wu are the ranking agents at the scene. Also known as Mr. Chen and Mr. Huang. Neither of them have ever even been to China—Durita is originally from outside Chicago and Wu was born in Jersey City. After we left Miranda at the hotel, we went to Jimbo's cabin and then we sent the recovery team to The Koolah Cliffs. When the climbers couldn't locate Rahman's body, I knew I needed Cleo's help. Christ, was I dreading that call. She knew that I was the man she loved, the man who had abandoned her and now the man who had the balls to ask for a favor.

"Thanks, Ms. Gallier," Wu says before he and Durita go to the group of climbers who are tasked with repelling down the cliff and recovering Rahman's body.

Cleo is shaking, so I give her my jacket. With us in the breezy Hawaiian night are Miranda and Jake, and Jimbo is there too, and Danny, and young Cleo. We are in a wide net of complexity and conspiracy. There's no fear and no laughing. But there is a sadness. We know this is our only chance. Both our bodies have adrenaline pumping through them. Inside of an afternoon, she'd killed her best friend after she found out he was the head of an Al Qaeda terrorist cell and then she discovered who I really was. On their own, just one of those pills would be tough to swallow, but one right after another would be too much for most people to wash down. She'd done what I had wanted to do. She killed that Al Qaeda motherfucker. She saved the island. She's the hero of this whole scenario and no one will ever even know.

"Take me home. I can't be here any longer."

I go over to Durita and Wu. I've never wanted to leave the scene of a crime so badly.

"Guys, I'm going to drive Ms. Gallier home. She's pretty shaken up. You guys take it from here."

We climb into my car, and once again, we drive in silence. Neither of us says a word until I pull into her house. I put the car in park and look over at her. Even in all her anger, anguish and angst, she looks beautiful. She *is* beautiful. I can't help myself. I lean in and kiss her, but she doesn't respond so I back off.

"Cleopatra?"

She pushes me away and tears start streaming down her face.

"I'm sorry, do you want me to go? I understand if you just want to be alone."

"How could I not know?!" she cries.

"How could you not know *what?*"

"About Jimbo! For God's sake, he was my very best friend and I had absolutely no idea that he was an international terrorist! He lived on my property for four years!"

"Hey..." I say softly, putting a comforting hand on her shoulder. "It's not your fault. Most people who—"

"I didn't want to kill him," she sobs. "But if I hadn't, he would have killed me. I saw it all over his face. He grabbed my arm fiercely as he said, 'You know I hate to do this.'"

Cleo covers her face with her hands, embarrassed that I'm seeing her like this, so emotional. But I don't care. I love this soft side of her. In a million years, Miranda would never let me see her so vulnerable. I lean over and wrap my arms around Cleo, holding her. And she lets me. Thank God she lets me. Her body heaves up and down as she continues to cry. After an eternity, Cleo has calmed herself down and all the heaving and all the crying eventually subside.

"You smell like you..." she says, finally looking up at me.

"Well, that's a relief." I smile.

"Wait here."

Right now, I'll do whatever she says. She gets out of the car and disappears inside her house. The lights from my car shine onto her front entrance. A few minutes later, she reemerges with a big striped tote bag.

"Champagne... Come on, I want to show you something."

"Okay," I say again.

Cleo has me drive down a sheltered road. At the end, we arrive at rock croppings quite reminiscent of the ones on Kilimanjaro. She hops out of the car without a word, never looking back but just expecting I will follow.

She keeps climbing. It isn't very steep and she seems to know where the footholds are, so I gamely start after her, carrying the tote bag. The only light is coming from the moon. Finally, she disappears, gone as she was after Africa.

"Up here," she calls out.

I climb up further and discover a small cave opening. I go in slowly and stop in amazement. The cave inside is painted white from floor to ceiling and there are large, matching pillows on a bright orange Turkish rug. Cleo is lighting candles and as each one is lit, I take in more and more of this remarkable cave she's made. On the white walls, there are photos of other cave houses.

"They're from Cappadocia. In Turkey," she tells me when I go over to admire them.

There is a vintage, silver Turkish tray table with short wooden legs next to the rug.

"Because it's Christmas. And because you smell like you," says Cleo, toasting me as she opens the bottle of Veuve Clicquot which she takes out of the tote. We both sit on the rug and she wraps her lips around the top of the bottle and takes a huge swig, and then another. A few drops miss her mouth and trickle down her cheek, down her neck, and eventually, down her cleavage.

"To Marc Antony and Cleopatra, whose ending was not happy either. But they at least had their glorious moments," she toasts again, taking another swig.

I take the big green bottle and a swig of my own, and another, before she grabs it back.

"This is great, what you've done," I tell her as I look around the cave. "Back in Africa, we would've had a much longer hike to get here. And there would have been bats, not Turkish rugs. And you would have been in your pink parka."

"You remember my pink parka?"

"I remember everything, Cleopatra of the violet eyes. Your pink parka, your pink lipstick. Your pink nail polish..."

She doesn't say anything, so I keep talking. I think that's what she wants. I've heard all about Danny from Cleo so I suppose it's my turn, for Tripp Regan to tell her how Danny Mortimer felt.

"I don't blame you if you never forgive me."

"Good."

"What I did… it was awful. But for what it's worth, I couldn't help myself, Cleo. You're pretty hard to resist, you know…" I smile.

"Yes, I am," She smiles back proudly.

"Everything except my name and how I made a living was real."

"Well, not everything…"

She means that Danny Mortimer didn't also have a wife and children at home, but she doesn't say it and neither do I.

"Right…"

I loved you then and I still love you now, is what I really want to say. But I don't. And I really want to reach over and take her. But I don't do that either.

"You're the only one I've brought here."

"I'm honored."

"I was furious when I found out who you were, you know."

"How did you find out?"

"Oh, it's a long story. Let's just say I have friends in very high places."

I nod. I was pretty sure her father, with the inconceivably higher clearance than mine, told her.

"I must admit, I did smile for a second when I realized you had had the tiny holes in your teeth capped."

"I'm very thorough…"

"And I must have been quite the surprise when you saw me on the beach with Jake."

"Jesus. Don't remind me. I could hardly speak. Then I worried you were an operative too."

She laughs.

"Well, you put me on the plane in Africa and then you were with me again here. At the time, it seemed like too much of a coincidence. And then, of course, killing Jimbo."

"You must be a very good spy. I really had no idea," Cleo says as she sips from the second bottle of Veuve.

"Even good spies get tripped up from time to time. But, Cleo... my life with—" I start.

"I know. I understand because of my father," she cuts me off mercifully.

"Your father?" I ask her, pretending not to let on that I already know he's in a similar line of work.

"Yes. He too leads a life with secrets under it."

I can't take it anymore. I have to have her and she is sending me signals that she wants me to take her. I am not scared as I finally lean into Cleo and kiss her gently. This time, she responds gently too.

"I am only kissing Danny, not Tripp." She pulls away. "And I am going to make love to Danny, not Tripp. Tripp is married and has children. Danny is in love with me."

I grasp this. And it is Africa again. Africa in this perfect, white cave. And it is her birthday.

Chapter Fifty-Seven
December 25, 2011

MIRANDA

Thank you, God. We're finally leaving this God forsaken island. I feel like doing a cheer—having the whole plane shriek, "We won, we won, we won! Home team! Home team! Rah, rah, rah! Gooooooo home team!" I'm so happy I could perform every single one of my college cheerleading routines down this plane's skinny, ugly, blue carpeted aisle.

I lean back in my seat as we take off smoothly, rushing down the runway, leaving Cleopatra Gallier below. My son and my husband are both safe now. I bet Cleo would say that a plane taking off is like a caterpillar shedding its chrysalis, turning into its real self, a butterfly. Or something ridiculous like that. Oh yes, she's fabulous. She's poetic. Yet, my husband left with me. Deep down, I know he really had no choice. He's with me, though I know a part of him isn't—but I know that part never was.

For me, it's enough this way; for I have him and she has nothing.

Last night, when we got back to our hotel from Cleo's, Tripp was quiet as he changed into his pinstriped suit, shirt and tie. As he walked out the door, he turned back to me.

"Miranda, you know this is a very important deal, right? I'd never just abandon you and the kids like this on Christmas Eve unless it was absolutely necessary."

"Of course."

"It was all set when I left China, but now it's all gone to hell and I have to play Mr. Fix It."

"I understand," I said, a bit more curtly than I normally would have.

"Depending on how long this takes, plan to either see me back here or I'll just meet you on the plane."

"Well, I hope it's the first one..." I smiled.

"Wish me luck." He kissed me. "Hey, why don't you come down and meet the guys? You can give them a piece of your mind..."

And this time, I did. Misters Chen and Huang were waiting for us in the lobby.

"Mrs. Regan," Mr. Chen—or was it Huang?—said as he shook my hand. "We so sorry to steal your husband on Christmas time," he said in a thick Chinese accent.

"Yes, so sorry. But we have serious problem and only Mr. Tripp can fix!" Mr. Huang—or was it Chen?—laughed.

I walked them to the front entrance and watched the three of them pile into a black SUV. Tripp's work does get in the way of our lives at times. When I was back in our room—so lonely— I went through his clothes and started packing, trying to stay busy. I had a feeling we weren't going to be opening presents and singing carols with Tripp on Christmas Day.

When that became a reality, I arranged a special brunch for the kids and me at Orchids, the Halekulani's elegant oceanfront restaurant. Wherever we are in the world on Christmas morning, it's family tradition that we eat a festive breakfast and I was not about to let our patriarch's absence get in the way. Other happy families surrounded our table and we finally got our carols. The staff was delightful as they served us every breakfast food under the Hawaiian sun—French toast, eggs benedict, blueberry pancakes, bacon and eggs, croissants and cheese Danishes, coffee and tea; I even indulged in a mimosa, another little Christmas ritual of mine. Food always lifts my spirits when I'm feeling blue, but today, it didn't totally do the trick. I felt like the giant clock in Times Square on December 31st, but instead of counting down the hours and the minutes until the new year, I was counting the seconds until my family and I were off this island once and for all. My children are grown but still, I don't want them to see their mother unhappy, especially on Christmas.

After breakfast, I brought the boys up to my room for present opening while Julia caught a few last rays of sunlight. Ricky put their favorite movie, *Home Alone,* on the television for background. Ever since the boys graduated from college, Tripp has given them the gift of the almighty dollar on December 25th. There's nothing that a twenty-something living in New York City wants more than a little extra cash in their pockets. Last night, before he left, Tripp filled out three checks and stuffed them in envelopes with Jake, Matt, and Ricky's names scrawled on them. They all seemed happy with my gifts—a new Tribe 7 lacrosse stick and Tiffany cufflinks for Jake, tickets to *The Book of Mormon* and a new Brooks Brothers blazer for Ricky, and an annual membership to the New York Botanical Garden and gardening tools for you know who.

Ricky and Matt were disappointed about their father for obvious reasons, but it hardly seemed to phase Jake. For the rest of the day, he watched the news incessantly. The big story was about the jihadist who had been killed and how his plot to blow up buildings on the island was foiled. My goodness, this must be related to the red alert from yesterday. People at the hotel were fascinated but Jake was obsessed. After presents, he holed up at the hotel bar, where CNN was playing on a loop. I wondered why, on his last day, he wasn't seeing Cleo? And it was her birthday too.

"Is there a reason you're so interested in this particular story, Jake?"

"Mom, hello... He almost blew up Pearl Harbor. In case you hadn't noticed, that's around the corner from us!" Jake cried. There was a strange look on his face, one I hadn't seen before. And I have seen all of my son's looks and expressions.

"I know, I know... It's terrible. I guess I just never pegged you as a news junkie." I smiled. "That's always been Ricky's field."

He rolled his eyes. The bartender came over but I waved him off, hardly in the mood for a second drink.

"Merry Christmas, Jakey. Meet you in the lobby at three."

"Merry Christmas, Mom." Jake managed a smile but his eyes were still glued to the screen.

The newest lovebirds, meanwhile, Julia and Ricky, had gone off to play golf again while Matt wandered around the gardens taking notes. I decided to walk the beach and I must say, for once on this trip, I enjoyed being alone and enjoyed that there was no drama.

It isn't until Tripp boards the plane home that I see him again. He gives me an 'hello' kiss and apologizes for missing Christmas. He smells of Cleo's perfume, but I know it couldn't be. My mind must be playing tricks. I met the Chinese men he was working with.

"One second," Tripp says as he goes to Jake, who's calling him over.

I look over my shoulder and watch my son grab Tripp's wrist and pull him close. I strain my ears as best as I can. Damn these seats, I can hardly hear a thing. Usually, I book the whole family in the same row in order to keep my eyes and ears on everyone the entire flight. It doesn't matter where we are, I just love it when we're all together, even if most of them are sound asleep or have headphones stuffed in their ears. Honolulu must have been a very popular destination this year because I booked these flights all the way back in July, and even then, there weren't six seats available together. And now, since all planes were grounded yesterday, the flight is completely full.

I deliberately knock my cell phone off the tray in front of me and onto the carpeted floor.

"I was right, Dad. I was right the whole time, wasn't I?" I can hear Jake say.

I pretend to fumble with my phone on the carpet, buying myself more time to eavesdrop.

"Not now, Jake. We'll talk about it later."

"But, Dad—"

"Jake. Not now," my husband says with a toughness in his voice. Tripp whispers something else to Jake but I'm too far away to hear. I could have sworn I heard him say her name though. *Cleo*. That name will haunt my nightmares until I'm a very old woman.

Hearing as much as I could, I recover my phone and sit up in my seat. It's now glaringly obvious that Jake won't marry Julia like I'd hoped, but some other wonderful girl his age will come along and he'll soon forget all about Cleo. Jake and Julia seem to have given each other up so easily that I have to believe it wasn't meant to be.

Before we take off, the captain comes onto the loudspeaker. "Good afternoon, folks, and on behalf of the entire flight crew, we'd like to wish you a very Merry Christmas. Count yourself among the lucky. Due to the storm, this is the first flight out of Honolulu in forty-eight hours." A few passengers cheer. "We're number three for departure. We're hoping for a smooth ride to Los Angeles."

About a half an hour out, while Julia and Ricky are happily playing cards, the turbulence begins. Awful, awful shaking.

Jake laughs tightly. "Pele doesn't want me to leave!"

Tripp does what he always does, and takes my hand. I hold it. I'm his anchor. "Pele" pushes too hard, shakes him up too much, so he holds onto me. I'll be sure he's not afraid; I'll be sure he's safe.

The pilot comes over the loudspeaker again. "Hi, folks. This is your captain speaking. Apologies for the turbulence but unfortunately, we're told it gets a lot bumpier up ahead. As a last resort, we may have to return to the airport. We'll be sure to keep you updated."

Oh God. Please no.

Jake laughs strangely. Will she be at the airport waiting for us? Tripp's face is impossible to read. He must see this as a sign from the gods. I'm forsaken. How can she have *this* power? I have them here, safe. She can't have them back. She can't. When we land, I'll have to pretend I'm really sick and have my family take me to a hospital until we can leave. I'll pass out and mention my heart. After all, it would be the truth. It has suddenly started to ache so much. Then they'll all stay with me until we leave. Would they call her for the name of a good doctor? She'll probably rush over in a candy striper's uniform and take their pulses, which would be racing in her hands. My total opposite, my only threat is Cleo.

But after a few minutes more of horrible bouncing, the pilot comes on again. "Okay, folks. Good news. We've been rerouted to avoid the severe weather, climbing to thirty-nine thousand feet, then continuing to LAX and then onto JFK. So sit back, relax, and have a good flight. We'll keep you updated."

Ha ha, she lost! She shook them to their truth, their roots, she almost got them back, but they rose above their instincts all the way to thirty-nine thousand feet to escape.

Jake slumps in his seat. Matt reads the notes he was making. Ricky and Julia pull out their cards to continue playing gin rummy and they laugh together. Maybe I will have her for a daughter-in-law, after all. Tripp looks at me and I smile my smile. The smile he needs.

Chapter Fifty-Eight
December 25, 2011
My Birthday

CLEO

Tripp pulled away from me at the very last possible moment to make his flight back to New York with his family. And I urged him to go. I had taken him to a magical place last night, a place he will never forget. He got a call while we were there to say they found Jimbo and they had taken his body and bike away. I flashed back to Jimbo's hand on my arm like a vise right before he tried to kill me.

The last thing I wanted to hear about was Jimbo's dead body. I turned to Tripp and whispered simply, "Please. Not now."

He nodded and hung up his phone.

I seem to need to release these men to get my power back. They are my temptation, the serpents in my garden of Eden, my danger, my spiraling away from my feminine power, from who I am. I could become my mother with these men who are so like my father in charm and looks. I could repeat history. But I did such a brave thing killing Jimbo. Tripp kept reminding me I was the heroine who saved this island I so love. It felt good to realize how many lives were saved because of me.

Because of my Krav Maga, because I had continued to do it all these years.

Just as on Kilimanjaro, we talked and talked the night away, but this time, there were no bats. This time, we were in a beautiful cave of my own creation and here we fed our bodies, not just our minds and souls. I think feeding our minds and souls is what allowed our lovemaking to reach a place unlike any other I had been to. It wasn't the lust as it was with Jake; it was the life force, the excitement of who he was, an agent fighting evil, a man I had loved in a different form. I asked him to make-believe he was Danny and to make love to me as Danny, not as Tripp. And he did, and that way I had my Marc Antony finally. I didn't want to make love to Tripp who was married and Jake's father, I wanted Danny who did not have a family and whom I had loved for so long. So, when he kissed me, he was mine only, and so I kissed him with all the yearning I had. We kissed for hours, and then like a bolt, we were touching one another not gently but with the terror that the other would go away. Then he kissed my breasts. He kept looking at them after he pulled my shirt off and said he could do this for the rest of his life. Then he was in me and we were finally together and I would happily have died at that moment.

Tripp will explain to Jake that he should never speak of what he saw at the cliffs. I was appalled when Tripp told me Jake had seen me kill Jimbo. And how undone Jake was by the "baking cookies" text I sent him afterward.

I call my father to tell him I am leaving to meet him in Dubai at our rendezvous place in the desert. I leave my house with the black kitten with the huge violet bow that somehow Tripp managed to have one of his agents sneak into my bathroom when Tripp and I were together last night. The kitten was next to a bottle of my perfume, Endgame. Endy is what

I will call the kitten for short. Endy is the perfect reminder of my night of lovemaking with Danny, and also of our breakfast at Amboseli in Africa years ago when that black cat walked out on the patio. He told me to use my power those many years ago. I did. I still do.

Danny and I had finally found our time.

Epilogue
December 24, 2013
Two Years Later

MIRANDA

It's Christmas Eve and we've all just come home from the Carol Sing at church. Except for two years ago in Honolulu, this is my favorite time of year and has always been a perfect holiday. As I put the key into the lock of our 62nd Street townhouse, I'm greeted by the smell of evergreens wafting from the wreath, the tree upstairs on the first floor, and the banister covered in garlands. I'm so happy and content, especially because all three of our sons came to church and are also joining us for Christmas Eve dinner.

Tripp also invited an ambassador from the UAE whom he met a few months back and who's alone in America for the holiday. He should hopefully be a great addition since he'll be able to provide his take on world views—though we all know ambassadors aren't always the most reliable as they have rather a natural bias.

I climb the stairs, fixing the red velvet ribbons on the garlands as I go up. At the top step, I nearly fall back down the staircase when I see the entire living room is filled with white roses. White roses everywhere. This can't be. It just can't—but her timing would be perfect, sending these at Christmas time.

Jake, who's behind me, also stops short, causing Tripp at the rear to smack right into him.

"Jake!" Tripp says.

I hear his intake of breath.

"Who sent these?" Tripp asks.

"I don't know, ask Maggie," I say, suddenly short of breath.

Jake, excited: "It has to be her! Who else would send them?"

And no one has to ask who HER is. We all know—Cleopatra Gallier.

"If she sent them, she is, as she might say herself, 'hurtling toward the eccentric,'" Tripp says calmly to me, but he's unable to hide his delight.

It's not so much Cleo reentering my son's life that worries me—he and Julia are long gone, just ask my middle son—it's my husband's. Jake would be catatonic if he knew about his father's mysterious involvement with his Hawaiian romance.

Jake runs to the kitchen and returns crushed, holding a card.

"Thank you for having me to your special festive celebration this evening. Sincerely, Ambassador Obaid Fayazid," he reads aloud, listlessly.

Thank God. I breathe again. Thank you, God.

The ambassador arrives shortly after and we thank him profusely for the lovely flowers. Since he doesn't drink and the boys all have plans later, we go straight into dinner. Ricky and Julia are going to be late—they had to stop at a holiday party for Julia's new job after church—so we start without them.

After we sit, Tripp starts carving the filet.

The Ambassador looks at the table crammed with flowers "You know, I sent the white roses because I met an amazing woman on horseback in the desert a few weeks after you offered me this lovely invitation. Her father, a friend of mine, was there and introduced us. I told them I was living in New York and returning there in a week's time.

"She asked if I had friends in New York and when I told her I'd been invited to a Christmas Eve dinner at my lawyer's, Tripp Regan, she advised that a very thoughtful present for his family would be white roses. And then she said something so poetic... 'did you know the Earth laughs in flowers?'"

Jake couldn't control himself.

"Where is she? Where is she right now?! What's she doing?!" It all came tumbling out of him.

Two years of pain came through in his voice. Poor Jake; she had demolished him and I thought he'd gotten over her, but I've been wrong before.

Matt chirps in, "I love these white iceberg roses, especially with the snow and ice tonight. I like that saying, "The Earth laughs in flowers." That sounds so Cleo. She was probably thinking of me since she knows how I love flowers."

Only Matt. And I know that saying is taken from some poet.

At this point, Julia and Ricky arrive. At Thanksgiving, they announced their engagement and we're all so thrilled.

"Did I hear the name, 'Cleo?'" Julia asks, beaming, her eyes as big as saucers as she sees all the white roses.

Jake averts his eyes—it's still a bit of an awkward subject between the old lovebirds. But I nod and smile at my future daughter-in-law.

"Really? I have to admit, I love Cleo now. She's the one who brought us together," Julia says sweetly to Ricky. "Maybe I should invite her to our wedding."

Jake abruptly changes directions. "Ambassador, does she live in the UAE? No chance you have her cell or email?"

"I'm sorry. I have to assume she lives in the UAE or Saudi Arabia. If I didn't know Didier, her father, I would've thought she might be a Saudi princess. She had a bodyguard, a stallion horse, and her burqa was diamond studded; the kind only royalty could afford. She had the most amazing violet eyes. When she and her father rode off into the desert, the burqa billowed behind her. It was quite a sight."

Tripp stopped carving while the ambassador spoke. He was about to begin again as his phone rang with a really odd ringtone. He was about to answer but I nudged him not to.

"Work," he explained as he opened his phone and looked down at it.

His face froze. Again in shock. The shock on the beach in Honolulu registering all over again. Cleo.

December 24th, 2013
Continued

TRIPP

I answer my phone, but instead of a voice, the username ENDGAME and a photo pops up. It's of a baby who looks to be about a year old, hugging a black cat with a huge purple bow. A girl baby with blue eyes and dimples. And there's a caption: ZELLI—YOUR EYES; MY DIMPLES.

Then the photo evaporates. It's on screen for no more than eight seconds before it is lost in cyberspace forever. I want to call and have the office trace it, but the entire table is staring. All eyes on me. I hate when all eyes are on me—reminds me of my drama class days with Mrs. Huneke.

"Wrong number." I shrug and continue carving the filet. She timed that beautifully.

She would've been sure I couldn't trace her photo so why even bother. Cat and Mouse. Or Cat and Child and Mouse. Coincidentally, the photo arrives two years to the day after I gave her the black kitten and obviously a child too, though I knew nothing about the latter until this moment. The baby girl must have been conceived on that one wonderful night under the stars in Honolulu.

Jesus, what's she been up to the last two years aside from giving birth to Zelli?

"What else did she say? How is she?" Jake continues to probe the ambassador. His new CIA training hasn't yet taught him to hide his emotions.

"We spoke about horses since Dubai is a mecca for them."

Jake falls silent and looks confused. The ambassador is pretending—I'm sure this is a setup—that he doesn't know anything else. He came to my law firm for advice—she was behind that too. Well, she sure has style, I can't deny her that. I told Cleo at breakfast at the Honolulu Marathon that if I ever had a daughter, I would've wanted the baby to look like her, and I would have called her Zelli. I hope my wish came true—I reach out and touch a white rose.

Of course I have to find them.

Acknowledgements

Those who helped this book come to life by cheerleading or by reading it or giving great suggestions

Patti Alling

Brenda Anderson

Alex Andrews

Katti Anstey

David Baden

Candi Bagby

Becca Bartels

Maria Bayazaid

Mel Berger

Jessie Bohonnon

Lia Bohannon

Terry Bovin

Dede Brooks

Alex Burlason

Cat Carlson

Beth Chamberlain

Mary Jo Chapoton

Crystal Chappel

Maureen Chilton

Maria Church

Susan Colby

Chris Cowperthwait

Heidi Cox

Marty Cox

Jeannie Daniel

Banany Dearborn

Michele DeFilippo

Alix Devine

Bobo Devons

Kathy DeWitt

Ruthie DuPont

Toddie Findlay

Mary Fisher

Stephanie Flynn

Anne Ford

Ellie Ford

Acknowledgements

Toddie Findlay

Charlotte Ford

Patsy Forelle

Rosie Gwathmey

Jeff Gygax

Julia Halberstam

Eleanor Hall

Kay Moore Harris

Marje Helfot

Isabelle Houghton

Maisie Houghton

Alexandra Howard

Jill Hurst

Martha Ingram

Michele Jacobs

Eaddo Kiernan

Suzie Kovner

Lucy Lamphere

Ellie Lowery

Betty Marsh

Meg Pearson Marenda

Helena Martinez

Mary McCormack

Jeanne McCutcheon

Kristin McGee

Grace Meigher

Annie Harris Milliken

Sophie Mellon

Suzie Moore

Mary Morse

Bree Mortimer

Siri Mortimer

Kathy Murphy

Jane Nickerson

Linda O'Connor

Nell Otto

Mercedes Ovalle

Danielle Paige

Kathy Parsons

Susie Parsons

Peter Pauley

Louise Patterson

Maria Patterson

Joe Plummer

Nathalie Plummer

Craig Pollock

Melinda Pyne

Sherry Ramsey

Ronda Rawlins

Barbie Riegel

Josh Sabara

Georgina Sanger

Acknowledgements

Ali Schiff

Cindy Scott

Courtney Simon

Sarah Slack

Hilary Smith

Maureen Smith

Abby Stokes

Matt Stoneburg

Nonie Sullivan

Emily Talamo

Nan Talese

Shannon Thompson

Anne Tracy

Genie Trevor

Edith Tuckerman

Cristabel Vartanian

Jane Vasilou

Candace Wainwright

Patsy Warner

Susan Wald

Helgi Walker

Cynthia Watros

Bonnie White

Caroline Williamson

Jean Wolf

Alicia Wolfington